CW00544922

Seb,

The moment I held this
hands for the first time w
moment I finally became who
meant to be. I hope your mom
finds you soon.

Louis Stephenson

The Boatmore Butcher

By

L. Stephenson

www.DarkInkBooks.com

First Published by Dark Ink Books, Southwick, MA, 2023

Dark Ink and its logos are trademarked by *AM Ink Publishing*.

www.AMInkPublishing.com

This novel is dedicated to Nikki, Katie & Holly.
Each one of you is Irreplaceable.

Part I
The Goners

1
Jamie Brooks, Pt. I

It all began that very night. The night he returned for the first.

Nineteen-year-old Jamie Brooks sat alone on the third story of the university library. The overhead lamp of his study cubicle shone down on him like a spotlight in the darkness as it was one of the few lights left working on the entire floor, courtesy of the evening caretaker. Those that burned on illuminated the great staircase that corkscrewed its way down to the revolving door entrance. By day its constant spin swept in as many bodies as it did out, but now, at this late hour, it lay still.

The tip of a pen hung frozen over an empty page of lined paper as Jamie stared at the screen of the phone sitting next to his notepad. Having vibrated obnoxiously a moment ago, the student looked around guiltily before tapping the device.

A message from NIGEL:

Are you okay? Everyone missed you at the meeting.

Of course. The LGBTQ+ meeting he was supposed to attend two nights ago. He had signed up on the first day of the opening semester. Even paid for a full membership. Such pride he had felt, being brave enough to walk right up to that table with the rainbow flag draped down the front. And so casually, too. He went to one meeting. He didn't approach anyone and no one approached him, so he spent the time sitting by himself writing melancholy song lyrics on his phone that he would never use until it was over.

By the following Thursday, as he stood across the street from the group's designated bar, all that pride and all that bravery was gone. He felt a cold and hollow sadness where he had always imagined the warmth of friendship and acceptance would be. When would he feel like he belonged somewhere? What would it take? He didn't know, and so he faded into the foot traffic of the night to lullaby the ache of his hungry belly. Halfway through gobbling his large portion of chunky fries and melted cheese, he cried his first tears of true loneliness.

Jamie jolted as he was startled by a noise. Like the sound of a door clicking shut, and shuffling. Someone running? Or creeping towards him at an alarming pace?

Seated close to the far wall, he had a wide view of the floor as he quietly leaned back in his chair and took a look around. All he could see were books, the shelves they rested upon, and the shadows that enveloped everything. Silence and darkness. He dared not call out. What if someone answered? What were they doing there, sneaking around and hiding like that?

He drew in a sharp breath as the lamp above him jumped. He squirmed as something snagged his foot. Fingers grappling the edge of the desk, he pushed himself away and peered beneath. Relief washed over him as he realized that he grazed the lamp's ugly gray power cord with the toe of his sneaker.

Shielding his eyes from the powerful bulb's blaze, it occurred to him that if there were someone standing on the other side of the brilliant white light, all he would see is a blinding wall concealing their presence from him.

But there was no one there. There couldn't be. There wasn't.

Was there?

A reminder alert caught his attention. The message again. A second review thawed him a little. Maybe there was still hope after all. With a half-smile, he swiped away Nigel's kind white lie and resolved that he would give the meetings another chance. Feeling encouraged by this decision, he hustled to his feet and brushed his pad and pen into his flimsy excuse for a satchel.

Turning to leave, he halted as the phone throbbed in his hand. The name MOM appeared.

"I'm leaving now," he told her as he walked slowly along the row of empty cubicles towards the aisle.

"Good boy," his mother's voice said. "Oh, I've missed you so much!"

"I've missed you, too," he admitted sadly. "Really."

"I know, dear," she soothed. "Did you get your tickets? I sent them to you."

"Yeah, yeah. I printed them earlier. I've been at the library, so..."

"Excellent! I can't wait to see your sweet face when I pick you up from the ferry tomorrow afternoon."

Jamie stopped when he reached the middle of the aisle. Swallowing dryly, he asked, "Will Dad be there?"

There was a moment of quiet on the other end, and then: "You know he has to work on the boat to provide for us."

"Okay…" His mouth trembled as he struggled for words. "It's just I haven't talked to him since I told him I was–"

His head snapped around as something slapped down on the floor somewhere behind him. A book had fallen from one of the shelves. By itself?

"What is it? Are you all right?"

"Mom, I need to go," Jamie said as he backed away from the towering shadows of the book cases all around him.

The groan of metal cut into him as the chair he had been sitting in tumbled over.

He staggered away, hearing the sound of another book hitting the floor as he turned and raced down the aisle towards the staircase. He dared not look back as he tore his way down to the ground level of the library. Not until he reached the revolving doors as they stood frozen in front of him. His eyes frantically searched the entire room behind him as it appeared to come alive, closing in, reaching for him. He made for the side entrance and pounded the green EXIT button. The door released. Forcing it wide open, he barged out into the night.

The university grounds were dark, empty, and wet from a gentle rain as Jamie pumped his way across them. He soon reached the main street where a town bus was just about to depart. Scurrying around the front of the vehicle, he jumped aboard as the doors closed behind him.

His phone pulsed again as he fell into a seat.

"Yeah, Mom, I'm fine," he assured her. "I gave myself a good scare, that's all. I'm just on my way to the station now. I'll call you when I get to the hotel, okay? Don't worry about me. I'll be fine."

* * *

The 19-year-old student only had seconds to spare as his connecting bus was already waiting at the station.

Announcements blared out and echoed along the walls of the great old building as a large round clock passed over the boy's head in his haste. An ever-changing blue television screen flickered as it listed off all the scheduled arrival and departure times.

The place was practically deserted at that late hour, save for a janitor who swept away with his wide broom and a drunk who could barely hold his balance as he stunk to high heaven.

Jamie had no time to acknowledge either of them as he heard the piercing hiss of his next bus preparing to depart.

"Wait!" he called out as he dashed back out into the freezing night air where he just made it.

Stepping on board, he smiled at the weary bus driver as he showed him his pass before taking a seat towards the back.

Rolling up his sleeve, Jamie smiled to himself. No matter who he was, and no matter where he was, he would always have at least one friend. Upon the delicate flesh of his left wrist was the name ELLA, his Grandmother's name. The only person who knew who he truly was, even before he did. As a growing boy, he would visit her every weekend and she would prepare him bowls of soup with plenty of bread and butter to sop it up while she sat contently in the corner and smoked her cigarettes.

As the bus set off, Jamie reached up and opened a window above the seats in front of him. Apart from the bus driver and himself, the bus was empty. He leaned back against the headrest and closed his eyes, taking in the cold night air as it washed over his face.

Just as he began to relax, he heard a loud cough coming from behind him. Jamie turned to look.

Was he there before?

Sitting at the back of the bus was a man in a pale hood staring directly at him.

Jamie faced forward, gripping the support bar in front of him. He tried to distract himself with the scenery as the city disappeared into the night, but his thoughts wandered back to the passenger behind him.

Was he hiding back there? The back seat was empty.

Unable to resist, Jamie slowly turned his head again.

The man was still staring at him.

Snapping forward, he froze as he realized something. The man was no longer sitting on the back seat. He had moved places when Jamie wasn't looking. The man was sitting closer now.

Holding his breath, he listened. He could hear the tires on the road, the night air coming in from the window, and the floor of the bus creaking quietly as the man moved even closer.

The next thing Jamie heard was someone breathing, deep and heavy. Tears surfaced as he realized the man in the pale hood was now sitting right behind him. Then he heard the flickering of paper. The strange sound was almost like someone playing with a deck of cards.

Jamie jumped hard as something dropped down onto the empty seat beside him. Flinching away from the object, he looked down to see what it was. His notepad?

He looked up again as the man in the pale hood got up and walked to the front of the bus.

Returning his thoughts to the notepad, he remembered hearing a second book fall in the library as he made a run for it, but he never saw what it was. It must have been the sound of the notepad falling out of his bag as he went. Which means...

He was there.

The bus came to a stop just inside the mouth of a great arched tunnel that curved its way beneath the derelict train tracks high above.

Jamie quietly got out of his seat and started to back away as he heard the man in the pale hood having words with the driver.

Their conversation ended quickly as the hooded man drew a black metal pipe from beneath his coat and smashed it over the side of the bus driver's face. Jamie held back a gasp as he ducked behind the nearest seat, his eyes searching frantically for a way out.

With chilling ease, the man in the pale hood ripped the bleeding bus driver from his seat and hurled him out of the sliding doors. There was a dull thud as the driver's body bounced off the wall of the tunnel. Staring directly at Jamie, the man pushed a button, automatically slamming the bus doors shut.

Jamie slid all the way down to the floor where he could feel the body of the vehicle humming beneath him, but then the engine stopped, the floor became still, and all the lights went out.

In the dark of that bus, all he could hear now was the man's footsteps, slow like a steady heartbeat as they got closer and closer.

With every step forward the man took, Jamie felt his throat tighten up a little more. He wanted to scream, but the grip of his own fear was too strong. He couldn't breathe; his lungs ached as they burned with their need for air.

The bus began to shake as the footsteps got heavier, louder, faster.

Petrified, he climbed back up onto his seat and curled into a trembling ball, hoping that he remained hidden.

In the distance, he could hear the sound of car wheels racing over the tarmac surface of the road. Jamie slowly edged his head around in time to see the entire back window of the bus illuminate as it captured the full beam of the car's headlights. He jolted with fright as the car's horn blared like the cry of a startled elephant. The squeal of its tires pierced the dense air inside the bus as the car swerved to avoid it.

Three more angry horns, followed by one long furious horn, blasted the night as the car sped off deep into the tunnel.

The footsteps had stopped.

Jamie squinted into the darkness in front of his eyes. His breath caught in his throat at the black shape looming over him. The light from the motorist's car had shown the hooded man exactly where Jamie was hiding. He smiled emptily as he reached out for him. An arm gently wrapped around his neck as a voice whispered, "Hello, my boy…"

As cold fingers scratched at his throat, Jamie screamed as he dove over the seat in front of him, reaching out for the metal handle of the emergency exit door. The headlights may have given away his hiding spot, but not without illuminating a way out. He yanked the handle and leapt blindly out into the middle of the road.

The impact of the landing kicked his head back at the same time as it threw him forward to the ground. The rough surface of the road shredded his palms and fingers. Ignoring his torn flesh, Jamie clawed himself to his feet and took off into the pitch-black throat of the tunnel, pumping his legs as fast as he could.

Jamie hurtled through total darkness, stumbling over potholes, loose pieces of brick from the tunnel walls, and even his own feet as his toes jabbed the surface of the road too steeply. Sobbing and whimpering, he pressed on, praying for another car to come by. He would flag them down and he would be safe. Safe from the man who, for all he knew, was only inches away from grabbing him.

He ran faster. His heart and windpipe seemed to fuse into one. Every sharp breath of air he took pulsed beneath his Adam's apple as if something was trying to punch its way out of his throat from the inside. Was he going to die here in this tunnel? In the dark? He felt like he was dying already, enveloped in that terrifying blackness, and then...

Light! There was light coming from the tunnel behind him. The car he had prayed for was on its way. Safety was now within his reach. He stopped in his tracks, wheezing, coughing, and smiling as he turned to flag the car down.

But there was no car, only the bus. The lights were blinding as its engine choked into life. Jamie shrieked into the beaming glow of the monstrous machine's headlights. They were like the devil's eyes burning into his soul, and the engine was its bone-splintering roar, beckoning him into the deepest of depths. Jamie screamed at the beast and the creature bellowed back. He turned and ran further into the tunnel. The bus growled as its wheels began to turn.

The boy's throat was ripped raw as he screamed every frantic step of the way. Contorted in his own fear, his body ran too fast, even for itself, as if his bones meant to burst free of their skinsuit. He stumbled and tripped and screamed and cried. All the while the bus behind him rapidly gained momentum.

Jamie looked to the shadows cast by the light of the beams. He searched for a maintenance door to charge through or a pillar to hide behind, but he found nothing. He fast approached a sharp bend in the tunnel that curved beneath the bridge.

The cry of the bus engine cut through the air like a power saw as it raced through the tunnel. Within seconds it was behind Jamie, beside him, and finally in front of him. There was a roaring crash, the sparking and shredding of metal on brick, the shattering of light fixtures and windows.

The boy found himself pinned up against the wall of the tunnel. He was unable to breathe, unable to move, unable to make a sound. The darkness, the pitch black, returned. It engulfed him. It had such a cold grasp, empty of warmth, empty of light, the suffocating end of all things. And so it came to pass: Jamie Brooks was dead.

But then he blinked his eyes and allowed his mouth to open and his lungs to inhale a much-needed breath of cool night air. He found himself standing face to face with a cold wall of metal. As he looked from side to side, he realized that the bus had cornered him at the curve in the tunnel.

Releasing the greatest sigh of relief, he kissed the name that was forever etched on the skin of his left wrist. He wiped away tears, for there was no time to stop now. He had to keep going. He had to keep trying.

Shakily but cautiously, he crept alongside the bus towards the front. The metal skin of the vehicle had mashed itself into the bricks of the wall. Turning, he limped in the other direction, finding the same result. The bus had fenced him in. The impact of the crash had fused the wall and the vehicle into a cage.

The boy froze as the lights inside flickered on. The man in the pale hood stood right above him with only a sheet of window glass between them as he raised the black metal pipe in his hand.

With one sharp gasp of panic, Jamie dropped to his hands and knees and scuttled under the bus. The road under him ate away at his fleshy knees and bleeding palms as he went. Clenching his teeth, he fought through the pain and the numbness. As he felt the night air blowing against his face on the other side, he sprang triumphantly to his feet.

Before he could take off running, two arms came down from above his head and wrapped themselves around the boy's throat as they ripped his body from the surface of the tunnel road. Jamie screamed for his life as he was pulled back through the emergency exit he had used to escape.

The exit door slammed shut, the screaming stopped, and the lights went out.

He had him. Finally, he was his.

The first.

2
Christopher Price, Pt. I

Eighteen Months Earlier

Liam Price and his wife, Ally, moved to the island three months before the birth of their son. The entire foundation of the move was based on the isle's promise of safety.

There was no crime to speak of, and in its entire history, there has never been a murder. All recorded deaths on the island of Boatmore, from its first settlers to the present day, were either natural or accidental.

Life there wasn't slow, but uneventful enough to make even the most monotonous occasion feel like a fiesta. Living on an island that small made the world feel small, as if that chunk of land were all there ever was, all there ever would be.

On that Saturday morning, Liam lay in his sun-filled back garden struggling to hear the football score from the radio poking through the kitchen window.

Beads of sweat trickled down beneath the whiskey-colored glass of his sunshades and into his pale blue eyes. His golden-brown fringe was matted against his wet forehead. Beneath a pit-stained white t-shirt, he wore cream shorts and dark blue beach sandals.

Finally fed up, Liam rose out of his deckchair with every intention of marching straight back into the house, but the view stopped him. It always stopped him.

Beyond the bent chain-link fence at the bottom of the garden, the town of Boatmore sloped down into a row of shops that sold old books, fish & chips, and island merchandise. Beyond those shops lay a row of pubs and restaurants, behind which was the fishing pier, and, finally, the sea.

Aside from the smiles of his loving wife and son, the sea was the most beautiful of all things in Liam's eyes. It held an unfathomable feeling of freedom and possibility. Most of all, it gave him a fantastic sense of satisfaction and accomplishment. He had managed to gift his family with a calm and easy life.

Stretching until his body shook in the sweltering warmth of the early afternoon sun, Liam slinked through the white patio doors into the kitchen.

Peeling his sticky shirt away from the hot skin of his back, his fingers raked open the first top drawer to his right. Boxes of AAA batteries toppled over each other inside, but all of them were empty. Shaking his head with a frustrated chortle, he chucked the lot of them into one of the recycling boxes by the back door.

If he was going to enjoy the afternoon the way he intended to, a short walk to the newsstand was just the thing, but he would have to be quick if he wanted to get back before halftime.

Scooping his wallet from the kitchen table still littered with the plates and cutlery of that morning's breakfast of eggs and toast, he marched for the front door.

As he trod noisily through the hallway past the staircase on his left, he cocked his head to the side and called up to the landing, "Ally? I'm just going to the shop, okay?" Liam stopped in his tracks before entering the porch. "Do you want anything?"

"No," his wife answered. "Can you check on Christopher?"

"Okay…" He hesitated as he peered into a deserted living room. "Where is he?"

"He's outside playing," the faint reply came, the dull purr of shower water echoing in accompaniment.

"All right," Liam said with a nod as he scratched the back of his neck. "I'll be back soon, babe."

He didn't even make it to the front door.

BANG! BANG! BANG!

The urgency of those knocks jolted him deeply. After taking a moment of pause, he answered them.

"George?"

The old man wheezed against the doorframe, his short-sleeved shirt clinging to his chest. Beneath his straw sunhat, his wrinkled face was turning dark pink, and the kind eyes behind those huge spectacles of his were puffy with tears.

"George, are you all right?" Liam asked as he watched the old man's body heave. "Can I call someone for you?"

A breathless George Hale shook his head vigorously as he massaged his aching chest.

"Do you need emergency services?" Liam clenched his fists as he became further unnerved.

George shook his head again, his bottom lip quivering.

A choking lump the size of a peach stone had grown in Liam's throat.

"George…"

The old man's mouth trembled open as he drew in a deep breath. "It's Christopher."

The lump in Liam's throat grew as he gently shifted George away from the doorframe and leapt from the doorstep. Whipping his glasses off onto the lawn, he jogged out into the road.

The street that he had known so well was suddenly an alien place to him, like a battlefield in a strange land. Even the sky didn't feel the same. Why was the air suddenly so thin? He had forgotten to breathe. His gasp was loud and shrill as he allowed himself oxygen.

The road was empty as he walked directly down its center. His legs did not feel like his own. The bones beneath the flesh seemed to be liquefying.

Tears began to fall as he pressed on, his heart thrashing the inside of his chest. His breathing became heavier in his silent agony, and far behind him, poor George made a valiant effort to keep up.

Liam screamed out the boy's name again and again as his eyes darted madly from lawn to lawn, house to house. His voice broke in his desperation, his cries becoming nothing more than raspy whispers.

Where was his son?

Vomit snaked its way up his throat, sizzling around the lump, but he could not feel it coming from his stomach, for his body had gone numb below the chest.

His mouth flew open as he gagged. Nothing came out. He gagged again. Still nothing. The convulsions forced his head forward, sending his skip cap flopping onto the road. It bounced once and then no more. He gagged a third time. The sickness was almost there.

Then it stopped.

He stopped.

Time, life, joy, pain, existence stopped.

The first thing that Liam Price saw was the man sitting on the road.

Leaning back against the bumper of a car, the man held his knees up to his chest, sobbing uncontrollably. His body shook as he wept.

Liam started to run. The world before him lashed from side to side in front of his eyes like a fishbowl in the hands of a cruel child.

The crying man drew closer. He could even hear his bawling and sniffing over the sound of his sandals slapping the surface of the road.

At the end of the street an ambulance raced around the corner, blue lights flashing, but Liam did not hear a sound as his heartbeat punched his eardrums, deafening him.

He was now close enough to see.

Beyond the man who sat weeping on the road, beneath the car he had curled up next to, was a little hand.

Liam choked out a horrified scream, throwing himself to the ground.

It was Christopher.

For a few moments, it almost looked as if his son's eyes were staring back at him. But they weren't. They were dead eyes. Empty and aimless.

If only he had held that lifeless gaze. Then he wouldn't have seen the torn clothes, the mashed skin and protruding bones, nor the twisted limbs, the blood and the urine. But he did.

And with that, he froze to the ground, still as stone. So still, in fact, that the responding paramedics mistook him for a casualty. Not even the calming scent of salt whisking in from the sea could revive him.

Refusing to let them turn him over, Liam's eyes remained on his son's body, wishing, begging, and praying unashamedly that this was someone else's child.

3
Jamie Brooks, Pt. II

Present Day

Somewhere on the island of Boatmore, a man in a pale hood laid the body of a boy down next to a field, and in the silence of the morning, blood ran thick as the man left his mark nearby for all to see.

* * *

Ben Braithwaite dragged his shaggy mop of mousey-brown hair across the solid chest of the man lying next to him before burying his beak of a nose in his boyfriend's armpit.

"Quit it!" Matt giggled, perfectly awake.

"Oh! I thought you were…"

"You have been up worrying all night," Matt yawned. "Do you have any idea how hard it is to sleep with someone who won't stop staring at you?"

"I'm sorry," Ben said as he snuggled into Matt's shoulder with a contented hum. "I like staring at you."

Gazing up at the high ceiling of that dark little shoebox of a bedroom, his eyes wandered down the walls until they arrived at Matt's naked body.

Deep in thought, his fingers traced the prominent veins of the long muscular arm that he rested soundly upon. Both arms were painted from wrist to bicep with the kind of wonderfully elaborate and beautifully colored tattoos one might expect to find defiling the flesh of the lead singer in a famous rock band. Ben's digits abandoned ship before they reached Matt's hair. Its controlled chaos unnerved him, but somehow he was comforted by the fact that it was finally taking shape, knotting itself into several thick dreadlocks.

"What are you thinking about right now?" Matt asked him.

Ben reached out a hand and the two of them connected, palm to palm as they gently locked fingers. "Do you ever wonder if we go together the way we do because we both came from the system?"

"I don't know." Matt caressed the back of Ben's hand with his free thumb as he pondered. "It helps, I guess: being with someone who just gets you, because they've been through the same stuff."

"Sometimes–" Ben had to stop himself as tears found his eyes. He took a deep breath. "Sometimes I feel we're like two broken parts…that shouldn't even fit each other, but when we meet, somehow, we just make each other whole…"

"Hey," Matt leaned in close and kissed him deeply. "It's okay. I feel it, too."

Ben laughed at himself with embarrassment, snuggling closer as a tear rolled down his cheek.

A few moments of peace passed between them.

"Now what are you thinking?" Matt nudged Ben playfully.

"I'm thinking…we're both gonna be late if we don't get out of bed soon."

Matt growled naughtily as he hooked his strong arms around Ben's slender frame and reeled him over until he rested atop him, bare, trembling, body to body.

"Would that be so bad?" Matt grinned, weaving his hips slowly yet hard at the same time as he held Ben closer.

"While you do raise a very good point…" Ben struggled to catch his breath as he fought temptation. "…I can't. I can't." He pushed himself away from the tongue in his ear. "No, really. I've heard it from a few people now: my new boss is a real piece of work."

Sliding off of Matt, Ben swung his feet over his side of the bed and wrestled on a twisted pair of boxer shorts. "Can't really say I blame him, though."

Matt sat up with a huff of disappointment. "And why is that?"

"They told me his kid got killed," Ben responded, without turning to look at him. "Just over a year ago."

* * *

Liam Price leaned against the back door of the ambulance drinking piping hot black coffee out of the plastic cup lid of his thermos as he awaited the rest of his team.

"Is this your first time as an acting paramedic?" Martin Fin glanced over at the new recruit as they stepped out through the entrance door to the station and came to a stop.

"Yeah," Ben Braithwaite replied quickly, clearing his throat noisily. "Yes, it is, but I did do a few ride-alongs on the mainland."

"Well, don't worry," Martin assured him. "You've been trained by one of the country's best and you've got it all up in your head. All you have to do is just stay calm and keep your ears open. Now, I'll warn you, since you're the new guy, Liam and I are pretty tough and dry, but we'll keep you on your toes. We've seen it all and there's nothing we aren't prepared for, so just follow our lead and you'll be fine."

Ben couldn't help but be enamored by his new co-worker's good looks. Even through their boxy green work attire, it was painfully obvious that Martin was in peak physical condition. Not only that, he had a face that Ben once believed could only belong to statues of Greek mythology—until now. Next to him, he felt like a mopey little weed of a man.

Martin nodded to Liam with a sarcastic grin as they made their way over. "Mr. Price."

Liam nodded back with a hint of a smirk. "Mr. Fin." He glanced over Martin's shoulder at Ben. "The new guy?"

"Ben," the young man said as he took a step forward and held out his right hand. "Or Mr. Braithwaite, if you prefer."

"Liam." Liam shook Ben's hand briefly and then climbed into the driver's seat of the ambulance.

Ben watched him go, frowning, as he did not know whether to feel welcomed or insulted. He turned to Martin, whose smile was ear to ear. "Tough and dry?"

"Tough and dry," Martin responded with a nod, patting Ben dismissively on the shoulder before climbing in next to Liam.

Ben's shoulders sank with a deep sigh as he followed.

"So, what have we got this morning?" Martin sighed as he watched the road rattle beneath them.

"We think it's a kid," Liam replied.

Martin looked to the driver with a skeptical frown. "We *think* it's a kid?"

"We're not sure," Liam admitted. "We weren't given too much to go on."

"So, we've no idea what the emergency is?"

"Nope."

"How do we even know where this kid is?"

"Dispatch said the call came from an SOS phone," Liam explained, "so we've got a pretty good idea where they are."

"An SOS phone?" Ben asked, cramped between Martin and the side door as he tried to squeeze into view. "That'll mean their injuries will be car-related, won't they?"

"The main cause of death on this island is either natural or accidental," Liam informed him, "but I've gotta say, this one is looking to be pretty suspicious. We've never had a murder here before. Not one. Until we know more, I'm not going to say anything that's gonna change that."

It was three minutes past six a.m. when their ambulance arrived at the scene.

Liam Price was the first of the three paramedics to step out onto the roadside.

The dawning sky glowed eerily and the chill in the morning air was sharp and unforgiving. Each man stepping out of the back of the vehicle shivered in the wake of its cutting icy caress.

Ben Braithwaite was the second out of the ambulance, adrenaline already coursing through his veins, causing his skin to crawl and vibrate. For the first time he felt the frightening state of being he had been dreading every nauseating moment of his medical training—a feeling that suddenly imploded violently in on itself, choking him. He froze where he stood as he first caught sight of the blood.

"Jesus…" Ben gasped as he pointed with a nervous finger. "Over there."

Liam and Martin turned their heads. They saw the blood almost immediately before locking wary eyes on each other.

About thirty feet up the grassy embankment stood a lonely orange SOS phone. The left side of the white telephone symbol was stained thick with blood. Blood in the shape of a hand. Its fingers smeared to the right. Deep red droplets streamed from under the palm down to the bottom edge of the pumpkin-colored phone box.

The three of them made their way towards it, carrying their gear at the ready.

Out of the silence, Martin remarked, "I'm going to take a wild guess and say that isn't paint," as he planted the spinal board under his arm upright on the grass like a surfer.

He and Liam came to a stop as Ben squinted at the handprint. He stepped in for a closer look. Carefully, he dabbed a finger across the area of its palm.

"Not paint," Ben confirmed as he looked from the bloodied SOS phone to the slimy, crimson tip of his gloved finger. "It's fresh, too."

He took one last look at the handprint made of human blood. The spot where he had dabbed his finger began to close up. In a few moments it would be as if he had never been there.

Liam cleared his throat. "Let's find who that belongs to, shall we?"

Shivering, Ben followed his colleagues along the embankment as they searched for a casualty.

Soon enough they spotted a groove that opened up through a small grassy slope by the roadside, like a passageway. Beyond the groove the land levelled out, lined off by a barbed-wire fence that bordered the farmlands on the other side. For now, the farmland appeared to be deserted. Even the animals didn't dare to tread there this morning.

Liam, Martin, and Ben stood at the mouth of the opening as they peered cautiously over at what could be ahead.

"I see them," Martin called out first.

They all saw the two feet on the ground to the left of the opening. Two feet, bloodied and dirty, lonely and unmoving.

"We should call someone," Ben managed, blindly searching the pockets of his uniform.

"Wait," Liam stopped him. "Look."

The feet were stirring. A weak voice groaned in anguish.

"Shit," Martin grunted as he led the way through the groove, followed by Liam, swiftly, then Ben, reluctantly.

Jamie Brooks lay as still as stone upon the grass, redressed in a filthy pair of jeans and a ragged white t-shirt. The t-shirt was half crimson down the left side as it clung to his body.

"Wasn't he moving before?" Ben croaked, his legs shaking beyond his control.

"Check his pulse," Liam urged him, as he set down next to the boy.

Ben could only stare.

"Check the pulse," Martin repeated, already on the phone to the authorities.

The young paramedic dropped to his knees. He reached out a hand but quickly withdrew it, realizing it was the one that touched the blood on the SOS phone.

Trembling, he pressed two gloved fingers of his other hand against the side of Jamie's neck. Drawing in a deep breath, he waited.

Meanwhile, Liam slowly began to peel the t-shirt away from the stomach, looking for a wound, an origin of the blood.

"It's there, but it's weak," Ben reported.

"What the hell?" Liam whispered to himself.

"What is it?"

"I'm not sure," Liam replied, digging into his kitbag. "We need to get this shirt open."

Finished with his call, Martin re-joined them. "What have we got here?"

Liam drew out a pair of scissors. "That's what I'm about to find out."

"How's the kid?" Martin asked Ben.

"Holding on."

"See if you can get him talking."

Ben nodded and crawled up to shoulder level with the boy as Liam started to cut up the middle of the bloodstained t-shirt.

"Hello?" he began. "Can you hear me? Can you open your eyes for me? Open your eyes if you can hear me."

Jamie's eyes flickered.

"He's responding!" Ben alerted them, tears surfacing.

"Good," Martin gave him the thumbs up. "Keep going until he's conscious. Get him looking at you. Get him talking."

Liam's scissor blades reached below the collar of the t-shirt. He handed them to Martin, and with one swift tug, ripped the t-shirt in two. Then softly, he laid the material back down before gently spreading each half away from the center.

Martin attended to the left side as it stuck to the boy's skin. Steadily, he peeled it away to reveal what Liam had been searching for.

"Jesus Christ…"

A sickly gash, a jagged, demented incision, ran down the side of Jamie's chest. Peculiar and careless stitches barely held the separated flesh together.

"What is that?" Ben gaped at the sight. "Some kind of black market surgery?"

"No…not this," Liam replied cryptically. "Even black market is better than this. This is just shoddy, torturous, and of the uttermost cruelty. He needs a hospital now."

"Right. Ben," Martin motioned to the spinal board as he got to his feet. "Me and you, we're moving him. Now."

"Wait," Ben stopped him.

"What?"

"I can't find a pulse." He doublechecked. "…I don't think he's breathing."

Liam sprang into action. "Okay, Ben, you do mouth to mouth. I'll do compressions. Mr. Fin, get ready to apply pressure in case we breach the wound."

Each paramedic manned their station.

"Starting compressions." Liam began to pump against the boy's chest. He paused and then looked to Ben. "Go."

Ben shakily blew short puffs of air between the boy's bluing lips.

Martin inspected the wound and informed them, "Nothing so far. We're good."

The three of them carried on this cycle five more times.

"Come on, come on, come on!" Liam huffed through clenched teeth.

Just then, a single thick drop of blood emerged from one of the stitches and ran down Jamie's heavily bruised skin to the grass below.

"Getting a bit of leakage here," Martin alerted them.

"Do you think we should stop?" Liam stared hard at him, his hands curled against one another like claws above the boy's chest.

"Nah, we're still good," Martin dabbed at the blood and then piled on the gauze with both hands as Liam and Ben carried on. "We need to m—"

Suddenly a high, sharp breath from the boy stabbed the air. Ben jolted away in fright. A deep gurgling built in the boy's throat, traveling up and up until a torrent of blood erupted from his mouth, splattering his face and painting his teeth red.

"Whoa!" Ben cried out, losing his balance.

"Get up. Check his airways," Liam ordered him. He looked to Martin. "Hospital."

The man turned and sprinted back through the groove.

"I can't get a good look," Ben reported, pocketing his penlight.

"Help me move him." Liam unbuckled the straps of the spinal board in a few fast clicks. He took the feet as he met Ben's gaze. "Ready? Go."

They lifted him over. The boy spluttered and choked as they set him down.

"Turn his head." Liam fastened him onto the board.

Taking it with both hands, Ben turned the boy's head gently. Blood spilled out of his gaping mouth and onto the grass.

"Okay, we're moving him. *Now.*"

Feeling the board against his lower back, Ben could see through the groove to the road where Martin pulled up with their rescue vehicle.

They moved quickly, but the boy spasmed violently before they could make it out of the opening. Ben struggled as he could feel the board slipping out of his grip.

"Stop?" he shouted back.

"Keep going." Liam had Martin in his sights as he opened the rear doors of the ambulance. "We're almost there."

And they were almost there as Martin stepped aside for them as they approached.

Then, another gurgle came from the boy.

His head snapped back as a second gush covered his face, staining the whites of his eyes as they remained in the back of his head.

"Stop, stop, stop!" Liam halted them.

They lowered the boy to the roadside as blood began to overflow through his nostrils. His rolled eyes returned, but not as they once were. They slanted off in different directions beneath half-closed eyelids as Jamie's body sank into lifelessness. The blood that filled his mouth to the brim bubbled as pockets of trapped air escaped to the surface.

A dense fog of silence engulfed them all, isolating them, constricting them.

Ben's tear-filled eyes drifted towards the emptiness of the farm on the other side of the embankment only to find a herd of cattle waiting beyond the barbed wire. All of them were resting on the ground, watching. Their ears twitching. Their eyes knowing.

The silence began to break under the slapping sound of Liam tearing off his medical gloves. He tossed them defeatedly to the ground.

Leaning over Jamie's body, he checked his pulse one last time. He noticed a name tattooed on the boy's left wrist. Did it belong to his mother?

With a disheartened sigh, he said, "He's gone…"

Ben choked out a single cry but quickly breathed it back in.

"No, let's keep going." Martin reached down to take Ben's end of the board.

"We shouldn't." Liam stood up, away from the body.

"Why not?"

"Kid's dead onsite, under suspicious circumstances." Liam's gaze wandered over to the SOS phone as it bled in the morning air. "He's part of a crime scene now."

Martin narrowed his eyes at his two colleagues as he crossed his arms. "So, no one is curious about what the hell just happened?"

"Of course I am," Liam admitted. "But I'm a paramedic, not a coroner. My job is over."

"Oh, so you're just going to ignore *this*?" Martin demanded, pulling the gauze away from the wound in the dead boy's chest. His mouth dropped. "Whoa, whoa!"

Liam's spine went rigid as the sight before him caused every hair on the back of his neck to stand up.

The three paramedics stared at the boy in horror and confusion as they realized that the left side of his chest had caved in.

"Did we do that?" Martin choked out.

"No. No way," Liam replied, shaking his head insistently.

"Then what could've done that."

"Osteogenesis...imperfecta?" Ben barely managed.

"Brittle bone disease?" Martin squinted at him before looking to Liam. "Do you think?"

"No, it can't be," Liam pondered. "I've never heard of something like this happening. We'd have known right away just by looking at him."

"Well, isn't it possible?" Martin pressed. "If the case were mild enough? How hard were your compressions?"

"What are you trying to say?" Liam said through a furious glare, fists balling and un-balling.

"I don't know," Martin retreated. "I don't know. This just seems a little screwed up to me. Last time I checked, people...people's ribs just don't give that easily. Not like that..."

"I'm sure we'll find out soon enough."

With an angry grunt Martin turned away from his friend when he clocked Ben staring. The sudden urge to snap at him quickly dissolved as he realized that young Ben was too dazed to even recognize what he was doing.

Instead, he asked, "You okay, kid?"

"I think so," Ben answered eventually. "It's so cold out here... Is it time to go home yet?"

"The police will be here soon," Martin told him as he carefully observed his colleague. "They'll want us to stay where we are, and they'll probably have some questions for us about what happened. Try not to move anything."

"If it's okay with you guys, I'd like to wait inside and warm up before they get here." Ben's words were almost a whisper as he began to slowly shrink away like a terrified child, desperate to run to its mother for comfort.

"I'll let you know," Martin replied. His voice low, he leaned towards Liam. "I think something's wrong with him."

"He's fine," Liam grumbled, "just a little shaken up. He'll come around. He just needs a little time."

"He's not going to last very long here, is he?"

"Can't say for sure."

4
Jamie Brooks, Pt. III

Officer Jennifer Colby settled into her car by the fishing pier, steam rising from the freshly grilled ham and cheese sandwich concealed within the paper bag cradled carefully on her lap. She gulped down half a can of Coke, took a deep breath, and sounded off an impressive belch before reaching happily into the bag for her morning meal.

Whipping her cap off, her curly red locks spilled down around her face as she took her first bite. Brown sauce glopped down the side of her mouth as she munched away, gazing out at the pier through the windscreen. The high stone wall that curved away to the right. The stacks upon stacks of empty fishing cages. The mother walking her two children to the end to look at the water, and the vacant docks of trawler boats already out at sea.

The touchscreen above her car radio lit up as the name NEWTON appeared next to a phone icon.

"Crap…" she muttered, answering with a loud sigh. "Morning, Newton. What's up?"

"We've got a body," a young man's voice blared through her speakers.

"Shit." Colby snapped forward in her seat, paper crinkling noisily as she clutched her grilled breakfast. "You're kidding. Where? And *who?*"

"It's Jamie Brooks."

"Barbara's boy?" She gripped her fiery locks in thought. "How is that possible? I could swear she told me the other week that he was still at the university."

"I don't know what to tell you about that."

Colby sank back against her seat. "My God, she'll be devastated."

"That's actually what I'm calling you about. We really need to get a jump on things. You know what this island is like."

"I'm well aware." Colby nodded to herself as she rolled her eyes.

"I'm tied up here at the scene so I need you to inform the family immediately before they hear it from someone else."

"I understand." She gulped soundly as she took hold of the steering wheel. "I'm actually close by right now."

"That's great. Thank you. You'll be much better at this emotional stuff."

"What the–!" Colby composed herself. "Seriously, Newton?"

"Sorry! I didn't mean it like that!" the bumbling officer stammered. "This has never happened to me before. Finding bodies like this."

"The 1950s never happened to you either, but you seem to be doing a great job there!" she scolded him.

Jabbing her finger at the touchscreen, everything faded to black as she hung up.

"Stupid ass."

Piling her hair atop her head, she refitted her police cap and took another bite of her food along with another swig of her Coke.

"Shit, shit, shit. Okay…"

Belching one more time, she dropped the can into a cupholder, started the car, and backed out of her parking spot.

* * *

Matt's dreadlocks peeked out the back of his work cap as he covertly smoked the final third of a joint outside the entrance to the morgue. Setting off the automatic doors, he hid the thing behind his back until it was time to inhale again. Earphones blaring, he sluggishly nodded his head to '90s metal.

Watching the road, he coughed as the ambulance that appeared on the corner caught him by surprise.

"Shit," he choked out, spinning and flicking his joint away. "Ah! Shit!" A small cloud of glowing hot ash burst into the air like tiny fireflies as Matt shook his finger in pain. "Fuckin' bitch…"

The ambulance pulled over to the side.

"Hey!" he lit up as Ben Braithwaite was the first to jump out of the vehicle. He held out his arms as his boyfriend jogged towards him. "What's up, bubble butt?"

"Don't call me that," Ben scolded him with a sharp whisper. He pulled on Matt's shoulder. "Bathroom. Take me, please."

"Okay, okay, okay." Taking him by the hand, he led Ben through the automatic doors. "Are you all right?"

Matt peered over from the row of bathroom sinks and mirrors as Ben retched loudly into the bowl of one of the cubicle toilets.

"Bad first day?"

"Matt…" Ben gasped and gagged. "I love you…but this is not the time to make me laugh!" He retched again, sitting

down on the floor as he caught his breath. "It was horrible…
There was blood…everywhere…"

* * *

Officer Colby's police vehicle fell still as she switched off the
engine and turned to look back at Mrs. Barbara Brooks.
Dressed in a smoky blue velvet tracksuit, the woman clutched
a packed lunch as it rested uneasily upon the edge of her
knees.

"We're here, Barb," Colby said softly.

"I made this for him." Barbara raised the packed lunch,
her eyes thick with dried tears. "He's always starving for
something to eat when he gets off the ferry."

"Barbara, we're not going to pick Jamie up from the
ferry." Colby's lip trembled as she turned to look at her
passenger through the reflection in her car mirror instead.
"Do you remember what I told you just before we left? Jamie
has passed away. He was found this morning. I am so sorry,
my dear. I understand if you need a few moments. Please take
your time. You tell me when you're ready, and I will take you
to see him."

Colby flinched in her seat as she heard the packed lunch
tumble onto the floor of her car. She turned to find Barbara
holding out her wrists.

"He gave this to me just last Christmas," the mother told
her as she tugged on the fabric of her tracksuit. "It's been my
favorite thing to wear ever since."

"It's lovely, Barbara." Colby smiled sadly at her. "You'll
have to tell me where I can get one of those."

The woman in the back seat opened her mouth to speak,
a smile nearing full bloom on her lips, but then it shrank away
when it occurred to her: "I'll never have another Christmas

with my boy. Or another birthday. Or holiday. Nothing ever again. All that time, all that love just gone. And I'm supposed to accept this is life? What a cruel joke."

"The cruelest," Colby said with a nod, "but there's always love, Barb."

Barbara's tears dried once again as her gaze fixed on the packed lunch that had fallen from her grasp. "Alastair… He should be here. He's still out on the water. Can we wait for him?"

"I told the station to radio his boat," Colby assured her. "They will call me back as soon as they can with an update."

"He needs to be here, or he'll never forgive himself."

The officer went to respond when she spied Martin Fin approaching her vehicle. "Barbara, I'm sorry. Just give me a moment, my dear. I'll be right outside if you need me."

"Hey, you," Martin beamed at her.

"Heard you were onsite with Newton this morning." Colby grinned back at him. "Your favorite officer of the law."

Martin chuckled through gritted teeth. "Boatmore's finest… Ha!" he scoffed. "You should've seen the wimpy little prick."

"Not if I can help it," Colby laughed. "Lemme guess. He didn't go near the body, did he?"

"Wouldn't even look at it." Martin smiled, but it quickly faded as his eyes widened in realization. "Oh crap. Can Barb hear us in there?"

"Can she hell!" Colby assured him. "The glass I had put in is thick as fuck. It's practically soundproof."

"I like the way my lady thinks," Martin said with a cheesy wink.

"Don't call me your 'lady'," she grimaced. "And don't wink at me, either."

"All right… *Fine!*" Martin raised his hands in defeat. "So…dinner tonight?"

"Sure."

* * *

The body of Jamie Brooks lay upon the embalming table as the coroner, Carl Oxspring, dialed away on the cordless phone.

The 52-year-old squinted through thin spectacles at the laminated contact chart next to the wall mount as a gloved hand scratched his head of short gray hair.

He hung up the second he spied Liam Price entering the morgue.

"Liam, what are you doing here?" He smiled, replacing the phone. "Are you all right? You look as if you've been through it."

"You could say that," Liam uttered glumly, hands planted firmly in his pockets.

"Is this one yours? From this morning?" Carl walked over to the open body bag. "Poor boy. Looks like some nasty business if you ask me."

"That's actually why I'm here. Could you let me know the cause of death on this one? We've no idea what happened to this kid. I figure it's better to know in case this ever happens again."

"Shouldn't be a problem," Carl replied. "Are you around this week?"

"Yeah, should be. Give me a call. I'll buy you a beer for your troubles."

"Sounds fun."

"Thanks, Carl." Liam patted the coroner on the arm.

He took one last look at Jamie before he made his way out of the morgue.

Halfway down the long corridor to the exit, Liam stopped, unable to take another step, as he remembered. He had made this walk before. He found it almost funny that he had actually walked into the morgue that day still wearing those damn beach sandals. Almost.

Suddenly he buckled. Catching himself on the wall, Liam sat down on the floor before he could collapse. Closing his eyes, he kept his breathing slow as he waited for the memory to pass.

5
Christopher Price, Pt. II

Seventeen Months Earlier

With a knock so weak that only a house of silence could hear it, Ally Price answered the door one late afternoon in her unwashed dressing gown. Her eyes, puffy and red, were raw with grief.

She opened the door to the tear-stained face of Bethany Wilde, who stood there on the step in a blueish purple anorak, clutching an embroidered handkerchief with shuddering hands that were deep pink from the freezing island winds that tossed about her gray curly hair.

Although Ally had every intention of turning the woman away, the morning's adverse weather conditions forced her to be a fraction, a broken shard, of her compassionate self.

"Come in," she muttered as she backed away.

"Thank you, Allison." Bethany hurried inside, pulling the door closed behind herself. "I won't keep you."

"What do you want?" Ally rubbed her eyes in her impatience.

"I thought you should know: Alec and I are leaving the island," Bethany told her. "He can't forgive himself for–"

"For running over my son." Ally was blunt as she finished the woman's sentence.

"It was an accident." Bethany choked on a sob. "Of the worst kind, no question, but it was. Lord knows, I understand. Sometimes, I'm not sure how I feel when I look at my Alec. But, Allison, you should hear the things people are saying to him. Just yesterday evening, I couldn't buy food because the cashier 'refused to serve the wife of a child killer'."

"That's not my concern, Beth," Ally replied emptily, her eyes disengaged and wandering the floor and the walls. Any excuse not to acknowledge the other woman's presence in her hallway.

"We're neighbors," Bethany reminded her with hurt in her wet eyes. "Friends, even."

"No…" Ally shook her head slowly.

"I've never repeated this to anyone…" Bethany braced herself as she took a deep breath. There was nowhere to sit in that quiet hallway, so she rested a hand against the wall. "Before Alec and I moved to the island, we had two children."

Ally Price finally met eyes with her unwelcome houseguest.

"We were young parents," Bethany continued. "I was working a long shift at the hospital. Alec was looking after the kids. Our five-year-old, Samuel, and our baby girl… Her name was Lily."

"That's a pretty name," Ally said quietly as the woman collected herself.

"He had just finished giving her a bath when he heard the fire alarm," Bethany went on, sniffing tearfully. "The food in the oven was burning. Alec put Lily in her cot and ran downstairs to quickly fix things. But not quickly enough…When he went back upstairs, the cot was empty. After a frantic search for her, he found her in the bathroom. Her big brother had put her back in the bath. He didn't hold her under, apparently. He just sat on the toilet and watched her drown. Alec did everything he could to try and save her, but it was too late. Our Lily was gone.

"The next day, they took Samuel away, and we were put under intense scrutiny for weeks. An investigation was opened because Samuel told them that he saw his daddy drown his baby sister. His story held weight because the report showed that Lily had fractured ribs. A medical expert told us that it most likely happened when Alec was trying to revive her, but that didn't matter to anyone.

"We lost all our friends. Family members. The whole town turned on us, much like they are now, but, eventually, they found that the accusations were just the lies of a scared little boy who didn't want to be punished for what he had done. It made no difference. The damage was already done. Our lives were in tatters. So, we left for the island, and we haven't seen Samuel since."

Ally approached her and put a hand gently on her arm.

"I'm very sorry for what happened to you, Beth," she said softly. "But don't you find it strange?"

"I don't know what you mean." The woman was oblivious.

"Bethany…" Ally removed her hand. "A child is dead. Again. Your husband is being blamed. Again. A town has turned against you, and now you're leaving. Again."

Bethany opened her mouth to speak, but no words came out.

"How many times does this have to happen for you to see?" Ally asked, holding her eyes. "Are you even sure that Samuel wasn't telling the truth?"

"No, no." Bethany started to tremble as she backed away. "That can't be right."

"You lost two children because of that man," Ally pressed as she stepped forward. "And now my son is dead."

Bethany Wilde could say no more as she burst into tears. Stumbling as she turned away from her neighbor's reasoning, she retreated through the front door as fast as her uncertain feet could carry her.

Ally Price watched the woman scurry down her drive and back up the street to her home. She didn't care enough to go after her. She wondered if she would ever care about anything ever again. And with that, she shut the door to the world.

* * *

Present Day

Liam's eyes were already open when morning came.

He watched the sunlight slowly brighten up the room as it radiated through the thin fabrics of the bedroom curtains. Observing the world coming to life gave him a near unbeatable urge to rip them open. His fingers twitched eagerly above the covers.

Turning cautiously onto his side instead, he stared at his wife.

Ally looked so adorable and peaceful when she slept. It reminded her husband of the way a child sleeps; quiet, perfect looking, chest slowly rising and falling, the remains of a smile from sweet dreams of the night before.

Watching her sleep, Liam forgot all about the world outside. He kissed her very softly on the cheek. The act was impossible to resist. So was lifting the covers to stare at her naked body and marveling at the miracle mound of flesh where her flat stomach used to be: Ally's heavily pregnant belly. He wished for the courage to make love to her the way he used to in their younger, happier days.

Their two souls combined could stir up a rapture so intense that reality swayed to and fro with every pulse of pleasure. Culminating in eruptions and voices, expressions of love, uncontrollable body tremors as the act drew to a close. Followed by sighs of amazement, strokes of appreciation, kisses of adoration, and, at long last, warm and sweaty laughter.

How Liam missed those times in their life together. As he looked at his wife's inviting body, his eyes moved over to the lifeless roll of skin between his thick thighs, good thrusting thighs. Thighs that were only good for running now.

"Still sleeping?" the beautiful voice beside him asked.

Liam dropped the covers back over his body as he sighed disappointedly.

"Sorry."

Ally reached over and squeezed his hand.

"We'll be okay," she said breathily as she ran her fingers up and down Liam's arm.

"*Are* you okay?"

"Of course I am," she assured him. "Why wouldn't I be?"

"I couldn't keep my hands off you the first time."

"Hey, I was just as crazy for it as you were," she reminded him. "Do you see me leaping over furniture to rip your clothes off this time around?"

"No…" Liam narrowed his eyes. "But I thought that was because of me."

"Nope." Ally shook her head. "I've got news for you, Mr. Price. I'm just as scared about all this as you are."

"You, too?" Liam asked in surprise. "Really?"

"Uh-huh." She nodded, kissing his shoulder. "I'm absolutely terrified. And do you want to know what the worst part is?"

"What?"

"That the both of us know, beyond a shadow of a doubt, that it would make us feel much better if we just did it."

Liam laughed with his whole body. He fought back tears as he held his wife's face in his hands as he kissed her warmly, sadly, deeply.

"I *love* you, Ally."

"I love you, too." Ally hummed before stretching and yawning as she lay back against her pillows. "Do you want me to make you breakfast?"

Liam leapt out of bed, semi-awake below the waist.

Ally's eyes shivered wide open with excitement as her mouth watered at its girth and its veiny-ness. She looked up into her husband's eyes as he smiled dirtily back down at her.

"No." He shook his head suggestively. "I want you to get in that shower with me and help me make some new memories."

"I'm already there," Ally said with a grin.

The two giggled mischievously as they raced each other to the adjoining bathroom.

That morning should have felt like heaven behind the leaf-patterned glass of those shower doors; the concentrated streams of high-pressured water beat down on their hot skin like dozens of lean and long fingers in an intense deep-tissue massage. It should have felt like heaven on Liam's flesh as Ally kissed the sweet spot on his neck with renewed love and desire, causing his eyes to roll and his limbs to stiffen and quake.

It did feel like heaven…until Ally spoke. "I'm so glad we're doing this."

"Mmm, me too," Liam replied as his head swam in euphoria.

"God only knows we won't get a chance when baby number two gets here," his wife joked softly as she ran her tongue up to his unresponsive lips. "Liam, love?"

In one single moment, Liam resisted the aching urge to punch a hole in the shower wall. Instead, he opened his eyes with a smile and engaged in the kiss. He wrapped his arms around her as she rested her head contently against his shoulder. His smile disappeared instantly.

Baby Number Two? There had to be a Baby Number One for there to be a Baby Number Two. And where was Baby Number One? Resting for eternity in the grave only a few miles' drive away from their door because they couldn't bear the thought of doing any more damage to his fragile little body. There was no Baby Number One, but there was a boy. A dead boy. And he was *his* boy; his poor, dead, baby boy; the only baby as far as he was concerned.

For a few seconds, Liam allowed his mouth to open for just one agonizing silent scream. Could he cry? The shower water would hide his tears. He had permitted himself, and he was ready, until he heard that sound.

Now that the two of them were locked in a long, warm, loving embrace, the high-powered streams were pelting the glass of the shower doors like deadly laser beams. They made a familiar sound, a horrible sound.

As Liam watched the streams splash apart into countless droplets on the surface of the steaming glass, he didn't hear the rush and impact of the water. He heard the rattling wheels of the ambulance gurney as he pushed it down the corridor that led to the morgue. The corpse of Jamie Brooks peeked out of the body bag that lay atop it.

Every passing second Liam heard that sound, the images in his mind shifted and changed. Suddenly the body bag was wide open. Jamie's bloodstained face looked almost blue. Liam continued pushing regardless. Jamie was now gone, leaving just an empty body bag. And still Liam pressed on.

"Daddy?" a child's voice uttered from somewhere beyond time.

The wheels of the gurney squealed to a halt. The sound stopped. Liam looked down to find Christopher's body in the bag, eyes still staring back at him as if they could see him.

Fighting back his wish to weep, he held Ally a little tighter, a little closer, and kissed her play-roughly on the side of her head as he exclaimed, "I love you!"

Husband and wife laughed at one another.

"I love you, too," Ally sighed as she rubbed her face adoringly against Liam's chest.

Once again, his smile disappeared.

Liam pulled a pair of navy blue shorts up his legs as Ally sat on the bed wrapped in a dressing gown, staring at her husband with concern.

"You tried," she said soothingly. "We both tried."

"Tried and failed," Liam muttered as he pulled on a white t-shirt. "Might as well've not tried at all."

"We were rushing things." Ally got up from the bed and crossed the room to her husband. "We were silly to think we could just jump back in. Obviously, this is going to take time."

"Time," Liam scoffed as he passed by his wife and sat on the bed with a pair of sneakers in one hand, a pair of ankle-high socks in the other. "We've got nothing but time on this island."

"At least we know that we both want it," Ally reminded him as she rubbed his shoulder. "That says something."

"Somehow, knowing that," Liam sighed as he finished tying up his sneakers, "makes it even worse…"

He got up and headed for the door.

"I'm going out for a run," he said miserably over his shoulder before disappearing through the doorway.

Ally shook her head until her eyes traveled down to find her beautiful baby bump. A smile graced her lips as she cradled the miracle mound in her hands.

"I would just like to know how this is so easy for you," Liam demanded as he barged back into the room.

"What the hell do you mean by 'easy'?"

"You're always so calm and collected about everything all the time," he accused her. "I'm sorry if I'm disappointing you, but I can't be like that. I wasn't raised by an upper middle-class family of robots who just sweep everything they don't want to deal with under the rug!"

"That is not fair," Ally said through tears. "You know what I've been through."

"I know, that's not what I'm saying."

"Then what are you saying!"

"You don't have to do that with us," Liam sighed sadly. "You don't have to keep how you're feeling a secret anymore. I want to know if you're in pain. I want to know I'm not the only one falling apart inside."

"I'm afraid to," Ally told him quietly as she pointed to her belly. "I've got this one to worry about now. I can't just let myself fall apart. No matter how much I want to. I'm scared, Liam. I'm scared of what will happen to her if I can't put the pieces back…"

Liam's arms and legs ran thick with sweat as his jog slowed to a finish a few doors down from the house.

As he breathed slowly in and out, the scent of salty sea air filled his mouth. He tasted it on his tongue as the morning breeze pushed and pulled the sweat across his sticky limbs.

The familiar purr of a familiar motor grabbed his attention as he stopped to take a breath. He rested his hands upon his hips.

Martin Fin's car was parked outside Liam's house.

He could see Martin sitting in the driver's seat, waiting for him before he spied Ally's face disappearing from the window at the front of the house.

Liam sighed in annoyance as he began to weigh his options. He weighed the chances of Martin being able to chase him down if he took off through the wide streets of the island. He weighed having to deal with a pregnant Ally's hormonally heightened disapproval and disappointment if he were to do such a thing, as opposed to having to deal with a pregnant Ally's tears when he scolded her furiously over dinner for giving Martin a call on his behalf.

A second sigh as Liam surrendered and walked over to the car.

Inside, Martin fought back a grin.

It suddenly occurred to Liam that he made the wrong decision.

"You know, if you're gonna keep parking outside my house," Liam remarked as he supported himself against the car roof, "eventually Ally's going to find out about us."

"I'm game if you are." Martin winked at him.

"Get lost," Liam said with a grin.

"Relax," Martin reassured him, "I've got our play worked out. You get in the car. We talk. Ally watches. We hug. You get out of the car. I leave. You go back in the house. You pretend the conversation Ally wanted us to have has been had. You kiss. You make up. You get your ass to work."

"And that's why it's always been you."

"Shut it and get in the car, ya wuss."

Liam laughed as he jogged around the front of the car and got in.

"So, is everything all right?" Martin asked considerately as he patted Liam on his clammy thigh.

Liam's mouth fell open. "Oh, you bastard." He reached for the passenger door.

"Liam…" Martin grabbed his friend's arm.

"It's Liam now, is it?" he said, astonished. "Aw, this can't be good."

"Everything's going to be fine."

"What in blue hell did she say to you?"

"Will you just listen to me?" Martin near enough growled. "*Everything* is going to be fine. You and Ally. Ally and the baby. It's all going to be all right."

Liam turned away from Martin. His eyes tried to find even a glimpse of his beloved sea view. Nothing. He bowed his head instead.

"You and I know what it's like," Martin continued. "You and I know what tragedy is. How often it happens. Who it happens to. Despite all that, if we've learned one thing from the job, we can't take anything for granted."

Liam said nothing. He did not move or show any sign of acknowledgement of Martin's words. He just pressed a finger down on the button on the handle of the passenger door. The car window on his side rolled down. He inhaled deeply through his nose as he closed his eyes.

"Are you okay?" Martin asked as he tried to make sense of Liam's reaction.

"I think so," Liam replied, finally opening his eyes. "To tell you the truth, I'm just relieved."

"Relieved?"

"Yeah. I thought Ally had called you over here to give a pep-talk to my penis."

With a loud, abrupt click, Liam opened the car door and slipped out.

Martin watched him walk around the front of the car towards the house, a look of bemusement all over his face.

L. Stephenson

"Huh?"

6
Callum Wright, Pt. I

Night fell upon the island's small town of Boatmore, and it was time to find the second.

Before sixteen-year-old Callum Wright's night of freedom could even begin, his father, Gary, decided that it was time for his son to learn what it felt like to have the side of his head bounce off the freezer door. If dinner wasn't ready when Daddy stumbled home from another full day of drinking, he got very angry. It didn't really matter as he always found some ridiculous reason to go off.

Still, Callum would forgive him that night the same way he forgave him every night: in his prayers before sleep came to dull the throbbing ache of the day's beatings. He would forgive the fists to the face, the cruel names and crueler words, the cold cans of beer hurled at his gut, the cigarettes to the back of his hands. And he'll continue to forgive him for the sake of his mother, because he wasn't like this before she left them both to be in heaven.

But tonight was Callum's night to escape it all. Even if it was just for a few hours. Tonight was his night of freedom.

His thick dark eyebrows scrunched miserably as he spun an empty beer bottle atop the table of his booth in The Golden Eagle, named after the majestic bird that took up residence on the cliffs of Last Point, one of the island's most popular beaches. Although he hadn't quite discovered what his scene was just yet, unfortunately, this bar most definitely wasn't it.

The place was abuzz with the drinking and laughter of mainlanders making the best of their long weekend. The atmosphere was warm and merry as the resident disc jockey played it safe with classic floor-fillers. The wine bar was always a big hit with the crowd, with its own selection of local wines to choose from. A pub during the weekdays, as its main seating area was hardwood flooring, just the clearing of a few tables and chairs turned it into a disco.

Sixteen-year-old Callum gazed indifferently at the crowded dancefloor from his corner, as less than sober girls gyrated up against their boyfriends to the icy beats of cheesy '80s electro-pop. Rolling his eyes, Callum dragged himself out of the booth and made his way around the dancefloor.

A man in a pale hood stepped out of the crowd and followed him. He watched as the young man walked around the perimeter of the dancefloor, nearing the exit.

The man began walking faster.

But Callum didn't use the exit, carrying on around towards the bar instead.

The man stopped in his tracks and observed Callum as he rested his elbows against the support railing, awaiting the tender's attention.

A moment later, the hooded man seeped back into the crowd.

Callum returned to his booth to find that mainlanders had rather inconsiderately taken up residency. Frowning, but unsurprised, he sighed and defiantly claimed one of the uncomfortable metallic chairs on the other side of their table. A table that now played host to over a dozen bottles, shots, and wine glasses.

He placed his glass of whiskey, two shots of vodka, and a chaser pint of ale upon the table. From that moment on, he wasted no time in getting to work. Down went one shot, a long sip of ale, a gasp for breath. Down went a second shot, a second sip of ale, a longer gasp for breath. He slowed down with a minuscule sip of whiskey that made his eyes water.

Already feeling a little bit more than fine, Callum drew in a long breath through his nostrils, closed his eyes, and swayed his head to the euphoric creeping bassline of another '80s dance number.

This otherworldly feeling ended abruptly when a drunken woman in her late forties tripped over a chair leg at the next table and crashed against Callum's shoulder. The impact shook his table, tipping his ale over his left leg.

Laughing uncontrollably, the woman picked herself up and cheerfully offered to mop up the mess she had made, while managing to grace Callum with the most ineffective suggestive wink he had ever witnessed.

He quickly brushed her desperation away as he made a quick escape from his table towards the dancefloor.

Callum waded his way through the thick sea of people while the odd patron pointed and giggled at the wet stain. He tried to smile it off, but his determination to get to the nearest restroom deadened his face.

Finally, he broke free of the crowd as he squeezed his way out on the other side of the dancefloor. With the bar in front of him, he headed to the right where both the Ladies and Gentlemen restroom doors lay.

A man emerged from the crowd behind Callum—the man in the pale hood. He followed the young man, watching the other exit directly behind the bar—the one that led out to the smokers' shelter—but the young man did not head in that direction.

Arms outstretched, Callum pushed his way through the Gentlemen's restroom door.

The man in the pale hood followed him in.

Inside the Gentlemen's restroom, Callum stood in front of the sink, exasperated, as he angrily tore paper towel after paper towel from the dispenser beside the mirror and mashed them against the soaked leg of his blue jeans.

He didn't notice the man who walked casually by him and into the stall beside the sink less than three feet away.

Pressing the side of his face against the wall of the cubicle, the man in the pale hood pulled the door open as far as the latch would allow it. He held his breath as he watched the young man at the sink.

Turning to the wall, he spied a small window that lay open.

Even if this room was empty for long enough, the window wasn't big enough to push the young man's body out of. There had to be another way.

He needed him.

There was the sound of paper rustling and then a thud.

He returned to the door gap in time to see the lid of the plastic trash can swinging back and forth as the young man pushed his way out of the restroom. He snapped the latch open and raced to the door.

Back in the pub, he slowed to a relaxed, devil-may-care pace. Across the room, over the heads of the pub's writhing patrons, he could see the young man already back at his booth making conversation. He gestured empathically, pointing to his jeans, pointing to the middle-aged woman at the next table who had spilled his drink on him and then made a pass at him. Once his story was over, he got to his feet once again. The young man shook a few hands and waved as he headed off.

The hooded man's fingers tightened up into fists as Callum's hand rested on the exit door of the pub. It opened.

Go.

* * *

The whiskey buzz was now taking full effect in the fast-food restaurant.

The fluorescent lights above Callum Wright's head seemed to blaze a little too brightly in his intoxicated haze. The color coordination of tomato reds, sea blues and daffodil yellows made his eyes throb. Squinting to dull the ache, he put his head in his hands as he rested his elbows against the counter. As the hissing of fat and oil under burger meat from the kitchen seared through his brain, he moved his hands from his forehead to his ears.

"Early night?" asked a man in a red cap behind the counter with a smile. Sweat glistened on his freckled cheeks, but his fiery, red, curled locks were untouched.

Callum looked up with a frown, smiled, and laughed.

The yellow name tag pinned to the left breast pocket of the man's blue shirt said GORDON in red capital letters, but with the state that his eyes were in, Callum couldn't read it.

"Looks like it," he replied.

Gordon frowned in confusion as he pointed over Callum's shoulder towards the window. "Is that your friend?" he asked.

"Who?" Callum asked tipsily, failing to look.

"Never mind." Gordon shook his head with a smile. "He's gone now, whoever he was."

He couldn't keep his eyes off the window the entire time he served Callum. Who was that? And why was he looking at his customer that way? And his stare. He had never seen anything like it. For the first time in the three years he had worked there, enveloped in the sweltering heat from the grills, Gordon felt a chill.

* * *

There was not a single soul inside the taxi stand, save for the man sitting by the little window in the wall at the back.

Callum Wright stood outside the front entrance, already halfway through the cheeseburger he had ordered ten minutes ago, as he waited for the taxi ride that he ordered two minutes ago.

Between bites, he knew in his heart and bones that from the moment he eventually got home that night, he would pay dearly for his little adventure out into the world for weeks and weeks to come, but until then there was the warm, oily, salty goodness of the overcooked burger meat and the tangy melted cheese swimming inside his starving mouth. As it all mashed softly under his teeth and curled deliciously around his tongue, it made his taste buds sing and his eyes water with joy. To him, this was the taste of freedom.

The streets were surprisingly clear, considering that he seemed to be the only one heading home early, but he could definitely hear their noise: their laughter, their off-key singing, their bickering over in which order they should visit their favorite pubs. Yet there was no one in sight. Apart from a trio of louts whose plan it was to raid the nearest liquor store and lurk outside the pubs that they had been turned away from for their past behavior.

Lowering his head, Callum took a deep bite of his half-eaten cheeseburger and held his teeth there inside the greasy meat. He even closed his eyes as he prayed that those three loud men did not come in his direction, that they did not spot him and engage him.

He had read many solemn articles in the newspapers and had watched so many shameful television reports on the news of men just like them causing trouble, bashing in elderly men, stabbing rival gang members, shooting young children, setting their vicious dogs on complete strangers.

The three men began descending down the street towards the liquor store directly across the street from the taxi stand.

Callum muttered a curse to himself. That long bite of his fast food was not going down his throat easily, and although he knew that a simple forced cough and clearing of his throat would help, he was certain that it would attract their unwanted attention.

They drew closer still. Out of the corner of his eye, Callum could see their heads already starting to glance in his direction. Soon their glances would become longer. They would begin nudging one another, pointing over to him and suggesting cruel things to do to him, all because he was alone and vulnerable.

He needed to get out of there. But to where? Back inside the taxi stand?

The road before him crunched as a taxi slowly ground to a halt right in front of him.

Callum's heart skipped a beat in relief as he checked the doors for the taxi stand's logo. He let out a rush of air through his nostrils in frustration as he realized that it belonged to somewhere else.

The back window of the taxi on Callum's side hummed as it rolled down. He made a quick glance up at it but then looked away just as swiftly.

"Hi," said a man's voice.

Callum looked up from his cheeseburger. A frown spread across his face as he noticed that the man was speaking to him.

"Hi..." he responded hesitantly.

"You look like you don't want to be here," the man said with a smile.

Or at least Callum thought the man was smiling. There were no lights on in the taxi and most of his face was shrouded in the shadow cast over him by the roof of the vehicle under the streetlight.

"Nope," Callum managed to force a laugh followed by a smile.

"Can we give you a lift?" the man in shadow asked.

Callum looked left and right as he took in a breath, uttering another curse. He turned back to the taxi.

"Where are you headed?" he asked with a sigh, hoping that the man would give the wrong answer.

Whether it was the right one or not, Callum's taxi still hadn't arrived, and he had genuine doubts about his safety if he remained on that street with the three other men who were just entering the liquor store across from him. If he went with the man in the taxi, by the time they came out with their beer and their spirits, he would be long gone.

"Well, if it's no trouble," Callum said with a shrug, praying that his apprehension hadn't cost him the man's offer.

"No trouble at all."

Relieved, Callum tossed the half-eaten cheeseburger into the nearest street garbage can. He ran around to the other side of the taxi where the door was already open for him and climbed in. As soon as he was strapped in good and tight, they took off.

"Thanks a lot," Callum said. "To be honest, I didn't feel very safe out there."

"Oh? Is someone after you?"

"Nah, not really," Callum sighed. "I don't think so anyway. I didn't want to stay to find out."

He gazed thoughtfully out of the window as the buildings on the other side of the glass were swept away into the night. "You just never know, you know?"

The shadowed man didn't respond.

* * *

"Stop here!" a man's voice boomed out of nowhere.

Callum Wright's elbow slid off the taxi door window. His eyes snapped open, but not soon enough to stop the side of his head from bumping the glass. He had been asleep for the last eleven minutes. Dazed and barely awake, he rubbed his eyes as they adjusted to the darkness inside the taxi.

They had come to a stop beside a grassy embankment on a back road. The looming shadows of towering trees lined a footpath a few feet in.

"You've been sick, son." The man's hand was on Callum's shoulder. "I think we should get you some air before we carry on, hmm?"

Callum looked directly into the taxi driver's side mirror as the man spoke. The driver drew something from beneath his coat, out of what appeared to be a leather holster. It was some kind of black metal pipe.

"No need to worry about a mess," the man assured the driver. "He only got it on himself, so if–"

Before Callum knew it, the man sitting next to him, the man who had been kind enough to offer him a ride, was slumping forward in his seat. The driver hit him again, hard. He could hear the blunt cry of solid metal on bone. The poor man's head bounced off the window beside him. Instead of shattering, it became a spider-web of cracked glass.

The man in the taxi driver's seat sheathed his weapon and pulled up his hood.

Suddenly the taxi shook as he erupted from his seat and tore out through the driver's door.

Turning, Callum clung to the headrests of both front seats as he tried desperately to haul himself to the front, to safety. But it was too late.

The door beside him ripped open with a shriek. The shock caused Callum to throw himself across the back seat, slamming his back hard into his unlucky rescuer's unconscious body. The blood still flowing from his head was cold and sticky against the back of Callum's neck as he grunted and kicked at his attacker.

The hooded man reached into the taxi with gloved hands and jagged fingers. The boy battered them with the soles of his loose sneakers, making little impact. Still, it was enough to make the man angry.

With a ferocious growl, the man in the pale hood clamped down on Callum's legs by the knees. He fell silent as the man loomed forward and over him like some form of dark serpent. The creature leered at him.

The boy recoiled as he heard a hum of satisfaction, but the sound was strangely muffled. As his eyes adjusted further to the darkness, he soon discovered why. It wasn't a real face looking back at him. Some kind of mask? Whatever it was, the only thing that looked real were those eyes. The rest didn't look even close to human, as its bloated lips were too warped to smile back at him.

The sight of the thing sent Callum into a frenzy of fear as he thrashed blindly with his free arms, his fingers searching for an escape. The man holding him down just laughed. Until the boy managed to release the headrest from the car seat next to him and jammed the metal shafts toward the man's eyes.

There was a howl as the man shrank back into the night.

Reaching back, Callum grabbed the door handle and pulled and kicked with all his might until both he and the bloodied unconscious body he lay against toppled out of the taxi and onto the road.

Rolling onto his knees, Callum yanked off a sneaker and tossed it across the grassy embankment towards the woods beyond. Spinning on his heels, he scrambled under the taxi, hiding himself directly beneath the body as it hung out of the vehicle. Once hidden, he tried with all the might he could muster to remain as silent as the grave. All he could do now was wait.

The road beneath his clothes was cold and wet, made colder still by the uncaring chill of the night air. He froze to the spot as the taxi shook above him only a few inches away from his face. His fingers dug themselves bloody into the tarmac as he listened to the madman thrash and scream and rage inside the vehicle that was on top of him. The maniac's tirade gathered such force that the broken window gave way, shattering to the ground.

The commotion ceased.

Callum held his breath. Clasping a hand over his mouth, he waited. He could hear the trees moving in the wind, the rustling of a million leaves.

Then, the footsteps. Slow at first. The sound came from the direction of the boy's feet, which meant the man was standing on the other side of the taxi. As Callum continued to listen, he realized that it was too quiet, which meant the man must be listening too. Did he know he was under there?

Please God, don't let him find me.

Suddenly the footsteps quickened. Callum lost his breath. The sound seemed to come from all around him as they raced around the taxi. The boy covered his mouth with both hands this time as the tears came thick and fast. He trembled in silence beneath the belly of that vehicle, convulsing with each heavy sob. This was it. The madman had found him, and now he was going to kill him. He closed his eyes and accepted the inevitable.

But nothing happened.

No reaching hands and fingers. No frightening faces. Just silence.

Allowing himself to remove his hands from his mouth, Callum's breath was shaky as he lifted his head back and took a look around, searching for the man's feet. And he found them right next to his face! Callum let out a sudden gasp as his body jerked away with fright.

For a moment he had forgotten that the unconscious stranger was still out there on the road. His body stirred as the man in the pale hood took a hold of him.

Refusing to be seen, Callum quietly braced both feet against the underbelly of the taxi and twisted himself until his entire body was hidden beneath the vehicle. As soon as he felt secure, he turned to watch his savior's body as it was dragged out onto the grassy embankment and left there. He had turned out to be the perfect gentleman after all.

The hooded man stopped as he spied something.

Callum tried to shrink away further, but the wet ground made it near impossible. He just had to watch as the man walked towards the trees. He stopped again and picked something up. The sneaker.

The man dropped the shoe to the ground as he turned towards the woods. Slowly, he crept into the darkness between the trees. He vanished from sight.

Callum exhaled with such relief that more tears came.

"Thank God…" he uttered under his breath.

With his next prayer he jammed his hand into his right jeans pocket. It had to be there. It just had to be. It was! He could have screamed with joy as he pulled out his phone.

It lit up instantly. Holding its luminescence up to his face, his fingers punched away at its touchscreen for the authorities. Placing the glowing phone to his ear, he didn't notice the rush of the wind outside getting stronger and louder. The taxi even bobbed gently over him. He paid it all no mind as he pressed the phone harder against his ear, listening desperately as it began to ring.

There was an answer! Or so he thought. He couldn't be sure. And a voice? It was too hard to tell. Was it the wind or a bad signal? Probably a bad signal. There were many horror stories on the island about people dying after an accident because they couldn't get any phone reception, and now he was going to be a horror story come true.

Callum kicked and cursed in his frustration. His left leg got stuck to something. Was it caught on part of the taxi? He tried to shake it loose with no success. He had no choice but to hang up his phone and shine the light on his leg.

He screamed as he found that horrible face from the taxi staring back at him. It roared as it grabbed for his other leg.

Dropping the phone, Callum reached out from under the vehicle with both hands, grabbing hold of whatever he could find, kicking and pulling himself with all the fight he had in him. As soon as he saw the night sky above him, he flipped like a pancake onto his front and threw himself, half-stumbling and half-running, across the embankment as he headed for the woods.

As he broke through the tree line, it was as if a heavy curtain of darkness had been dropped over his eyes. The ground was soft beneath his feet and the air was thick, wet, and warm as it passed through his nose and mouth. He had the moments to observe all these things because the woods would not allow him to run as fast or as far as he needed to. There were clawing branches in his path and tricky roots under every step, and the farther he walked the stronger the darkness grew. Even the sky was blacked out by the treetops.

Callum quickly decided that if he couldn't go far, then he would hide instead. He prepared to crouch until a branch caught the arm of his sweater. Wincing in his haste, he turned and tore the branch loose, leaving a shred of his clothing behind.

He turned back to find the man in the pale hood standing right in front of him as he raised the metal pipe high above his head. The man pummeled the boy at a vicious speed, one limb at a time, until he crumbled whimpering and weeping to the woodland floor. As the flesh of his limbs vibrated with agony, Callum was helpless as the man stood over him.

The pipe came swinging down. The boy's cry of fright cut short as the weapon struck him. There was a split second of pain, a moment of gloom and agonizing blur, and then complete darkness.

Back out on the empty road, the man in the pale hood climbed into the driver's seat of the taxi and closed the door. Moments later, the engine started up and he sped off into the night with the body of Callum Wright lying beaten and bloodied in the back seat.

He had him. Finally, he was his.

The second.

7
Jamie Brooks, Pt. IV

The following evening The Golden Eagle pub was set up as it would have been on any regular weeknight.

The chestnut wood panels, the deep red leather bar stools, the yellowish-orange glow of the lights, and the stained-glass window fixtures above the green pool tables were all combined, all intended to create a relaxing safe haven for its patrons to unwind, sit back, and have a drink or two.

Unfortunately, the warm ambience was of little comfort to Liam Price as he picked at the corners of his beer coaster. Removing his half-finished pint, he continued to peel at its center.

Martin Fin joined in the fun. He flipped the food menu continuously, looking through the items that he knew by heart and had never ordered. Flipping it one last time, he slotted the laminated sheet of folded card, with all the cheesy font that Microsoft Word could muster plastered on it, back in between the salt and pepper shakers and returned to his bottle of water.

"You not going to finish that?" he asked Liam as he cleared his throat and capped the bottle at the same time.

Liam stared blankly at his pint of beer. "Why? Do you want it?"

"No." Martin shook his head instantly and patted his flat stomach. "I don't want a beer gut."

"This will not give you a beer gut." Liam rolled his eyes and shook his head at the half-empty glass.

"Maybe, but one will lead to another, and before you know it–"

"Yeah, I get it," Liam quickly cut in, raising his right hand in defeat, "You're a health freak." He sighed as he lowered his hand onto the table. "But you're not going to live forever, you know. Nobody does."

"Well, that may be so! But I'll live longer than you, you grumpy shit."

For the first time that evening, a smile formed on Liam's weary, unshaven face. "You asshole… Go order me some fries."

"Yeah, sure," Martin stretched and got to his feet. "Anything else?"

Liam nodded. "Don't forget the ketchup!"

"Hey, who do ya think ya talkin' to?" The hilariously bad gangster impression gave them Liam's first laugh of the evening.

Before he could sink back in his seat or even catch his breath from what he hoped would be the first of many chuckles that night, Carl appeared at their table with his hands pushed firmly into the pockets of a depressingly ugly, bright gray jacket.

"Liam," Carl nodded to him politely.

"Carl!" Liam straightened up, looking for a server. "Are you ready for that drink?"

"We should discuss this outside," Carl responded insistently. "I won't keep you."

With every intention of arguing that the man take a seat and share some of his chips, Liam turned back to Carl and any hint of cheer left his expression when he caught sight of the look on the coroner's face.

"Outside it is." As he picked himself up, he looked over to the bar. "I will be back momentarily, Mr. Fin. Hold down the fort, if you please."

Still fastening his coat as he stepped outside, Liam found Carl already perched on the bench across the street lighting up a joint.

"Jesus Christ, Carl," Liam laughed in his surprise as he jogged across to him. "Where the hell did you get that?"

"From Matthew. Where else?" Carl replied as he took his first puff. "He's also exceptionally good at rolling them."

Shaking his head in disbelief, Liam dropped down beside the coroner. "I guess that assistant of yours is good for something after all."

"Oh, Matthew's a bright boy, really." Carl smiled. "He's taken quite a shine to your new recruit, it seems."

Liam chuckled. "Well, if there's anyone who needs something to take the edge off, it's Ben."

"He seems like a nice boy, too," Carl said, continuing to stall.

But Liam cut to the chase. "I thought you had something to tell me."

Carl took the joint from his mouth and exhaled with a sigh. He watched his escaping breath as it caused the tip to glow orange.

"You see many things in my line of work…many strange things, dark things," the coroner began. He then placed a firm hand on Liam's arm. "There was no way you could've saved that boy, and from my findings, somebody definitely didn't want you to."

"So, I didn't… I mean, we didn't…" Liam couldn't finish his sentence.

The relief washing over him was palpable. He bowed his head, running his hands through his hair, catching his breath as he resisted the temptation to crumble into tears.

"You didn't kill him, son," Carl reassured him, putting a hand on his friend's back.

Collecting himself, Liam released his hair and dusted it off with a grunt.

"So, what did?"

"Whoever did this, the cruel bastard separated the poor boy's ribs," Carl explained. "Cut right through the bone of each one, at just the right angle to make the ends as sharp as possible, and then sewed them back up inside him. Any amount of pressure, they would collapse inwards, rupturing any organs in their path."

"When we found him on the side of the road, he stopped breathing," Liam recounted. "We performed CPR, chest compressions. Standard procedure."

"Any amount of pressure, son," Carl repeated, "I'm surprised he was still alive when you got there. That boy's ribs skewered his insides like he was a human shish kabob."

"But why? Why would someone do something like that?"

"After a while, you'll find there's no real answer to that question. Not one that'll sit right, anyways."

"He would've lived if we had never touched him, though."

"No!" Carl said sternly, slapping Liam on the back. "I said you didn't kill him, and I meant it."

"There's more to it, isn't there?" Liam insisted.

"While we had him open, we also found a little baggie lodged down in his pipes."

"A baggie?" Liam was puzzled. "Drugs?"

"That's what I assumed at first, but after testing, it turned out to be a mixture of some very deadly industrial poisons."

Liam was at a loss. "I don't get it. Again, why?"

"Well, I'm no detective," Carl puffed, "nor am I a gambling man, but I'd bet my reputation that if you had chosen to intubate that boy instead, it would've ripped right through that baggie, poisoning the young boy in the process."

Astounded, Liam lay back against the bench. "Jesus…"

"As I said, somebody made sure you couldn't save that boy."

"Son of a bitch," Liam muttered at the evening sky.

Carl offered him a puff of his joint, but he declined with a polite shake of the head.

"That thing you said earlier, about seeing many strange, dark things," Liam began and sat back upright. "What did you mean by that?"

The same look he saw on Carl's face when he first came to the bar appeared again. The coroner took another puff in place of a response.

"What is it?" Liam pressed, nudging at him with an impatient elbow.

"Aye, that's right. I have seen many strange and dark things." Carl stalled with yet another puff. "But not on this island. Not in a place like this. Something…something about this feels personal. Whoever did this to that boy isn't finished. A colleague once said to me, when it comes to things like this, when you know, *you know*."

"Well, I'll tell ya this much," Liam began and shivered as he got to his feet, crossing his arms to protect his hands from the cold. "I hope you're wrong."

Carl chuckled. "So do I." He took one last puff and flicked the joint into the drain. "So do I."

Liam stretched as he extended a gentleman's helping hand out to his coroner friend.

"Come join us in the bar."

"No, I'd better get home," Carl said, accepting Liam's hand as he declined. He stared at the smoking drain. "Those things are marvelous, but they do leave you feeling rather famished."

"You can have my fries," Liam offered.

"Fabulous!"

Liam laughed as he patted Carl, who excitedly linked arms with him.

They stopped to watch the road between them and The Golden Eagle just as a police vehicle pulled up in front of them. The body was in pristine condition. Smooth and glossy beneath the light of the streetlamps, its spotless reflective surface of silver, blue, and yellow illuminated with the gleam of a dozen glowing eyes.

Carl nervously checked the drain, relaxing as he discovered that the joint had since extinguished itself.

"Good evening, gentlemen," said Officer Jennifer Colby as she rose out of her car.

"Officer," Liam nodded respectfully.

"Hello, Jennifer." Carl smiled warmly. "Sorry. Ma'am."

"S'better," Officer Colby let him off with a quick wink as she joined them on the pavement.

"Official business, I presume?"

"You presume correctly," Colby nodded, sliding her hands into the warmth inside her thick police vest.

"First things first," Liam said, crossing his arms as he inspected her vehicle. "How do you keep this thing so clean?"

"Pride," she said simply.

"Ah. Well. What can we do for you, officer?" Liam asked as he leaned his head closer with genuine concern.

"Gary Wright's boy went out drinking last night," Colby told them. "According to him, he hasn't been home since. Far as we know, he was last seen here at The Golden Eagle. So,

I'm here to talk to the owner, a couple of the regulars. Take a look around."

"You'd be better off starting with Gary himself," Liam advised her.

"What do you mean by that?" Colby probed with narrowing eyes as she produced a pen and pad from the front pocket of her uniform.

"Let's just say the boys on the night shift have paid that house the odd visit over the years," Liam replied. "They'll tell you: Gary's boy hasn't come home because he doesn't want to go home."

"Can you give me their names?"

8
Callum Wright, Pt. II

A handful of island folk assembled directly across the street from Murray's Tool Supplies, the only tool supply store in Boatmore. There was an air of unrest as they paced, loitered, and fidgeted endlessly on their phones to friends and family. Passersby were stopped and hounded as the group forced their attention to the shop across the way. Most took no notice and they walked on, but others rushed on into town to spread the word.

A police vehicle was parked outside as Officer Colby took Murray's statement. They both stood close to the entrance while a customer of his sat handcuffed in the back seat of Colby's car. One of the rabble stood at his window trying to communicate with him amongst all the commotion.

"Sir!" Colby called over to him. "Sir, please can you go stand over there with your friends right now? I won't ask you twice."

The man held up his hands as he complied, returning to the group as they hooted, hollered, and wolf-whistled at him and the officer like schoolchildren. Much to her relief, their ruckus died down quickly as the ambulance appeared at the corner, coming to a stop around the side of the store.

Some of them called out Liam's name as he led his team towards the entrance. Though he found this strange, he gave the small crowd a wave of acknowledgment. The gesture earned him a few short claps. The brief applause was even stranger.

"Good morning, Jen," Liam said, smiling as he approached. "Where can we find our injured party?"

"Morning, Liam," Colby nodded to the store. "He's inside with his wife."

Murray, a short man with huge spectacles, a bald patch, and baggy maroon trousers handed him the keys to the shop.

"Past the cash register; the room in the back," he told him. "I had to lock them in there, or they would've killed them. With my damn tools, too!"

"Thanks, Murray." Liam patted him on the shoulder. "I'll get these back to you when we're finished."

"No problem."

Liam headed inside before Murray could delay him any longer with idle island chit-chat. Ben followed him in straight after without saying a word while Martin stayed behind to visit with Colby.

It was dark in Murray's Tool Supplies, as the store had already lost the sun's light. Still, Liam wasn't much concerned about finding the switch as he wandered up the middle aisle. He stepped over a large wrench on his way towards the back.

"I'm guessing that's our murder weapon," he remarked, unbothered whether his present company found him funny or that they even got the reference.

Ben remained silent. Evidently not.

Squeezing past the cash register with his equipment bag, he placed it behind the counter before knocking gently on the door.

"Hello, sir," he called.

No response.

"This is the paramedics. Please don't be alarmed. We are here to treat you."

Pushing in the key, he turned the lock.

"Liam, don't!" Martin shouted from the entrance of the store, jogging inside.

"I'm coming in…" Liam looked back over his shoulder as the door opened and creaked inward. "What?"

"Do me a favor?" Martin asked as he hurried past Ben in the aisle, coming to a stop in front of the cash register. "Just…please don't go in there. Let me take this one, will you?"

"Why?" Liam narrowed his eyes.

Too stubborn for his own good, he shoved the door to the back room wide open to the sound of a woman gasping with fright. The gasp came from Bethany Wilde, who stood there holding a bloodstained handkerchief to her husband's head.

"Don't hurt him," she pleaded, sobbing. "They attacked *us*. We didn't do anything wrong."

"I…" Liam had to fight for words as he suddenly felt light-headed. "I didn't know you were back on the island…"

As he looked upon the man bleeding in the old wooden chair, he could feel the pounding of his heart in his ears and the burning sickness snaking its way up to his throat. It was exactly the way he felt the day he saw the very same man sitting in the road, weeping against his car. The car that killed his boy, Christopher.

"We returned a few weeks ago," Bethany uttered tearfully as she dabbed away at the wound. "We thought enough time had passed, but it's like we never left."

Alec Wilde could barely look at him as he sat there in his tweed suit and chaotic gray hair. He always did look like an eccentric English teacher.

Liam found Martin's huge hand upon his shoulder.

"Come on," he said quietly. "Let me take care of this one."

Stepping back out of the room, Liam pulled the door with him as he closed it tightly.

"Did you know they were here?" he demanded of his best friend with a scowl.

"You would be my first call," Martin assured him as a grin formed across his face. "But I guess now we know why you got such a warm reception on arrival. They think you're gonna kick his ass."

Liam rolled his eyes as he laughed away his scowl.

"Unfortunately, we have to treat them like every other decent citizen on this island."

"Says who?"

"Call me when you're done," Liam instructed him as he planted Murray's shop keys in Martin's hand. "We need to take them out the back way. Avoid that mob out there."

Leaving the equipment bag for his colleague, Liam started back down the aisle. As he passed Ben, he happened upon the same large wrench on the floor. He stopped for a moment and stared at it, wondering if he should pick it up, take it to the back room of that store, and finish the job. Instead, he kicked it to the side and kept on walking.

* * *

As the front bell rang through the open back window of the Crispy Chicken & Burger Bar, a tired and perspiring Gordon Starkwood gave up halfway through his cigarette break without complaint.

Flicking his smoker's lunch over the back wall, he made his way through the kitchen, smoothing his sweat-soaked, curly red hair up under his work hat as he carefully weaved through his co-workers as they cooked and cleaned.

Smile at the ready, he greeted his latest customer at the counter.

"Good afternoon, officer," Gordon chirped. "What can I get for you? Free coffee?"

"No, no." Officer Colby waved away the offer. "But thank you. I'm here to ask your staff a few questions. I believe I spoke with your manager earlier this morning?"

"I'm afraid he's out for lunch," Gordon informed her.

"Oh, I see." Colby creased her brow in her annoyance. "That's unfortunate. He did say he would be here most of the day."

"I understand. Sorry about that…" Gordon awkwardly bit his lower lip. "Can I help you at all?"

"Yes, as a matter of fact." Colby drew something from her vest. "A young man has been missing since the weekend, and according to a couple of witnesses, this was one of the last places he was seen at."

"Wow, that's terrible," Gordon said thoughtfully.

"Were you working here late on Saturday?" Colby asked.

"Yes," Gordon replied. "I was here all weekend."

"Do you remember seeing this person at any point that night?" Colby handed Gordon a photograph.

At just a glance, he recognized the boy immediately.

"Oh yeah, I've seen this one," Gordon passed the picture back to the officer.

"You're sure?"

"Definitely," Gordon confirmed, his service smile completely vanishing. "Can't forget those eyes…"

"Whose eyes?" Colby scribbled away in her tiny notepad. "The missing person's?"

"No." Gordon's eyes shifted as his hands searched for support from the counter. He gripped on tight as he continued: "There was someone else, out there. The lad came in for a burger, and as he was ordering, I saw those eyes in the window… They were staring at him from outside. I've never seen a look like that before. If I'm honest, I hope I never see anything like it again."

Gordon Starkwood cried out as someone banged on the front window. His hands jolted free of their grasp on the counter with fright, knocking over a box of napkins. They blanketed the grease-speckled maroon tiles beneath his squeaky sneakers in white, like freshly fallen snow.

"I'm sorry," Colby said as she headed for the entrance. "Please excuse me for a moment."

"Sure…" Gordon looked up from the mess to find the officer already standing on the other side of the window, speaking with Ben Braithwaite.

"Do you mind?" Colby frowned as she crossed her arms. "I'm conducting a serious police investigation here."

"Oh, I'm sorry," Ben cowered easily, holding up a bulky plastic carrier bag filled with soda cans, crisps, and sandwiches. "I was just getting lunch for the boys, and I thought I'd say hi."

"Ben, breathe. I'm kidding." Colby chuckled with amusement and a hint of pity.

"I knew that," Ben lied, lowering the bag sheepishly. He noticed Gordon gazing at them from inside.

"I'm not mad," Colby reassured him. "But I am working."

"Okay," Ben said as he started to back away. "I'll tell the guys you said hey."

"Thanks, Ben." Colby smiled sweetly, granting him a nod.

The young paramedic gave her a silly salute as she went back inside to resume her questioning.

"Do you think you would be able to provide us with a detailed description of the man you saw at the window?" she asked.

"No, not really." Gordon shook his head. "Just the eyes."

"It doesn't have to be facial features," Colby said softly. "Those can be difficult to recall sometimes. It can be anything at all. Like, how tall was he? Was he thin or bigger? What was he wearing? His skin color?"

"Uh, I think he was white."

"That's good," Colby said, scribbling again. "And his height and build?"

"Pretty much the same as that guy you were talking to," Gordon said.

Colby shot him a curious look from over her pad and pen.

"Except, maybe tougher looking," he clarified.

"That's great," she said encouragingly with a smile. "Now, can you tell me what this man with the eyes was wearing?"

"I'm not sure…" Gordon struggled as he scratched the moistened curls at the back of his head.

"Try and remember what was around those eyes," Colby pressed him, her stare boring into him as he concentrated.

"Some kind of weird hood," he answered.

"A hood?"

"Yes," Gordon nodded slowly. "It was weird because it looked like he made it himself. You know, like a knitted sweater or something. My grandma used to knit sweaters and things like that for me when I was a kid."

"Excellent." Colby put away the pen and notepad. "Thank you…?"

"Gordon Starkwood."

"Thank you, Mr. Starkwood," Colby laughed in her embarrassment.

"All this is confidential, right?" Gordon asked for peace of mind.

"That's correct. Super top secret," she assured him with a grin. "It's probably nothing."

Reaching the post office at the end of the street, Ben rounded the corner into the parking lot, expecting to find the ambulance sitting in wait for his return.

Ben stopped still as the vehicle was already peeling out onto the road. He jumped back as it came to a sharp, abrupt stop next to him. The passenger door opened as Martin Fin held it ajar for him.

"Come on," Martin said as he took the bag. "Looks like we got another one."

"Seriously?" Ben's mouth fell open in his dread.

"Get in!" Martin barked.

Ben jumped. "Shit! Sorry!"

It was all he could do not to dive into the vehicle head first as Martin pulled the door closed securely behind him.

The ambulance set off. The emergency sirens screamed through the streets of Boatmore as the team headed out past the town limits.

Heeding the words of the island coroner, Liam braced himself for what lay ahead.

* * *

The loose stones of the country road crunched under their boots like gravel as the team crossed over to the field entrance on the other side.

Out there in the seemingly endless miles of farmland, the air was calm and quiet. Even the island winds were absent.

Not even a breeze. The only sound was the call of the wildlife that surrounded them. And in the clear sky above, the sun burned white.

Liam and Martin approached the gate as they took a look around. Save for the cattle that had assembled on the opposite end of the field with their young, the two paramedics observed nothing more than the hoof-trodden grass and scattered patches of mud and dirt. But something else caught Ben's eye.

"What do you think, Mr. Fin?" Liam finally asked as he leaned against the top bar of the gate.

"Couldn't be a prank," Martin replied. "Who would know to do this apart from us?"

"Fair point," Liam said, nodding slowly as he pondered. "The call was more or less the same. So, where are they?"

"They're here," Ben said quietly.

His colleagues watched in silence as he walked between them. He ran his hand carefully over the sign attached to the center of the gate. Of the two screws that remained in the battered thing, the one on the right was old, rusted, and loose. Most likely the original. The other was brand new and just barely holding up the left side.

Although he hesitated at first, Ben plucked the screw out. The sign swung down to the right. And there it was. The handprint made of blood.

"Okay then, let's get a move on," Liam said as he unlocked the gate.

Its steel hinges squealed as he managed to brace it open wide enough for them to enter single file.

The high-pitched shriek of grinding metal sent a shudder through Ben's upper body. It began on the side of his neck, just below his chattering jaw and rattled down from the joints of his shoulders to the tips of his fingers, as if his own fear had invaded the nerves and bones beneath his flesh. He told himself that the cold was responsible for the tears in his eyes…despite the fact that there was no breeze out there.

"Come on, Ben," Liam said as he squeezed his way past the gate with his medical kit bag.

Letting out a deep sigh through his nostrils, Ben closed his eyes for a couple of moments before following Liam through the gap.

The view from the other side was no more hopeful than where they began as they spied the same livestock occupying the same landscape. Nevertheless, they pressed on, but their search only yielded more grass and more clumps of earth. The three of them came to a stop when they reached what they believed to be the rough center of the field.

"Does anybody see anything?" Liam asked, failing to mask the bleak tone in his voice.

"Not a damn thing," Martin muttered through his teeth in his frustration.

"No…" Ben shook his head quietly, eyes searching intently.

"Me neither," Liam informed them.

"I say we all take a direction and keep going until one of us finds something," Martin suggested.

"That's not a bad idea," Liam admitted as he turned to Ben. "Do you think you can handle the animals?"

"I can do it," Ben insisted, trying his best to avoid sounding insubordinate whilst attempting to ignore Martin's amusement at the same time.

With his back turned, he could feel both of them laughing at him as he walked away. Clenching his fists, he fought the fear, refusing to let his tears be his humiliation. Instead, he let them burn with anger and resilience as he quickened the pace.

The peacefulness was palpable as the young paramedic heard all the noises that were normally hidden by everyday life: the breath on his lips, the grass beneath his boots, the chafing of his uniform, the quickening beat of his heart. Then there were the groans of the herd.

Before a determined Ben could slow his approach, a boy stumbled out into view. Half-naked, dirty, and bloody, he limped over uneven land, mouth frozen agape in a silent wail.

Both the elbow and ankle on the right side were black and blue against his paling skin as they bent away from his body at a sickly angle. The good arm was caked in a thick, steaming dollop of cow shit as his hand clutched at his chest. Little black flies buzzed about him noisily as he could barely utter a whisper.

"I found him!" Ben managed through the choke of his own horror.

"Quiet!" Liam hushed him with a low rasp as he started towards them. "You'll spook the herd."

"Okay…" Ben whispered back as he set his kit down, trembling as he crouched on the ground beside it. His fingers hovered over the bag in his uncertainty.

Somehow the boy managed an intake of uncaring country air loud enough for his rescuer to hear. With most of them lost to pain and fright, what tears he had left to cry ran a flesh-colored stream down through the dirt-speckled surface of each cheek as his working arm reached out for Ben.

The young paramedic heard that stifled call. Rising to his feet, he too reached out as the boy desperately employed every last ounce of his strength to form decipherable words with his dry and splitting lips…but no words came out. Only huffs, wheezes, and globules of bloodied saliva and thick mucus that slurped in and out of his mouth with every harrowing heave.

"It's okay…" Ben said soothingly as he took a step towards the boy. "I'm here with the ambulance. I'm here to help you."

Closing his bruised eyelids for just a moment, the boy wept with relief.

"I'm just going to have a quick look at you," Ben told him as he carefully examined the boy's misshapen limbs. "Then we can get you out of here. Get you all good and bandaged up, all right?"

"What's going on?" Liam asked as he stood by Ben's kit, arms crossed.

"There's an odd curve to the bruising around the breakages," Ben spoke quietly as he stepped back towards his leader. "I'd say he's been trampled on. He's scared and disorientated, so I'm guessing it must've happened while he was left out here unconscious."

"Right, quickly now, go get the spinal board," Liam ordered. "This poor lad has suffered enough. I'll–"

Just then, a terrible noise pierced Ben's soul.

His head wrenched back around to the boy as he heard an awful, wet snapping sound. He saw the blood-red bone glistening as it now protruded from the boy's leg. He saw the agony in the boy's face as he shrieked at the top of his lungs. He saw the cattle jolt with panic as they started to move.

A thunderous stampede began as the herd bounded towards them. It found the boy first as he disappeared from sight. Hopelessly engulfed, hundreds of pounds of solid muscle, meat, and bone churned and crushed his near-naked frame. The breath was squished from his lungs before he could cry out. Bones splintered and vital organs ruptured and burst inside him as he was battered to the ground.

Hands grabbed the back of Ben's uniform as Liam dragged him into a sprint. The ground that wasn't ripped up by the rush of startled hooves rumbled under their soles.

Liam guided him off to the side, never letting go, praying that they weren't followed. They didn't stop until they reached the barbed wire fence. Their trail was followed by a few feckless straddlers, but the creatures soon lost interest, returning to their usual docile selves.

Catching their breath, they turned to find the charge already dispersing. Cows scattered about all over the place, flicking their ears and swishing their tails as if nothing had occurred.

Avoiding eye contact with them, Martin waved to his colleagues as he walked as speedily as he could to the boy's aid.

"You go clean up your stuff," Liam instructed Ben.

"Yeah…" Ben agreed as he spotted the trail of medical supplies leading up the field to where his kit bag had been mashed down flat.

Liam hauled it out of the ground and tossed it aside for Ben to collect as he reached Martin and the boy, but there was little for them to do, as the poor lad had been stomped to a pulp. His top lip hung loose, the lower half of his mouth had been crushed in on itself. One eye appeared sleepy while the other remained strangely intact, as most of the socket surrounding it was missing. The rest of his body was littered with several bloody craters, like finger marks in clay.

"It's Callum," Liam said sadly. "Gary Wright's boy."

9
Michael Ketler, Pt. I

The air in the house was thick with the scent of succulent meat and sweet vegetables as Liam Price emerged from the bedroom, wearing a pale blue shirt and a glob of shaving foam hanging from his left earlobe. Rubbing his drying hands on the back of his dark blue jeans, he took in the delicious aroma, sighing loudly with contented satisfaction.

"Liam." A sweet call from the kitchen.

"Yeah, babe." Liam made his way towards the sound of his wife's voice.

Ally appeared at the end of the hallway. "Can you watch the cooking for me while I finish getting ready?"

"Of course, my sweet." Liam smiled warmly, wrapping his arms around her, kissing her as he tried to sneak his tongue past her bee-stung lips.

"I need to get ready," Ally giggled as she kissed him off and headed for the bedroom.

Liam watched her go, shaking his head before strutting gleefully into the adjoining living room and kitchen.

Taking a beer from the fridge, he snapped it open and then peered into the oven as it hummed along. All appeared to be well inside its warm, orange glow. On the stove, the boiling bubbles had amassed to a white froth over the sliced carrots and broccoli, threatening an imminent spillage. With all the indicating miniature diagrams rubbed away, Liam rectified this by eventually turning the correct nozzle. Seconds later, the creeping foam receded. All was well. Unsure of how long this mini ordeal took, Liam double-checked the oven. All was still well.

Already mentally exhausted, Liam relieved himself with a congratulatory first sip of his beer. While taking a second gulp, he noticed through the patio doors that the long wooden sun table out in the back garden had not yet been set.

"Shit," he grumbled, setting down his bottle as he swiftly got to work.

The cutlery drawers rattled like chains as he carelessly dug out dinner knives, spoons, forks, teaspoons, a corkscrew, a bottle opener, and a pizza slicer that he quickly put back. Heading for the garden, he cursed as he tripped through the patio doors. He cursed again when he realized that the corkscrew had pierced the pocket of flesh between his thumb and his index finger. Ignoring this mishap, he set the table and then headed back inside for placemats and napkins.

"Are you ready yet?" Liam half shouted, half moaned towards the hallway.

"I'm just putting on my makeup," Ally replied casually.

Annoyed by her blasé attitude towards his crisis, Liam laid out the placemats followed by the napkins. As soon as his back was turned to go inside, the napkins were swept off the table by the slightest of breezes.

The phone rang.

"Oh, what now!" he growled, grabbing the cordless from the wall. "Hello!"

"Mr. Price…" Martin responded.

"Mr. Fin," Liam beamed. "Are you not on your way? Dinner is nearing readiness as we speak."

"I'm afraid not."

"…I beg your pardon."

"I'm not coming."

"Oh. And why not?"

"I have a date with our favorite lady police officer," Martin announced proudly.

"Oh, do you now?" Liam asked, skeptical.

"Mmm-hmm," Martin confirmed, sounding very pleased with himself.

"So, it's just gonna be me, Ally, and the kid?" Liam said, his grip tightening around the beer bottle in his good hand.

"Looks like it," Martin said, amused and unsympathetic.

"Fan-fuckin'-tastic," Liam muttered, putting down the bottle before he did himself his second injury of the evening. "Well, God knows he deserves a cooked meal after *that* mess."

"It'll be fine," Martin assured him. "He's a good kid."

"That may be," Liam admitted, "but you do know you're going to have to pay for this…in several units of alcohol."

"Aye, I will," Martin chuckled, "but until then, have a good night!"

"You bastard!" Liam hissed in jest.

As Martin's chuckle erupted into fully-fledged laughter, Liam could not help but smile.

"What has the lovely Ally whipped up for you all?" Martin finally asked.

"Well, for starters we're having lentil soup…" Liam paused as his eyes widen in a realization. "Aw shit, the soup!"

The cordless phone hit the counter as Liam dashed with the grace of a polar bear back to the stove.

* * *

Martin Fin shook his head with a chuckle as he switched off his phone for the night, stuffing it into the side pocket of his baggy, sand-colored shorts.

Colby, off-duty and out of uniform, handed him back his cigar just as she blew smoke rings with her own. She wore a mint-colored vest above a flowing, deep purple, three-quarter-length skirt and black sandals. Her curly red locks floated around her shoulders.

The two occupied a picnic site that overlooked the waves of Yellow Bay as they sat atop one of the wooden tables like a couple of mischievous teenagers.

Martin's arms looked especially bulbous in his pale blue cycling top as he held one softly around Colby's waist.

"Now, don't think I don't know what's been bugging you these past few days," he said softly as he leaned in and kissed her delicately on the cheek. "I didn't mean what I said about your…situation. It was just a big surprise, you know, because we've always been so careful."

"I know, it is a lot, but it's handled now, so neither of us has to worry about it anymore." Ash flew from Colby's cigar as an island breeze picked up.

"And you're sure you're all right?" Martin held her close. "Don't be holding out on me now."

"I'm fine. Thank you." Colby returned his kiss as he ran his big fingers through her fiery hair.

"So, shall we dig into this wine and takeout I brought along for us?" Martin motioned with his eyes to where his car was parked nearby.

Colby frowned at him playfully. "If you even look at my food this time, I'll cut that dick *off*. It's been getting me into *way* too much trouble lately."

* * *

Michael Ketler stood in the center of his living room with one hand on his hip and the other holding the phone to his ear as he listened to his mother, Suzie, lay down another lecture about his responsibilities in the upkeep of the family home.

"And could you please do me a favor, just for once, and have all the dishes washed and dried and put away by the time I get home?" she instructed him.

"I will, I promise," he said, trying not to whine like a spoiled child. He failed miserably.

Michael used to have friends when he was younger. In fact, there was a time when his house was considered a mecca during weekends and summer holidays. All eight of them had packed the very living room he stood in now and watched Spielberg's classic *Jaws* so many times that they'd lost count. On Saturday nights, he would have sleepovers after renting classic '80s horror movies such as *A Nightmare on Elm Street 3: Dream Warriors* or *Halloween 4: The Return of Michael Myers* and spend half the night laughing and screaming the house down.

But Michael was the fussiest of eaters as a growing boy; aside from breakfast, every meal he ever had never went without a worrying amount of cheese. He loved his sausages, his beans, his bacon, and his burgers. His diet was a never-ending Sunday morning fry-up. Soon enough his weight, his skin, and his hairline suffered. Lacking the will and the motivation to change, Michael lost his confidence and his health declined considerably. It didn't help matters that he had suffered from asthma since he was a baby.

Now that his friends were grown, all they wanted to do was go out. Island life became all about keeping active for them. They swam the seas. They dove from cliffs. They surfed the waves. They ran, they trekked, they climbed, and they cycled. Unfortunately, Michael couldn't do any of these things for very long without bringing himself to the brink of an attack. It was humiliating. His skin would burn red. He would sweat and wheeze heavily. His chest would ache so terribly that he would cry from the pain when nobody was looking.

But they were always looking. They would never stop looking, and so, more often than not, the pain would become agony.

Michael was happy for his friends, that they were enjoying life. He was always glad to have them over whenever they had the time, but they soon stopped coming around, and so, at home was where Michael stayed. He had shelves full of horror DVDs and cupboards full of treats, but no one to watch and eat them with, except himself. Somehow, he had become content. Most of the things that made him happy hadn't changed. He still had friends out there somewhere on the island, waiting for him, and he knew that if he really wanted, if he really tried, then one day he could have them all back. And he would, one day. But he wasn't ready. Until then, the living room, the horror movies, and the food would remind him of times when life was truly good, of when he had friends.

"Make sure you do this time, Michael, because you're always doing things at the last minute, and then when I get home from a long shift at work, the first thing I find myself doing is drying and putting away your dishes."

"Just ask me to do it, Mom, and I'll do them."

Suzie laughed. "Oh, God forbid I interrupt you when you're on that computer of yours!"

Her son couldn't help but laugh along with her. He respected his mother for always telling it like it is. She was too busy to fabricate a good lie. She was the hardest working person he knew. The least he could do for her was put away a few silly little dishes.

Just then, the door to the back room creaked open, stopping Michael in his tracks before he could lean against the mantelpiece. At one time they had intended the back room to become a spot for dining and entertaining, but as the Ketler family were never in the house at the same time for very long it had eventually become a graveyard for old chairs, books and exercise machines. Nobody ever went in there. Or so he thought.

"Mom…" Michael whispered.

"Yeah."

"Could you stay on the phone, please, for just a minute?" Michael asked her, locking his eyes on the opening of the backroom door and what appeared to be the shape of a man staring out at him.

"Okay, but I can't stay for long. My cigarette break is nearly over."

"Thanks…" his voice trailed off as he slowly side-stepped back into the center of the room. Like the eyes of a painted portrait, the shape behind the door appeared to follow him wherever he moved.

"Hello?" he called out to it.

It didn't respond. It just stood there.

Michael put the phone back to his ear.

"Mom…?"

There was no one on the other end but the dial tone. He was all alone.

Hanging up the phone, he shook his head, disappointed in himself. He had seen enough horror movies to know if an intruder was in his house or not. Despite his certainty, there was a slight wheeze at the back of his throat as he approached the shape staring at him from behind the backroom door. He took a breath for his health's sake and then pushed the door all the way open.

It turned out to be just one of his mother's old coats hanging from the handle of an elliptical machine. Unsurprised, Michael rolled his eyes at his overactive imagination and hauled the backroom door shut.

Chewing on some string cheese, he selected a horror movie from his extensive library and settled down on the sofa to watch it. As the credits began and the creepy music started, he was relieved that he had made a conscious decision not to opt for a movie with a home invasion theme. Michael was never one to tempt fate if he could help it.

Halfway through the movie, he noticed that the backroom door had opened itself again, and even though Michael Ketler knew better, the dark shape in the doorway still made him feel as if someone was standing there, watching him, waiting.

* * *

Ben Braithwaite and his plus one, Matt, sat across from Liam and Ally Price in their back garden at a beautifully lit dining table. They were just tacky Japanese lanterns, as Ally had explained when they all sat down to eat, but the fact that they glowed different colors gave their meal a seasonal vibe, as they reminded everyone of Christmas tree lights.

They were just finishing their main course of shepherd's pie with homemade gravy when Liam Price decided that he had had enough alcohol to ask the question that had been on his mind since Mr. Braithwaite and Matt, the coroner's assistant, arrived for dinner.

"So, Matt, I didn't expect to see you here tonight," he began, trying to appear nonchalant. He failed, coming off snooty rather than casual.

Before anyone had the chance to respond, Ally butted in.

"And how do you know–" she started to ask Liam, suddenly switching her attention to her guest. "I'm sorry, do you prefer Matt or Matthew?"

"Just Matt is cool." The boy smiled politely, pushing back a giggle.

"Okay. And how do you know 'Just Matt' here?" Ally asked, back on Liam.

"He's Carl's assistant," Liam informed her.

"Carl? 'Carl the coroner' Carl?"

Liam nodded with an "Uh-huh."

"And why weren't you expecting him? You didn't invite him?"

"Oh, someone did invite him. Right, Ben?"

Ben looked at Liam as if he had just pulled a gun on him.

"Uh, yeah. I mean, yes. Yes, I did," he stuttered in his response. "You did say to me at work, if I had someone special that I was to bring them along."

Like a magician executing a magic trick, Matt spread his arms with a cheesy grin and exclaimed, "And here I am!"

"Aw, that's sweet." Ally's eyes glistened over her smile as she put a hand to her cheek in admiration.

Taking another sip of his white wine, Liam gave himself a moment to take it all in. "So, when Carl told me you two had taken a shine to each other, he meant you'd *really* taken a shine to each other?"

Matt nodded emphatically. "The old geezer's pretty boring for an undertaker, but he's surprisingly open-minded."

Liam pursed his lips and shrugged in agreement.

"I'm impressed," Ally said, beaming as she raised a glass to her two dinner guests.

"That's pretty fast work, Mr. Braithwaite." Liam caressed his wife's shoulder. "How did you two meet, anyways?"

"Well, we…we met each other on…online?" Ben somehow managed.

"Ooh! On a dating site?" Ally asked excitedly.

"You could say that. It's a site for men to…I mean, it's a site where men can—"

Matt put him out of his misery. "We whacked off to each other on the web; that's what he's trying to tell you."

Ben was horrified. "Jesus Christ, Matty!" He tried feebly to hide behind one of the paper plates, but Matt gently snatched it from him and tossed it back onto the table.

"You did what?" Liam was just lost.

"They had webcam sex, babe," Ally quickly clarified for her husband as she nibbled at a small chunk of well-cooked mince.

The look of horror that filled Liam's face was priceless. "How do you know what that is?"

Struggling to swallow her food and sound offended at the same time, Ally angrily retorted, "I watch TV. I read the news. I believe they also invented the internet."

"It's actually called camming," Matt informed them.

"That's good to know!" Liam frowned sarcastically.

Ally shook her head as she looked over at Matt's date. "Ben, are you okay?"

"He looks like he's about to be sick!" Liam burst out laughing.

True enough, young Ben had his head in his hands, with a cold sweat on his brow and a brighter shade of pale on his skin.

Matt rubbed Ben's back tenderly. "I've got just the thing to calm my baby down." He revealed his left hand balled into a fist with a joint slotted in between each finger. "I brought us all some party favors!"

"Aw, I'm afraid I can't attend this party," Ally said, firmly but friendly, rubbing her belly as she turned to Liam. "But you can."

Half-an-hour later, their seasonal dining scene had become a charming shambles. The table shoved to one side where Ben now lay atop it, curled up and using the tablecloth as a blanket. Liam, Ally, and Matt remained in their chairs, slouched back and gazing up at the night sky.

"So, Mr. Braithwaite is a gentleman's gentleman. I knew it!" Liam giggled.

"Liam! You did not," Ally scolded him. "I'm sorry, Ben. Do not listen to him. I'm sure that's just your boyfriend's weed talking. Isn't that right, babe?"

"Isn't what right, sugar plum?"

"That you're stoned."

"I am not," Liam whined, becoming agitated.

"You are *so* stoned."

"I am not stoned! I am drunk. There's a difference!" Liam roared, but then quickly settled. "Anyways, Ally…don't embarrass me in front of the boys."

"Oh, I am not. You're embarrassing yourself," Ally said, dismissing him.

Matt clutched his stomach in pain from laughing. "You guys are awesome."

"Well, thank you, Matt." Ally smiled as she took hold of Liam's hand. He smiled back at her as he rubbed her big, pregnant belly. "You're awesome, too."

"We're all awesome." Liam squeezed Ally's hand.

"Yay…" Ben moaned weakly from atop the dining table.

In their merry haze, they all laughed.

It had been a wonderful night. It really had been. But Carl's words of warning from that night at The Golden Eagle still weighed heavily on Liam's peace of mind. And as he knew all too well, nothing stayed wonderful for very long.

* * *

BUH-BANG! BUH-BANG! BUH-BANG!

Michael's body twisted in his bed as he jolted out of sleep. He sat up immediately. What was that sound?

Grunting in his confusion, he forced himself to his feet. He grasped the banister as he came to a cautious stop on the landing.

BUH-BANG! BUH-BANG! BUH-BANG!

Was it coming from the front door? Was someone trying to break into the house? Only one way to find out.

Drawing his set of house keys from the pocket of his sweatpants, Michael descended from the landing to the front door. He felt too off balance from sleep to peek through the letter box, so he unlocked the door and opened it. Nobody there. Just the night outside.

BUH-BANG! BUH-BANG! BUH-BANG!

He finally realized where the sound was coming from. Pushing the front door shut, he quickly made his way down the hallway, across the kitchen, and around the refrigerator to the back door. Past the back door lay the washroom. As his mind continued to awaken along with the rest of him, the sound was all too familiar. It meant that someone had overloaded the dryer.

Sighing in annoyance, he yanked open the machine door and the sound was no more. He gave the contraption a childish kick as payback. A chill washed over the back of his neck. Shivering, he turned to find the back door standing silently open. If someone was standing out there, he was trapped in that room. The back door was the only thing between Michael and the rest of the house.

He felt the set of keys still in his hand. Clutching them firmly, he marched to the back door and pressed it shut. Jabbing the key into the lock, he twisted until he heard the

CLICK! Breathing a sigh of relief, he gave the door a pat before he made his way back through the kitchen.

He stopped in his tracks.

The front door was wide open. He had forgotten to lock it.

Clenching his keys within a balled fist, Michael started down the hallway. His face contorted as it was torn between disbelief and fear, and pain. A hoarse growl sounded from the back of his throat as his lungs felt deflated and heavy inside his chest. He took hold of the door handle and steadied himself as he lay his face against the cool stained-glass window. The front door closed softly under his resting weight.

As Michael turned his head, he spied the light coming from the living room.

He had switched everything off before he went to bed. Hadn't he? He was too tired to remember.

Locking the front door, he pushed his way through to find he had left the television on, but he didn't switch it off. Instead, he took a moment to rest on the big comfy sofa. The only safe place he ever really knew in his whole life.

He took a look around the room where he had made so many wonderful memories with his friends. Once again, the backroom door was ajar; his mother's coat still looked as lifelike as ever. He just had to tear down that damn coat and then he could rest his mind. Before he could pull himself up, Michael noticed his mother's coat on the floor.

Then came that demented rasp.

His gaze moved slowly up from the coat to the dark shape that stood staring at him from behind the backroom door until it met the two eyes glaring back at him. They bulged and trembled in their madness.

The boy screamed in terror as a man in a pale hood burst into the room, snarling like a wild animal. His gloved hands clawed at the terrified teenager's belly as they scrambled for his throat.

The throat of the third.

10
The Boy by the Lake

Lagan Lake had been one of their favorite places to play on the island when they were children.

Twins Molly and Sarah Miles never liked the sandy beaches that surrounded most of the coastline, whereas the shores of Lagan Lake brimmed with pebbles of all colors: blacks, whites, and grays, as well as browns, oranges, and even, sometimes, greens. They loved to spend their afternoons collecting the prettiest ones for their mother to judge in competition. The result was always a draw, after which their mother would take both girls out for ice cream cones with Cadbury Flakes and strawberry sauce. What they loved the most was to feed Lagan Lake's feathered little inhabitants: the common pied oystercatcher. They had become accustomed to calling them Pinocchio birds because their beaks looked like long thin noses.

Now those days were gone. The years moved on and they stopped wasting their time playing and started thinking about how they should do their hair, which makeup to use, what clothes to wear. And boys. Time to stop eating ice cream and start to exercise. Time to find out about the world through magazines, social media and its vloggers. Time to start preparing to leave their old island life behind. Or at least, that's what reality TV told them…

Molly felt like her twin sister was always in too much of a hurry to grow up. After all, they were barely fifteen.

It was another chilled sunny morning. A thin veil of mist blanketed their side of the great sea inlet. The Miles sisters were out early on one of their exercises. Molly was bundled up like a much older sensible woman. Sarah, however, sported body-hugging gear with the vain hope that it would accentuate curves that have yet to exist. Still, Molly was happy that her sister was aiming for curvy.

"Look over there." Sarah directed Molly's attention over to Lagan Lake as the two of them powerwalked the roadside together.

"Over where?" Molly hoped for once that she was talking about the birds or the pebbles. Maybe even the ice cream?

"There!" Sarah pointed harder. She was referring to the free-floating dock that sat perfectly still above the surface of the water. "Jessica told me some of the older kids like to take a boat out there and make out with each other. She says Hannah Wilson even lost her virginity there."

"You're joking." Molly's face scrunched up in her disapproval.

"Na-ah." Sarah shook her head. "She did it with Jessica's sister's best friend's brother."

"But why would someone do that?" Molly failed to hide her disgust. "Everyone can see you."

"It's not like they did it in the middle of the road." Sarah frowned at her sister's attitude that morning. "What is up with you, anyways?"

The girls slowed down to a walk, and then a break.

"Nothing," Molly huffed. "I'm just hungry. Aren't we supposed to eat to get energy or something?"

"Yeah, if we want to throw up everywhere."

"Good point."

Sarah laughed, squinting as she tried to look at her sister in spite of the morning sun. She held her hand over her brow like a visor and took a look around while she waited for Molly to catch her breath. She stopped still as she spotted something.

"Hey, look over there."

"No more sex stories..." Molly whined.

"Seriously, just look, will you!" Sarah urged as she grabbed her sister by the shoulder and twisted her in the direction of her discovery.

In the distance, a man stood on the other side of the road covered in a red sheet that whipped in the wind. The man, however, remained as still as stone.

"What is it?" The sight drew Molly forward as she started to walk again.

"I don't know." Sarah followed. "I haven't seen it there before, have you?"

"Nah…"

"Do you think it's a statue?"

"It could be a scarecrow?"

"That's creepy." Sarah frowned. "Who would leave a scarecrow on the side of the road like that? They're not scaring anyone."

"I know," Molly agreed, picking up speed. "That is just weird."

"So weird," Sarah said with a nod, her eyes searching as she puzzled over the strange display and where it came from. "You know, I bet this is a prank set up by the boys."

"Well, if you're right, then they just failed."

"Oh my god!" Sarah exclaimed excitedly. "I'm gonna film their fail with my phone and post it online!"

"This is one of those few moments in life where I like the way you think," Molly remarked both proudly and shadily.

"What is that supposed to mean?" Sarah glared at her.

"Nothing. Just get your phone out."

They came to a halt as they looked both ways before crossing. They didn't know why they even bothered with road safety tips anymore. Sometimes living on the island felt like living in a ghost town. Still, it was better to be safe than sorry.

The red sheet flapped noisily in front of them as they approached the scarecrow. Sarah held her phone out, already recording. She kept a little bit of distance so that everything was in shot while Molly crept in closer.

"Sarah," Molly whispered. She pointed at the ground. "Look."

Sarah lowered her view to the roadside. She zoomed in. The scarecrow was wearing sneakers and a pair of jeans. Whatever was hiding under that red sheet definitely wasn't made of sticks or straw.

"Molly," Sarah whispered back. She mimed a tugging motion with her free arm. "Pull it off him now!"

Grinning from ear to ear, Molly snatched hold of the red sheet. Fighting the wind resistance, she tore it away as hard as she could. She fell to the ground as the sheet flopped over her head.

Sarah started screaming.

Molly ripped the red sheet from her face. She lost her breath as she caught sight of the body of the dead boy, now swaying unsteadily against the weakly planted post he was tied to.

His skin was a sickly pale grayish-white color. The lips were dark blue, verging on black. His eyes were clouded over. The hair on his head was an ugly rat's nest of spikes, curls, and tufts. The head hung limp as the right arm was propped up to the side.

There was a *SNAP!* as the ties gave way. Both girls screamed with fright as the dead boy's body toppled towards Molly. In sisterly unison, Sarah grabbed the back of Molly's baggy coat and pulled as Molly took hold of Sarah's arm and scurried backwards. *THUD!*

They sat there on the roadside, breathing heavily as they stared at the boy's corpse only a few inches away from them.

"Oh my god," Molly whimpered.

"Molly…" Sarah managed.

"Yeah?"

"I don't think this is a prank…"

"Sarah, we need to call the police."

Sarah checked her phone. She ended the recording.

"Aah! I can never get a signal on this stupid island."

"What about that one over there?" Molly pointed across the road.

"Oh yeah!" Sarah left her phone with Molly. "Now don't freak out. I'll be right over there."

"Okay…" Molly cuddled her knees as she tried to avoid staring at the body.

Looking both ways before she crossed, Sarah jogged over to the other side of the road. She picked up the receiver of the orange SOS phone, failing to notice the bloody handprint dripping on the side of it.

* * *

A circular groove of coarse black rock cradled a makeshift barbecue as the coal below sent white smoke billowing into the fresh air of Green Water Bay. Sausage and chicken meat were cooking nicely as they lay upon the well-worn grill.

Twenty-year-old islander Nicola Reade lay soundly upon a tartan picnic blanket. Sheltered by a blue and white-striped windbreaker, she rested her eyes behind a pair of candy-cane-colored sunglasses.

Her boyfriend, Ashley Newton, split his attention between the food and the waves as they gently rolled in. He watched the crash of saltwater and sand colliding, and the fizzle of bubbles as the foam spread and receded, with childlike fascination.

Nicola noticed and smiled.

"My god, you can tell you don't live here," she laughed, unfurling as she rose from the blanket.

"What?" Ashley turned to her with an open trap, oblivious.

"The way you stare at the water."

"I guess so," Ashley admitted as he knelt at the grill. "Well, I look at screens all day, don't I? At the station, I spend hours typing up reports, searching databases… It's tedious as hell."

"My boyfriend, the police officer," she beamed proudly.

Leaning her head to the side, Nicola gazed at him with a smile of sad love and sympathy. She blushed and chuckled silently to herself as her heart swelled.

"I can watch the food," she offered with moist eyes, "if you want to go in for a swim."

As the sun above hit his eyes, it blinded Ashley from spying his girlfriend's tears.

"Really? You don't mind?" he doublechecked as he dusted the sand from his knees.

"Yeah. Go on." Nicola took a deep breath as she swallowed a little piece of her spirit. Her only consolation was to imagine that the smile he flashed her before he left was his way of saying 'I love you.'

Ashley walked only a few feet from their barbecue when he spotted something out in the water. It appeared black beneath the blinding sunlight as it bobbed on the surface.

"Nicky, babe, can you grab my binoculars?" he called back over his shoulder.

Too excited to wait, he turned and ran back to camp.

"What? What is it?" Nicola shielded her eyes, looking towards the waves as Ashley rummaged around in his gym bag. A bag that he elected to double as his holiday hold-all.

"I think I saw a seal," he told her as he untangled his binoculars from a set of earphones.

Tossing the wires back into the bag, he jogged back to the place he had stood mere moments ago as Nicola followed close behind. He looked again, straining his vision. Whatever it was, on closer inspection, Ashley was pretty sure that it wasn't a seal.

"What the hell is that thing?"

"I'll take a look?" Nicola held out her hand. "Maybe I'll know."

"Yeah, of course. Go ahead." Ashley stepped around the back of her and rested his hands on her shoulders, squeezing and massaging them in curious anticipation.

Grinning to herself, Nicola took a look.

"Ash-bear…" She looked gravely into her boyfriend's eyes. "We need to call the coast guard."

She handed him the binoculars before sprinting back towards their spot on the beach.

"Why? What's wrong?" Ashley asked as he took one final look.

His mouth fell open as he stumbled backwards over his own feet. He managed to catch himself, but his legs started to shake. As he walked shakily back to camp with his heart pounding, he could taste the acid in his throat, an unwelcome gift from his empty stomach.

If only he hadn't looked. If only he hadn't seen what he saw. Amongst the blackness of that shape floating out in the water was a human hand.

As Nicola was on the phone with the coast guard, Ashley took one look at the meat sizzling on the grill and vomited onto the sand of Green Water Bay.

* * *

Molly and Sarah Miles sat side by side on the floor at the back of the ambulance, their feet firmly on the roadside as Ben Braithwaite examined their eye responses one by one with his medical pen torch. Liam Price observed from close by.

Across the road, black and yellow police tape cordoned off the spot where the two sisters had discovered the body. Beyond the tape, a wall of white tarpaulin stood crinkling in the wind around the perimeter of the crime scene. Martin Fin was taking a peek over the top. Officer Colby shooed him away as she approached Carl, who was already perched by the body carrying out his preliminary examination. His assistant, Matt, was crouched across from him. Colby stood quietly behind them.

"Do we know who this is?" Carl asked her as he gently lifted up the dead boy's jumper as he remained face down.

"It's Gordon Starkwood," Colby replied glumly. "Age seventeen. We didn't even know he was missing... I interviewed him about the Callum boy just the other day."

"Our resident island mangler strikes again."

"So, what do we have here?" Colby pressed, ignoring Carl's remark.

"Bruising and abrasions on the ankles and wrists suggest the victim was bound. The discoloration of the back suggests the victim did not die here, but that he most likely died in captivity."

"That's strange," Colby stepped in for a closer look. "Why would he kill him before laying him out here?"

"Well, it was and remains my expert opinion that we are not dealing with a medical professional. Whatever he is doing to these poor boys…" Carl trailed off, but quickly collected himself. "It's a miracle that any of them survive this amateur form of butchery."

"Do we have a cause of death?" Colby continued softly.

The coroner took a breath. "Exsanguination." He pulled up the nearest sleeve of the boy's jumper to reveal his arm.

"Self-inflicted?" Colby asked as she gazed into the deep and jagged torn gashes in the corpse's dead flesh.

"It's possible." Carl recovered the arm. "Whatever did it must've been very blunt, and it would have been excruciatingly painful."

"I can't imagine wanting to die that much," Matt said quietly as he looked into the bluish whites of Gordon's deceased clouded eyes.

"This is the kind of sicko we're dealing with here, Matthew." Carl got to his feet and ripped off his medical gloves.

"Is there anything else you can tell me?" Colby struggled to mask the desperation in her voice.

The coroner sighed as he motioned over the back of the dead boy's head.

"Oh, his nose and a couple of teeth; all broken post-mortem." He moved in close to whisper in her ear: "But I think you can thank his two new best friends who dislodged him from his display for those injuries."

Carl nudged the officer with an amused smile on his face before he walked away. Colby turned to Matt.

"Is he okay?"

"He will be." Matt grinned stupidly as he mimed the smoking of a joint.

"I'll pretend I didn't just see you do that." She walked in the opposite direction to find Martin Fin beaming back at her from the top of the tarp. "Marty?"

"So, is it our guy?" Martin winked at her.

"You know I can't tell you that."

"Bullshit!" Martin exclaimed. "I've seen you naked, woman!"

Matt cut short a loud laugh. He wisely walked away at a fast pace when Colby spied him. She turned back to Martin.

"You've got to be fricking kidding me!" the officer growled under her breath. "There are young witnesses, young *female* witnesses, not ten feet away from you. What do you think you're playing at?"

Martin held his hands up in concession as he backed away from the tarp.

Officer Colby watched him disappear before glancing over her shoulder at Matt who covertly slipped Carl a joint.

"I am working with idiots…"

* * *

Colby crossed the road as the coroner and his assistant loaded Gordon's body into the back of their van. The Miles sisters remained in the back of the ambulance. Sarah had been given a blanket for warmth while Molly tried desperately not to embarrass herself by sucking her thumb. Colby crouched down in front of them.

"Don't worry, girls," she assured them. "I'm going to take you home now to see your mom. I just need her permission to ask you a few questions about this morning, if that's okay with you?"

"You don't need to," Molly mumbled.

"I'm sorry?" Colby leaned in.

"You don't need to ask us anything."

"Molly...!" Sarah nudged her sister.

"I'm afraid I have to," Colby pressed. "I need you girls to help me–"

Molly cut her off. "We filmed everything."

"You did, did you?"

Molly nudged Sarah back. "Give her your phone."

"Molly!" Sarah snapped. "No..."

"I'm sorry, young lady, but if this is true then I will have to confiscate your phone into evidence," Colby insisted.

"What if I just send you the video?"

The officer narrowed her eyes at the young girl.

"That could work." She held out her hand.

Sarah reluctantly passed the phone to her.

Colby drew her own phone out from her jacket pocket as she flicked over the girl's touchscreen. She tapped Sarah's phone one last time. Her phone emitted a *DING!* sound as it vibrated.

"Ah, there we go." The officer smiled as she returned Sarah's phone. "I'm afraid I had to delete your copy, young lady."

The girl nodded, more than happy just to have her phone back.

"Will you take us home now?" Molly asked as she chewed at her thumbnail.

Colby looked over her shoulder to a car that had just parked up a few yards away from the ambulance. She waved to its inhabitants, hoping that they spotted her. She turned and motioned the two girls out of the back of the ambulance.

"Actually, I believe you know your neighbors, Mr. and Mrs. Morris." She pointed to the couple who now stood at their vehicle waving back. "Well, they sometimes do volunteer police work with me. They will be more than happy to take you home."

11
Michael Ketler, Pt. II

With Molly and Sarah Miles bundled into the back of the Morris' car, Colby sent them on their way. As she watched them drive into the distance, something felt off.

She turned to look at the bloodstained SOS phone behind her and then across at the crime scene, still shrouded in white tarp.

"You okay?" Martin came to her side. He reached for her hand, but she didn't take it.

"Something doesn't feel right," Colby replied, deep in thought.

"What do you mean?"

"This guy, what he does to these boys," Colby began, "There has to be a reason behind it, a message. Carl said that they're lucky to be alive when we find them. I don't think he wants to kill these boys. I think he wants us to save them."

Martin snorted doubtfully. "If that's the case, he ain't making it easy."

"That's the whole point." Colby returned her attention to the tarp. "You've seen his calling card. Why is this one different?"

"I don't know."

"I just feel like I'm missing something, and it's staring me right in the face."

"Did you get anything out of the girls?"

"I have a video recording of them finding the body."

"Watch it," Martin suggested. "You never know."

Colby wasn't hopeful, but she took out her phone nevertheless to search for the file. She found it and pressed PLAY. She watched as Molly crept towards Gordon's body draped in the red sheet. She watched her pull the sheet away to reveal his corpse. She flinched as Sarah's scream blared out of the phone's speakers.

"They found him propped up like that?" Martin asked from over her shoulder.

"They did," Colby sighed as Gordon's body toppled towards the screen. "As Carl put it, they dislodged him from his display."

"Then it must mean something." Martin jabbed his finger at the phone. "Wind it back."

"Yes, sir," Colby teased him as she tapped the touchscreen. She looked again at the body tied to the post.

"Okay, freeze it," Martin instructed her. She obeyed. "Now take a look and tell me what you see."

Shaking her head, she looked at the body again. Her mouth fell open. "Oh my god..." Colby started to run across the road towards the tarp. She hadn't seen it before. How could she have been so stupid?

"What? What is it?" Martin called after her as he followed.

Colby began tearing down the entire tarp wall. "Help me with this, will you?"

"Are you going to tell me what's going on?" Martin joined in.

"You'll know in a second." Colby stepped over the used tarp and examined the post that Gordon Starkwood's body had been tied to. She motioned at the coroner's van. "Matt, get over here!"

The coroner's assistant came running. "Yeah?"

The officer directed him to the post. "Could you stand with your back against there, please?"

"I'm still completely lost here." Martin put his hands on his hips as he shook his head.

"Can you raise your right arm until your hand is at shoulder level?" Colby continued. Matt complied. She held the frozen video image up to Martin's face. "Look."

Martin's eyes widened as they looked from Matt to Colby in realization. "He was pointing at something."

Nodding, Colby then followed the direction of Matt's arm. She crossed the road, her eyes fixed dead straight ahead. She walked around the ambulance, mounted the concrete curb, and stepped up onto the small stone wall that separated the pavement from the pebbled shores of Lagan Lake.

The officer drew a set of binoculars from her belt and peered through them. And there it was. Right out in the middle of the water: the free-floating dock. Atop it was another sheet, dark green this time. There was no doubt in Officer Colby's mind what lay beneath it.

"Another body?" Martin asked her.

Colby turned to find everyone standing by, ready to assist. Despite being momentarily flustered, she was glad to have their company. She jumped down from the wall.

"That's not a body, this is a victim," Colby informed them. "The deceased was meant as a sign, pointing the way to the real danger. However, thanks to our two young friends and their wannabe internet sensation antics, we have lost a lot of precious time. He could be dead already, but until we know otherwise we need to get you guys out to him as soon as possible. So just sit tight while I call for some assistance." Colby tossed her binoculars to Martin before she rushed away towards her police vehicle to make contact.

Martin handed them to Ben. "Get a good look at that dock, Mr. Braithwaite. See if you can find any signs of life."

Ben and Matt took a stroll down to the edge of the beach to get a closer look.

"Kid's gotta be dead by now, right?" Martin looked to Liam.

Liam Price looked out over Lagan Lake. "It's not looking good, but why don't we hope for the best, anyway?"

"I can do that." Martin smiled at his friend's optimism.

"Shit!" They heard Colby cry from her vehicle.

Ben and Matt ran back up the beach as the officer rejoined the group.

"What's wrong?" Martin asked.

"There's been a drowning at Green Water Bay." Colby was breathless in her frustration.

"They do have some killer waves," Matt said, nodding to himself.

"Matthew!" Carl scolded him.

"They're on the other side of the island?" Liam clarified before throwing his hands up as he walked away.

"Calm down, Mr. Price." Martin made a swipe for his back but missed.

"By the time they send us someone, it'll be too late..." Colby leaned against the stone wall. She pulled down her police hat to hide the fact that she was on the verge of tears.

"Can't we just pull it in?" Matt asked.

"It's a free-floating dock, Matty," Ben explained to his boyfriend. "The point is we can't pull it anywhere."

"A point, I'm sure, that our resident island mangler was counting on," Carl added.

"We have a boat!" Liam cried out of nowhere.

They all turned in the direction of his voice. In his aimless wanderings away from the group, Liam had spotted the little vessel sitting by itself on the shore, complete with a pair of oars, no visible signs of leakage, and, best of all, it had an outboard motor.

The team joined Liam on the beach as they gathered around the boat.

"I think we can all agree, under the circumstances, we can worry about who this belongs to later." The fight was back in Colby's eyes.

"I don't think that'll be a problem," Liam assured her, pointing to the side of the boat which was carved end to end with initials, plus signs, love hearts, and exes. "I hear tell that dock is somewhat of a make-out point for the kids in town. This must be the boat they use to get out there."

"Even better." Colby thanked him with a wink. "Is there enough fuel?"

"I have some spare in my van, if need be," Carl volunteered enthusiastically. "I still like to do the odd bit of fishing from time to time."

"Thank you, Carl."

"There's not enough room for the three of us *and* our equipment," Martin assessed.

"There's barely enough room for all three without it." Liam scratched his chin.

"Who goes out?"

"You two will." Liam pointed out Martin and Ben. "Carl and I will advise from afar." He started back towards the ambulance for the supplies and equipment. "Mr. Braithwaite, you can help me load the boat."

Both Liam and Matt were up to their waists in the waters of Lagan Lake. Together they had aided the boat out of the shallow end of the pebbled shore.

Matt pulled himself along the side to the bow where Ben sat, clutching the sides. He rested his hand upon Ben's tense white knuckles.

"Remember," he said softly. "Relax. Take it easy. Don't freak out. You'll be fine."

Matt withdrew his hand from Ben's and replaced it with a single kiss.

Liam and Martin watched them before turning to each other.

"I'll be on the walkie-talkie if you need anything," Liam reminded him. "This guy is a tricky bastard. Let's beat him at his own game."

"We're gonna save this one," Martin agreed with determination.

The two shook hands. They held on tight before the gesture broke.

"Matt, come on. We can't waste any more time here," Liam called over.

There was a splash as Matt waded back to him as quickly as the lake would allow him.

"Let's back it up," Liam warned everyone.

As soon as they were far enough away, Martin secured the mounting bracket to the stern and fired up the motor. The propeller roared as the boat moved across the water. Once Martin took control of the tiller, the vessel took a sharp swerve, sending up a glistening wall of icy foam as it picked up momentum.

Liam and Matt rushed for the shore as Martin and Ben glided over the water's surface towards the free-floating dock. Pebbles flew like ricochet under their boots as they stumbled up the beach to join Carl and Officer Colby, who watched and waited from behind the stone wall.

"Do you think there's still time?" Colby asked anyone.

"We'll find out soon enough." Carl patted her shoulder.

"I wish he'd sit down." Colby shook her head at Martin, who used the tiller to balance himself while he struck a heroic sea captain pose.

"Boys will be boys," Carl chuckled with amusement.

Liam held his hand out to the coroner with a smile. Carl nodded as he passed over the walkie-talkie.

They all looked on as Martin and Ben closed in on the dock. Nothing could be heard except for the hum of the outboard motor. Colby cupped her hands over her mouth and nose as if in prayer. Matt chewed his fingers while Liam switched the walkie-talkie from one hand to the other and back again. Carl observed it all quietly with the knowing stance of a great owl.

Without warning, the boat bucked violently, stern first. The sound was like an explosion as it echoed across the lake. The force dislodged the motor from its mounting bracket. It clipped Martin across the side of his head before it tumbled overboard with a loud *PLUNK!*

Ben clung to the bow in disbelief. His mouth hung open with the shock of seeing such a muscular brute as Martin Fin on his stomach out cold.

"Jesus Christ!" Liam cried. "What the hell was that?"

"Ben!" Matt screamed out at the lake.

"He can't hear you, Matty." Colby took hold of his upper arm. "He's too far out there."

"Well, he can sure as shit hear me," Liam growled as he switched on the walkie-talkie and tuned it in. "Mr. Fin, what the hell is going on over there?"

Ben scrambled over their equipment as he heard Liam's voice crackling and buzzing from beneath Martin's unconscious body. He pulled the walkie-talkie out from Martin's front breast pocket.

L. Stephenson

"This is Ben," the young paramedic said shakily. "Can you hear me?"

"Yes, Ben, I can hear you," Liam's voice replied. "Tell me what happened."

"I'm not sure," Ben responded breathlessly. "We hit something, but I don't know what."

"Are you both all right? Is anyone hurt?"

"I'm okay, but Martin hit his head, and the motor...we lost it. We lost the motor." Ben quickly ran his eyes around the base of the boat. "And no leaks, as far as I can tell."

"We'll worry about the motor later. First things first, is Martin conscious? Is he breathing?"

"He's unconscious." Ben unhooked the medical safety glasses from his uniform's shirt as he leaned over Martin. He held one of the lenses under the man's nose. After a few seconds, they fogged up. "And yes, he's still breathing."

"Okay, good. Now we need to be sure of your safety. I want you to tell me if you can see what hit you."

Ben peered out over the water. Something dark lurked under the surface.

"I think I see it."

"Can you tell me what it looks like? What is it doing?"

"I can't really see it all that well, but I think it's black and maybe round, and it's just sitting there in exactly the same place, like it's weighed down or something."

"Could be a dummy mine," Carl interrupted.

Liam looked back over his shoulder at the coroner. "A dummy mine?"

"Completely harmless," Carl went on. "Non-explosive. Usually filled with sand. They were a nuisance tactic during the war. Mostly used to waste our time."

"It's working!"

"Liam?" young Ben's voice whimpered from the walkie-talkie. "I'll soon be drifting close enough to board the dock."

"Understood. See if you can tie the boat to the dock so Mr. Fin doesn't go sailing," Liam joked.

"Okay," Ben laughed nervously in return.

Liam smiled warmly. "Ben?"

"Yeah?"

"Just keep that thing with you and I'll be there to help you every step of the way."

"I will."

As the walkie-talkie went quiet, Liam held it to his heart and bowed his head. *Please give us a win. We need a win this time.*

With his legs shaking and his heart thumping, Ben carefully unloaded the medical equipment onto the free-floating dock. Using interlinked straps from patient restraints, he connected to the dock via one of its wooden beams and an outrigger from the boat. After he was sure that it all seemed to hold together well enough, he climbed over with walkie-talkie in hand.

"I'm here," Ben alerted them as he lifted the dark green sheet away from Michael Ketler's body.

"We're here, Ben," Liam came back. "Now, tell us what you see."

"It's like I'm looking at the Brooks kid all over again."

As if trapped in a recurring nightmare, there the boy's body lay, seemingly lifeless, wearing the same filthy white t-shirt with the same dark stain of blood streaming down the left side of his torso.

"I need you to get a better look at his chest."

Lifting the scissors from his medical kit bag, Ben pushed the sheet away and began cutting up the middle of the boy's t-shirt. He reached the collar and tore it apart with both hands. He found what he was looking for. Someone had cut this boy open and stitched him back up, but it wasn't as dirty or inflamed. It looked more recent.

"It's what you thought," Ben reported. "It's got the same shitty incision and everything."

"Okay, remember, you're not going to be able to do compressions."

"Trust me, I will never forget that." Ben reached for his bag.

"And you're not going to be able to intubate him either."

Ben fell back into a seated position on the dock, causing it to wobble. "You're kidding me... So, what can I do?"

"You've got your AED with you?"

"Yeah..."

"Use it, and don't forget the manual override."

"Okay..." Ben took a deep breath and then scrambled to his feet. "Okay, okay, okay."

"Come on, Ben. You can do it," Liam whispered to himself, clutching the walkie-talkie over his chest.

"He's done this before, right?" Colby shot a frown of concern at him.

"In training," Liam replied after swallowing an inaudible gulp like a ball of worry.

Double and triple-checking that the pads were securely in place, Ben knelt in front of the semi-automated external defibrillator. The contraption was the color of a cartoon bumblebee and closely resembled a toy spell-checker with no letters. Just one big round orange button above which Ben's nervous finger hovered.

"I'm ready," he informed Liam.

"Go for it."

"Are we sure about this?"

"Yes. Press it now!"

He did, and with the slightest of sparks, it began.

All Ben Braithwaite could do was watch in stunned bewilderment as a translucent veil of blue flame washed over the entirety of Michael Ketler's body. With a jolt of the limbs, he awakened, screaming in agony as he burned alive.

"He's on fire!" Ben cried. "I've just set him on fire!"

"Put him out!"

His breaths escaped him in high-pitched squeals as he clawed at the green sheet. He tugged at it, covering the shrieking, kicking boy. It didn't work. Pulling it aside, he tried one of their blankets, but the fire burned away. The flesh that was once as pale as steamed chicken was now dissolving into a searing red rawness.

"I can't put it out!" he yelled in his panic. "Nothing's working!"

"You need to do something, or that boy is going to burn to death, and it will be your fault!"

"No!" Ben screamed.

Protecting his hands with the emergency blanket, Ben roared as he heaved the burning boy over the side of the dock and into the lake. Before he could jump in after him, he noticed that the dock had also caught fire. It spread to a far corner as if following a trail, happening all too quickly for young Ben's mind to comprehend.

Suddenly, the sound of a second explosion. Except this one was bigger. Big enough to lift the dock out of the water. Big enough to rip the whole thing in half in mid-air. Screams could be heard from the pebbled shores as all the medical supplies and equipment fell into Lagan Lake, along with the body of Ben Braithwaite.

12
Ben Braithwaite, Pt. I

Liam's mind felt like a bubble of concentrated hate and anger as he sat in the hospital waiting room. He ignored the smiles of strangers passing by. He tuned out the hushed voices of his friends and colleagues, numbing himself to any embrace of comfort.

It had never occurred to him how detached it felt to be in such a place. The area was brightly lit like a clear winter morning, and yet there was no warmth. In the worst hours of someone's life, they were expected to sit among people they have never met. All jammed in side by side, caged in their seats like livestock. Trapped by fear, wondering with every passing of a nurse or doctor when it will be their turn to be let off of this morbid, businesslike assembly line.

As hard as he tried to hate the system, the bubble collapsed. He turned to Martin Fin, who sat dumbly next to him with a bandaged head. "I should've been on that dock. Not Ben."

"But then you'd be dead," Martin sighed. "And what good does that do?"

"It's natural that you feel this way," Colby tried to reassure him. "Anyone would." The officer's hands cradled a hot but pitiful looking cup of black coffee from the hospital drinks machine.

Liam granted her a smile and a nod to let her know that he appreciated her concern.

The three of them turned to the sound of heavy footsteps approaching to find Carl arriving, closely followed by Matt. They rose to meet them with hugs and handshakes.

"Can I get you some coffee?" Martin asked as they all took a seat.

"Thank you, son, but that can wait," Carl replied cryptically as he pulled a chair from the opposite row and seated himself facing the rest of the group. "We've been had again."

"How?" Colby leaned in.

"I spoke to one of the doctors treating the Ketler boy. He's a good friend of mine," Carl explained. "The incision and stitching on the upper torso...completely for show. No internal damage whatsoever. No obstructions in his throat either."

"But why?" Martin was puzzled.

Liam answered. "He wanted to make sure that we'd defibrillate."

"And the explosion?"

The coroner edged in closer. "It appears that both the boy and the dock were doused with some type of odorless accelerant. Parts of the boy were still igniting when they were trying to treat him, but it looks like he's going to make it."

The harsh squeal of a chair leg scraping the waiting room floor disrupted the group.

"I can't do this..." Matt whispered, standing weakly before them. He pointed to his right shoulder the way an infant would to a sore spot. "His head was there this morning. He sleeps...like an angel, or something. He's always so uptight. It was cool to see him peaceful for once." With his hand still holding his right shoulder, he looked at the floor. "I don't know what I'll do if I can't have him back here..."

Matt sat back down as Colby walked over to the trash to throw away her empty cup. In those few steps in which her back was turned to the group, she crumbled, crying hard into her free hand and disguising it as an itchy nose. She dried her eyes in secret before she returned to a different seat. She took the empty chair next to Matt and held his free hand. The other was still clinging to the place where Ben had last slept.

* * *

Ally Price liked to rest her pregnant belly on the handlebar of the shopping trolley whenever she visited the supermarket or the local newsagent. She would lift her t-shirt up slightly so that her hot skin could be soothed by the coolness of the metal frame. Sometimes she would let her belly maneuver, as if the child she carried inside were already big enough to push the trolley for their mommy.

It was funny to Ally how long little girl fantasies last into adulthood. The fairy tale of happily ever after. Love, marriage, children. She wanted it all, and although they began as dreams and wishes, there was never a doubt in her mind that she was born to be a mother. A good mother.

She wanted to be able to count the number of children she would have on both hands, taking up every last finger and thumb. She wanted boys and girls of all ages. She wanted photo albums bursting with pictures of birthday parties and school dances. She wanted their graduation caps hanging from her kitchen wall, all stitched together like a 'Welcome Home' sign. She wanted to be front row at their weddings—gay, straight, and everything in between. She wanted to be there for the births of her children's children. The births…

Ally stopped cold in front of the frozen food section.

The births… Birth…

"Oh shit…"

She dropped the milk in her hand. The carton burst open over her comfy sandals, mixing in with her broken waters.

"Oh gross…"

* * *

"Ben Braithwaite," Dr. Ellison called out as she approached the waiting room. Ellison, a woman and specialist greatly respected in her field, a miracle worker to some, hid her long blond hair beneath her surgeon's cap.

Martin took a look at all the sad and exhausted faces that surrounded him. He slowly got to his feet.

"I'll go."

The team watched as Martin Fin stood with his big hands clasped on his hips, nodding as he listened closely to every word that Ellison had to say. He stayed firm, unwavering. He took it all in. He scratched the back of his head once. As the exchange concluded, he cleared his throat.

"Thank you, Dr. Ellison, for everything that you do," Martin commended her as he gladly shook her hand. "I know your work very well. You're the best in my eyes."

Ellison responded with a smile. She welled up for a moment, as she always did. This was how much she cared, but she had taught herself to blink it away in an instant. These moments belonged to her patients and their loved ones, not her. Dr. Ellison, a true professional with a heart through and through.

Holding Colby's gaze, Martin returned to the group. They rose to meet him. He smiled at Colby, and she smiled back, and then his smile disappeared.

"He didn't make it." His head hung low. "He died on the table."

"Oh god…" Matt lost his breath and then the strength to stand.

Carl grabbed hold of the young man and pulled him in close. Matt slowly curled his arms around the coroner as he wept into his chest.

"His injuries were too severe," Martin went on. "Too much damage had been done. There was nothing they could do to save him."

"Jesus…" was all Liam could think to say as he descended back into his chair.

Colby put a hand on Martin's shoulder. "I'm sorry, you guys. I know how close you were getting."

"We weren't *that* close," Martin remarked bluntly, brushing a hand over his face.

"It's okay to be sad," Colby said softly. "You worked with him, side by side. You saw him every day. Like family."

"We held his hand," Martin sniffed. "It was like working with a kid."

"Or a brother."

Martin didn't respond. He chewed his bottom lip while he pretended to be distracted by noises from across the room that hadn't even occurred.

With a sigh, Colby looked to Liam. "Is there anyone we need to call?"

"No…" Matt replied, his voice muffled by Carl's hug.

"Sorry?" Colby looked to the two embracing.

"Ben was an orphan," Carl informed her. He looked down at Matt's head as he comforted its messy locks. "They both were."

"Jeez, I'd never have guessed that one." Martin frowned in his surprise.

Liam shook his head silently in his agreement.

"He had a pretty hard start to life," Carl said quietly. He lowered his voice to a whisper. "The kind that most people never want to talk about."

Gasping and sniffing, Matt pulled himself away from Carl's comforting hold. "Can we go see him?"

"They'll send someone to get us when he's ready," Martin replied, apprehension in his voice. "But we need to be prepared. He's not all there."

"What do you mean? He's dead," Matt sobbed. "That's about as 'not all there' as you can get."

"They had to make some amputations...during surgery. He'll be missing both his legs."

Matt's mouth fell open as he started to gag and choke on the vomit that was filling up his throat. The young coroner's assistant doubled over as he was sick on the floor.

Liam got back on his feet, ready to help. He scanned around the area for the closest place to take poor Matt to get cleaned up.

A nurse approached just as he was glancing over his shoulder.

"Liam Price?"

He turned to her with a friendly smile.

"Yes?"

"If you would just like to follow me, your wife is in delivery." The nurse turned and began to lead the way.

The smile on Liam's face vanished. He froze, but only for a moment. There was no time to freeze. There wasn't even any time to mourn. He faced the group and then looked to Martin.

"Clean him up," he ordered him sharply as he pointed to Matt.

Like a good soldier, Martin complied.

Satisfied that this situation was mildly under control, Liam Price followed the nurse on to the next.

* * *

Ally Price lay in her bed, soaking head to toe in perspiration. Her body was a pulsing, vibrating beacon of pain. Her face was flushed with a deep pink color as she breathed long and slow and heavy. And on her chest, tiny and wrapped in white, the new arrival rested. Ally was a mother once again.

"I missed it…" Liam Price said quietly.

"You missed the first one, too." Ally's exhausted eyes opened slightly. She barely managed a smile. "She came…so fast… I barely got in the building before I had her… Your daughter was almost born with waffle face…"

Liam chuckled as he held a plastic cup of cool water under his wife's chin. She slurped it noisily as he smiled warmly down at her.

"Well done, love."

Ally coughed and spluttered as she shooed the empty cup away. She cleared her throat as she pointed to their newborn baby.

"Hold her."

The plastic cup crushed into a ball in his grip. The last time he held a baby was with Christopher. He had politely refused or found strange excuses to avoid how he might feel if he ever held another, and now she was finally here. *Why did Ben have to die today?* So much had happened in the last few hours. He had done so much. Said so much. Felt so much. What if he was all out of feeling?

When all was said and done, he was her father and she was his daughter, and the time to take her up and hold her was now. Liam Price picked up her little body with his big strong hands. He took a breath, and he looked at her. *Oh my god…*

"She looks… She looks…" The tears were thick on his words as he couldn't bring himself to finish.

"Like the double of Christopher," his loving wife finished for him. "I thought so, too."

"Oh god…" Liam couldn't control his shaking as he cried with his baby girl in his arms. "I'm a daddy. I'm *your* daddy. Oh, I'll never let anything happen to you. I promise, I promise, I promise. I'll always keep you safe. I'll always be there for you. Forever and ever."

Weeping with joy, and pain, and love, he kissed his newborn daughter on the forehead.

* * *

The Price family shared Ally's hospital room as she slumbered soundly on her side, hands together between her cheek and the pillow, as if in prayer. Liam sat beside her, one foot on the bed and the other planted firmly on the floor as he watched their new baby girl sleep in her cot by the wall. Before he could soak in another wave of blissfully ignorant happiness, there was a gentle knock at the door.

Liam looked over to the window with tired eyes to find Officer Colby waving and motioning for him to come out into the corridor. Stretching, he nodded, kissed both of his girls, and left the room as quietly as he could manage.

"How are they doing?" Colby asked, holding a weak smile.

"They're fine, Jen," Liam replied gruffly, crossing his arms as he leaned against the wall. He rested his eyes for one more moment and then reengaged. "What's up?"

Colby's smile disappeared.

"I thought it best that you know, since you have a history with the couple…"

"History? With who?" Liam pressed his temple as if their conversation was causing his head to ache.

"Our drowning victim over at Green Water Bay," she reminded him. "The one that held up our rescue assistance?"

"Yes, I remember," he gestured as he hurried her angrily. "That was this morning."

The officer pressed her lips together for a moment as she let him off. It had been a hard day for all of them.

Finally, she told him. "Liam, it was Bethany Wilde."

Liam's eyes seemed to freeze open, wide and alert, spine straightening up as he stood away from the wall. "Beth…?"

"I could be sacked for telling you this, but…" Colby doublechecked the long corridor, up and down before saying, "…we're having a bit of trouble locating Mr. Wilde."

"You think he killed her," Liam stated plainly at the officer. "Because of the boys. You think he killed her so that she would take his secret to the grave."

"You forget there are a few possibilities to be considered here," she asserted. "Accidental drowning. Suicide. Maybe he drowned with her. We just haven't found the body yet. Or maybe he's dead, on the floor of his own home, from natural causes, and that's why no one answered. Or maybe he's just away somewhere, for whatever reason, and has no idea that she is even…"

Liam slid both hands into the pockets of his trousers and tilted his head at her with one eyebrow raised.

"But then I considered…" Colby's shoulders sank. "Whoever is responsible for kidnapping and doing that to those boys. It could easily be shrugged off as an unlikely coincidence that some psycho has taken an interest in you and your team, but knowing what I know about what went on between you and Alec, as well as his entire troubled history with kids, and now his own wife turns up dead?"

Offering her a half-smile, Liam reached out and squeezed her forearm, but she moved it away, taking hold of his hand instead.

"So, yes. I do," Colby looked him in the eye. "Alec is our guy. He should've been put away years ago. Before Christopher. Before all of this. But I'm going to make it right."

Tears rolled down Liam's face.

"So, I was right…" he sobbed. "After all this time. It wasn't an accident. He killed my boy…"

"I'm going to make it right," Colby said one final time. "This I can promise you."

13
Ben Braithwaite, Pt. II

Great red curtains draped down from the ceiling to the floor of the pulpit of the church, and in the center of it all was the coffin of Ben Braithwaite.

It was a small service; in attendance were Liam Price and his wife, Ally, Martin Fin and Jennifer Colby, Carl and Matt, Michael Ketler's mother and father, and finally, a handful of doctors and nurses that Ben had managed to get to know during his short time on the island.

The weather outside was beautiful, and warm for once—something they were all grateful for as they waited on the church steps to be called inside.

The priest presiding over the service was a dear and well-respected man. A little plump but forward-thinking, with a broad sense of humor; an absolute darling. The piece that he had chosen to recite was perfect, apt, and he delivered it with such a solemn grace that it touched all who were present to hear it.

Sniffs echoed in the church as it became time for friends and family to give their eulogies. Matt recited the lyrics of a song that he and Ben both loved. Michael Ketler's mother, Suzie, followed briefly, giving her thanks to the dearly departed stranger who saved her son at the expense of his own life. She called him 'her hero.' When the time arrived for a third speaker, there was silence.

Believing that Ben Braithwaite deserved better than that, Liam Price got to his feet and made his way to the steps of the pulpit, but on turning to all the familiar faces staring at him, waiting for him to speak, he instantly regretted his decision. And therein he found his inspiration.

"Life can be full of many regrets," Liam began as he recalled the cold reception he had given Ben the first time they met, "and one of mine is that I know a lot more about Ben now than I did when he was…" He looked upon the coffin. "…when he was with us."

Returning his gaze to the congregation, he continued. "Don't get me wrong, I worked with him every day, for hours on end. I even shared a meal with him at my home. I'd like to think I knew something about him. He wasn't the best paramedic. He was squeamish. He was forever second-guessing himself. I'll be honest: he was absolutely terrified half the time, but he did it anyway, because that's what he wanted to do with his life. He wanted to help people. I know that I am comforted in knowing that he left us doing just that."

Martin smiled and nodded in agreement as he bowed his head.

"My wife Ally and I, we had a son once, as you all know." His voice began to waver as tears found his eyes. "And the other night, after we had an excellent dinner together," Liam recollected, "and we'd sent him on home, we shared a thought. And that thought was if Christopher was still with us…and had a chance to grow up, he'd probably be a lot like Ben. We would want him to be, and we'd be proud of him."

* * *

The church parking lot was nearly empty as most of those in attendance were already on route to The Golden Eagle for the wake. Liam and Martin stayed behind with Ally and Colby as they waited by the entrance for Carl, who waved the last of them off.

There was a shiver in the air as the day was nearing its evening early. The sun cast a beautiful beam of reddish-orange light over everything. The only thing as magnificent as the firelit sky as it met the molten lava glow of the sea was the church itself. The only one on the island, its inhabitants had become accustomed to calling it Boatmore Church. It made the most sense, as the town was the nearest settlement, after all. Although built a reasonable distance from its surrounding cliffs, it was decided that a six-foot picket fence be put in as a safety perimeter around the edges that were closest to the holy structure.

Ally put her arms around the coroner as he returned to their group and kissed him on the cheek.

"It's kind of you, what you've done here," she told him. "Doing all this for Ben."

"Who else was going to? My assistant?" Carl chortled. "He had no one else. There was no one to call when he passed."

"Shouldn't Matt be here?" Colby asked.

"He's leading the charge into town," Carl informed them with a sad smile. "Brave boy is playing host until I get there."

"Is there anything we can do?" Liam offered.

"Nah, everything's paid for," Carl said, shooing him away until it occurred to him: "The church does take donations, though!"

"You heard him. Everyone open your wallets," Liam ordered heartily, holding his funeral program out like a collection plate in one hand while he dug around his suit for his wallet with the other.

They all chipped in, and they did so quite generously.

"Well, this is just embarrassing!" Liam exclaimed with laughter as he turned to go into the church. "I'll just go give this to the priest, and then we can all get going."

It was not lost on Liam how different the place felt when it was empty as he marched up the center of the nave. His footsteps resounded as he passed a row of pews with each stride. As he approached the chancel, he scanned the walls for a donation box, as the priest had already retired to the sacristy. He spotted one nailed to the wall on the far left, just before a large mahogany door with a black iron door handle.

He was almost there when the sight of Ben's coffin brought him to a standstill. Not the coffin itself, but the bloody handprint that was on the lid. The program fell from his hand as a mess of bills fluttered and heavy coins clanged and jangled loudly against the stone church floor.

Liam failed to notice the iron handle of the sacristy door slowly starting to turn as he rushed over to the coffin and flipped it open. The rank and rotting stench of death repelled him as he backed away from the decomposing corpse inside, crying out in shock and disgust. He took one last look at the red eyes, distended tongue, and sickly yellowish-gray color of Alec Wilde's skin before he slammed the coffin shut with both hands. Choking on the putrid stink that still hung in the air, Liam froze as he noticed the great sacristy door standing fully ajar.

Suddenly, his body buckled against the coffin as something thrashed him hard across his lower back. A second blow to the ribs, as Liam tried to steady himself, sent him rolling down the steps of the pulpit, landing on his back on the chancel floor. He cradled his aching side as he struggled to catch his breath. Rapid footsteps closed in on him. A gleaming shoe came down, stamping on his free wrist, pinning it to the cold stone. Liam groaned as he spied the other shoe preparing to kick him in the jaw.

"Please, stop…" His plea was met with hushed giggling from above as he gazed up into the face of his attacker. "Matthew…?"

The coroner's assistant stood over him with an amused grin on his face and a metal pipe clasped in his hand as he twirled it by the side of his leg, itching to put it to use.

"Wait…" Liam only needed to glance at the coffin for a moment before his eyes snapped back to Matt as he made the connection. "You're Alec's boy… Samuel?"

"Hmmm…" Samuel nodded as he pressed his foot harder into Liam's wrist. "Did you like your gifts, Uncle Liam? I hope you enjoyed them. I hope you loved each one of them in their own special way."

"Gifts?"

"Yes…" Samuel hissed furiously, his spit raining down upon Liam's face. "I know Auntie Allison told you my story. How else does someone like me show their appreciation for the gift you gave me?"

"Someone like you?"

"You know what I am." Samuel beat the elbow of the arm holding Liam's rib.

His scream echoed along the ceiling of the church. Unable to tend to his throbbing limb, he breathed his way through the agony.

"And what did I give you?"

"You brought *them* back to me." Samuel sneered at him. "Hoping that I'd changed. Hoping that I was the boy they always wanted. The boy they thought I was before they sent me away. As you can imagine, I didn't take too kindly to being rejected all over again. Even less so when they tried to have me put away for the rest of my life. So, when they ran all the way back here where they thought they could hide from me, on this shitty little island… I followed them."

"What about Ben?" Liam questioned as he balled and un-balled the hand of his battered arm. "He was about as innocent as they come."

"The last time I held something that innocent in my arms…" Samuel's eyes drained of color as he sighed. "…I drowned it."

A bible dropped down from nowhere, clapping against the stone floor as if it fell from the heavens.

Samuel looked up in time as Martin Fin's fist socked him hard across the cheek. His body crashed against the coffin. The thing toppled over as he clung to it, trying to scramble to his feet. He lost the metal pipe as he flailed over the side of the pulpit, retreating through the open doorway to the sacristy.

"Matt?" Martin puzzled it over as he pulled Liam to his feet.

"Samuel Wilde," Liam explained as the two began to give chase. "He killed Alec and Beth. He did it all."

They came to a stop as they reached the priest's office.

Ben's body lay across the desk, posed as if still inside his casket. The priest himself lay sprawled behind it all, sporting a great purple lump above his right eyebrow that bled from his forehead down to the floor.

"You check the priest," Liam said, directing Martin to the unconscious clergyman, as he headed for the back way out.

"Go get the little prick."

Liam soon found the rear exit flung wide open as he burst out into the cold evening air.

Samuel tore across the greenery like a mad sheepdog chasing an invisible flock as he made his way towards the picket fence perimeter. Liam was not far behind as he bounded after him.

"Get him, Liam!" Martin cried as he joined the pursuit. "If he makes it over that cliff, we'll lose him!"

As he reached the fence, Samuel kicked a hole in the weatherworn wood with ease and squirmed his way through. He screamed as he was met on the other side with empty animal eyes. The Alpine goat's cry was shrill, its steaming breath visible in the chill of the red sun. Its tufty white fur rippled in the island winds as it stood there gawking.

The startled beast scurried away as Liam barged through the broken fence, knocking Samuel over the edge of the cliff. Liam landed hard on his chest as he grabbed the falling man by the wrist with both hands. Martin appeared with no time to spare as he clamped his arms around Liam's waist.

"I got you!"

"You might as well let me go," Samuel shouted up as he hung loose and heavy from Liam's grip.

"The fall won't kill you." Liam strained against the man's weight as it got heavier with every passing moment. "Trust me."

"I could still drown myself." Samuel reached up with clawed fingers. "Same way I made Mother do it."

"You're not going anywhere," Liam told him through clenched teeth.

"I deserve to rot." Samuel dug his nails into the flesh of Liam's hand. "Just like Christopher."

"That's not gonna work." Liam braced against the sting as big beads of his own blood started to drip down onto Samuel's head.

The eyes of that blood-speckled face darkened once more.

"If you don't let go," he whispered with a deep rasp, "I will kill them all…including your baby girl."

Samuel gasped as Liam hoisted him up with one hand, a strength he didn't know he had. The muscles bulged from his veiny arm as Samuel dangled there helplessly. The other arm reached for Samuel's throat. He grabbed the necktie and wrapped it tightly inside his balled fist. When he looked back into Samuel's eyes, the darkness was no longer there. What was left could almost be described as human.

"He made me this way—"

Liam didn't know if Samuel was referring to God, Alec, or even the devil. It didn't matter to him anymore. He let go of Samuel's hand before he could finish his final word. As he started to fall, Liam wrenched the tie skyward.

There was a sickening *CLICK!* as Samuel's neck broke in mid-air. The young man let out a single strange gulping sound. His feet did a twitchy little dance as his eyes rolled red and white, and his tongue hung out over his teeth.

With a heavy sigh, Liam dropped Samuel into the sea below.

"What the hell happened?" Martin demanded as he heard the sound of Samuel's body connecting with the water.

"Couldn't hold on," Liam replied breathlessly. "He just slipped out of my hands."

Martin looked Liam over for a moment and then got to his feet.

"Okay then," he said as he started stripping out of his funeral suit, preparing to jump in after Samuel.

"Okay then…" Liam repeated warily.

As he began to take off his funeral wear, he peered over the edge of the cliff. He found Samuel's body still floating close to the surface.

14
Ben Braithwaite, Pt. III

It was Saturday afternoon, and Liam and Ally Price were holding a barbecue in their back garden to officially celebrate their precious new arrival.

A great white banner reading WELCOME HOME BABY KLARYSSA in big blue-on-pink balloon letters was pinned to the clothesline.

"It's Clarissa, except with a K and a Y instead of a C and an I," Ally happily repeated every time someone asked, and sometimes when no one asked at all.

The weather that day was so perfect that every time a hint of cloud passed over the sun Liam Price looked up from the closely guarded grill and shook his barbecue tongs like a grumpy old man with a walking stick and growled, "Don't you fuckin' dare…"

Content with his own company, Carl gorged himself on burgers in buns dripping with the greasiest melted processed cheese.

Ally and Jennifer sat at the table talking about a million things at once. They talked about Klaryssa's future, about the nights out they were going to have now that Ally could drink alcohol again, about their handsome men, about everything they loved and everything that annoyed them, and about Ben.

Martin Fin stood behind the barbecue, pretending to listen to Liam as he stared across the gathering at Colby. Liam went on about how they should do things like this more often: fishing, hiking, making the most of their island life.

Eventually, Liam realized that Martin's mind was elsewhere. With a laugh, he shook his head and picked up his glass, tapping it loudly.

"Can I have everyone's attention please?"

The party's conversations promptly died down.

"Ally, take it away." He took his place by his wife, resting an affectionate arm around her waist as she stood by him.

"Firstly, of course, I want to thank everyone for joining us in celebrating the arrival of our baby girl." Ally smiled tearfully. "It means the world to us that you could all attend. I know there is someone special who we all took into our hearts that isn't here today, but I would like everyone to know that he is still with us—in one special way in particular. Liam and I are proud to announce that we have decided to name our new baby girl Klaryssa *Ben* Price."

The party was moved by this sweet dedication as they gave gentle applause.

"Secondly…" Ally continued as she and Liam stepped aside. "Martin, if you will."

"Thank you, Ally." Martin cleared his throat nervously. "Congratulations on the newborn. She is a real beauty, but I'm afraid she's just not as beautiful as a certain someone who is here today." He turned and looked to Colby amidst a few playful laughs and boos. "Jenny, I know I have this reputation for being some self-absorbed, dickhead pretty boy. Growing up… All I ever saw were dull gray buildings where I came from. All in this never-ending row. Like tombstones. Nothing to do but just wait to die. Everybody dies. Nobody escapes. No one ever gets out. But I got out. I was able to do that by never letting anyone tie me down. That's all behind me now. I'm sorry this isn't the big romantic speech that you definitely deserve. Believe me, it's not for the lack of trying. I didn't want to steal someone else's words. I wanted this to be my own.

The truth is I couldn't find the words to describe how you make me feel. Nothing was good enough. All that I have for you is...I love you. So much that you take all my words away. You make me speechless."

Martin Fin slowly fell to one knee in front of Colby as he presented her with an engagement ring. "So, if you wouldn't mind having a silly brute like me around for the rest of your life, will you marry me?"

A sobbing Colby fell to her knees in front of Martin. He bowed his head in a flood of tears as Colby wrapped her arms around him and kissed him on the forehead.

"Yes," she whispered.

"She said yes!" Martin cried as he closed his muscular arms around his new fiancée.

The party filled with laughter and clapping, cheers and whistles, as they all set off party bangers that startled the engaged couple, who broke down in giggles together.

Liam ran over to his newborn as the loud popping noises set her off crying. He picked up the tiny treasure and cradled her as he spoke soothingly to her. He danced slowly around, singing softly to her as he held her close.

In the few short days following his death, stories and rumors among the townsfolk about the murders committed by Samuel Wilde had earned him the name 'The Boatmore Butcher.' Now that he was gone, their peaceful way of life was restored to order. And as before he and his crimes had darkened the shores of their merry isle, it was widely known, or more so believed, that there were only two causes of death on the island: either natural or accidental.

Life was full of accidents, most of them terrible, but every now and again, a beautiful, natural accident came to be, such as the unplanned yet wonderful miracle that Liam held in his arms at that very moment.

Finally, he realized that the best he could do from now on was to cherish this gift, to love his wife, Ally, and to continue rebuilding their life together as a family. He assured himself that he would be prepared for, but not be consumed by, the fear of whatever accidents may lie ahead. And he had no choice but to accept that death, however it comes, accidental or otherwise, would always follow. Naturally…

Until that day came, Liam Price had a promise to keep.

"Forever and ever," he whispered to his child before taking in that beautiful sea view. The way he always did. The way he hoped he always would. For the rest of his days.

* * *

Ally Price wandered around her back garden, clearing away all the disposable party wear as the party itself continued inside.

"Congratulations," Martin Finn uttered as he stepped tipsily from the house. "That's a beautiful baby girl you've got there."

"Thank you." Ally smiled politely, continuing on with the clean-up. "Congratulations to you, too. Getting engaged."

"I know." Martin sipped his can. "Weird, isn't it?"

"We're both getting on with life." Ally started to become breathless. "There's nothing strange about that."

"Did I tell you that Jen had an abortion not too long ago?" the man blurted out.

Ally stopped still. "You shouldn't have told me that, Marty. That is a deeply personal experience for a woman."

"It was mine as well."

"Oh, don't pretend like you were trying for one!" she scoffed as she looked right at him.

Hurt, Martin leaned in as he whispered, "I guess I can't succeed every time, huh?"

He turned to the party banner with Klaryssa's name on it as it still hung in the garden before turning back to Ally with a dirty grin and shooting her a wink.

She marched straight for him. "You shut your fucking mou—"

"Hey, you two," Liam called merrily from the house. "Hurry up and come inside. You're missing all the fun."

Ally glared at Martin as she slowly barged past him. "I think I've had enough fun for one night."

* * *

Officer Colby wore a pair of pale blue medical gloves as she sealed the polythene bag carefully with thick red tape. Laying it down flat on the smooth and shiny surface of the embalming table, she patted down a sticky label titled 'EVIDENCE.' After filling out all the other necessary details, next to the word 'Description,' she wrote the words 'Bone Saw' in black marker.

Ripping off the gloves with a huge sigh, she tossed them into a nearby trash can.

"Thanks for those." She smiled at Carl, who sat across from her, greedily chewing on a long stick of licorice. "And thank you for submitting your tools for testing. It's much appreciated."

"Oh!" Carl exclaimed as a finger shot up. He climbed out of his stool as he reached under the table for something. "You forgot one last piece of evidence."

The coroner smiled excitedly as he slid it over to the officer. Her eyes widened in amazement at the contents of the bag.

"Oh my god, you found it!" she exclaimed, holding it up. "This is the 'strange hood' that Samuel was said to have worn while hunting for his victims."

"The very same!"

"Except I never told you about that." Colby's eyes narrowed as she squinted at Carl in confusion. "So, how did you know?"

Even though she uttered the words herself, she still couldn't bring herself to comprehend what was right in front of her.

"Because it's mine," Carl revealed. "That's the hood I wore when I grabbed those boys."

Her good friend's smile was unchanging as his hand raised something high over his head. The light of the morgue cast a shadow from the post-mortem hammer across the officer's disbelieving face as she opened her mouth to cry out. The coroner swung for her temple, making an unpleasant meaty whacking noise as cold hard metal hit warm skin and bone. The officer slumped down onto the tiled floor.

"So, one evening, after class, my school teacher takes me back to his place," Carl began as he wheeled an old television and VCR in from the corridor. "I was ten going on eleven at the time. Anyways, when we get there, he asks me to get in the bathtub with my clothes on because he wants to take pictures of me lying underwater. Says it's 'his thing.' He tells me to keep my eyes open and to make sure I lie as still as I possibly can. He promises me money, promises me candy, if I do a good job for him."

Colby lay upon the embalming table, unconscious, her shirt torn wide open and the bra removed as Carl finished plugging in his video equipment and switched on the TV. The screen filled with silent chaos as streams of silver, black, and white static fired back and forth. Finding the remote, he aimed it at the television, but then he paused, letting his arm drift down by his side.

"I think I was supposed to die that night..." he uttered in a thoughtful tone suspended somewhere between questioning and wondering. "Instead, he gets me out of that tub and he's down on his knees. He holds my face in his hands as he speaks to me. He offers to dry me off and wash my clothes. I say no. He starts to cry. I don't want my teacher to be sad, so I hug him. He thanks me. Gives me the money, some candy, and sends me on home."

After placing the remote upon the table by Colby's leg, Carl picked up a VHS tape and sat it carefully on top of the VCR.

"He committed suicide the next morning," the coroner said matter-of-factly. "Threw himself off a building. A letter he mailed to the police led them to the bodies of three missing boys, but I think there were more. There's always more...

"In the years that followed, I became more and more obsessed with what happened that night," Carl continued as he stared blankly at the TV static. "I wanted to know why. I had to find a way to see what he saw when he took those pictures. I waited. And I studied. I became an expert in human biology like him. Even found a passion for forensic sciences. I became a public schoolteacher like him. I did everything I could to get inside the head that had fascinated me for so long."

Carl slowly rubbed the back of a gloved hand across his eyelids before he slotted the VHS tape into the mouth of the VCR. The peeling label read 'JAMIE B. #1' as the mechanism swallowed the tape whole. It buzzed, it whirred, and it groaned until moving images finally filled the glass screen above.

The eye of a camcorder gazed down upon a little boy, no older than four or five, as he gazed back up from beneath the surface of the water. He was dressed in his play clothes as his bony elbows pressed against the sides of the bath, holding himself under. As the boy lay submerged, the water's skin gave his widened eyes a doll-like glaze, making him appear lifeless.

"It wasn't until I took home young Jamie here that I first saw it." Carl was unable to mask the trembling in his voice. "For the first time, I saw the sickness in me. It had been with me ever since I got in that bath all those years ago. And this was the moment I passed the sickness on to Jamie. The instant we put our heads below the water...we were gone. Callum, Michael. Even Ben after he went into the lake that day."

Carl let out a deep sigh before he ripped apart the sealed evidence bag to reclaim his electric bone saw.

"Meeting Samuel made me see things differently, though," he said with a smile. "The times we spent in this very room as he spoke of his plans of killing his own flesh and blood. He inspired me to take action. Rather than spending the rest of my days being haunted by this disease, I decided to change what I saw in those boys. By cutting and mutilating them, they became something else entirely. We all went under the surface, but none of us came back. We are just what's left behind. We're the goners..."

Plugging in the bone saw, Carl stood over Colby's body as the blade hovered up and down her naked torso. He switched it on. It buzzed furiously in his grip as he lowered it towards the officer's exposed flesh.

Part II
The Butcher

1

The Dark Room

July 1977

The mold in the walls was heavy on the boy's lungs as he crept silently down that long, thin hallway. He fought to stay quiet as he tried not to choke on the filthy moisture that clung thick to the roof of his mouth and lingered like a spider in the hollow of his throat. The light overhead was dim and seemed to grow dimmer still the further he inched his way towards the door at the very end.

It lay open to the right of a bookcase that nested its way up to the ceiling. Towering over all like an ancient tree, the wood was as black as infected teeth and filled with over a dozen old marionettes.

Their smiles were white, wide, and lifeless beneath their pointy bobbled hats. They sat on the edge of their shelves in their frilly, striped, and polka-dotted outfits. Their painted eyes did not follow him nor anyone. They were dead, blind to the world of shadows all around them in that dark and dank hallway.

The boy possessed the good sense to keep well away from such strange circumstance as what lay before him…but he'd heard a noise. On his way out, on his way to freedom, he'd heard a sound. A very particular sound. It was the unmistakable sound of another child. A cry cut short by something, or someone. And it came from that door on the right, at the end of the hallway, next to the bookcase full of little wooden nightmares.

Finally, the boy stood at the doorway. Not only was the door ajar, it was wide open and waiting for him to take a look inside, but he dared not take another step. The room itself was darker than the bottom of the deepest pit. A void, empty of light. Empty of life. If there had been a child in that room, they were probably dead before the boy made it to the door.

The only thing he could see was a bone-white rotary dial telephone. It sat upon what could have been a desk, but he couldn't be sure.

"Carl," a man's voice called from the other end of the hallway.

The boy turned his head. "Yes, Mr. Walker."

"That's not the way out."

The boy blinked innocently. "Sorry, Mr. Walker."

"Go on home now."

"Yes, sir," the boy said with a nod as he turned back to the dark room.

Perhaps his eyes moved too quickly, or perhaps his mind was playing tricks on him, but for a moment, he thought he saw a wall. And against this wall was a person, not a child, standing there, staring back at him. He dismissed it as just his imagination. Until he took one last look at the phone.

Dripping down the pale handset was a bloody smear in the shape of a hand. The blood was fresh and new, and the hand was the size of a child's.

2
The Autopsy

Forty-Two Years Later

Martin Fin drained the last of the sea water from the body bag into the sink. Rolling it up, he turned and headed for the door when he was stopped by the sight of his friend, Carl, standing over Samuel Wilde as he lay lifeless upon the embalming table.

Even after they had suffered through one of the longest days of their lives, they had yet to change out of their funeral attire. Martin's clothes clung to him as his skin was still wet from rescuing Samuel's body from the sea. Carl's, on the other hand, were bone dry.

"You shouldn't be doing this," the paramedic remarked thoughtfully.

"The police have already called someone in from the mainland," Carl reassured him. "Don't you worry about me. You get back to the others. They need you more than I do right now."

"You could come with me, you know," Martin offered. "I'm sure they'd like to see you, too."

"That's sweet of you to say, my boy," Carl said, smiling, "but I'm needed here."

"You're sure?"

"Of course. They're coming in tomorrow," the coroner explained. "And there's much to prepare."

"If you say so," Martin conceded as he went to leave. "You know where we are if you need us."

"I do." Carl gave him a nod of appreciation. "Thank you, Martin."

The door creaked to a close as Martin Fin exited the morgue.

Lifting a stethoscope from the nearby instrument tray, Carl placed it around his neck and began unbuttoning Samuel's soaking funeral shirt. Donning the device, he listened to the body's bare chest. There was nothing. He knew full well that this would be the case, but still, he needed to hear it for himself. He needed to hear the nothing. There was no escaping the truth. Samuel really was gone.

Tossing the stethoscope back onto the tray, Carl walked to the end of the embalming table where he stood and stared at Samuel's body in silence. All sound emptied out of that room, and all other things in existence along with it. He ran a finger across the ankle and placed it between his lips. Suckling on the flesh of his fingertip as if it were a baby bottle, he could taste the salt from the sea water on his tongue.

Finally, Carl removed his funeral blazer and began neatly folding it up. Upon completing such a simple task, the man uttered a noise that fell somewhere between laughter and tears. And words. Words he could not say that were now lost to them. He shook his head at his own foolishness. Dropping the folded blazer to the floor, the coroner climbed up onto the embalming table and lay down next to his deceased assistant. Laying on his side, he placed a hand upon Samuel's shoulder and closed his eyes. As the drops of water steadily dripped from the young man's sea-drenched hair, Carl wept soundly beside him as he wished that they were the sound of a living heartbeat.

* * *

Four people attended the autopsy of the Boatmore Butcher: Officer Jennifer Colby; her superior, Sergeant Cunningham, who had journeyed over from the mainland that very morning; and the afternoon's acting pathologist, Irene Birchwood. Also in attendance was the resident island coroner, Carl Oxspring.

The body was prepared, lying in wait beneath its sheet upon the table. A tray of the necessary instruments for the day's task was also laid out ready. Everything was clean. Everything was in order. Everything was cold.

Dressed head to toe in his best official attire, Cunningham was a short but broad and angry looking man, thanks in no small part to a career that had steadily twisted his bushy gray brows into a permanent scowl.

He extended a handshake to Carl just before the proceedings were underway. "We appreciate you taking the time to join us in a consulting capacity."

"You're welcome," Carl said. "It's my pleasure."

"Thank you for doing this, Carl," Colby chimed in.

He offered her a mischievous wink to which she responded with a soft giggle.

Briefly shaking his head at her, Cunningham then motioned Carl's attention over to Irene. "I understand the two of you already know each other?"

Beneath a head of fading strawberry blonde hair and wiry-framed spectacles, the older woman wore a pine-green bowtie between a pair of berry-red trouser braces.

"Why yes, of course," Carl confirmed, clapping his hands with delight as he walked over to greet her. "We attended the same university together. Took all the same classes. We became fast friends."

"We speak on the phone quite regularly, you see," Irene confessed to the sergeant, grinning from ear to ear. The two laughed heartily as they embraced and shook hands.

"Right, well." Cunningham's patience had clearly worn thin. "Shall we get started, everyone?"

Colby rolled her eyes at him. She had become experienced at doing such things and going undetected. Not that this was difficult in such a man's presence.

Both she and Cunningham respectfully stepped to the side as Irene and Carl readied themselves to examine the deceased. Carl switched on the table's overhead lighting while Irene produced a Dictaphone. The device emitted a hard *CLICK!* as she pressed RECORD.

"3 p.m., Tuesday, March 19th, 2019," the pathologist began, her mature croak ringing loud and clear. "This is Dr. Irene Birchwood and I will be performing the autopsy of Samuel Alec Wilde. Also present are Officers Colby and Cunningham. Assisting me is Dr. Carl Oxspring. I will now begin my preliminary examination."

Irene smiled across the cold metal table at her old friend as she slowly circled the body like a cunning predator closing in on its prey. Finally, she lifted the white sheet away from Samuel and pulled it down until his head and shoulders were exposed. She picked up a scalpel from the tray; the gleam caught Carl's eye. He winced at first, but then his breathing halted, making way for the growing drum of his heartbeat as he watched the glistening blade glide close to his assistant's dead flesh.

From that moment, whatever resolve he thought he had possessed drained out of him along with the color from his face. As his own body became numb, he felt a faint sensation in his stomach as if his guts were melting inside his belly and were now spilling out of him like warm wet paint.

"Subject is a Caucasian male, twenty-four years of age, according to documents provided to me by the local police department. Samuel is 181cm in length and weighs approximately…158 pounds. There appears to–"

"I am so sorry!" Carl exclaimed abruptly, forehead soaking in sweat. "I thought I could stomach this, but I need to leave."

Unable to wait for a response, Carl marched out of the room, tearing away his gloves and apron as he went.

* * *

Dr. Irene Birchwood watched silently from the entrance of the morgue as Colby's vehicle drove out of sight. Reaching into her coat, she approached her colleague, who rested against the wall of the building with his hands jammed into the pockets of his trousers.

"For you," she said as she held out the mini cassette tape from her Dictaphone.

Carl's lips parted in surprise. "But–"

"I record with my phone nowadays," the pathologist explained, patting the breast pocket of her coat. "My niece showed me how."

His gaze fixed, Carl held the micro-sized cassette between his fingers the way a nervous child would hold a precious Christmas tree ornament.

"You cared for this one," Irene said in realization as she watched Carl carefully pocket the tape inside his cardigan. Looking into the coroner's sorrowful eyes, Irene placed a hand tenderly upon his cheek. "Do you have any idea how rare that is, my friend? I am so glad you were able to find someone. And even sorrier that you lost him."

Reluctantly removing her hand, Irene turned to leave.

Carl watched the shadow under her shoes move across the ground as Irene made her way over to her car.

He called out to her: "I don't know what to do now that he's gone."

"Listen to the tape," his friend called back from across the hood of her car. "You'll know what to do."

After he waved Irene off, the coroner was left with the emptiness of the morgue's parking lot, and the faint cry of great, foaming waves crashing into the island's rocky shores in the distance.

* * *

That night, the overhead lamp above the embalming table was the only light on in the morgue. It shone down harshly upon Carl Oxspring, who sat hunched over in a stool with a Dictaphone in hand as he waited for the courage to press PLAY. Breathing deeply, he turned to gaze at the drawer where Samuel's body was being kept. Heeding the words of his friend and colleague, Carl let out a long sigh as he bowed his head and hesitantly pressed the button to start the tape.

At first, the words of Dr. Irene Birchwood were like distant echoes, faded signals too weak to infiltrate the coroner's mind inside its mighty cage of pulsing flesh, surging blood, and solid bone. Until her findings confirmed the suspicions that had taken root in his brain the moment she lifted away the cold sheet from the boy's lifeless face. The swelling of the neck, the abrasions, the ligature marks, the ruptured vessels in his eyes. *Such beautiful eyes...*

As the tape continued, only the fragments he had needed to hear remained with him.

"...believe the subject died from a cliff fall, did you say?"

"...simply no trauma to support such a theory."

And finally, "…subject's injuries are consistent with a hanging."

The tape came to a STOP. He had heard enough.

From the depths of a heart drowning in rage, a whisper rose.

"*They…killed…you…*"

The Dictaphone cracked as Carl's grip tightened around it until its outer casing split wide open.

Shrieking at the ceiling in all his fury, he hurled it at the wall. The contraption shattered into dozens of tiny plastic pieces, but it wasn't enough. The coroner's bones and muscles began to twist and contort. He bared his teeth like a wild animal as he dragged his fingernails over the metal surface of the table. He needed more, and his gaze glared ferociously as he hunted for it.

"Aah!" the man rasped, grabbing a particular item from the instrument tray. The tray clattered loudly behind him as it toppled from its stand to the tiled floor.

Hissing through his clenched jaws, he threw open the nearest cabinet and tore the drawer inside out of the wall until it would go no further.

His breathing slowed, quieting down until all was still. Silently, he tugged lightly on the sheet that covered the corpse and let it fall softly to the ground.

Approximately eleven minutes later, Carl retrieved the cordless phone from its wall mount by the door. He dialed as he walked back to the embalming table. Putting the phone to his ear, he began drumming the metal surface with the ends of his fingernails as it rang.

Colby's voice answered with a "Hello?"

"Officer Colby," the coroner said, smiling. The drumming stopped.

"Carl! What can I do for you?"

"I just wanted to apologize for this afternoon."

"Think nothing of it. Everyone understands."

"Oh, thank you for that."

"Now that I have you, we will need to take your tools into custody to examine as potential evidence. Just to give you a heads up."

"Oh, I see. Is it possible that you might grant me a day or two so that I can make the necessary arrangements? Otherwise I won't be able to do my job!"

"That shouldn't be a problem. Tell you what, Klaryssa's Welcome Home party is tomorrow, so why don't I swing by the next day after my shift?"

"I don't see why not. I'll be sure to be ready for you."

"Perfect!"

"Officer Colby?"

"Yes, Carl?"

"I happened to hear that Dr. Birchwood found that Matthew's—sorry, I mean Samuel's—cause of death was due to a hanging?"

"I know. It's the strangest thing. Those cliffs are pretty jagged though. Perhaps his clothing snagged on something when he fell."

"That certainly would be strange…"

"Yeah, well… Anyways! That's all sorted now, so if I don't see you at the party, I will see you in the morgue."

"Can't wait."

"Bye, Carl."

"Goodbye, Officer Colby." The coroner sighed deeply as he ended the call.

His smile gone, Carl walked back to the wall mount by the door and replaced the cordless phone before returning to the body on the open drawer, all the while keeping a pace that was both cool and calm.

The deceased was an islander of average build with dark hair and pale white skin. According to his toe tag, he was in his mid-forties. *Samuel would never reach his mid-forties*, Carl realized as he looked upon the limbs of the corpse that he had smashed to pieces. Thick wads of loose rotten skin were torn as the sharp ends of broken bones skewered through dead flesh this way and that. The man's belly had been caved in until it resembled some sort of macabre human doggy bowl, and beaten with such a vicious force that the body had shit out its own internal organs.

Carl raised the instrument he had used to perform such a barbaric act, a post-mortem hammer. He hit the corpse in the neck. He hit it again, and again, and again. And he did not stop until he completely severed the man's head from the rest of his body.

* * *

Two days later he used that very same hammer to render an unsuspecting visitor unconscious.

Head throbbing furiously as she slowly awakened upon the embalming table, the first thing that Officer Jennifer Colby saw when she opened her eyes was a child, a young boy, floating in front of her. The sight appeared to glow somewhere in the distance. As her vision cleared, she realized the image was coming from an old television screen. She saw Carl standing there, too, staring at it, completely transfixed. He held something in his hand. Some kind of videotape.

My god... What the hell is he watching?

A groan escaped her lips as she tried to look around. Did she just give herself away? She lay still as she shut her eyes and waited. After a few moments, she opened them again. Carl hadn't heard her, but then again she couldn't hear herself either. He must have damaged her left eardrum when he struck her.

I can't believe he did this to me! She couldn't believe any of it.

Her fingers scrambled as they searched the table she lay upon for a weapon. They found something hard and plastic. Another videotape? It would have to do. She closed her eyes again as the coroner made his way over.

Carl let out a deep sigh before he ripped open the sealed evidence bag to reclaim his electric bone saw.

Colby knew that Carl had been talking since she regained consciousness, but only now that he was standing right beside her could she hear what he was saying.

"Meeting Samuel made me see things differently, though," he said with a smile. "The times we spent in this very room as he spoke of his plans of killing his own flesh and blood. He inspired me to take action. Rather than spending the rest of my days being haunted by this disease, I decided to change what I saw in those boys. By cutting and mutilating them, they became something else entirely. We all went under the surface, but none of us came back. We are just what's left behind. We're the goners…"

Plugging in the bone saw, Carl stood over Colby's body as the blade hovered up and down her naked torso. He switched it on. It buzzed furiously in his grip as he lowered it towards the officer's exposed flesh.

Just then, a leg rose up as she bent her knee. A second later she let it drop back down.

The menacing whir of the bone saw fell silent.

Carl jolted with fright as something rattled on the tiled floor at his feet. It was one of his VHS tapes. A hand grabbed his arm as Colby snapped upright and headbutted the side of his face. With a snarl, the coroner sawed into the woman's neck as she tumbled to her feet on the other side of his table.

There was a scream. A spurt of blood. The officer flailed wildly as she staggered towards the door, her red spray speckling the walls of the morgue. She grabbed the phone from its mount before disappearing into the corridor.

She didn't get far before she let out a cry of horror. A corpse strung up against the entrance door was blocking her exit. The body's stomach was collapsed inward and its limbs were a broken mess of protruding bones and hanging meat. As for the head, it was nowhere to be found.

Keeping a trembling hand clasped against her wound, she made her way towards the entrance, regardless. She dialed and waited for an answer while trying every door handle with her elbow that she walked past. Everything seemed to be locked up tight. And with her blood oozing thick and fast down the center of her bare chest, she could feel it filling her underwear and spilling down her legs as she slipped on it with every despairing step she took.

It was only when she reached the mangled corpse that she finally realized that someone was standing right behind her.

"Officer Colby…"

She hadn't heard him. *Was he following me this entire time?*

She spun around with a gasp, swinging the phone for his face. He grabbed her wrist with ease, snatching the phone from her weak grip. She yanked a loose bone from the corpse hanging behind her and held its sharp point out like a knife. Carl knocked the weapon out of her hand with a single swipe.

"Listen, Jennifer," Carl sighed with pity. "You can either come with me and I'll fix up that nasty cut I gave you, or we can both wait until you pass out–"

"Fuck you, Carl," Colby sneered defiantly.

A grin spread across Carl's face. He nodded. He even laughed. Then he grabbed her by the shoulder and beat her back into unconsciousness with one fist.

He stopped only when he was interrupted by the shrill ring of the cordless phone in his other hand. Shoulders rising and falling, Carl caught his breath first before he answered the call.

"Irene!" He shook his aching hand as he looked down at Colby's body. "Yes, I listened to the tape. And you were right." Carl peered around the torso of the mutilated cadaver at Colby's police car waiting outside. "Listen, I'm going to be needing your assistance with something. I will explain everything in a few days when I come over to the mainland."

3

The Lake

Some stories are not always told the way that they happened. Take the events that took place on that fateful day at Lagan Lake. The discovery of seventeen-year-old Gordon Starkwood's body, the rescue of sixteen-year-old Michael Ketler, and the explosion that ultimately claimed the life of young paramedic Ben Braithwaite. All this had since become known as the Lagan Lake Massacre—a gruesome, gore-soaked bloodbath that claimed the lives of no less than eight people. Eight lives violently snuffed out by the Boatmore Butcher himself. With an axe, he swung, and with a cleaver, he hacked. Every islander that told the story had a friend of a friend who knew one of the victims. And to every islander that listened, the evil Butcher of Boatmore lived on in their minds. Even in death, they believed that he still stalked the night, searching for his next victim.

"Should've brought a coat," Hannah Wilson said, pouting at her boyfriend as she sat at the rear of the rowboat. Her arms were crossed tightly around her thin pink sweater. "What am I even doing here?" she muttered to herself.

The soft bite of the evening raised the goosebumps from the flesh that shivered beneath her sleeves. The darkening blue sky that stretched above them appeared navy against a cold and piercing moon. Besides the slow trickle of lazily rowing oars, the winds were stilled and the lake was quiet.

In the distance, a shadow moved silently along the shore.

The boat came to a stop as Ryan Reade hauled his shirt over his head. "Same reason I am." He held it out to Hannah with a smirk. "Because there's nothing else to do on this frigging island."

Hannah let out a short laugh, smiling warmly as she draped his chivalry around her shoulders. "Did you bring my cigarettes?"

"Like I'd dare forget."

Ryan was slim but handsome, and remarkably kind for a boy his age. A trait that a lonely Hannah needed as her natural beauty left her subject to jealousy and rumor.

Lighting one up, she took her first drag of the evening. Leaning against the side of the boat, her eyes wandered along the surface of Lagan Lake as it surrounded them, frozen and unmoving. "God, it's so quiet."

"Can I get some of that?" Ryan extended a hand.

Hannah turned, frowning at him in her surprise. "You don't smoke?"

"I know," he said with a shrug. "I just wanna see if it's better when we both taste the same."

"Oh," Hannah sat upright. "Well, in that case." Passing it over, she waited and watched him with a hint of bated amusement on her lips. She snuck out her phone, hoping to capture the show about to unfold before her.

The shadow on the shore was no longer moving. It lingered there, unseen, as it leered out over the water.

"Don't forget to inhale." Hannah covered the grin on her face as she made certain her boyfriend was in the frame.

"I know what I'm doing," Ryan insisted, fumbling the cigarette between his unsteady fingers. Tobacco spilled from the tip as they bent and split the paper. The burning ash end had already broken off and extinguished itself upon the wet floor of the boat.

His girlfriend giggled as she leaned in closer.

Suddenly the figure in the dark took off running, and it was fast, tearing madly down the pebbled shore as it charged straight for the lake.

A sharp gasp escaped Hannah. "What was that?"

"What was what?" Ryan finally dropped what was left of the cigarette.

Hannah clutched the side of the boat as she peered overboard. "I felt something bump into us."

"We must be in the right spot," Ryan remarked cryptically.

"What do you mean by 'right spot'?" Hannah sighed as she lowered her head, already knowing the answer. "Ryan, please tell me this isn't why you brought us out here."

"Yep," Ryan responded with a defiant *pop!*

"What is wrong with you?" She scowled at him.

"What?"

"He killed your sister."

"You know Nicola isn't dead!" Ryan scoffed. "She just hasn't been back since she found that old lady's body at the beach."

"She was his mother, right?"

"Yup," Ryan confirmed, his face changing as he fell deep into thought. "At least, that's what the police told us. They came to our house just after they got him. Told us he forced her to walk into the water and drown herself."

"That's horrible…" Hannah said solemnly. "I can't even think about it."

But that did not stop her mind from trying. All she could think of was the body of Bethany Wilde twisting and thrashing helplessly as the tide dragged her into the crushing, rolling dark of the sea.

Looking over the side, Ryan discovered a charred piece of plank and a torn shred of green sheet clinging to it as they bobbed by the boat, just out of reach. He turned to Hannah excitedly. "Hey, look what I–"

The boy's words whimpered to nothing as a bloodcurdling scream ripped through the air. Their eyes met in a moment of dread and panic before they looked to the shore, the echo of that horrid cry still stinging their young ears.

"Ryan…" Hannah could barely speak as she took her boyfriend's hand and held it tight.

"Don't worry," Ryan whispered, squeezing her fingers reassuringly. He gulped quietly as he tried not to vomit. "Long as we're out here, we'll be okay."

"Okay," she repeated as she reached out to him.

Ryan gently guided her over to his seat. Hannah sobbed as he pulled her in close. He wrapped his arms around her and kissed her softly. As she hummed soundly into his shoulder, Ryan kept a watchful eye on the shore.

"We shouldn't have come out here," Hannah fretted, furious at herself all of a sudden as she pushed her way out of his grip. "Have you seen my cigarettes?"

"Probably where you were just sitting, maybe?" Ryan snarked at her.

Keeping her arms spread out for balance, Hannah carefully sidestepped towards the stern of the boat. She found them beneath her seat on the wet floor. Smiling to herself, she shook off the pack, placed a cigarette between her lips, and lit it up, relaxing as she took in those first few drags.

"Hannah, sit down," Ryan pleaded in his confusion. "Someone might see you."

"Who's going to see me?" Hannah looked around. "We're way out here. There's no one else but us."

That's when Hannah Wilson saw something impossible. Out there on the lake. Out there in the dark, someone was standing atop the water, staring back at her.

She let out a scream of fright. Tripping over her own feet, cigarettes flew into the air like cheer batons at a pep rally as she tumbled. There was a dull *CLINK!* as her head clipped one of the oarlocks. Reaching out to grab her, Hannah wilted into Ryan's arms, out cold.

"Oh shit! Hannah… Hannah?" He tried to stir her. "Okay, I'm just gonna lay you down like this." He spoke softly to her as he set about gently placing her body into the recovery position. "You're gonna be all right. I'll take care of you. Don't worry."

As Ryan grew concerned over the small pool of blood spreading from Hannah's head, the man hiding in the dark moved closer. He glided silently over the lake, his feet never touching the surface as he headed straight for them.

Removing his left sock, Ryan dipped it into the clear water surrounding them before ringing it out. Folding it, he crouched down low as he held it firmly against the wound on Hannah's forehead.

The man from the lake appeared behind him. A smile widened beneath his pale hood as he brought down the black metal pipe. The weapon grazed Ryan's shoulder. Crying out, he fell back against the other side of the boat.

Bracing himself, he peered through the shadowy curtain of night at the horrid face in front of him. Although its features appeared too twisted to be human, Ryan could tell it was smiling at him.

The man held up the pipe, ready to strike.

"You're him, aren't you?" the Reade boy said shakily. "The Boatmore Butcher?"

Instead of delivering a second blow, the man pointed the metal pipe directly at him.

"Please don't kill me," Ryan said sadly. "My mom. She's sick. I don't want her to die alone."

The man was still for a moment, and then the pipe pointed to Hannah.

Ryan shook his head, "No, don't take her. Please. I'm sorry. I'll go with–"

Suddenly Ryan hurled his loose shoe at the man's face and then lunged for the nearest oar. Batting the shoe away with his arm, the man caught the boat oar as the boy swung for his mid-section. He forced the oar back into Ryan's stomach, knocking him over the side. Unable to breathe or swim in his battered and bruised condition, Ryan thrashed around blindly in a panic, coughing and spluttering as water filled his mouth and spilled into his lungs.

The man in the pale hood floated soundly around the rowboat to where the boy was drowning, twisting, and writhing in the nothingness. His head tilted in his curiosity as he watched Ryan desperately fighting to breathe, hands reaching and grasping at the side of the boat for a way out to no avail. The man tossed a rope over Ryan's head and pulled it taut, tightening it around the boy's throat. Ryan choked and wheezed as he clawed at his own neck in an attempt to loosen it, but the water made that impossible. He spun around as he could feel the man looming over him.

"Please…" the boy begged, his tears hidden by the lake and the darkness.

He was met with a cold smirk as the man in the pale hood brought the oar down on top of his skull with a blunt *CRACK!* Ryan fell limp, bobbing there in the water like a dead trout.

Fishing the boy out of Lagan Lake, he placed him onto the platform of the motorized raft. He returned the oar to the rowboat, setting it down carefully by Hannah's side. Then he removed the rope from Ryan's neck and dropped it into the water. The motor started up and the raft began to move.

The Butcher sped off into the night with the unconscious body of Ryan Reade lying at his feet.

The fourth was his.

#4.

4
The Husband & The Father

A red sun glowed with a fury that scorched the sky, burning it to a shade of crimson. The clouds became the color of bruised flesh, and far below the sea was blood. Deep, dark blood.

A body clothed in a black suit rose from the waves that crashed against cliffs made of jagged iron. The corpse free-fell upward, stopping only when it came to hang by its own necktie. Its distended tongue slithered back between its teeth. Its eyes were white and lifeless as its broken neck snapped the head upright.

Samuel Wilde smiled through the blood stains splattered across his face.

"I deserve to rot," he uttered. "Just like Christopher."

For the briefest of moments, his face was that of Christopher Price. So young. So beautiful. So precious. And then the boy was gone. Returned to whatever kind sleep held him now.

"I will kill them all," Samuel growled as the blood spots on his face burned holes into his flesh. The air filled with the screams of infants. "Including your baby girl."

The deafening cries sounded from a great white church that towered in the distance. Its entrance doors flung wide open as it bled from every window.

"You made me this way," Christopher's voice whispered from Samuel's lips, "…Daddy."

The blood sea surged up to meet the scorched sky.

"*You killed me.*"

Liam Price startled awake, his face soaked with tears as he gasped for air.

"You're all right, you're all right, you're all right," Ally soothed him, breathless, as she cradled and comforted her trembling, sweat-covered husband.

The newborn in the crib mere feet from their bed began to cry.

"That was Carl on the phone," Ally informed Liam downstairs as he rested back against the kitchen counter, sipping contently from a mug of hot black coffee.

The steam smoothed away the cold sweat from his brow as the aroma flavored the air around him so deliciously. The clearing of his throat felt like ruffling warm silk.

"Oh really?" Liam responded dreamily. "What did he want?"

Ally sat adjacent to the kitchen area, barely keeping herself awake as she yawned from their cozy dining table, a baby monitor never more than an arm's length away from her. For a moment she was too tired to form words.

"I dunno…" The moment had passed. "But it sounded important." Another deep howl of exhaustion accented what remained of her reply. "He said he wants to see you and Martin as soon as you can both spare yourselves."

"Can I make you one, love?" her husband asked thoughtfully as he wandered over to her.

"Oh God, no," Ally said, shaking her head. "Thank you, but no. If I have any of that stuff I will never sleep."

She hummed as Liam stood by her, rubbing her back with his free hand.

"I wish I could help more," he said softly.

"I know, but you do more than enough," Ally said, gently squeezing his wrist, "considering the hours you're working."

"You're amazing," Liam told his wife before kissing the back of her neck. Pulling over a chair, he perched by the corner of the table, as close to his beloved as he could get.

Ally slowly traced the veins of his arm with her fingertips, never touching the skin.

"You had another nightmare," she said without meeting his eyes. "Another dream, about Samuel?"

She didn't need to lift her gaze, for she could feel the warmth washing right out of the man sitting next to her like blood in a rainstorm.

* * *

It was a good hour before their day shift the next morning as Martin Fin and Liam Price stood cross-armed and waiting by the side of the coroner's embalming table. Having stepped in from the familiarity of fresh salty sea air only moments earlier, the uninviting scent of disinfectant stung their senses.

Facing away from his trusted guests, Carl Oxspring was unaware that he had neglected to properly fasten the waist ties of his apron around his work uniform. His visitors smirked in their amusement as they watched each tie dangle shoddily on either side.

"The police had the kind decency," Carl began, "to knock on my door in the dead of night." He turned and placed something upon the spotless surface. "To give me this."

The paramedics only needed to take one look at the bag in front of them. Their faces fell and gaped in their confusion and alarm as its presence sank in.

The body bag sitting on the embalming table wasn't the regular kind. This one was smaller. The kind they themselves had used once or twice before, for small children and infants.

The breath in Liam's throat turned to thick nausea.

"It isn't…?" he looked to Carl with watering eyes.

"It's not," his friend assured him as he dragged the zipper of the bag from one end to the other. "Someone found *this* floating in Lagan Lake."

The coroner met the eyes of both men.

"No…" Martin shook his head in disbelief.

"I'm afraid so." Carl nodded cryptically.

The material of the bag crinkled as his gloved hands spread it wide open. Beneath the slimy, once-charred flesh of half a shin was a human foot. Swollen from its time submerged in the lake, three of its toes had been guzzled down to the bone. The skin appeared rubbery while it barely clung together, covered in a swarm of tiny holes created by the countless bites of the creatures that lurked below the water's surface.

Liam lifted a hand to hide the remains from his sight.

"Are you saying that's Ben?"

Carl managed a sad half-smile. His silence was all that was needed for confirmation.

"Jesus…" Martin muttered as he bowed his head.

Liam lowered his hand as his eyes lowered to the floor.

Ben Braithwaite, the man who died the same day his daughter was born. Like an exchange of energy, the world maintaining its ever-delicate balance. One soul moving on to the next life as another soul began its existence in this one.

"I thought you boys deserved to know," Carl finally uttered.

Liam chuckled dryly through wet eyes. Overwhelmed, he turned away, quietly retreating towards the door to collect himself.

"Who found it?" Martin asked.

"Heather Miles," Carl replied as he draped each side of the body bag over the severed foot. "She's the, uh, mother of the twins who were there that day. Said she thought she was rescuing a drowning dog. Screamed half the neighborhood awake, apparently. When she realized what it really was, that is. Ha! That must've been quite a shock."

"The twins," Martin recalled at first. "Molly and Dolly, or something?"

"Molly and Sarah," the coroner corrected him with a grin as he zipped the bag closed once and for all.

Lifting it from the embalming table, he caringly ferried it over to an open drawer where he placed it inside and pushed the cabinet door shut. Next to it, Martin noticed another door left ajar. He spied a pair of feet in black work boots. Women's work boots.

"You left one open," he pointed out.

Carl glanced over at it. His shoulders jumped as he chortled.

"Oh!" he stared back at Martin. "I'm keeping that one warm for now."

"Who is it?" the paramedic asked as he started towards the open cabinet. "Anyone we know?"

Tilting his head forward, Carl narrowed his eyes while he sidestepped into the man's path.

"Come on now, Martin, you know better than that," he said quietly. "Show a little respect for the dearly departed, won't you?"

The obnoxious blare of a *BLEEP!* slowed Martin's approach. He looked back over his shoulder as the commotion was followed by the buzz of a distorted voice echoing from the far corner of the room.

"Mr. Fin," Liam called from the doorway, radio in hand. "Looks like we're going in early."

Stopping in his tracks, Martin turned to face his work partner.

"Already?"

"Yep. We need to go now," Liam asserted impatiently. "We've been called out to Lagan Lake."

* * *

The lake now felt like an alien place to him as Liam Price walked alongside the stone wall they had stood upon while they watched the events of that day unfold. It had always been a peaceful place to visit until he heard the explosion that shattered whatever illusion of tranquility he had left. Until he heard the screams of horror and disbelief from his friends who stood beside him, it had become a part of his little island paradise, but now, Lagan Lake was nothing more to him than a watery grave. One that he had not visited nor even dared to acknowledge since that day.

Patricia Morris, "Patty" to those who know her, climbed the pebbled shore in her floral-patterned pajamas to meet the paramedics.

"Morning, Patty, are you not cold?" Liam asked her as he watched her purple-rinsed curls whipping around in the wake of a stiff island breeze.

"Harold will be out with a coat for me in a moment," she told them as she rested a hand against Martin Fin's broad chest. Pivoting in her loose-fitting slippers, she pointed to the young girl draped in a dressing gown sitting on the side of a rowboat shivering by the edge of the shore. "He's just fetching her a nice cup of tea. Poor thing is freezing cold. We tried bringing her up to the house to get warm, but she said she was feeling very dizzy, so we thought best to wrap her up and wait for you boys to get here."

"Let's get to her then," Liam pressed, setting off down the shore.

"Thank you so much for keeping her warm, Patty." Martin took her hand from his chest and squeezed it before following his colleague.

"No worries, dear," Patty called after him. "Can I get you some tea and biscuits?"

"Don't trouble yourself, my love," he chortled delightedly. "I'll pop around for a visit later."

"Oh, that would be lovely," Patty beamed before heading in the opposite direction. "I'll just go see what's taking this old goat so long."

Fifteen-year-old Hannah Wilson cradled the side of her head with one hand while she shoved Liam's penlight away from her eyes with the other.

"Don't, that hurts," she groaned.

"Sorry about that, Hannah," Liam said softly. "Can you move your hand so I can get a better look at your head?"

The left side of the girl's face was caked in dried blood. Slowly, she removed her hand to reveal a furious dark gash. It jutted out and away from her forehead like a pair of gory pouting lips.

"That looks pretty sore," Liam remarked as he fished a little gauze and a vial of fresh clean water out of his medical kit bag. "Is it okay with you if I just give this wound a quick clean and plaster it up before we take you to the hospital?"

Hannah avoided his gaze, but nevertheless nodded for him to proceed.

"Patty said you were feeling dizzy?" Liam started to dab away the blood from her cheek.

The girl's expression was as blank as the unwritten page as she responded with a confused "Who…?"

The paramedics frowned at one another in their concern.

"How about your memory?" Martin asked her. "Do you remember how you got here?"

Hannah's mouth suddenly fell open as her body snapped around to the side. She retched across the rear seat of the rowboat.

"It's okay, it's okay," Liam soothed her as he gently rubbed her back. "Just breathe, just breathe."

Martin offered her some dry gauze as she sat back upright.

Coughing and gasping for air, she wiped away the unpleasant mess from her mouth. And when she finally caught her breath, she managed three words.

"I remember everything."

* * *

Ally Price was too tired to remember to close the bedroom curtains when she lay herself and baby Klaryssa down to sleep. It was dusk outside her window, and that was all the darkness she needed. Overwhelmed with relief, she sank into her bed as she sank into slumber.

The first thing Ally saw was the empty space next to her in their comfy double bed as she slowly awakened a few hours later. The digital alarm clock read 3:50 a.m. upon the bedside table. Where was her husband? *He should have been home by now.*

It was only by the dull orange glow of the street light that she noticed the shadow of someone else in that room standing at the foot of the bed. Ally erupted from the covers without letting a single sound escape her lips.

The man stood with his back to her, holding something in his arms. He also didn't make a sound. Ally crept closer as her eyes adjusted. It was Liam cradling their newborn daughter. Letting out a sigh of relief, she put a hand upon his shoulder and ran it down his bare back.

"Hey, you," she whispered, kissing the spot where she had first laid her hand. When Liam didn't respond, Ally wandered round to meet him face to face. "Are you okay?"

Liam just stared straight ahead, unblinking, as if she were not there.

"Liam?" Ally tried again. "Liam, can you hear me?"

She waved her hand in front of his line of sight, but his gaze remained the same. With the greatest of care, Ally lifted the baby out of his arms. When they were empty, they fell by his side. By some wonderful miracle, Klaryssa was unharmed and still fast asleep. Unable to call out his name, Ally slapped him across the face.

Her husband grunted as he dropped down onto the edge of the bed.

"Hey, what was that for?" he asked innocently, holding his cheek like a scolded child as he looked up at his wife.

"You really don't know?" Ally frowned in her concern. "You were gone. Like you were sleepwalking. While holding Klaryssa."

"Nah, I don't sleepwalk," Liam said, dismissing her as he got to his feet. "Never have. I probably just nodded off."

"While holding Klaryssa," she repeated.

"Klaryssa is fine." Liam kissed her upon the forehead as he scooped the baby out of her arms and lowered her into the crib. "Now let's get to bed. God knows we both need it."

"I heard you treated the Wilson girl," Ally said as they lay together.

"From your nurse pals, I'm guessing." Liam rolled his eyes.

"Yup," Ally admitted. "Apparently she had quite the story to tell."

"She certainly did," he said, trying to stall, as he knew exactly where the conversation was going.

"What did she say happened to her?"

A few moments passed as Liam fell silent. If he didn't say it, maybe it didn't have to be true.

"Babe?" Ally persisted. She placed a hand upon his chest. "What is it? What happened to her?"

Liam could not bring himself to say what he prayed to God wasn't true.

5
The Great Rock

Early the following morning, beneath a gray overcast sky, residents came from all across the isle of Boatmore to join the search for fifteen-year-old Ryan Reade at Lagan Lake. The boy was given a day to either return home or be discovered safe and sound. Once the twenty-fourth hour of his absence had passed, every telephone on the island had rung by the closing of hour twenty-five.

Presiding over the search party was Sergeant Cunningham. He was joined by Rori Fin, elected official.

Officer Ashley Newton approached his superior and handed him a clipboard. "That's the information of everyone present, sir."

"Did you get a headcount?"

"I think we're looking at around sixty people."

"Confirm that for me, will you?" Cunningham ordered him. "If something goes wrong, I don't want to have to coordinate a search party to look for the search party." The sergeant dismissed the officer with a single nod, but then stopped him as he recalled. "The missing boy. He's your lady's little brother, isn't he?"

"Yes, he is."

Cunningham leaned in closer. "How is she?" he asked quietly.

"She's worried, obviously," Newton told him. "I made the call. She's on her way back to the island."

"Give her my best," the sergeant said with a nod. He dismissed the officer again only to stop him a second time. "I heard you threw up when the two of you found the Butcher's mother floating down at Green Water Bay."

The officer's shoulders sank. "Yes, sir."

"Try not to do that when you find this one," Cunningham remarked dryly.

"Yes, sir," the officer repeated, dismissing himself.

Switching on the megaphone hanging by his side, the vertically challenged Cunningham boarded a sturdy stepstool, placed in front of him by one of his officers so that he could be seen by all that gathered that morning at Lagan Lake.

Clearing his throat, he lifted the megaphone to his mouth as he addressed the volunteers. "Ladies and gentlemen, I'd like to thank you for giving up and devoting your precious time to helping the department in the search for young Ryan. We've got a lot of ground to cover, so if you could please split yourselves into groups of five, we will provide each group with a map, which will have your assigned area marked down for you. This morning we will be searching every area surrounding the lake, which means each group will start on the shore and work your way outwards." Cunningham motioned over to a nearby police van. "If I could just draw your attention over to Officer Newton, he will supply you with everything you need to begin your search. And next to him, you will find food and drink provided by our voluntary police team."

Beside the van, Patty and Harold Morris smiled at their neighbors as they stood behind two long foldout tables filled with bagged sandwiches, canned soda, chocolate bars, and crisps, as well as an assortment of fruit and bottled water.

"Can the first two groups of five please join me?" Officer Newton called out. "Everyone else please wait, and I will call over the next two groups when we're finished. Thank you very much."

As the first 2 groups approached, Newton hauled open the sliding van door to reveal a rich host of supplies.

"Okay, first of all, each group gets a backpack," Newton began as he took up one of the packs and opened it. "You're gonna need it for everything that I'm about to supply you with."

"Good of you to join us this morning, mayor," Sergeant Cunningham said as he handed Rori Fin a Styrofoam cup of tea.

"These are my people," Rori said matter-of-factly. "I show up for them, just as they show up for me." Blowing on her cup, she watched intently as the residents of Boatmore began their search for the missing boy. "So, what's the plan, sergeant?"

"Well, if we don't find anything around the lake, the next thing to do is look *in* the lake," he told her bluntly. "But we'll wait until our volunteers have gone home before we do anything of the sort."

"Do you think we'll find anything?" Rori asked as she watched the man gaze miserably at the water.

"Around the lake, no. In the lake, most likely."

"You don't believe the Wilson girl's story?"

"I witnessed the man's autopsy with my own eyes." The sergeant spoke through gritted teeth below his dense and bristly moustache. "Whoever she saw that night—if she did, in fact, see anyone at all—it certainly wasn't the Boatmore Butcher."

"I'm sure my people will turn up something," Rori spoke optimistically, letting out a long sigh of pride.

"Will you be joining them?" Cunningham's shoulders jumped as he huffed out a laugh at the legs of the mayor's purple business suit as they fluttered about wildly in the island winds.

"Damn right!" Rori exclaimed, handing her tea back to the sergeant. Dragging the zippers down the sides of her suit trousers, she tore them away from a pair of thigh-high beetroot Wellington boots. She removed her business blazer, folded them both up together, and dropped them into Cunningham's arms. "I love a good reveal, don't you?"

With a cheeky wink and a smile, Rori galloped over to the van where Officer Newton was waiting. "I'll take a backpack, please, kind sir."

"Yes, of course," Newton stuttered as he sprang into action. "Anything for you, mayor."

"Call me Rori."

"As you wish, Rori."

The search groups tittered as the officer blushed.

* * *

"Liam…" a voice called.

Only shadows lay before him.

"Liam…"

No, more than just shadows.

"Liam, what are you doing?"

A room in the dark.

"Liam…"

And a wall that dropped down below the floor.

"Liam, wake up!"

Liam followed the wall down. It disappeared into a ceiling. Below the ceiling stood his wife. Her arms reached out to him. Her mouth was open in a scream, but no sound came out. His eyes continued down. It was then that he realized that he was standing on the edge of the top step of a staircase.

Baby Klaryssa balanced upon the ends of his fingers as he held her tiny body out over the drop. Crying in silence, his newborn daughter started to roll away from him.

"Liam, wake up!" Martin shouted again, beating the inside wall of the ambulance.

"What?" Liam coughed as he sat up, half alert, dazed and teary eyed. "What is it, Mr. Fin?"

"We're here."

At the far end of Windygo Bay, beyond tumbling sand dunes and warm island streams, you will find almost nothing but rock. Jagged dark towers that appeared black against the pale sand. Sand that lined the narrow avenues that paramedics Liam Price and Martin Fin now navigated through like the ruins of a long-lost labyrinth.

"So, what are we looking for?" Martin asked, keeping the spinal board hoisted over his head so that he could fit through the landscape's rocky passageways.

"Caller said they heard screams coming from the top of one of these rocks," Liam informed him. "And that there'd be a marker so that we'd know which one."

Gazing upwards, Liam could see only charcoal gray walls, coarse and cavernous on either side of him. He couldn't help but notice that their voices did not echo there. The very thought made the spaces seem a little smaller. He felt eyes on him. He looked back over his shoulder just to be sure. He looked up again just to make certain that no one was watching them from above, following them. The walls seemed tighter. He lost his breath for a second as he heard the spinal board scraping the side behind him.

In that moment, the passage finally opened out. And it didn't take the pair long to spot a child-sized scarecrow planted in the sand at the base of the rock before them. The rock itself was over fifty feet high. As they drew closer, they realized that the marker wasn't a scarecrow at all. Upon a cross made of sticks, there hung the skeleton of a seagull. Its feathered wings were spread out wide as if frozen in flight, tied to the wood with slippery blades of seaweed. Jellyfish tentacles mimicked muscle tendons as they spilled from the eye sockets of its shattered skull and coiled down through its bones.

"Please tell me some kids made that…" Martin muttered fretfully. Setting the spinal board down, he shook the stiffness out of his arms.

Liam didn't answer. The stem of the cross snapped easily beneath his boot, toppling the crude creation over. With a curse on his breath, he kicked it across the sand. The thing flew apart as it rolled away.

Martin extended an arm as if making a weak attempt to stop it. "The police will probably want to take a look at that…" he began to say, but his voice trailed off as he watched Liam snatch what was left of it out of the ground and hurl it through the air with an angry grunt. He gave his colleague a few long moments to collect himself.

Gently closing his eyes, Liam listened to the bay. The island winds picked up, carrying with them the thundering power of the waves as they lashed against the other side of the great rock. The sound was so crisp that he could hear the rich sizzle of the bubbling foam.

"Any idea on how we're going to get this one down?" Martin asked, trying to get a good look at the peak.

"Let's assess that after we've made the climb, shall we?" Liam replied, oblivious to the small rocks that started to tumble down all around him.

"Li–" Martin didn't even have time to scream his name as he grabbed the collar of Liam's uniform and wrenched him backwards. Liam landed on his back with Martin's boot caught under his shoulder. There was a sharp slapping sound as something hit the wet sand.

First he saw the boy's shoe. Then he saw the boy.

"Oh, no… No, no, no…" Liam wailed as he struggled to his feet.

The boy was dressed in Samuel's funeral clothes as he hung by the neck from the great rock.

"Is this really happening?" Liam's voice trembled as he spoke. His legs barely held him up in his disbelief.

"Yeah, it's happening," Martin assured him from where he sat in the sand. "Why is he dressed like that?"

Liam couldn't say it. He could barely bring himself to think it.

"I don't know," he lied.

"Well, somebody knows." Martin pointed up at the boy's body.

The noose that stretched his broken neck was fashioned from decking rope, which creaked loudly as he swung slowly from side to side. His hands appeared to be missing, engulfed by the long sleeves that were meant for the taller frame of their previous owner.

Liam Price couldn't deny the truth to himself any longer. After all, it was as plain as the bloody handprint smeared across young Ryan's lifeless face.

* * *

Mayor Rori Fin was nearby, ankle-deep in the cold mud when she heard the cry of the whistle as it pierced the morning air. Accompanied by Officer Newton and the rest of their search group, they followed the direction of the sound through a sparse tree line and onto a dirt road.

"Over there." Officer Newton pointed to a small huddle of islanders thirty feet down the track.

As they made their way towards the other group, the officer blew a short blast from his own whistle to alert them of his presence. Their heads turned in his direction.

"Officer," one of them called out as the huddle opened out into a crooked line.

"Thank you, all of you," Rori said as they reached the group.

"Can you please show me what you found?" Newton asked, holding a pair of disposable gloves ready in his hand.

"Here, sir," responded a man in a royal blue rain jacket, scraping his boot noisily against the ground, drawing the officer's attention to the puddle at his feet.

Newton crouched down as he carefully inspected the brown puddle of muddy rainwater. Floating in the center was a torn piece of white shoelace, the end of which was stained a reddish pink. Gloving up, the young officer produced an evidence bag and collected the lace.

"What do you think?" the mayor asked in a hushed voice as Newton got to his feet. "Is it evidence?"

Wary of the islanders around them, the officer ushered her to the side of the dirt road.

"It's the same color as the shoes the boy was wearing that night," Newton began with a whisper. "There appear to be bloodstains."

Bloodstains.

Rori didn't dare repeat the word as she searched the faces of those around them, tracing their features for any sign that they had heard it, too.

"So, what happens now?"

"We're going to have to clear the area," Newton informed her. "There's likely to be more potential evidence around here. This spot is now a crime scene."

"Do you think he could still be alive?" The mayor's eyes lit up with hope.

"I wouldn't rule it out for now." The officer fought a smile. "Chances are we won't have to look for him in the lake."

"I've been waiting to hear those words all morning." Rori chuckled in her relief as her phone started to ring. She glanced at the screen and answered. "Sergeant Cunningham! Did you hear our whistling?"

Officer Newton watched the light fade out of her as his superior gave his reply.

"Oh no…" she uttered sadly as she listened on. "Where did they find him?"

* * *

Within minutes, the mayor and her police escort arrived at the great rock on Windygo Bay. Sergeant Cunningham took Rori's gloved hand as he guided her footing over the last tricky step out into the open. There, she found three firefighters standing around an inflatable cushion set up at the base of the rock. Another two steadied a ladder against its face as a sixth made his way up towards Ryan's body with a pair of long-handled rope cutters.

"What is happening here?" The mayor's concern was stifled by her confusion as she addressed them. "Can someone please explain this to me?"

"Mayor," Captain McKai called out as he marched over to meet her. He offered her a nod of respect before he continued. "I apologize for how this looks, but as you can see, the terrain makes it impossible to transport in our equipment."

"Thank you, I do realize that," Rori Fin said, unable to take her eyes off the hanging boy. "But I have two devastated parents and a family in pieces."

"I felt this was the quickest and safest way to get the job done, ma'am," the captain told her.

"Sorry, I certainly appreciate your expertise." Rori sighed as her eyes ventured over the great rock. "Not even if you came around from the other side?"

"No, ma'am." McKai shook his head insistently. "There's just no way. Not only would the conditions of the beach not support the weight of our vehicles, but we'd also run the high risk of losing them to the sea. I wish I had something better to tell you, but we're doing the best we can under the circumstances."

"I understand, captain." Rori shook the man's hand "Proceed as you see fit."

McKai turned back to his team. "Cut him down, Henry!"

The three firefighters working the landing cushion readied themselves as Henry carefully slid the blades of the cutters around the rope.

Off to the side, Martin Fin slipped on his sunglasses and stared down at the wet sand. "I can't watch this."

Liam Price, on the other hand, couldn't look away.

"Poor fella."

"Okay, he's coming down!" Henry warned them as he closed the blades on the rope.

They sliced through. The boy's body lurched forward. And stopped in mid-air. Gasps of shock and disbelief sounded from below. Henry caught himself before he could lose his balance.

"What's going on up there?" McKai called up to him.

Clutching the ladder, Henry shuffled closer to the body. Out of a hole in the back of Samuel's funeral blazer, a dark gray wire traveled up and disappeared into the deep cracks of the great rock.

"Henry?" his superior called again.

"Hold on a second," the firefighter replied, but only loud enough for himself to hear.

Henry reached a gloved finger into the opening in the blazer and slowly tore it wider. The back split open to reveal a harness.

"Captain, I think this kid is still a–"

Ryan screamed awake, his head bucking as he choked out a fishing line and a bloodied hook. Weeping with fright and disorientated, he tried to speak but the line in his throat gagged him, forcing him to cough out a red spray that caught the wind and speckled Henry's face.

"Get him down now!" McKai ordered.

"He's choking, sir," Henry reported as he reached out for the line and grabbed hold. "I'm just gonna help him."

He pulled.

"Don't touch him!" Liam bellowed from the earth.

The firefighter could only watch in silent horror as something hissed from inside the boy's throat. A cloud of thick smoke appeared on his tongue as it blistered over. His limbs jumped and flailed as his body pumped out its own stomach contents. His bladder and bowels emptied themselves and ran down his shaking legs. He began to convulse. His eyes rolled back. He bit off his own blistered tongue as his jaw locked shut. Blood spurted from between his teeth and overflowed through his nostrils. He seized violently, veins rising from his flesh. His body arched, tensed, and trembled as if it were about to snap itself in half. Then it fell still as the boy hung limp, crying crimson tears as he bled from the eyes.

Down on the sand, Liam fell to his knees, curling into himself, while Henry stood frozen upon the ladder, wondering if he would ever find the courage to climb back down.

"What the hell happened?" Sergeant Cunningham barked his demand as he marched up to the landing cushion.

The mayor dug her fingers into her wet silver hair and tugged at the roots. "What am I going to tell his mother?"

Their questions went unanswered as the firefighters, the police department, and the paramedics stared at one another in stunned silence.

"Where the hell is that damn coroner?" Cunningham growled soundly at Officer Newton. "Or didn't anyone think to call him the first time he died!"

The sergeant winced in disgust as he spotted a piece of the boy's severed tongue sitting in the center of the safety cushion.

6
The Journalist

The office was abuzz when Quinn's boss approached him. Phones rang as story leads were chased, pens clicked, staplers snapped, photocopiers and personal printers hummed, and coffee machines bleeped and hissed. Thanks to the usual commotion, he didn't clock the man until he was already towering over the wall of his cubicle.

"You know this island, Boatmore, don't you?" he asked.

It was the rarest of occasions when his boss actually addressed him directly, which was why it took Jordan Quinn a moment to realize that the tall fellow in the loose tie and thinning hair wasn't speaking to someone else.

"I used to go there every year for the summer holidays when I was younger…" Quinn mentioned tentatively, removing the pen that was starting to crack between his teeth.

"Then I imagine you know full well about the recent deaths there."

"I've heard this and that," Quinn said as he nodded, "but it's a nowhere, nothing little island that no one's ever heard of, so only a few outlets local to the area are covering it. Which is why nobody is paying attention."

"Well, they should be!" His boss had a glint in his eye as he sat on the corner of his desk. "Because these aren't just any old deaths. These are murders. And apparently they're the first to happen in the island's entire history."

"Wow…I had no idea."

"Exactly." Quinn's boss grinned in his excitement. "The story may have already broken, but I think we can blow it up. This is where you come in. I need someone who knows the island."

"I...guess I'm your man," Quinn responded hesitantly in his disbelief.

"That's what I like to hear." The man practically slapped him on the back. The entire cubicle creaked as he got up to leave, but then he turned, leaned in close, and whispered, "Find out everything you can, because if what I'm hearing is right, we could be looking at a goddamn serial killer." Finally, his boss turned and left him with a throbbing shoulder blade.

"Serial killer..." the young journalist repeated to himself as he gazed dreamily at the wall of his cubicle.

Their conversation played over and over in his mind later that afternoon as he tossed item after item into a travel bag back at his single bedroom apartment.

"Can you believe it?" he shouted through the open doorway as he sidestepped back and forth between the closet and the bed, stuffing fresh clothes into the bag without folding them. "He picked me for this assignment. Me!"

With toiletry bag in hand, Quinn marched out through the thin hallway and into the bathroom.

"Half my life spent being dragged to that fucking island every summer while all my friends stayed home. Who'd have thought all that boredom would come in handy one day, huh?"

"I miss those days..." a melancholy voice sounded from the living room. "Why did we stop going?"

"Because we got older and we got our own lives." Quinn bared his teeth in disgust as he assessed the accumulation of blue and pink disposable razors in the trash.

The voice came again in a child-like moan: "When are you coming back?"

Leaving the toiletries in the sink, Quinn followed the whine through to the living room where he found his sister, Wendy, lying with her feet up on the sofa. Her face was red, puffy, and streaked with dried tears above a fluffy baby blue dressing gown decorated with pink dolphins. The polar bear slippers on her feet shook nervously as her older brother appeared in the doorway.

"I don't know..." He pouted sympathetically as he leaned his head against the frame. "Until I have everything I need to make it a great story. This could be really important for me."

Ignoring her brother's words, Wendy's arm shot out as she passed her phone to him. "Mom wants to speak to you."

Confused, Quinn held the phone to his ear. "Mom?"

"Jordan, would you like to tell me what you are thinking abandoning your sister at a time like this?" his mother scolded. "You know she's not doing well. She needs her big brother."

At that moment, he wanted to mute the call and give Wendy a piece of his mind for ambushing him with such blatant emotional blackmail, but when he turned to find his baby sister sobbing into her mug of hot chocolate, he knew that he didn't and could never have the heart to kick her when she was down. He loved her, so much that her tears were like fire and knives inside his chest.

"I need to do this for me, Mom." It made Quinn sick to utter the words. "I will be back to take care of her as soon as I can. I promise. Love you."

Hanging up, he did his best not to give Wendy a look as he passed the phone back to her.

"I can't even go with you?" she asked, even though she knew the answer.

Quinn shook his head as he sat down next to her. "It's just not realistic. I wouldn't be able to do my job properly. I'd be constantly worrying about you. You'd be alone most of the time. Plus, I hear the phone signal sucks out there, and the internet service is dicey at best. You'd have nothing to do. Nobody to talk to."

"I could always pack a DVD player and a few boxsets," Wendy joked.

"You binge a full series faster than I eat dinner," her brother chuckled.

"Shut up!" She gave him a weak punch to the arm. She fell silent for a moment and then took his hand. "I'll miss you."

"I'll miss you, too." He squeezed her fingers softly. "Call your friends. And call Mom. You'll be okay. I'll be back sooner than you know it."

"You better be," she warned him playfully, tossing his hand aside.

"This could be really good for us," he told her excitedly as he hopped off the sofa and jogged out of the room. "Remember, don't watch anything sad or scary. Happy stuff only!"

"Whatever," Wendy sighed as she set down her mug on the glass top of the coffee table.

Unfolding her laptop, she opened up an internet search engine and typed in just two words:

BOATMORE ISLAND

* * *

The light of the evening sun, warm and golden, cast long shadows over the street as two friends shared a few cold beers on the front lawn.

Ally Price appeared with a blanket in one hand and a baby monitor in the other. Stepping over Martin Fin, who sat on her doorstep, she snatched herself a bottle and fell onto the bench beneath the front window. Her husband joined her as she draped herself with the blanket. She took a sip of her beer and then rested her head upon his shoulder.

"This is nice," she sighed.

Liam hummed in agreement as he nuzzled his face against his wife's frizzy blonde hair with affection. The two of them shared a soft kiss.

"Will you pervs put it away," Martin said playfully. "There are children on this street."

"I'm looking at one now," Ally muttered under her breath.

"Still haven't heard from Colby?" Liam asked as he tried not to laugh.

"*Heard* from her? No," Martin replied, taking out his phone. "Got plenty of texts from her, though!"

"She's still dealing with her 'family emergency'?" Ally joined in, suddenly alert.

"Apparently so," Martin uttered miserably. "Either that or she's having second thoughts on the engagement. A possibility that the lads on the nightshift have no problem pointing out to me."

"Don't listen to those idiots," Liam said as he reached over and patted his friend on the shoulder. "They don't know what the hell they're talking about. They're just winding you up because they can."

"Yeah, maybe," Martin grumbled to himself as he picked at the label on his bottle.

"She must be having a difficult time," Ally reassured him. "Some families just don't get along at all."

"I know," Martin said thoughtfully. "It's one of the things we actually have in common."

"I'm sure she'll call you when she's ready, buddy," Liam tried to say comfortingly.

Shrugging at Ally, she attempted to echo his words when she was interrupted by a distorted wail as it crackled from the baby monitor beneath her blanket.

"One sip…" she rasped through gritted teeth. "I had *one sip*… This child wants me to be sober forever…"

Liam stopped her from getting up. "I'll see to her, love."

"Thank you, babe." She smiled, squeezing her husband's hand before he went.

Her smile quickly faded as she realized that she had been left alone with Martin. Taking another sip of her beer, she didn't say a word to him. Instead she snuggled under her blanket on the bench and gazed into the golden glow of the sun as it hung low in the distance.

Upstairs, Liam reached for his daughter with a half-smile, but then stopped. His fingers receded as he lowered his arms. Smile gone, he backed away slowly. The wicker creaked beneath his weight as he sat in Ally's reading chair on the other side of the room, unable to do anything except stare at the crying infant.

* * *

Jordan Quinn had never felt so far from civilization as he traveled through the deep valleys of the countryside. It reminded him of how he used to feel when he visited the island, the very place he was heading to now.

He drove carefully as the slopes above and below seemed dangerously steep. As he marveled at the wonderful scenery, he soon came to realize that the narrow road was the only sign that other people had ever been there. There were no fences or electrical poles. Not even a single guard rail or safety barrier.

Eventually, he passed through a tunnel where the path widened as it wound down through tall bare trees. He felt swift relief as it soon led him over a small stone bridge to a main road. There, he found pavements, street lights, and a sign with the promise of a gas station only three miles away.

With no lights or another driver in sight to tell him what to do, Quinn sat there with the engine purring, drumming the top of his steering wheel as he stared at the sign on the corner. Back in the city, he had never been much of an eater, but this was his first big assignment. The stakes were higher, the stress greater. And he would need supplies after all. This wasn't gluttony. This was necessity. Satisfied with his reasoning, he turned onto the main road.

To his disappointment, the selection was not much different from the vending machines he and his co-workers had been living off of for the past two years. The bags were just bigger. For the time being he stuffed three of everything that caught his fancy into one of the green plastic baskets provided to customers at the shop's automatic entrance and made his way towards the counter.

"Thank you," he said to the bored looking cashier as he set down his items in front of the man.

As the register bleeped away, something on the news rack that hung from the back wall caught Quinn's eye.

"Can I have a look at that paper, please?" he asked as he pointed.

The cashier frowned at him, looked over his shoulder, and then back at him again. "You buying it?"

"Yes, yes, of course," Quinn assured the odd man in the ugly shirt. "Can I see it, please?"

"Sorry," the cashier said as he retrieved the paper and handed it to him. "Had to put them back there because people kept reading them and then putting them back."

Quinn paid no attention to the man as he read the paper's banner headline:

KILLER'S FUNERAL TO BE HELD THIS WEEK

"I take it you've heard of the Boatmore Butcher then?" the cashier asked, a hint of amusement in his voice.

"Is that what they're calling him?" Quinn looked up from the paper. "I didn't know he was dead."

"You thinking of going to the island?" The cashier started to pack the food. "To Boatmore?"

"On my way there now, as a matter of fact," Quinn volunteered. "Catching the last ferry. Do you know anything about these killings?"

"Only what I've read in these," the man said, gesturing to the rack behind him. "Guy's one sick son of a bitch. Can't understand why anyone would want to do something like that."

"There will never be a good enough explanation for why these people do what they do," Quinn said as his eyes bored into the picture of the Butcher himself, Samuel Wilde. "Just be glad that this one is no longer with us."

"He's not dead," the cashier told him. "They never are."

"I think that's only true in the movies," Quinn said, smiling.

"Nah, I think they got the wrong guy."

"What makes you say that?"

The cashier fell silent as he narrowed his eyes at his customer.

The newspaper crunched as Quinn's grip tightened around it. He began to back away from the counter when bright light flooded through the shop window.

"Whoa, hey, hey, speak of the devil!" the cashier exclaimed excitedly to the sound of screeching tires outside his shop. "You see this pig car out there, just coming in now?"

Quinn took a step back to catch the gleam of a police vehicle pulling in to one of the station's gas pumps. "Yeah?"

"This police chick stops here every time she visits the mainland," the cashier told him. "Hot redhead, too. She's been patrolling the island for about a year now, maybe. Keeps her car in *pristine* condition. I tried to touch it once and I swear she nearly took my goddamn arm off."

"I think I'm going to go introduce myself," the young journalist said, leaving a pocketful of change for the paper as he scooped up his shopping and headed for the automatic door. "Thank you, by the way."

"Wait, are you some kind of reporter?" the cashier asked, narrowing his eyes again.

"Something like that," Quinn said and winked with a grin. "Nice talkin' to ya!"

"I knew it!" the man laughed.

The cashier leaned an elbow against the register and watched Quinn through the window as he carried his bag of food back to his car. He watched as Quinn left the bag in the front seat before he walked over to the police vehicle with the newspaper tucked under his arm, but just as he approached the driver's window he suddenly stopped in his tracks. He stood there frozen for a moment. The newspaper fell to the ground. A moment later Quinn jumped back and took off running back to his car.

"What the?" The cashier watched as his last customer tore out of the station. He listened until the roar of the car's engine faded away to nothing. After letting out a single chuckle, the man got back to work. "Guess he changed his mind."

Jesus, what the hell was that? Quinn could barely catch his breath, holding a hand against his chest to feel the rapid pounding of his heart. He checked the mirror to see if anyone was following him. There were no police lights. No lights of any kind. Just the empty main road disappearing behind him.

What he saw back at that station, its face, it didn't look human. It had to be a mask. Whatever it was, it saw him. It looked right at him. That's when he knew he had to run. He could only hope that he could run fast enough and far enough so that no matter how hard it searched, it would never find him.

* * *

Christopher Price stood at the bathroom sink as he brushed his teeth. He was barely tall enough to see himself in the mirror as he stood on his tiptoes. He stopped to giggle at a bubbling sound that was coming from behind him. Looking back over his shoulder, he smiled and laughed at his father who sat upon the closed lid of the toilet grinning back at him as he made the sound.

The boy returned to brushing his teeth. Once more he heard the bubbling noise. Laughing, he turned to his father, but this time he sat there perfectly still. The grin was gone as he stared emptily at his son. Christopher heard the noise again. The sound was not coming from his father. Confused, the boy ignored this as he tried to continue brushing.

Soon, he realized that he could hear nothing except the bristles as they rubbed against his teeth. The sound had stopped. When he looked back over his shoulder, this time there was no one there. Turning away from the sink, he searched the room for his father, only to find that he was nowhere to be seen.

That's when the bubbling noise started again. And it was coming from the bathtub.

"Daddy?" the little boy uttered as he slowly approached the tub.

Clutching the side of the bath, Christopher took a breath and closed his eyes. He counted to three in his head and looked down into the water. He let out a scream. Floating just below the surface was baby Klaryssa's body.

There was a loud knock on the bathroom door.

Liam Price just managed to steady himself as he stumbled awake next to the bath. Water roared from the taps, as they were on full blast, sending thick white clouds of steam billowing into the ceiling. And in the middle of the tub, one of Klaryssa's teddy bears lay underwater. *Did I put that there?*

Another knock on the door as Liam turned off the taps.

"Liam?" Ally's voice called from the hallway. "Are you coming to bed?"

Lifting the teddy bear out of the tub, he couldn't help but grimace with guilt at the sorry thing as it dripped on the mat.

"Yeah…I'll be right there." Liam tried not to groan before tossing the soaking bear into the bathroom sink.

* * *

The sea and sky seemed to merge into one endless black space before Jordan Quinn's eyes as he stood outside on the upper deck of the 8:30 p.m. ferry to the island. Sailing farther and farther away, the mainland, once so solid beneath his feet, slowly broke apart into a cluster of ever-shrinking shadows, almost too faint to make out under the clouds as they softly put out the stars.

Although he could hear the water rushing out from behind the vessel's propellers, the darkness that surrounded him was of little comfort as he guzzled a large bag of cheese crackers by the railing. He still couldn't shake the face of the thing he saw back at the gas station from his mind. As he consumed mouthful after mouthful, he managed to convince himself that if he shoveled enough junk food down his own throat, somehow, he would forget everything, burying it all beneath a mountain of salty fatty goodness.

He let out a muffled cry as his jeans pocket vibrated. Pulling out his phone, he answered without checking the screen.

"Hello?" he croaked and cleared his throat. "Hello?"

"So, I'm looking online, trying to find out what all the fuss is about," his sister's voice began. "And I can't find a single thing... What is it you're not telling me?"

"Why, yes, sis, I'm doing just fine," Quinn quipped. "Thanks for asking!"

"I'm serious, Jordan," Wendy growled in annoyance. "It's something dangerous, isn't it?"

"I promise you, there's no danger," he croaked again.

"What's up with your voice?" she continued. "You sound weird."

"Hmm?" He was confused for a moment until he realized. "Oh! Looks like I've picked up an old habit of ours again. Eating my feelings. Like sister, like brother, huh? It's been a while."

Quinn chuckled, licking away at the cheese-flavored powder that coated his fingertips.

"You're eating your feelings?"

"Yup."

"Why? What's wrong?"

"I'm just a little nervous, that's all," he said, trying to reassure her. "Like I said, this thing is important."

"This thing that you won't even tell me *a-a-a-bow-ow-out*," her voice crackled as it broke up.

"Wendy?"

"*J-or-or-da-a-an*?"

"Hello?"

No reply this time.

"Damn it!" Quinn held the phone up high, searching for a signal. "I'm not even there yet and it's like I've already fallen off the face of the fucking earth. Wendy, can you hear me?"

There was no response from his baby sister, only distortion. The connection broke. The call ended.

A gust of wind swirled about him, tipping the bag in his hand and dumping all that remained inside overboard.

"Shit!" he cried in frustration, jamming the empty bag into his jacket before the wind could take that, too. Letting out a heavy sigh, he checked his phone again. "Come on…"

"That won't help you where you're going," a friendly voice said.

Quinn turned from the side railing to find an older man sitting by himself on one of the benches of the outer deck.

"Oh, believe me, I'm well aware!" Quinn smiled politely at the stranger.

"Ah, you've been to the island before then?" The man sounded surprised.

"Many times when I was younger," Quinn told him. "Family tradition."

"Perhaps I knew your parents," the man suggested. "What was the name?"

"Quinn."

"Sorry, it doesn't ring a bell." The stranger got up from the bench and held out his hand. "Nice to meet you. I'm Carl, island coroner. I handle the dead."

"Hi, Carl. Nice to meet you, too." Quinn shook the man's hand. "I know this might sound strange, but I feel like I was supposed to meet you."

Carl smiled.

The light in the lounge of the upper deck was dimmed but warm as Carl Oxspring and Jordan Quinn sat side by side at the corner bar. The glistening glass of the bottles that lined the wall behind the pretty barmaid clinked soundly as the sea rocked the vessel like a mother gently lullabying it to sleep.

"So, who are you, Jordan?" Carl asked before taking a sip from his glass. "What brings you back to Boatmore?"

"I'm here on assignment actually," Quinn responded in a hushed voice as he looked carefully over his shoulder at the rest of the lounge. Finding nothing but elderly couples resting side by side in rows of comfy armchairs, he deemed it safe to continue. "I guess you could say I'm a budding journalist."

"Ah, on the rise," Carl said as he nodded.

"Uh-huh," Quinn hummed, finally feeling calm enough to take the first swig from his beer.

"And you think there's a story here on our little island that's going to make you a star."

"Oh, I don't think it, I know it." Quinn set his bottle down upon the bar and faced his drinking companion. "Just like I know that you know exactly what I'm talking about."

Carl held the young man's eye as he took another sip. "The Boatmore Butcher…"

"Samuel Wilde." Quinn spoke the name before he leaned in with a whisper. "He's with you, isn't he?"

The coroner didn't need to utter a word, his steely gaze boring into the man staring back at him.

Without quite knowing why, Quinn had to turn away. "I hear you're burying him this week. Is that right?"

In defiance of the unflickering glow of firelight cast across his face, Carl's eyes darkened. "We're hoping to keep it a private affair, Mr. Quinn. I hope that you will respect those wishes."

"Of course," the journalist replied as he smiled out of the side of his mouth.

After taking his third sip, Carl cleared his throat and got up from his stool at the bar. "I shall return momentarily."

Quinn watched the man go as he finished the rest of his bottle. He winced in disgust, almost toppling the thing over as he dropped it back down. His reaction caught the attention of the pretty barmaid who stood to the side of him, drying off a pint glass with a dishtowel.

"I'm sorry, but do you have anything like an orange juice or something?" he asked her. "That's just left a weird taste in my mouth."

The maid ducked behind the bar, reemerging only moments later with a tall juice carton and a smile. "Not a beer lover?"

"I like *good* beer," he remarked, guiltily hunching his shoulders. "Sorry..."

"Say what you want," she chirped cheerfully as she poured him half a pint. "I don't brew it, I just sell it."

"Fair enough," Quinn said and smiled.

"On the house," the maid said, sliding the glass over to her handsome customer. "Any more and I'll have to start charging you again."

"You're sure?" Quinn frowned in his surprise.

"Yeah, it's fine," the girl assured him as she returned to her work chores. "To make up for the bad beer." She flashed him a wink that made him blush.

Or was he blushing? The sensation that seemed to begin on his hot cheeks spread across his face. A strange heat that thinned the air on his lips and drew the sweat from his temples. His stomach dropped as he started to feel the pull and sway of the vessel around him as it rode the sea waters below. He took hold of the bar to stop himself from falling. He felt the orange drink bubbling its way up, burning the back of this throat. He reached out for the pretty barmaid's attention, but went unnoticed. Before he could gather himself to call out to her, he saw the face.

Standing at the window, on the other side of the lounge, that horrid face from the gas station stared back at him.

When the barmaid finally acknowledged Quinn's odd behavior, he was stumbling away from his seat, slurring words and pointing at something outside. When she turned to look, all she could see was the black of night.

Meanwhile, Quinn shoved his way through the exit door on the other side of the lounge and retched over the railing. Spitting out the last of it, he realized that he was at the top of a staircase. He could just barely make out the words of a sign with a green arrow pointing downward:

THIS WAY TO VEHICLE DECK

Using the railing to steady himself, Quinn hauled his body forward, the toes of his shoes dragging across the ferry floor as he went. He came to a halt at the top of the stairs, hesitant on chancing that first step down. Clutching the banister as hard as he could in his state, he readied himself. He lifted a foot, bent a knee, and strained forward, but his concentration broke at the glimpse of a shadow moving dead ahead.

Draped in a pale hood, it appeared once again, leering at him from around the corner. It stepped out into view, watching him, enjoying his distress. Even as the world tumbled and fell around him, Quinn could feel it smiling at him.

Letting out a childlike groan, he lunged his body forward. He lost his footing, whacking his lower back against the blunt corners as his heels scraped their way halfway down the staircase. He choked on a grunt of agony as he vomited over his shoulder, plastering the wall with his own stomach acid. Tearful and spluttering and throbbing with pain, he forced himself onward.

The sound of the sea was drowned out by the constant hum of the vehicle deck as Quinn poured himself through the doorway. Under the pale light, its cargo seemed alive, like sleeping machines that could awaken at any moment.

He fumbled his way along the cold metal walls, dropping and catching himself, bashing his knees repeatedly as he continued to lose further control of his legs. Struggling to recall his parking spot, he wrenched his car keys out of his jeans' side pocket and aimed. Yellow lights flashed up ahead. Almost crumbling to the floor in his relief, Quinn collected himself and headed in their direction. He soon found his car parked behind an old caravan, a thick red stripe running along its side. Close to breaking his key off in the lock, he managed to get the door open and fall into the driver's seat. Pulling the door closed, he locked it again with the push of a button.

Fighting to remain conscious, the silence in that car was filled with his heavy breathing as he watched it fog up the glass of the windshield. The cloud of condensation grew and grew as his head began to swim and nod. Once…twice…

Quinn cried out as a screeching noise startled him upright. Flustered, he turned to find someone standing at the passenger door dragging the end of a black metal pipe across the window. The glass shrieked as it slowly grated its way around the outside of the car. Sobbing, he winced at the piercing sound as he watched their every menacing step until they were right outside his door. Quinn wept and screamed indecipherable gibberish as he beat at the car horn. Although it wasn't much, it was enough to send the thing slithering back to where it came from. He watched it seep away into the shadows between the horde of sleeping machines.

Clutching the steering wheel, he craned his neck to make certain that the coast was clear when Carl Oxspring stepped out of the doorway to the upper deck. With a thankful ease, Quinn unlocked the car, pushed his door open, and called out to him. Carl easily spotted the young journalist and hurried over.

"I wondered where you had got to," the man chuckled as he slid into the passenger seat.

He reached over Quinn and pulled the driver's door shut before relieving the frightened young fellow of his keys. Closing the passenger door, he pushed the button and locked the car.

"So…" Carl sighed deeply as he removed something from his coat. "You want to know about the Boatmore Butcher?"

Quinn's eyes lowered to find the mask clasped between the coroner's fingers. The face of the thing that had followed him through the night, the face that had stalked him on both land and sea. He let out a silent gasp. He went to reach for the door, but Carl easily guided his heavy limbs away from it and laid him back against his seat.

One last tear fell down Jordan Quinn's cheek before sleep finally overcame him and everything faded to black.

7

The Monster

Forty-Two Years Ago
  RUN HOME. NOW!

That's all a ten-year-old Carl Oxspring could think to do. He knew he saw someone standing in the shadows of that dark room, but he couldn't be sure. Not until they started moving towards him. And so he ran, shelves of puppets watching him as he fled. Back up that dank and moldy hallway, past the bathroom where Mr. Walker was still sobbing, down the stairs and through the front door to freedom.

He couldn't believe the sun was still out. Its rays speared his vision through the trees on the front lawn as he clambered down the driveway. Even when he reached the middle of the street, he did not stop for a breath. He turned and ran up the road, his drenched school uniform clinging to his little body.

It was the summer of '77 in the town of Gabvey. Although the holidays were just around the corner, there were no children playing outside. The evening was bright and the air was warm, but the park, the woods, the rivers, and streams were silent. The streets of Gabvey were empty.

Carl slowed down to a creep when he neared the family home, afraid that his parents might hear the sound of his wet shoes as they slapped the pavement, but it was harder to quiet the squishing noise they made as bathwater sloshed around between his pruning toes.

The radio, which always played the evening news while his mother stood at the kitchen sink washing dishes in her apron, was switched off as her son snuck into the house. She had a cigarette in her mouth. Although Catherine Oxspring was a smoker, she didn't usually light up until she settled down for the night in the living room, where she would finally have time to read the paper and her magazines in her armchair across from Mr. Oxspring as he watched television with a glass of beer.

Hopping from doorframe to doorframe, Carl closed in on the stairs when he suddenly froze mid-step.

"Go see your mother, boy!" his father's voice boomed from the TV room.

Head hanging low, Carl slinked nervously back to the kitchen. His mother gawked at him as he stood dripping in the doorway. The cigarette dangled from her pink lipstick for a moment before it plummeted into the sink. There was a hiss as it extinguished itself amongst the bubbles.

"Where have... You're absolutely soaked!" she exclaimed, pulling open a drawer next to the sink. "You've been playing in the woods, haven't you?"

Carl gave no reply.

Unfolding a fresh dishtowel, she dropped it gently to the floor in front of him.

"Stand on that!" she ordered him as she pointed to it.

Her son did as he was told.

"Wait here." Catherine sighed heavily as she marched out of the room, shaking her head as she went.

Carl could see that his dinner had just been served. Steam rose from the meat and vegetables on his plate as they sat waiting on the small round kitchen table. He was glad to see it. Not because he was particularly hungry, but because it had occurred to him as he ran through the streets of that quiet little town that he may never get to eat another homecooked meal ever again.

He lost his breath as something dropped down onto his head and shoulders. It was a bathroom towel.

"Dry yourself off," said his mother's stern voice, surprising him.

She plonked a pair of neatly folded pajamas on the table across from his hot meal. Returning to her son, she crossed her arms as she watched him obey her command.

"What were you thinking worrying me like that?" Catherine continued. She was too angry to refuse lighting another cigarette. "You know you've to come home straight after school. Do you know what you put me through? With all those boys going missing? I nearly called the police."

"I'm sorry, Mom…" Carl muttered, ashamed as he held out the towel and his wet clothes to her. "I promise I'll never do it again."

His mother could hear the sincerity in his voice as tears welled up in his eyes. She could have held him at that moment, but she had not been that kind of mother for years. Carl was her only child, but that had not always been the case.

Back in the year of '72, Catherine Oxspring had fallen pregnant with her second child, a girl. In anticipation of the new arrival, she bought her unborn daughter a doll. From the moment it entered the house, all Carl wanted to do was play with this new toy. Catherine would always refuse his never-ending requests, insisting that the doll must remain in its box until his baby sister was born. In the winter of that year, she suffered a fall on the stairs of their home. The incident was so slight that she didn't think to cause a fuss by going to the doctor. Two days later, Catherine miscarried the baby. On returning home from the hospital, she finally let Carl have the doll. Every time she watched him play with it, she would be reminded of the daughter she would never meet, never raise, never love. The following year, her husband asked her if she wanted to try again, to which she sadly replied, "No more."

Eventually it did occur to Catherine that she had not held her son since that time. The realization had made her feel guilty at first, but over time it became just one of the many worries she smoked away each evening as she thumbed through her magazines. And behind her armchair, in the corner of the living room on the top shelf of the bookcase, sat the doll, for she did not have the heart to throw her away after Carl ultimately lost interest in playing with her. She did not care to look at her, but somehow, she liked knowing that she was there.

"Put on your pajamas and eat your dinner before it gets cold," she told him as she took the washing out of his hands. "I want you to have a bath before bedtime, young man."

Later that night, Carl did not make a peep as he sat at his writing desk full of comic books. Turning the pages, his mind barely registered the illustrations and the speech bubbles; the dialogue simply did not exist to him. Quickly giving up, he glanced over his shoulder at the room behind him. Instead of reading about superheroes and faraway planets, he thought about the man in the closet, and the monster under the bed, and how he used to be afraid of them in his younger days. That night, for the first time, he began to wonder what their stories were. What they had to say. How they felt. Did they even feel anything at all?

He was startled from his thoughts by two knocks on his bedroom door.

"Carl?" his mother's voice called softly from the hall. "Bath time."

His face felt clammy as the warm and wet air of the bathroom clung to his skin. He had stood by the door—for how long he could not be sure—staring at the bath that had been made for him.

"Are you all right in there?" Catherine asked as she knocked.

"I'm okay," Carl replied, collecting himself.

Taking a deep breath, he sighed and approached the bath, staring straight ahead at the tiled wall, stopping only when his toes touched the side of the tub. Reluctantly, he gazed down into the water. It was still. Harmless, even. He looked further. Beneath the surface, his shadow loomed over the bottom, and for a single moment, a flicker, a face that he did not recognize looked back at him.

"What are you doing in there?" called his mother again, knocking harder this time.

"I'm okay," Carl repeated.

Backing away from the water, he faced the bathroom sink, turned on both taps, and set a towel down at his feet for him to stand on. That was where he would wash himself that night.

"Turn that lamp off!" his father scolded from the doorway as he lay in his bed. "I'm not having you running up the electric bill."

Carl switched off the light and pulled the covers over his head as darkness surrounded him. Closing his eyes tight, he fought back tears, praying that there wasn't someone standing against the wall watching him from the shadows. Whether he liked it or not, a new monster had made its home in his room.

The next morning, Carl munched on a slice of buttered toast and gulped down a glass of fresh apple juice as he waited for his mother to drive him to school. Catherine busied herself at the kitchen counter as she made ham and cheese sandwiches for his lunch.

"Be ready to go in just a minute," she told him. "I've got a lot to do today."

They were almost out the door when the phone rang. His mother's mouth fell open soon after she answered, and before Carl knew it, the call was over before it had even begun.

"Oh my goodness," Catherine said to herself, holding a hand to her chest.

Her son stood there dumbly gawking at her with a plastic lunchbox in one hand and a schoolbag in the other.

"Stay there," she told him as she brushed past him.

He watched as she hastened her way into the living room. It wasn't until he heard her switch on the television that he crept after her and listened from the hall. There was a burst of music, followed by the sound of another woman's voice.

"Hi, I am Lezlie Graham Jones with the morning news. Respected schoolteacher Alan Walker committed suicide after confessing to the murders of three young boys who had been previously reported missing from their local area since late March of this year. Walker's confession came in the form of identical letters that were sent to the police, the media, and his employer. The letters contained specific details to his crimes, including the location of their remains. The families of the victims have been notified and have declined to comment at this time. Eyewitnesses say that Walker leapt to his death from the top floor of this parking structure opposite the Gabvey town shopping center in the early hours of the morning. He is survived by his wife and–"

"What are you doing?" Catherine snapped as she appeared in the doorway.

"Nothing," Carl said, wincing and stuttering. "I was just coming back from the bathroom. I forgot to wash my hands."

"Oh…well, good boy," she said, softening, as she returned to the television and changed the channel to weekday morning cartoons. She then guided her son into the room and sat him down on the sofa. "There's no school for you today because classes are canceled, but I still have lots of errands to run in town. You're old enough to be left by yourself, I think. You've got your lunch anyways for when you get hungry. I will be back as soon as I can."

Carl waited until he was certain that his mother was gone before he picked up the remote control and switched the channel back to the news.

As Catherine drove to the final stop on her trip, she noticed a worker in overalls still trying to get the stain off the pavement across from the town shopping center. As she searched for a parking spot, she discovered that the top floor of the building had been blocked off by red and white tape. As she locked up her car, she looked down upon the street and spotted Carl standing outside the center across the road, staring back at the building.

"Carl?" she said to him as she approached him.

He glanced at her only for a second before his gaze returned to the top floor of the parking structure.

"How did you get here?" his mother asked him.

"I took a bus," he responded blankly.

"Why?"

He did not answer.

It was almost dinnertime when Catherine noticed that something was out of place. As she walked past the living room, she realized that there was something missing from the top shelf of the bookcase in the corner.

"Have you seen Emma?" she asked her husband.

"Who?" he croaked, frowning back at her in his confusion.

She was on her way to her son's bedroom when she saw the light coming from the bathroom. The door was already slightly ajar, so she walked in.

There was a flash.

She found Carl standing in a full bath of water, taking pictures of her doll with his father's Polaroid camera. She could tell from the mess in the sink that he had cut off most of her hair.

Catherine Oxspring closed the door to the bathroom without saying a word. What was left of her unborn child was now gone, and so now too was her love for Carl.

That night, when all the lights were out, instead of cowering under the covers, Carl crawled out of his hiding place, sat on the edge of his bed, and gazed into the dark. He looked upon the monster standing against his wall.

"Hello," he whispered, no longer afraid.

8

The Hearse

Jordan Quinn stirred to the sound of rain. Heavy rain. No, not rain. Rushing water. *Lots* of rushing water.

As his eyes slowly adjusted, he found nothing but solid wall in front of him. From the slimy glimmer of shiny paint on metal, he realized that he must be somewhere outside one of the upper decks of the ferry.

Although he could blink and see, and listen, his limbs were not moving. He felt the pressure of the safety railings behind him as they dug into his body. His head rested upon someone else's shoulder as they held him close. Most likely to appear as if they were both locked in a lovers' embrace to any unexpected passerby. Their cheek brushed against his ear as they whispered to him.

"You're not one of my boys," Carl said emptily as he hoisted Quinn's body onto the top railing. "Back under the surface you go."

A single push, a moment of falling, and then cold, cold darkness as Quinn rolled beneath the belly of the great sea vessel. His screaming eyes were blinded by the icy salt water as he hurtled towards something big. Something spinning.

* * *

"Thank you for doing this," Carl Oxspring said to Martin Fin the next morning as the old hearse rattled around them on the road. "I know you had plenty reason to turn me away. When it came down to it, I just couldn't bring myself to do this alone."

"I get it," Martin said thoughtfully. "He was your friend. He was a friend to all of us. Before we knew better."

The coroner hummed in agreement before he turned and gazed back over his shoulder through the small window to where Samuel's casket gently rocked from side to side.

"This wasn't your fault," the tall brute in the driver's seat said suddenly. "I thought you should know that."

Carl turned away from the coffin as he listened intently to the man sitting next to him.

"I came from a shit heap," Martin began, his eyes drawn in by the hypnotic winding of the road beneath them. "Before I even learned to walk, my dad kept me in a locked room until I was thirteen years of age. All I had to wear were diapers, even in the winter. When he remembered to feed me, it was mostly dog food. One night, a girlfriend of his snuck into the room absolutely wasted. She took my virginity. I was just ten years old. I didn't even know how to ride a bike. It stopped when Auntie Rori found out what was going on. This was before her transition. When she found us, Dad had choked on his own vomit and I had just about starved to death. I was fading, barely holding on. I can't remember this ever happening, but according to her, when I first saw her, I asked her, 'Are you an angel?' And then I died right there in her arms. Lucky for me, she knew CPR and she managed to revive me. She saved my life that day. That's why I do what I do now. God knows I'm not perfect—I've made plenty of big mistakes—but I think I turned out pretty well, considering what I came from. My point is you can't save someone from their childhood. Only they can decide the kind of person they want to be. So, like I said, this wasn't your fault."

All fell silent in the vehicle for a few moments as Carl looked through each of its windows, watching the road, the sky, and the land disappearing behind them like seconds in time. Just then, the steeple of Boatmore Church rose into view, lifting him from his thoughts.

"Thank you, Martin," he finally managed to say, patting the paramedic on the lap. "You're a good friend."

Martin smiled warmly at him, but it quickly disappeared when his concentration returned to what lay ahead of them. "Ah! What's going on here then?"

In front of the gated entrance to the churchyard stood Mayor Rori Fin between Sergeant Cunningham and Officer Newton.

"This can't be good," Martin remarked to the coroner.

Braking to an abrupt halt, he turned off the engine and climbed out of the hearse.

The island winds refused to rest as they whipped the long grass that grew against the stone wall perimeter to the church entrance. In the distance, by the surrounding cliff's edge, Martin noticed that the hole in the tall white fencing through which Samuel attempted to make his escape on the day of his death had been boarded over.

"I'm sorry, gentlemen," the mayor sighed as he and Carl approached, "but no one's being buried here today."

"Ma'am?" Carl struggled to control a trembling lip.

"What?" Martin squinted at his aunt in his confusion. "Are you serious?"

A single glance over her shoulder told him just how unwelcome they were. Blocking off the entrance to the church were a half-dozen island folk. With their bloated bellies, belt buckles, and faded jeans, they stood in a firm line. Their demeanor poised and their stares locked on the hearse, they needed only a simple signal from their leader to launch an attack. Martin recognized Patty's husband, Harold Morris, on the end, squinting through his huge spectacles and sporting one of his wife's famous knitted cardigans. He granted him a wave, which Harold returned, reluctant but friendly.

"I'm afraid so," Rori responded. "The people of the island have spoken, and they are not having it."

"So, what, if we don't leave, you'll set the dogs on us, is that it?"

The mayor didn't answer.

"Sergeant?" Carl looked to Cunningham, his eyes reddened in a state of sad bewilderment.

"They won't stand for it," the sergeant informed him. "Not after the things he's done."

"B-but I spoke with the priest—" a flustered Carl persisted.

Rori gently cut him off. "I'm sorry, Carl, but the priest's incredibly kind gesture was regrettably premature. Considering everything that poor man went through, I'm surprised that you would even attempt to take advantage of his forgiving nature."

"Are you really gonna do this?" Martin asked the human blockade. "Matthew was his friend. Can't you let him say goodbye to the person he knew?"

"*Samuel Wilde* was responsible for the deaths of at least 6 people on this island," Rori reminded him as she stood her ground.

"That we know of," Cunningham added. "The Ketler boy will certainly be suffering from his burns for years to come."

"And it doesn't stop there."

"I'm not following, mayor," Carl sniffed, raising an unsteady hand to shield his wet eyes from the cutting breeze.

"You're talking about the kid on the beach?" Martin asked as he couldn't help but laugh to himself. "You think the dead guy did that?"

"Not directly." Rori narrowed her eyes at her nephew before motioning to the sergeant by her side. "But I've been caught up to speed on your friend back there and his gruesome calling card. Just like the one left all over the poor Ryan boy's face. You were there. You saw it. He may not have done it, but his crimes have set something in motion."

The coroner could feel his heart sink into the earth as his eyes traveled over the church behind the mayor. Over the stone bricks and stained-glass windows, the wooden doors, frames, iron bolts, and hinges. Once it was a haven for the lost, and now it was a fortress for the just.

"We all owe this man better than that," Martin said, shaming them and guiding his friend away by the shoulders. "Come on, Carl. We'll work something out. I promise."

Shaking his head in disappointment, he led the man back to the hearse.

Before they could reach it, they were startled by a sharp *CLINK!* as a rock bounced off the rear side window, cracking the glass.

"Who threw that?" Rori roared as she spun on her heels to face the church guards. "Officer Newton, if you please!"

"Yes, ma'am." Newton obeyed, slipping through the gates.

The mayor turned back to the coroner. "Carl, I'm so sorry. I'll see to it that you get a replacement before the end of the day."

Carl hovered a hand over the fractured glass. On the other side rested Samuel's casket. There were no floral arrangements, no flowers of any kind. His coffin lay bare. Turning, he took one last look at Boatmore Church, the island winds growing around him. Sighing deeply, he stopped himself from patting the broken window of the hearse and climbed back into his seat where he began to ponder the mayor's words.

No one's being buried here today.

* * *

Anthony Morris, son of Patty and Harold, carefully smoothed over the adhesive tape that aided in holding the brand new rear window to Carl's hearse in place.

"I'd let that set for a day," he let Carl know. "Just to be on the safe side."

"Thank you, Tony," Carl said as he handed the glass fitter a fresh cup of hot tea. "I'm just surprised at how swiftly this came about."

"When our mayor makes a promise, she sees that it gets done," Anthony told him as his eyes wandered over the garage door that hung over them. "This isn't the first car window I've replaced for her, and it won't be the last. Bless her."

"Indeed…" Carl uttered as he looked back at the empty space where Samuel's coffin had been earlier that day. "You were there, at the church, when they threw the rock. Did you see who did it?"

"Sorry, no," Anthony quickly replied. "It just came flying out of nowhere. I hope you know that Dad and I would never…"

"Of course not," Carl said distantly, still fixated on the empty vehicle.

"Do you think she's right about there being another butcher out there?" Anthony asked.

Carl turned to find the man staring at him fixedly over the crescent of his tea cup as he took a long sip from its sugary warmth.

"I think the people on this island can get easily drawn into things," the coroner noted, "which can lead to some people doing some very stupid things."

"Very true, very true," Anthony nodded. "Like who?"

"Well, let me see now," Carl pondered. "Come to think of it, that lovely Officer Colby girl was looking into Gary Wright when his son first went missing."

"I remember that!" Anthony said. His eyes lit up in his excitement. "I was there that night at the Golden Eagle when she came around asking questions."

"As was I," Carl said, grinning behind his cup as he finished a gulp. "At the time, the word around town was that Gary liked to hit the poor boy quite regularly."

"He never was right after the wife died," Anthony said, shaking his head. "Shame that a lad loses his mother like that. Being stuck with a man like him for a dad… And then being trampled to death in a field of all things!"

"I know, such a senseless way to die…" Carl sighed, secretly amused by each change of expression on Anthony's face. "I always did think she was onto something with him."

Anthony hummed thoughtfully before he took in a loud breath and handed a half-finished cup back to his customer. "Thanks for the tea, Carl. Wish I could stay, but I need to get going. There is much to do."

The glass fitter's walk down the driveway towards his car quickly turned into a jog.

"Thanks again, Tony." Carl smiled before calmly finishing his cup of tea.

He was disturbed by the sudden blasting of a horn from the car waiting at the end of his drive. Gritting his teeth, he glanced down the length of the gravel to find Anthony beckoning him over from the rolled down window.

Grunting soundly in his annoyance, Carl rested both tea cups upon a high wooden shelf in the garage before approaching the car.

"Friendly bit of advice," Anthony offered.

Carl nodded with a pained smile.

"Be careful where you scatter the remains," Anthony warned him. "The people don't even want his ashes on this island."

The hand behind Carl's back trembled with its clawed fingers. If only he were still holding one of those tea cups. He could break it against the man's cheek and then grind the remaining broken pieces into the glass fitter's face.

"Oh, don't worry," the coroner assured him. "I will take him somewhere no one can disturb us."

"No one?" Anthony edged closer in the driver's seat in his intrigue. "Where is that then?"

"Nowhere in particular…" Carl sighed with a wink. "Just somewhere abandoned. A place not even the kids in town will venture to anymore. Like that old lighthouse on the other side of the island, for example."

"Headless Ben?"

"Yes, yes. That's the one! I don't think the seagulls even go there anymore. I'd have all the time I need to say my goodbyes, and no one to bother me."

Leaving the man with his thoughts, Carl walked back up the driveway and pulled on the garage door, lowering it to a close.

9

The Dreamers

Ally Price wept at nightfall, her faint silhouette accented by the half-hidden moon as she trembled upon the edge of Green Water Bay.

Out of the endless black beyond her, the sea roared as the waves tore up the sand, trillions of jagged icy teeth shredding over each other as they devoured the beach. Her long dark dress whipped back and forth while the hissing waters ate at the flesh of her ankles. Shaking uncontrollably in her tears, she reached out to the man before her. The man with her baby in one hand, and a knife in the other.

"Please… Please…" Ally cried over the furious sizzle of the crashing foam. "Don't hurt my baby…"

The man smiled as he held out the blade, pointing its tip towards the starving sea as it begged his permission to consume the rest of the wailing woman. She began to back away, further into the fate that awaited her.

"Liam!" he heard her scream. He enjoyed it.

Again.

"Liam!"

He wanted more. Needed more.

"Liam!"

Carefully tracing circles around the buttons of the sleeping infant's pajamas, the man desired the most sorrowful cry its mother could muster.

And so, with the tip of his dagger, he punched the baby in the chest.

A primal howl ripped through the Price residence in the early hours of the morning, shredding what was left of Ally's already rattled nerves to raw strips of the tenderest meat.

With baby Klaryssa clasped to her, she managed to gently bolt from the kitchen area to the bedroom she shared with her husband within a moment without spilling a drop. Only when they arrived did her daughter release and let out a howl of her own.

Breathless, Ally sidestepped the bedcovers lying at her feet, soaked beneath an empty drinking glass. The bedside cabinet on Liam's side was overturned, leaving a dent in the wall, the lamp broken, and their alarm clock flashing zeros. And on the floor by the corner, she found her beloved weeping by the side of their infant's cot, its crossed wooden legs jumping from the carpet with every tearstained convulsion.

"Oh love, you can't go on like this," she sobbed as she fell to her knees by his side.

Face red-raw and wet, Liam gasped for air as he turned to face his child. "Is she all right? Is she all right?"

"She's fine. She's fine," his wife reassured him, raising their screaming newborn into his view. "See. She's just a bit upset because I've interrupted her feeding. Haven't I, baby girl?"

Liam crumbled with relief, his face toppling onto Ally's shoulder where she hushed him with kisses and caresses.

"Talk to me, love," she begged as she continued to feed their child. "You *have* to talk to me. *Please*. Tell me what's going on."

Her husband took a moment to collect himself before he sat up, trembling as he looked away from her.

"I don't know–" he tried. He sobbed. He tried again. "I don't know why I thought having her would change anything.

He's still gone. And I miss him every day. I know she's not a solution. I know. I know that. I *love* her. I *do* love her. *So much.* I've never questioned that, but sometimes I catch myself thinking…do I hate her because she's here and he's not?"

"Is that what you've been dreaming about?"

Liam looked right at her. "I killed him."

"You did not kill Christopher."

"No, I mean Samuel."

Ally's heart missed a pump of blood. "What?"

"I killed Samuel that day at the church."

"Go on."

"It was the things he was saying," Liam explained. "About how he wanted to hurt you. How he wanted to hurt our baby. I rung the life out of the evil little bastard, and I just let him fall. And then I lied about it. I killed him."

Ally lost his gaze once again, so she placed a hand on his cheek and brought him back to her.

"*Good!*" she said, pressing her forehead against his for just a second. A kiss of the flesh. "You did what you had to do. You did it to protect your family."

"Still makes me a killer, Ally." He braced against her touch, wanting to pull away, but he lowered his eyes instead. "Sometimes it feels like that's who I am now. I've let all these people die. Christopher, Ben, those boys."

"That's simply not true, love," Ally told him. "They all had circumstances that were completely out of your control. That doesn't make you a killer."

She kissed him, holding on until she felt his body relax. Humming, she let go and said, "That makes you our hero."

"I love you," Liam sighed, wrapping his arms around his family. "I love you both. Forever."

* * *

The evening schedule began as dinner was being served and drink orders were being taken. The Boatmore Hotel's restaurant was alive with excitement, laughter, and good company.

Rebecca Hayes, the co-manager of the hotel, couldn't help but smile as she glided gracefully past the great wide arch entrance to the dining area. Passing out of sight, she met with Kathy, her best friend and the restaurant's maître d', as they linked hands and quietly squealed with glee.

"This is wonderful!" Rebecca rejoiced. "We have been at full capacity for two weeks now. And we're booked solid for months."

"I know!" Kathy cheered, adopting a hushed tone. "Those crime enthusiasts really do like a good murder destination, don't they?"

"Whatever it is, we'll take it!" Rebecca laughed, turning her head as she noticed her son Paul approaching in his waiting staff outfit. "Hello, dear."

"Hi, Mom." Paul smiled as he gave his mother a peck on the cheek.

"Hey, don't forget your Auntie!" Kathy jested, sticking out her chin.

Twelve-year-old Paul Hayes laughed and did as he was told.

"How is he doing?" Rebecca asked her maître d'.

"Oh, he's having a great first night," Kathy beamed as she hugged the young waiter with pride. "You know you've got a hard worker when someone asks for a job for his birthday."

"Let's not get carried away," Rebecca reminded them. "My boy doesn't become a teenager until *next* weekend."

"So you keep reminding me," Paul rolled his eyes.

"Leave your mom alone," Kathy said as she ruffled his hair. "You won't be her little boy anymore, so let her enjoy what time she has left."

"It's all right, Kath." Rebecca smiled sadly as she watched her son go back to work. "He'll always be my little boy."

Hours later, after Paul finished clearing up the last table, he found his mother by the front desk staring into space.

"Mom?" he whispered as he put a hand on her shoulder.

"Yes, dear." Rebecca drew in a breath, blinking her eyes. "Sorry. Mommy's just a little tired."

"It was a good night." Paul gave her a hug.

"It was," Rebecca sighed.

"I'm gonna go to bed now," he told her, signaling over his shoulder as he backed away.

"All right then, go. *Go*!" his mother joked in her exhaustion. "Abandon your mother."

Paul giggled as he pushed through the door to leave.

"I love you," he said.

"I love you, too," she said back.

"Goodnight."

Paul let the door swing shut behind him as he began the long walk home through the hotel's main corridor. Slipping a piece of bubblegum into his mouth, he started chewing noisily, looking from door to door as he made his way down the lengthy hallway.

He was halfway down that long corridor when a door far behind him clicked open. A man stepped out into the hall, and started to follow him.

* * *

It was 4:05 a.m. in the managerial live-in quarters of the Boatmore Hotel when twelve-year-old Paul Hayes jolted upright from his pillow, a cold sweat beading his clammy forehead. Realizing that he was safe and sound in his own bedroom, he let out a grateful sigh as he took a look around.

He looked towards the open door to his bathroom at the end of his bed. He let out a gasp of fright as he snapped on the lamp on his bedside table and looked again. His mind must have been playing tricks on him, as he was certain that he had seen the black shape of a tall figure standing in the doorway.

Shaking his head, he turned off the lamp and curled up beneath his covers, posting online to his friends and followers that he 'had that dream again…'

'The one where you're lying underwater?' someone replied, perhaps a little tactlessly.

Never one to leave a soul out, Paul responded with a simple, 'Yop.'

'Why do you think you are so afraid of the water?' another asked.

'I don't know. Ever since I was little I would be too scared to have a bath because I used to think if I ever got in one I would die. Weird, right?'

'Weird? Sure… Was gonna go with CREEPY!!! But sure. Let's call it that!'

'Hahaha!'

Watching words of love and support pour in, he soon returned to his slumber, snoring like a contented kitten.

At 4:58 a.m., Paul sat up for the second time that morning. He looked to the break in his curtains, hoping for a hint of daylight, only to find none.

Feeling for his tablet, he froze at the sight of the same black shape lurking in the wide-open doorway of his bathroom, looking right at him.

The lamp went on. Once again, the figure vanished.

"Nope," Paul said under his breath.

Hurrying out of bed, he pulled the bathroom door closed, his breath heavy and his heart pounding as he went. Double-checking that it was shut firmly, he nudged a wooden door wedge into place with the side of his foot. As he did so, something touched the back of his bare leg.

Yelping, he leapt away from the bed, the beat of his heart like a hammer inside his temples. He relaxed when he realized that it was just a fold in the bed covers jutting out. Embarrassed, he kicked at it, climbed back into bed, and began scrolling through the comments on his last post.

'If you don't turn that light off, you'll never get to sleep,' one read.

Paul glanced at the orange-yellow glow of his lamp. Uninterested in games, he screenshotted the user's comment, followed by their profile page, and then reported and blocked them. Dropping his tablet, he switched off the lamp and eventually drifted back to sleep.

At 5:29 a.m., something woke him. A sound? A *THUMP!* maybe? Paul blindly looked around with a yawn before sinking back onto his pillow.

At 5:35 a.m., the sound came again. This time it was definitely a *THUMP!* Lighting up the room, he patted the sheets for his tablet, finding nothing.

Where did it go? The gadget was another early birthday present from his parents. An expensive one!

He leaned over the side of the bed and found it on the floor. That had to be the sound. Picking it off the carpet, he viewed a new comment from a follower.

'If you're not going to talk to me, can you at least let me out?'

Paul looked to the bathroom door. Oblivious to the object that suddenly landed on the bed covers in front of him. He looked down to see the wooden door wedge resting on his lap.

BANG! BANG! BANG! The bathroom door quaked against its frame.

Springing up with a shrill gasp, Paul forced the wedge back under the door and called for assistance as he set off running, the covers brushing his legs as he went, but not covers made of fabric. Covers made of skin, bone, fingers, and nails.

Paul screamed for help as another hand emerged from under the bed and clasped around his leg. Abandoning his phone call, he chopped at the knuckles of the claws that dug into his flesh with the blunt corners of his tablet. One hand lost its grip. Paul's freed leg started stomping and kicking the remaining arm.

Then, a black metal pipe shot up from the floor directly into his face. The boy's nose exploded with blood as the back of his head smacked against the bedroom wall. Sliding down to the carpet, Paul Hayes appeared as if he simply fell asleep watching the screen of his tablet.

The man in the pale hood slithered out from under the boy's bed and stood there, marveling at his bleeding unconscious body.

The body of the fifth.

#5.

10

The Paramedic's Wife

Wearing nothing but loose boxer shorts and a stained t-shirt, Liam Price stood in the warmth emanating from the kitchen oven cradling Klaryssa in his arms as he calmly fed her the bottle. He marveled at her little face, tiny and empty of worry as she suckled soundly on the rubber nub.

Ally beamed at them proudly over her shoulder from the sink as she rinsed a plastic strainer full of crunchy leaves of iceberg lettuce.

The countertop groaned as Liam's phone vibrated over its marble-like surface. He squinted at the screen as it illuminated for a few moments and then faded. His wife watched him read as she set down the strainer. He muttered a single curse to himself.

"What's the latest from Martin?" she asked him as she pulled the kitchen towel out from the handles of the cupboard doors under the sink.

"One of the guys on the night shift," Liam told her. "He thinks he saw Jennifer's police vehicle on the last ferry back to the mainland."

"So, she left him…" Ally nodded, deep in thought. Her eyes slowly wandered the room as if they were carefully searching for something.

"It's not just that, Ally," Liam said dejectedly. "She's left the island. She's left us all."

"That's right…" Ally sighed and shook the aimlessness away, dropping the towel into the dry sink as she headed out of the kitchen area. "I'll be back in a minute."

"Okay," Liam mumbled, wincing as he tried to shake off the beads of sweat that clung to his clammy forehead. "Hoo! It's getting a bit too steamy in here."

Mindful of the pans on the boil, Liam balanced the bottle on the baby's belly as he reached for the stove hood. The sound of gale force winds filled the air as the extractor fan hummed to life. Turning to the foggy window glass, he pursed his lips.

"I think I'll open the back door a little, what do you think?" he said, consulting his daughter as he turned the handle.

The hinges creaked from the cold as Liam let the heat out and the night in.

Crouching upon the stone tiles of the patio, the man in the pale hood observed the smoke and steam as they seeped out of the doorframe and vanished into the shadows above. He reached out with a bloody gloved hand that glistened in the light from the kitchen as he rose to his feet. He took a step forward and pressed it silently against the glass. He waited, watching and listening to the father and child through the window.

Backing away, the man peeled his hand slowly away from the door, his flesh clinging to the sticky redness. It very nearly clicked its way closed, but the sound from the exhaust fan was far too loud for the parent inside to notice. The man smiled as he continued to back away. Before he reached the fence, he turned and slipped quietly round the side of the house.

The front door opened easily. It amused the man how hard it was to kill the bad habits of a safe neighborhood. As long as the danger wasn't on your doorstep, it couldn't possibly ever happen to you. *Well, here I am*, the man in the pale hood grinned to himself as he reached for the bathroom door.

* * *

Headless Ben, an island legend in its own right, got its nickname as the result of the great storm of December 31st, 1999, in which the entire outer structure of the top level was completely destroyed by a single bolt of lightning. Although restoration plans had been pending for the past decade or so, it remained disused to this very night. And parked at the base of the building on this very night were two islanders, one police officer, and a suspect.

"You can't do this to me!" Gary Wright lisped through the swelling of his busted lips as Officer Newton dragged the man stumbling and struggling through the missing entrance door of the old lighthouse.

Father and son Harold and Anthony Morris followed close behind. A nervous Harold found only darkness as he checked that the coast was clear before stepping inside.

Fearful cries echoed up through the shadows of the staircase that spiraled high above them. Wires, ropes, and long slithers of plastic sheeting coated in years of dust and filth dangled down through the center of it all.

"Why are you doin' this to me?" the pathetic little man wailed in Newton's grip as the officer pinned him to the far wall. "Please, I just buried my son. Leave me be!"

Gary was a short shrivel of a human being wasted away by his years of hard drinking with nothing to show for it but a bulbous pot belly and the constant reek of something sour on all of his clothes.

"And I just watched my girl's baby brother seize himself to death because some fucker poisoned him!" Newton hissed fiercely through clenched teeth, driving his knuckles up into his prisoner's jaw. "What did he ever do to deserve that, huh? Tell me!"

"I don't know!" Gary screamed at the ceiling. "I didn't do it! I didn't hurt anyone!"

"You're a fucking liar!" Anthony yelled over Newton's shoulder. "You hit your boy! Every night! Everyone knows that!"

"Ryan was only fifteen years old," Newton growled as he wrapped the collar of the man's vest tightly around one fist. "Same age as your boy was when you left him to die. You got a thing for hurting young boys? You sick bastard!"

Newton delivered the first blow, snapping Gary's head to the side.

"Well?"

A second sent him staggering along the wall.

"Do you?"

The third blow took him down hard.

Gary did his best not to choke as he puked up a little mixture of vomit and stomach acid. Groaning like a pregnant cow in labor, he spat out a mouthful of blood along with a few of his own teeth onto the dirty black and white tiled floor.

* * *

Heard the news from Liam. Hope you're okay, x.

Ally stood at the bathroom sink as she stared at the small screen clasped between both hands.

Yup, it's official. My bride-to-be has gone and ditched me. Swallowed me whole and shat me out faster than spicy takeout!

Snickering to herself, Ally quickly thumbed her response.

LOL. Let it never be said that you don't have a romantic side! You would know.

Ally's smile faded fast as she turned away from the bathroom mirror.

We're not going to talk about that.

Shaking her head, she lowered the phone as she gazed at the bathroom door. It seemed a lot closer than usual. Taking a deep breath, she flinched as the next message from Martin came through.

Suit yourself. But how long do you think it will take him to realize that's not his baby?

All of a sudden, the space felt much smaller as Ally lost the air in the room for a moment. She spun back to the mirror, clutching the sink as an icy wave washed over her flesh. Her skin continued to crawl as she made certain of the words that were on the little glowing screen in her hand. Her eyes avoided her reflection as unsteady fingers scrambled to delete the conversation from her phone.

Two hard knocks on the bathroom door took her by surprise. She jolted with fright, gasping as the phone slipped out of her hand.

"Shit…" she muttered quietly as she heard it crack in the sink. "I'm coming!"

Before leaving, she reached to retrieve it, but then decided to leave it where it was. Out of her hands and broken where it could do no harm.

Behind her, as Ally made her away across to the kitchen area, a pale-hooded figure seeped into the bathroom.

She found Liam standing by the back door, swaying gently, as he held baby Klaryssa upright against his chest.

"What is it, love?"

"I didn't say anything," Liam replied soundly, softly caressing the back of his child's head.

"You knocked on the door."

"I don't know what you're talking about," her husband said, frowning at her with his grumpy brow. "I've been here the whole time."

"Very funny," she said, sarcastically commending him as he moved to the side, revealing a handprint on the door. A handprint made of blood.

Letting out a shrill grasp, Ally watched in a moment of paralyzing panic as the mark she had heard so many horror stories about over dinner dripped down the window on the other side of the glass.

"The door…" she uttered, just barely.

"What?" Liam gawked at her.

"Liam, the door!" she yelled this time, pointing.

Her husband spun round, his back grazing the countertop and stove dials as he caught a glimpse of the handprint on the door. With one arm he pushed it shut, locked it up tight, and pocketed the key. Grabbing his phone from the counter, he handed both baby and device over to Ally, who was anxiously ready and waiting.

"I want you to call Martin and then the police, okay, love?" he instructed her as he retrieved a long heavy flashlight from one of the upper cupboards before moving for the back door.

"Liam Alexander Price!" His full name stopped him in his tracks. "If you leave your family alone in this house right now, so help me God, I'm a' beat two weeks' worth of shit out of you!"

Liam turned and faced her with a smile, raising his hands in compliance. "I'm just going to take a quick look around."

"Didn't you hear me before?" Ally stood firm as she took charge. "Someone knocked on the door while I was in the bathroom, and it wasn't you. So, if you want to look around anywhere, start with the inside first. You can go elsewhere when Martin gets here."

"Call him," Liam urged as he left the kitchen area to search their home.

Within five minutes, both he and Ally stood close by as Martin inspected and puzzled over the handprint that was still drying on the glass of their back-door window. Stepping away from it, he turned to face his friends. His perfect hair was disheveled, and his fine-shaven stubble was becoming that of a short beard.

"It could be a prank," he suggested.

"That's a possibility," Liam said.

"I know it's been the talk of the town," Ally said, still comforting baby Klaryssa as they followed her gaze back to the handprint, "but do people even know about *that*?"

"A small few."

"What else do you think?" Martin asked them.

"A warning," Liam replied solemnly.

"Maybe…"

"How can that be?" Ally's lips were thin with worry as she held her child closer. "And from who? Samuel is dead. Everyone on the island knows that. The Boatmore Butcher is dead."

Liam and Martin exchanged a glance before their eyes rested upon the handprint one more time.

There was a knock at the front door.

Ally left their little circle with her baby girl. And as she went to answer the door to the police, both she and Martin exchanged a glance of their own.

"There's something you boys aren't telling me," she grumbled as she turned the handle.

Just then, both men were jolted by a sudden buzzing noise as Liam's phone shredded across the wooden surface of the empty kitchen table. He caught sight of the screen.

"Fuck me!" he winced in a whisper. "I completely forgot we're on call tonight."

"Shit! Yeah," Martin said, keeping his voice low.

Pressing callback, Liam looked across at Ally as she greeted the responding officers.

"What am I going to tell her?"

Martin Fin didn't quite know how to answer his friend as he looked in the same direction. At the same woman.

* * *

Four Months Earlier

Five minutes after a joyless Liam Price had left for his morning jog, Martin Fin's car came to a stop outside his home. Seconds later, Ally Price scurried out, down the drive in her bulging dressing gown, and climbed inside.

A few moments of silence passed between them as the expectant mother watched the tiny droplets of winter rain gently land upon the windshield. Her labored breathing fogged up the glass as she fought back tears.

"He still won't come near me," she started, her heavily pregnant belly barely an inch away from crushing the glove compartment. "He hasn't touched me since… God, I don't even remember when."

"Maybe he knows." Martin smirked as he quickly adjusted Ally's gown to cover up her exposed chest.

She huffed with embarrassment. "It's not that."

"I just have to say: this is a bold move asking me, of all people, for help with…*this* situation," he remarked as he shook his head slowly back and forth.

"You also said we could still talk to each other about things," she reminded him with an accusatory tone that he ignored effortlessly.

"How did you even convince him…" the man said, frowning as he waved his hand over the painfully obvious, "…about *that*?"

"There were a few nights back when he was at his worst," Ally recalled with sad eyes and wilted shoulders. "When he would drink himself to sleep, so I just told him it must've happened then."

"That's a little messed up."

"Maybe," Ally sighed as a tear fell. "But then again, what about this isn't messed up? At least it got him to quit the drinking."

"If that's how you want to look at it," Martin said coldly, chuckling to himself.

"I have no choice!" Ally snapped, her eyes enflamed as she glared at the man sitting next to her. "I had no one else to talk to! No one else who knew what we were going through!"

"And that's my fault?"

"You could've stopped me!" Ally screamed at him. "Consoled me! Shook me out of my moment of madness! Instead of saying all the right things… Holding me. Kissing me–"

"*You* could've stopped you!" Martin threw back at her. "You knew how I felt! Maybe that's why you came to me. Couldn't get it from him, so you went straight for his best friend."

"That's not what I wanted to happen." Ally sniffed and sobbed, her head in her hands, wet hair falling everywhere.

"Yeah, you've made that pretty clear." Martin crossed his arms like an angry little boy. "Why are you even having that fuckin' baby, anyway?"

His breath caught in this throat as soon as he said the words.

Ally Price didn't even look at him. Her tears vanished as if they had never been shed as she sat up, got out of the car, and marched back up her drive to her home without closing the passenger door.

That was the last time they would ever mention their unborn child to each other. And the last time Martin Fin felt that someone truly loved him.

* * *

"Thank you for checking the house for my baby and me. I feel much more relaxed now." Ally smiled as she waved her goodbyes to the responding officers. "Like I said, my husband shouldn't be too long, but I promise I'll call if there's a problem. Even if I have the slightest suspicion. You can be sure of that!"

Laughing politely, she locked the front door and joyfully collapsed against it, rolling her eyes in her relief.

"Finally…" she sighed as she started dance-marching towards the kitchen area. "Coffee, coffee, coffee! Woo! And I – need a – shower! Woo! Where's my phone – I need music! Woo, woo!"

Remembering, she quick marched back the way she came. "Bathroom, bathroom, bathroom!"

She reached for the handle.

The bathroom door opened by itself.

The man waiting inside had already removed his pale hood for her to see.

Ally fell back against the hanging coats on the opposite wall, screaming.

The thing staring out at her was the death mask of a young boy, stretched taut over the face of a fully-grown man. A cast of a long dead drowning victim. Decayed, bloated, and warped by the waters that had become his final resting place.

"Hello, Ally…" rasped the voice of a man while the face of a dead boy smiled down at her.

11
The Lighthouse

"Call came from Harold," Liam Price informed his buddy as the dark island road rumbled beneath the tires of the ambulance.

"Uh? Huh? What?" Martin Fin stirred as he snapped out of his daydream. "*Harold?* As in Patty and Harold? Morris?"

Liam nodded. "I heard he was there when you and Carl tried to storm the church."

"We didn't try to storm the church," Martin said, rolling his eyes.

"What was that about, anyway?" Liam questioned. "What were you even doing there?"

"I don't know..." Martin admitted distantly with a shrug. Lying back in his seat, he stared blankly out the window at the passing nothingness.

"Okay," Liam muttered as the ambulance rounded through an open field gate, vibrating over a cattle grid as it went.

They came to a stop behind a black jeep and a police car as they pulled up to the old lighthouse. Towering over them like the chess piece of a titan, the two paramedics geared up and made their way towards its doorless entrance.

"Christ!" Martin flinched to the side, his boot stomping loudly on the concrete bridgeway that carried them over the building's shallow but rocky moat. "I didn't see that before."

Liam rested a hand upon the rusted brown metal of the side railing as he peered over at the ghost with no eyes.

Amongst the surrounding black rock, a tall figure in a white sheet stood watch.

The cry of a desperate man came from inside the lighthouse.

Martin looked back at him with a look of recognition on his face. "Was that—"

"Go!" Liam bucked the man forward with his chest. "Go, go!"

"Ye— Okay, okay! Ya fuckin'…dick!" Martin scowled at him in annoyance as he shuffled uncertainly into the building.

They both came to a sharp halt side by side as they immediately happened upon the scene unfolding within the walls of Headless Ben.

The disused visitors' foyer was stained with the blood of Gary Wright, who cowered on the tiled floor as Officer Ashley Newton mercilessly pummeled him by the far wall. Harold and Anthony Morris, who bore witness to the beating, froze as they spotted the new arrivals.

"What is this?" Liam demanded in his horror.

Newton leapt back from Gary in surprise like a child caught stealing chocolate from the kitchen cupboard. On the verge of tears brought on by a sudden wave of shame, he slowly collapsed to the ground on the other side of the room.

"What the hell is going on here?" Liam said under his breath as he crossed the foyer to Gary's aid, sending tattered tourist pamphlets flying left and right in his wake.

Martin eyed Harold and his son as he approached Newton. This time he did not offer the old man a wave. "Really?" he scoffed as he crouched down to examine the shaking officer's hand. "You had to go and be the big man now just 'cause everyone knows you lost your lunch?"

"Don't you want to know what happened to Colby?" Newton asked him.

"What about Colby?" Martin ignored him while he fished around in his medical kit bag.

"She's not coming back." There was a sadness to Newton's cryptic words.

"Well," Martin sighed heavyheartedly. "That's up to her. Not you. Or me… Give me your hand."

The officer complied. "She's not answering or returning any of her calls. Cunningham wants everything kept quiet until we can find her. Or until she turns up somewhere."

"You're serious…" Martin said with realization, his hands falling by his side. "You guys really think she's gone missing?"

"Think about it," Newton said, sitting upright away from the dusty wall, spiders fleeing in all directions as their webs clung to the back of the officer's police jacket. "There's still someone out there on the island killing people. And no one's heard from her in days."

Collecting himself, Martin set to work tending to Newton's torn knuckles.

"Sounds like more island gossip to me," he concluded, firmly dismissive in his reasoning. "I'm sure she's fine."

The officer laughed hopelessly to himself as he shook his head. Settling, he watched as the paramedic cleaned the blood from his furious open flesh.

"How'd you know we were here anyways?" he asked him, wincing from the sting of the watery solution being dabbed onto his battered hand.

"Same way we know where everyone is," Martin told him. "We got a call."

"From whom?" Newton withdrew his hand. "No one else knew we were out here."

"Well, we got a call from someone," Martin maintained, his gaze shifting to the father and son who lurked close by.

"Not from them," the officer insisted.

"If you say so," Martin said, frowning at the pair, unimpressed as he looked them up and down.

"He's right, Martin," Anthony confirmed. "None of us made that call. None of us could have. We haven't been out of each other's sight since we got here."

Martin looked to Harold, who corroborated his son's story with a simple but sure nod.

"None of you…" The paramedic fell silent as he got to his feet.

Looking to Liam, who was still busy tending to the beaten and bloodied Gary Wright, Martin made his way towards the entrance of the lighthouse. He went to step outside when something stopped him dead in the doorway.

"Jesus!" he cried out, grabbing the doorframe to save himself from tumbling backwards from fright.

Liam raced to his side. "What is it?" he asked as he looked out into the night.

The tall ghost with no eyes now stood in the center of the bridgeway. Its white sheet draped over the railings on either side as if it were trying to keep everyone inside from leaving.

"There's someone out there." Martin pointed as he backed away from the door. "That thing didn't just move on its own."

Already on the other side of the foyer, with fists digging into his hips, Liam approached Newton. "Officer, if you think you can pull yourself together, we've got a situation unfolding outside that we could use your help with."

Taking each other by the wrist, the paramedic pulled the police officer to his feet.

"Okay, everyone," Newton said, addressing the room as he dusted off his uniform. "I'm going to go take a look, see what's going on here. Harold, Tony, one of you call for assistance."

The officer drew his firearm. "Liam, Martin, with me."

Weapon aimed and ready, Newton edged through the open doorway. "Where the hell did this thing come from?"

"It was somewhere else when we arrived," Liam explained. "It's moved since then."

"And I'm guessing the same person who called you is the same person that moved it," Newton concluded as he stepped in closer. "So, what do you think, guys? You think someone's under here?"

Liam and Martin exchanged a look.

"I'll do the honors…" Martin said reluctantly, stepping slowly out in front of the officer. Ducking down, he took hold of the bottom of the sheet. "Ready?"

"Ready," Newton exhaled, steadying his grip on the gun. "Okay."

Martin started to lift the sheet.

Shoes. Trainers. White. Muddy, but white.

Socks. Thick and folded down around the ankles for warmth. Also muddy. Also white.

Bare legs. Pale. Dirty. Stained with fallen tracks of dried blood.

And above a pair of bruised and bloody knees, a denim skirt.

"It's a girl?" Martin's voice cracked in his disbelief.

Unable to wait any longer, he tore the rest of the sheet away from the young teenager's body.

"Shit…" Newton gasped, lowering his weapon. "It's Hannah Wilson."

The girl's eyes were red and empty between the blueness of her swollen eyelids. Her right arm was raised above her head, the wrist tied down to the rowing oar that her fifteen-year-old corpse was bound to.

Holding the index and middle finger of his gloved hand to her neck, Martin checked the girl's carotid artery for a pulse that he knew he would never find. He didn't feel the need to share his findings with his colleague, even after he confirmed the results with a stethoscope to the chest.

"I don't understand," Liam said, his voice tremoring. "Why her? I thought he only went after…"

"Remember the day we lost Ben?" Martin reminded him. "There was a witness."

"Witness?"

"Hannah claimed that she saw the Butcher take the Ryan Reade kid," Newton filled in.

"Oh, she didn't see anything!" Liam raged, clipping the doorframe with his fist. "She just wanted a little attention, like any child. I cleaned the head wound myself. She was knocked clean out. She didn't see a thing!"

"Liam…" Martin attempted to calm him.

"She's just a baby!" Liam yelled into the night sky.

"Mr. Price!" Martin grabbed his friend by the shoulder.

"Fuck that 'mister' crap," Liam seethed in a whisper as he swiped away the man's hand.

"Hey!" Martin squared up to him.

"Stop it, I know this has happened before," Officer Newton interrupted as he holstered his firearm and stepped in between them. "I've seen the report. Samuel Wilde isn't the Boatmore Butcher, is he?"

Neither Martin nor Liam were willing to offer the officer a response in that moment, but their silence was all he needed to hear.

"Perfect." Newton threw a hand up as he stepped out from between them. "Can either of you at least tell me why he's positioned her like that? I mean, is it some kind of symbol, or what?"

Finally breaking their stare-down, the two paramedics turned to look upon Hannah's raised right arm as it appeared to point skywards.

Martin's mouth fell open before he turned and ran back into the foyer with Liam following close behind.

"Wait, what's happening?" Newton called out as he jogged in after them.

He was met by Harold and Anthony instead.

"Did you get through to anyone?" he asked the father and son while Liam and Martin scrambled around behind them collecting their medical gear.

"Yes, connection was bad," Anthony reported. "They're headed for the wrong lighthouse."

"You're kidding." Stunned, Newton barely had time to react as Liam and Martin started ascending the spiral staircase. "Wait, that's not safe! Stop! What are you doing? Stop!"

"There's someone else here," Martin responded without stopping. "We have to find them. *Now!*"

A morally powerless Newton cursed to himself while Anthony and Harold looked on in their unnerved confusion.

"It's Paul Hayes," the officer blurted out.

Martin halted. "Hotel Paul Hayes?

"Jesus, they're getting younger…" Liam shook his head, kicking at the step in front of him.

"We had no idea," Harold uttered.

"The father wanted it kept quiet, for the business," said Newton. On hearing his own words, he decided to surrender. "So, go on. Get up there! I'll handle things down here."

Liam and Martin continued their ascent at a quickened pace.

"Go get 'em, boys," Harold said as he watched them go. "We're behind you."

The darkness made their climb harder than expected as they waded through the deceit of low-lying shadows, trying to find invisible steps with their uncertain feet. As they drew ever nearer to the door that would lead them up into the lantern room of the lighthouse, Liam and Martin happened upon a pile of rubble on the spiral staircase blocking the way up.

The large heap of broken stone and brick lay coated over by one of the lengthy plastic sheets that hung down from the ceiling like slaughtered animal carcasses.

"Keep to the wall," Liam instructed him. "All it takes is one wrong foot."

Martin seethed with sarcasm as they both scaled the stony mound single-file in just a few steps, the plastic crunching under their soles.

As they neared the entrance to the lantern room, Liam looked over the side railing and down the 170-foot drop to the floor of Headless Ben. From that height, the four men waiting below were so small that they could barely be said to have existed at all.

Taking hold of the door handle, Martin looked back at Liam as he opened it. "Let's find out what happened to old Benjamin's head, shall we?"

Gale force winds ripped the door from Martin's grasp, pulling his shoulder as it crashed against the wall. The rattle of tremoring metal filled the air as the lantern room's steel storm panels appeared to still be intact. With everything from the ceiling to the lantern itself being either destroyed or removed, only a great gaping maw of glass teeth now surrounded them. In the center of the room was a body. Martin instantly recognized the long and wavy red locks.

"Jennifer!" He fell to his knees next to Colby as she lay there, her police shirt split open, baring her bloodied torso. He patted her cheek frantically as he tried to revive her. "Jennifer? Jennifer? Jennifer?"

The helpless giant's tears fell in an ever-growing stream, flowing faster with every time that his injured fiancée failed to respond.

Liam squeezed his buddy's shoulder before he set himself down on the other side of Colby and turned on the white blaze of a rescue lamp, illuminating her unconscious body.

"Mr. Fin?"

"Come on, Jen," Martin sobbed. "Wake up. I'm here. It's me, your big idiot. Jennifer, wake–"

"*Marty*," Liam said sternly, grabbing his friend's attention. "I'm just going to open her shirt so I can see what we're dealing with here, okay?"

Before Martin could give his consent, Liam started to lift the shirt away.

A feeling of nausea flooded his throat as he rested his gaze upon the horrid incision that snaked its way up the side of her belly to her chest. The attempt to close it up was even uglier than he remembered, with torn flesh and fraying stitches. The rescue light caught the glint of stray needles left inside the crevice of the wound, hidden well enough by its enflamed, infected edges.

"It *is* him, isn't it?" Martin managed. "He's been out there this entire time."

Liam didn't answer as he placed Colby's shirt back over the nightmarish gash on her side.

"What's that?" Martin said as he spotted the shadow of something on Colby's neck.

Turning the light, Liam reached over to inspect. Another slit. More stitching.

"Why'd he cut her there?" Martin twisted and turned on his knees, edging one way and then the other as he struggled to hold himself together.

"I don't know, this is new to me." Liam examined further. "We need to decide what to do, and soon."

"Why isn't she responding?" Martin's breath hissed through clenched teeth as he tugged on his own hair. "They always respond, right? That one kid was even up walkin' around, remember?"

"Marty, you need to calm down."

"*Don't tell me to fucking calm down!*" his best friend screamed at him. "Fucking *do* something!"

Liam sat frozen while Martin wrestled with his stethoscope.

"Fuck it! *I'll do something!*" he snapped as he searched for a heartbeat. "I can't hear anything up here!"

"Marty, let me—"

"I'm gonna do a precordial thump." Martin mounted Colby's stomach. "I'm not losing her."

"What? Wait, no!" Liam pleaded, taking hold of the man's wrists. "You know what this guy does. We do the wrong thing and she's dead. That's it. No second try."

"You got a better idea?"

Releasing his arms, Liam backed away. "You got this," he said as he gave him a nod.

Martin shaped his fist ready. He raised it.

"Come on, love," he said as he brought it down.

He thumped her.

Thumped through her.

All the way through her.

There was nothing inside. Only a hollow pit where Colby's heart should have been.

Martin wailed in horror as he tumbled off her body.

"What happened?" Liam cried.

"I don't know!" Martin howled back.

They were both silenced by a loud *CLANK!* as the floor began to vibrate with the heavy hum of machinery coming to life.

"What the fuck is going on?" Martin scrambled over to join Liam, grabbing at his uniform for safety.

"I don't know." Liam shined the rescue light around the derelict lantern room as he searched for the cause. "Maybe you pressed something?"

More clicks and clanks sounded from beneath them. And then, slowly, Colby's body started to rotate.

"No... No, no, no, no, no." Martin reached for her, utterly powerless. "What is this? How do you stop it?"

Liam's mouth fell agape, the rescue light slipping from his fingers. He didn't know what to do. He was finally out of answers.

Beneath Colby's spinning corpse, the mechanism that once turned the lighthouse lantern itself had been converted into a motorized winch. Its winding drum began to collect rope around it more and more, pulling it tighter and tighter, until it went taut, causing the hanging plastic sheet that covered the pile of rubble on the steps to shift and fall away, revealing a cargo net.

The winch hoisted the net full of rubble until it swung freely over the center of the spiral staircase, rising up and up and up. The weakened rope across the bottom creaked as it separated.

Before it could reach the top, the net burst open, sending chunks of rock and brick hurtling down the long drop towards the four islanders watching curiously from below.

Harold Morris and Gary Wright were obliterated instantly, crushed flat into the tiled floor while Anthony was tackled to safety by a quick-thinking Newton.

A thick gray cloud engulfed the two as Anthony screamed for his father. The officer blocked his way when he tried to go back into the lighthouse.

Meanwhile, on the bridgeway behind them, Hannah Wilson's scarecrow corpse came to life as she climbed down from the rowing oar that her body hung from.

"Let go of me!" Anthony yelled, coughing from the dust. "Dad! Dad!"

"It's not safe in there!" Newton braced against the hysterical son.

THWACK!

"Da…" was the last thing Anthony Morris uttered as he collapsed onto the officer, his immense weight pinning him to the doorframe of the entrance.

Hannah dropped the rowing oar onto the bridge with a proud smirk.

"Tony?" Newton watched blood rain down Anthony's face as his eyes rolled away. "Tony!"

Straining, the officer carefully laid Anthony down on the ground. Then he sprang around to face the person responsible, reaching for his holster, but he froze in the wake of what he found.

Hannah Wilson. Alive. Aiming a spear gun at his face.

"For Sam," she said as she dropped her aim.

There was a sharp *THUD!* as the girl shot Officer Ashley Newton in the heart. He lost his breath, gush after gush pumping out of his chest like a drinking fountain. The officer stumbled backwards into the lighthouse, finally resting atop the fallen rubble.

Dropping the empty spear gun, Hannah marched in after him. Before he faded, the girl stood over his body.

"You wouldn't let us bury him," she told him as she crouched down next to him, "so now I bury you."

Removing the gun from the dead officer's holster, Hannah left the lighthouse and found a peaceful spot by the water.

"I'm coming, baby," she said through tears of joy.

She put the gun in her mouth.

BANG!

The shot echoed along the coast as fifteen-year-old Hannah Wilson's body fell into the sea.

Liam Price and Martin Fin watched from the top of Headless Ben as the sirens started to arrive.

* * *

One Week Earlier

Some stories are not always told the way that they happened.

"Have you seen my cigarettes?" Hannah asked as she pretended to search the floor of the boat, keeping her eyes on the lake around them.

"They're probably where you were sitting earlier," Ryan Reade said as he kept watch.

Hannah smiled as she saw the man in the pale hood hovering over the surface of the lake as he emerged from the darkness.

"Hannah, sit down," Ryan pleaded. "Someone might see you."

The girl gasped as she cowered next to the boy, pointing. "I think I saw something out there."

"Where?" Ryan walked to the edge of the boat and peered out across the lake. "Are you sure? I can't see anything. It's too —"

Ryan's body nearly plunged overboard as Hannah struck him hard across the back of his head with their rowing oar. Grabbing him by the waist of his jeans, she laid him down on the floor of the boat.

By the time she had gathered herself, the man in the pale hood was already waiting for her in the water.

"It always used to make Sam so jealous, the way Ryan would look at me," Hannah recalled with a smile as she dumped the Reade boy onto the man's raft. "Do you miss him as much as I do?"

The man in the pale hood did not respond.

"See you around, I guess," the girl sighed as she watched the man disappear into the night with Ryan Reade's body.

Hannah Wilson sat in the boat alone, smoking her cigarettes through the night until the first sign of daybreak. Then she shuffled along her seat to the nearest oarlock and pulled her hair back out of the way. Taking hold of the lock, she braced herself for a moment and then threw her head forward.

12
The Morgue

"You didn't kill her, son," Sergeant Cunningham informed Martin Fin as he sat in the back on the ambulance floor.

On hearing this, his head fell into his hands as Mayor Rori Fin sat by her nephew's side, comforting him with a hand on his back.

"I had a look at her with the coroner myself," Cunningham went on. "Maniac carved a hole right through her, from the front to the very back. Most likely—as you say—so that you could inadvertently activate this…lighthouse of horrors that we now see before us."

The cavalry was out in full force that night. From the police to the fire department, from rescue workers to island volunteers. Nearby, an inconsolable Patty Morris was led away by a close friend and an officer, in search of medical attention, having just learned of the deaths of her husband and son.

"And neither of you saw anything?" The mayor looked to Liam Price who stood, arms crossed, next to the sergeant.

"It was too dark, and we were too high up," Liam told her. "We heard a few noises, but nothing that we could make out. We even thought we heard a gunshot at one point."

"Officer Newton's firearm is missing," Cunningham mentioned.

"Do you have any idea why he would take the Wilson girl's body?" Rori asked.

"No," Liam said firmly. "And I wouldn't want to know if I could."

"You and me both," Martin muttered, finally looking up as he quickly dried his eyes.

"Well, gentlemen, I know it isn't pleasant," the sergeant said. "But in light of tonight's events, I think it's safe to assume that Officer Jennifer Colby has indeed been missing for the past two weeks without our knowledge. And so, with that in mind, I must ask you both: when was the last time that either of you saw Officer Colby?"

Martin went first. "It was just before her last shift. She let me know that she would be home late that night. She didn't say where she was going. Or why. And I didn't ask her… That was the last time that I saw her…"

"Thank you, son," the sergeant said solemnly. He turned to Liam. "And you?"

"The day before. At Klaryssa's 'welcome home' party. I'm pretty sure that's the last time that Ally saw her as well."

"I see." Cunningham noted it down. "Right, I'll leave you boys be for now. I'm sure you've been through more than enough tonight. Martin, again, I'm so sorry. My condolences."

"Thank you, sergeant," the paramedic said with a weary nod of acknowledgement.

"I should go speak to a few people," Rori said as she and her nephew got to their feet and embraced. "I'll be back to see you off, okay?"

"It's all right," Martin sniffed. "Go do your mayor thing."

Rori laughed as she went on her way after the sergeant.

Liam sighed heavily as he stepped over and stood next to his buddy.

* * *

The ambulance shuddered like a theme park ride preparing for launch as Liam took the drive back slow.

On the passenger's side, Martin had the window down as he held out his hand to the night air until it lost all feeling. He brought it back in and stared at it while he tried to move his fingers. He decided to lean his head out instead and waited for his mind to go numb from the cold. Perhaps the pain that awaited him would help him think of something else.

"You know you're welcome to stay with us tonight," Liam offered, switching his attention between his friend and the road. "Maybe longer if you need to."

"Thank you..." Martin responded absently as he lay against the edge of the glass.

"I should let Ally know before we go barging in there." Liam held his phone against the steering wheel as he drove, switching the thing on with his thumb.

Expecting a handful of missed calls, it surprised him to find only one text message on his screen. He opened it and read. "She's at the morgue?"

Martin grunted with confusion as his head snapped away from the window.

"What the hell is she doing at the morgue?" Liam tried to call her. "Damn it! Voicemail."

"I'll keep trying." Martin took out his phone.

"Come on, Ally, what are you doing?"

"You don't think...?" Martin turned to him, a grave look on his face.

"Let's just get there first."

Tightening his grip on the wheel, Liam picked up the speed as the ambulance raced on through the dark island.

* * *

"I don't see our car anywhere," Liam remarked as they swooped down the lonely street of the morgue.

"Maybe she got a ride," Martin said hopefully.

"Yeah, but from who?"

They were nearing the entrance to the parking lot when shrieking tires pierced the night. The windows of the ambulance shattered as something huge battered their vehicle to the other side of the road.

* * *

"*Daddy…*" uttered the voice of a little boy.

Liam was unresponsive.

The voice came again. "*Daddy…*"

"Chris?" he began to stir. "Christopher?"

Tossing and turning now.

"*DADDY!*" the boy screamed.

"Christopher!" Gasping, Liam awakened to find himself alone in the ambulance. "Marty?" He looked around. The great white supply truck that had rammed them into the curb hissed with steam as it sat jammed against the passenger's side.

Undoing his seatbelt, Liam touched at his throbbing forehead. He found fresh blood on his fingertips. Folding down the sun visor, he checked his reflection for anything serious. Satisfied that there was nothing to cause alarm, he folded up the visor and lay back against the headrest with a weary groan.

And then, a voice. "Daddy…"

"Huh?" Liam's eyes darted back and forth over the road in front of him.

He wasn't dreaming this time. The voice was real.

"Hello?"

He winced in pain as he climbed out onto the pavement. Balancing against the accident-warped wall of the vehicle, Liam hobbled round to the front of the ambulance.

"God…"

Just up ahead there was a car stopped in the middle of the road. A car that wasn't there before. It appeared to be empty as it faced out at a strange angle. And lying in front of the car was the body of a boy.

"Not again," Liam huffed breathlessly as he hurried towards him. "Please, not again."

He was only a few steps away when he recognized the corpse of fifteen-year-old Ryan Reade under the light of the street lamp.

Dressed like a toddler, in summer shorts and a t-shirt, his arms and legs had been separated into halves at the knee and elbow joints. The only things holding them together were the metal hooks and rings that were jammed into the decaying flesh of their stumps.

Liam crumbled as he sat down on the road next to the boy with the broken limbs, trembling as he started to weep.

"I'm sorry…"

"Daddy." A man's voice.

With his breath caught deep in this throat, Liam slowly turned his head and peered into the shadows beyond Ryan's body to find a man sitting in the dark. Curled up against the side of the car, wearing a tweed suit, the man sobbed into his hands, just as Alec Wilde had done on the morning that Christopher was killed.

"What is this!" Liam took off crawling towards the crying man. "Who are you?"

The man looked up.

The face of a drowned child with the body of an adult stared back at Liam as he stopped in his tracks, frozen in utter horror. For he knew the face of the dead boy all too well. It once belonged to his son.

* * *

"Wake up." A jagged whisper. "Wake up, Marty."

Martin Fin blinked himself awake as he lay upon the cold hard floor of a brightly lit room.

"Wake up, Marty," the whisper repeated with a distorted buzz.

Snapping upright, he spotted the baby monitor sitting against the wall in front of him, laughter hissing from its speaker as its little lights flashed bright green. He recognized it to be the same model used for Klaryssa.

"Ally…" he uttered, suddenly recoiling as his nostrils caught the stench of something sickly sweet in the air. He turned to search the rest of the empty storage area for the source of the smell. The space had no windows and no doors, just brick. And at the other end of the room, the body of twelve-year-old Paul Hayes hung by the wrists from the ceiling.

Getting to his feet, he slowly approached the half-naked boy. Nose caved in and black, he wore nothing but a stained diaper. A bloody handprint marked his young chest while his belly had been split open down the center to reveal something shiny inside. On the floor, beneath the child's dangling bare toes, was a slippery pile of what appeared to be feces, but Martin knew from the familiar jelly exactly what it was, because the things that glittered inside the walls of the poor boy's hollowed out stomach were used cans of dog food.

The sight was more than he could bear. Collapsing to the ground with a whimper, his boots screamed against the laminate flooring as he scrambled and kicked himself away until his back was flat against the wall on the other side.

Unable to peel his gaze away from Paul's dead body, he picked up the baby monitor and held it close to his heart as he shut his eyes tight.

"Is there anyone there?" he asked the small plastic speaker between his hands. "Auntie Rori? Can you hear me? Auntie Rori? Can anyone hear me? Auntie? Anyone there? Auntie? Anyone? Auntie? Auntie? Please hear me…"

* * *

Under a violent sky of swirling clouds and blazes of brilliant white light, the unquiet sea swelled up the rocky coast and barreled towards the southwest boundaries of the town of Boatmore.

On the other side of the island, a single gust of wind hit Mayor Rori Fin from behind, whipping up her spine and blowing through her silver hair as if it were whispering a secret into her ear. A terrible secret.

"Something's wrong…" she said, turning to Cunningham. "Sergeant."

He handed her his pair of binoculars from the Velcro belt pocket she had pointed to. "Ma'am?"

Holding them in place, she looked to the sea.

"My God!" She grabbed the nearest megaphone as she started to run in the other direction. "Run now! Everyone, run! Come on, as fast as you can! Run!"

With the monstrous roar of steel drowning out their hopeless screams, a 280-foot ferry was lifted onto the island, disintegrating Headless Ben with the left side of its bow and grinding the residents of Boatmore into the earth as it spun inland like the blade of a giant aquatic lawnmower.

Back on the southwest corner, the first building the sea found was the morgue. Cabinet doors flew open and the drawers rattled out as the morgue quaked from the impact. Windows broke and doors busted open as the room began to flood, the water rising and swirling, collecting everything that wasn't held down into a whirlpool in the center of the room.

The second impact was greater. Ceilings fell, cabinets gushed water like ruptured pipes. Displaced corpses were dragged from their storage and battered from wall to wall as they were carried down the corridors of the morgue in a river of death.

"Liam?" Ally's voice. "Liam, wake up! I can't move. Liam!"

"Ally?" Liam said groggily as he lay upon the embalming table of the island morgue. "Ally, is that you? What happened?"

He tried to get up, but found himself held down fast by several restraints up and down his body.

"There was someone in our house," she told him.

"Where's Klaryssa?"

"I'm not sure," Ally replied tearfully, "but I can hear her in the room somewhere."

Craning his neck, Liam managed to peer back over his shoulder. "Aw, thank fuck! I can see her."

"Thank God!" Ally cried with relief. "Where is she?"

"She's by the sink in her little car seat. She's fast asleep."

"Oh good…" Ally sighed and then looked around the room. "Liam, why are we in the morgue?"

"I don't know," Liam grunted as he continued to brace against the straps that held him down. "I remember this is where Colby thought that Samuel…liked to take his boys. Have you seen Martin?"

"He's not with you?"

"Someone rammed us just as we got here. I haven't seen him since."

"Where the hell is Carl?"

"He was working at the lighthouse when we left. He must still be there."

"The lighthouse? How bad was it?"

"There was an accident… A big one. Harold and Tony are gone."

"Oh no…" Ally cried.

"A couple of others. Young Hannah Wilson."

"No…"

"And Colby, too."

"No," Ally gasped.

"But she and Hannah were gone before we even got there."

"You've got to be joking! What was she even doing there? We have *got* to get out of here. Gah! I can't get out of these fucking straps!"

"We'll keep trying," Liam said. "I'll get you out of this, I swear."

"Love you."

"Love you, too."

* * *

Martin Fin jolted awake to the sound of the baby monitor hitting the floor of that storage room. Snatching it before it skidded away, he caught sight of the body in front of him. He emitted a groan that rose into a yowl of grief.

The pile of stinking dog food was gone, as was the hanging body of Paul Hayes. In his place was Colby's corpse, propped up like she was standing on the other side of the room waiting for him. The back of her torn police shirt was visible through the large hole in her chest.

Climbing to his feet, Martin teared over, sniffing as he edged his way towards his dearly departed fiancée.

"Jen…" He took her hand as it hung rigid by her side. Her flesh was ice cold. "I really loved you. I never would've hurt you. I'm sorry I never told you about Ally and the baby. I know it happened before we met, but that doesn't make it right. I hope you can forgive me for that. Your big idiot. Jesus, I can't believe you're gone. If the Butcher was here right now, I swear to God I'd—"

The little speaker fizzed furiously as the baby monitor came to life in his hand.

"*I killed him,*" Liam's voice blared out. "*I killed Samuel that day at the church. I killed him.*"

"What?" Martin fumed, lifting the baby monitor to his ear.

"*I killed him. I killed Samuel that day at the church. I killed him,*" the recording repeated. "*That's who I am now. I let these people die. Christopher, Ben, those boys. Makes me a killer. I killed these people.*"

"Liam?"

"*I don't know why I thought having her would change anything. He's still gone. And I miss him every day. I hate her. I do. I hate her so much. I hate her because she's here and he's not. I know a solution. I kill her. I kill her. I kill her. I…KILL…HER…*"

There was a high-pitched shriek as the baby monitor fell dead.

Martin jumped back as a bare arm slowly emerged from the great hole in Colby's chest. It wore a medical glove as pale as its blood-drained skin as it reached out to him, holding something.

Is this a dream?

Before his mind could even begin to answer the question, he was pulled away by the creak of a door hidden in the wall behind him. He walked towards it.

"I hear someone coming." Ally alerted Liam as their friend stepped out of the wall and into the morgue.

The wall sealed itself behind him.

"Marty! Hey, buddy!" Liam cheered. "Aw, thank God for that! Get us out of here. We gotta go before he gets back. Bastard took Ally *and* Klaryssa. She's fine, though. She's over there. Hurry up, buddy. Hurry."

"You're not going to touch her," Martin said blankly as he silently raised the scalpel and plunged it into Liam's abdomen.

"NO!" Ally shrieked.

Martin raised the scalpel again as the door to the morgue burst open.

"Martin, stop!" Carl yelled from behind Sergeant Cunningham.

"Drop it, Fin, or I'll shoot!" the sergeant warned.

"I'm sorry, I can't let him hurt her." Martin braced.

"Sergeant, don't–" Rori screamed as the scalpel fell.

Cunningham fired.

13
The Box

"Hi, I am Lezlie Graham Jones with the morning news. First and foremost, I would like to thank you, the viewer, for joining me on my final broadcast day. This morning we bring you the latest on the Boatmore Butcher.

"Life on the island seems to be returning to normal as the case of the Boatmore Butcher has finally been laid to rest. Although initially Samuel Wilde, a 24-year-old coroner's assistant living on the island under an assumed name, was believed to be solely responsible for the deaths of six people, a second suspect came to light as the Butcher's reign of terror continued, bringing the death toll up to a total of fifteen people. Shot dead by police while attempting to murder close friend and work colleague Liam Price, along with his wife and newborn child, an official search of his home residence revealed island paramedic Martin Fin, nephew of Mayor Rori Fin, to be Samuel's accomplice in the Boatmore Butcher killings.

"Today, a new message of hope fills the air as people from all over gather in the town hall to celebrate the christening of baby Klaryssa Ben Price. The positive atmosphere is palpable, something that the good citizens of Boatmore most certainly deserve after living through such terrifying times.

"I am joined now by the man appointed with the wonderful honor of being baby Klaryssa's godfather, close family friend, Carl Oxspring, a long-time island resident who is also a well-loved and trusted member of the community."

* * *

Irene Birchwood finished locking up the entrance to the building before she joined her old friend by the opening of the cremator. Standing across from her, Carl Oxspring placed a box onto the gurney—a box full of video tapes.

"These are?"

"My boys, yes."

Unable to resist, Irene rifled through them with her pointy fingers, reading the labels to herself. *MICHAEL K. #3, JAMIE B. #1, RYAN R. #4,* and *CHRISTOPHER P. #.* No number.

"Christopher Price was one of yours?"

A strange smile formed on Carl's face as he held his hand out to her. She surrendered the tape to him, watching as he looked upon it wistfully.

"You know, some children can just sense it in you," he told her. "The way animals can sense danger. When Christopher saw me approach that morning, he knew exactly what I wanted from him. He took off running immediately, fast as he could, calling out for his mommy and daddy. He ran right out into the road, and that's when Alec's car hit and killed him. I'm the reason Christopher died that day."

"What do you intend to do with the rest of the family?" Irene asked him. "The Boatmore Butcher is dead, and your revenge is only half complete."

"Well, Irene," Carl sighed as he dropped the tape back into the box, "before this all began, the main cause of death on the island was either natural or accidental." Shoving the box into the cremator, he closed the door. "So, I guess I'll just have to bide my time and wait for a few little accidents to happen."

Part III
Ghosts of
Boatmore

1
The Child

I let one of them scream.

How could I be so careless?

But Mother was quick. She silenced the child with one hand and delivered my punishment with the other. The side of my face throbbed as I tasted blood. I heard sobs of terror and gagging as Mother forced the steel bit into the back of the child's throat and belted it into place.

There were footsteps in the hall. Too light to be Father's. They had to belong to the boy he brought home from school.

I couldn't stop my hands from shaking as I quickly turned off the light and then set to work helping Mother hide the child from sight.

We were in Father's study as Mother swept the central rug aside with the tip of her shoe before lifting a hidden door that opened up a coffin-sized compartment beneath the floor. That's why Father's desk was set aside so close to the doorway of dim light.

The boy in the hall was so close now.

The sobs only got louder as we lowered the child into their shallow box. As Mother closed the floor and replaced the rug, I wondered if there was enough air for them to breathe under there.

Before I could decide either way, I turned to the door and there was the boy.

I froze.

I saw him, but could he see me?

I drew in a breath as I felt my mother's hand close over my mouth. She gently guided me away from the door, away from the light, until we were flat against the wall, her arms wrapped around me.

The boy was about my age as he stood there in his wet school uniform. He wasn't afraid to look into Father's study, but he didn't dare take a single step closer. His curious eyes searched the darkness between us until they rested upon the pale telephone on the corner of Father's desk.

"Carl," a voice called to the boy, distracting him.

"Yes, Mr. Walker." He was looking away.

What if he tried to use the phone? I couldn't let that happen.

"That's not the way out," Father told him as I crept towards the desk.

"Sorry, Mr. Walker," the boy said as my slippery fingers reached for the handset.

"Go on home now."

I held my breath as it was in my grasp.

"Yes, sir," the boy spoke as something grabbed me from behind and pulled me back into the dark.

Mother's nails dug into my flesh as he took another look into the study.

It wasn't until he spied my blood upon the phone that he turned and ran. I heard the front door slam shut as the boy made it out of the house.

That night I watched from the stairs unseen as Mother and Father had a long discussion. When it was over, Mother stood over Father, reading from a notebook in her hands as she dictated a letter to him. He then sat alone as he wrote two more. After he was finished, Mother rejoined him at the dinner table to envelope and address each one.

"I will do everything that you ask of me," Father said as he took her by the shoulders. "I have only one condition."

The staircase creaked suddenly as I leaned in too hard to listen. I wasted no time in sneaking back to my bedroom as fast as I could. There I waited and I prayed, but no one followed me. Somehow, I had escaped punishment.

Very early the next morning I awoke to the sound of the front door slamming. The air was cold for summer, and it smelled like rain as I looked out of my bedroom window. It was Father. I watched as he walked to the end of the street with the three envelopes in hand where he disappeared. I assumed he had gone to post them at the letterbox just around the corner, but he never came back. I didn't know then that this was to be the last time I saw him.

Mere minutes after he had left, Mother called me to the kitchen where she sat me down and told me that Father wouldn't be coming home. I didn't cry. In that house it was just safer not to.

She then placed something on the table beside me. It was a photograph of the boy we let go. Mother pressed the tip of her finger into his face.

"We are to watch over him," she told me coldly.

"Why?" I dared to ask.

"This one is different," she said, unconvinced. "Your father believed that he will be just like us one day, and must not come to any harm by our hands. That was his final wish."

"Do you believe he will be like us one day?" I asked boldly.

Mother removed her hand from the photograph, her fingernail taking half of the boy's face with it.

"That was his final wish," she repeated bitterly as she crushed his picture with a bony fist.

A few hours later, the police showed up at our door. They spoke to Mother in the living room whilst I hid up in my bedroom. I listened through the floorboards above them as they informed her of my father's passing. When I heard that there were more people waiting outside to search through our house, I decided to sneak out the back and make myself scarce until everyone had left. But where would I go?

At first, I wandered the surrounding streets like a lost pet. The further I walked away from home, the more I wondered whether or not I would ever be able to return there. Would they find the child in the floor? Did they know more than they were letting on? And could we really trust the boy we let go to keep our secret?

It was at that moment that someone familiar ran across the end of the street right in front of me. It was the boy himself. I raced to the corner where I found him further down the road as he took a seat at the bus stop. The boy wasn't going to school today. Of course he wasn't. How could he? Still, somehow, I knew exactly where he was going.

I waited until I saw the bus coming up ahead to approach the stop. The boy boarded first, followed by a woman pushing her kid in a stroller, an elderly couple fussing over a missing purse, and then me. I sat behind him for the journey. Not too close by, but not too far away either.

When we reached our stop, I walked ahead of him. We were going to the same place. There was no need for me to follow him.

It was too easy to slip under that police tape and sneak up to the final floor of that parking garage. I guess that's why so many of us go missing. We're just too easy to lose, especially if we don't want to be found, and even more so when someone else doesn't want anyone to find us.

As I stood close to the edge and looked down upon the street, it occurred to me: this was the last place my father was seen alive. And that was the first time the boy really saw me. Standing by himself just outside the entrance to the Gabvey town shopping center, he stared right up at me, and I stared back.

For the longest moment, it felt like he was the only one that could see me. Could Father be right? Was he just like us?

Just then, a woman appeared next to him. She looked worried. Frightened even. She had to be the boy's own mother. I couldn't let her see me. Only the boy could see me. I vanished from sight.

"How did you get here?" Catherine Oxspring asked her son.

"I took a bus," Carl responded blankly.

"Why?"

The boy gave no answer as he continued to stare up at the top level of the parking garage across the street.

That evening I stood outside the boy's house.

From the outside it seemed like one of those regular, happy, warm homes you see on all those funny shows from the television. Inside though, I felt a coldness not so unfamiliar to the one I have felt for as long as I can remember.

The boy's father remained planted in the living room enjoying the comforts of married life, whereas mine would stay rooted to the desk up in his study. What he did in there, I had yet to learn. Mother will have hidden every last piece of paper from the police. I could only hope that she will show me his things one day—that's if she hadn't already destroyed everything he left behind.

I soon found the frightened woman from the shopping center in the kitchen putting away the last of the dishes. There was a softness to her that I had never seen in my own mother.

And something else. Something broken. She would look for things in empty spaces. A chair, a doorway, on the floor. Something important was missing, and no matter how many times she looked, she would never find it.

Moving up to the second floor of the house, I discovered the boy in the bathroom standing over the sink as he scissored away lock after lock of a doll's hair. A Polaroid camera rested upon the corner of the bathtub behind him.

"Have you seen Emma?" I heard his mother's voice ask from below.

Moments later her footsteps were on the stairs.

I backed my way into what had to be the boy's bedroom and closed the door gently after myself before she could see me.

I waited on the other side and held my breath as I listened out for what was going to happen next. The floor in the hallway creaked soundly as the boy's mother reached the open bathroom door. I heard the heavy *CLICK!* followed by the mechanical whine of the Polaroid camera. She now saw what I had seen...and yet nothing. Not a word was said between them.

She started to move again. I looked over my shoulder. The carpet was riddled with the boy's dirty clothes that she could come in to collect at any moment, but as the door handle turned I had already slipped into the boy's closet.

It wasn't until after the boy's bedtime that I finally emerged from my hiding place crouched behind a large toy chest beneath a tower of board games.

As I crept from the closet, the boy sat up in his bed and watched while I made my way to the door.

"Hello," he said, unafraid.

Surprised by his calm greeting, what else could I say in return but, "Hello."

"Are you a monster?" the boy asked me.

Me, a monster? Was I? Was he one, too? Is that what we were? Monsters?

While I pondered this, I decided that, although I would only allow him to see me, I thought it best if he didn't believe that I was anything more than imaginary.

I replied, "Yes."

2
The Yard

Present Day

How did the time get away from her? Fiona Mayfair wondered at the sudden realization that it was already dark outside. Grabbing the clothes basket from the kitchen counter, she could just make out the white of her bedsheets as they hung out there, watching her move through the house like lonely ghosts.

Her hip vibrated before she could reach the back door. She stopped by the kitchen table with a sigh as she took out her phone.

A message from her daughter, Jo:

Just finished at the movies.

On my way home now.

Love you x

Leaving her phone upon the table, Fiona flipped the switch for the patio lights to come on. She halted as nothing happened.

She tried the switch again.

Still nothing.

And again.

Still no light. Only darkness.

Dropping the empty basket to the floor, Fiona unlocked the back door and slowly pushed it ajar as she leaned her head out to take a look, but she could barely make out the light fixture as it sat twelve feet above the yard at the far corner of the house.

Pulling the back door shut, she retrieved her phone from the kitchen table and fumbled through it until the flashlight blinked on.

Outside, the yard was darker than she realized as she felt it cover her with its heavy curtain. Raising her phone, its blinding beam lit the way as she followed the stone garden path to the corner.

Fiona glanced around the side of the house to the street.

All seemed to be well.

Aiming the phone up at the patio light, she squinted at the socket in confusion. She took a step closer to be certain of what she was seeing.

The bulb was missing.

Maybe it fell out?

The light of her phone flashed back and forth as she searched the path for its shattered remains, only to find no traces of broken glass.

Someone must have removed it.

Fiona turned as she caught a glimpse of something moving past the front of the house.

Probably just a neighbor walking their dog.

Dismissing what she had seen, she returned to the kitchen and snatched a set of keys from the wall. Patience dwindling, she wrestled open the padlock to the garden shed and marched inside.

The wall rack was a shrine of long forgotten holiday memories, from ice skates to rollerblades, from bicycles to paddling oars.

Fiona gritted her teeth as she tried not to think about the tiny creatures crawling across the ceiling falling into her hair and running up and down her clothes.

She eventually happened upon the drawer of replacement bulbs, but as she fought it open, she found only empty boxes.

"Of course," she sighed.

Composing herself, she locked up the shed, left her phone on the kitchen table, and stepped back out into the yard with the basket underarm.

Placing the washing at her feet, she set about unpinning the first of the sheets as they hung silently from the clothesline. Reaching blindly, she knocked the pin bag from its hook. She heard it land upon the grass somewhere to the side of her. Scolding herself, she crouched down and searched the ground with her fingers, collecting pin after pin as she went.

Rising to her feet with as many as she could find, she fitted the pin bag back onto the line when she heard a sound: something softly scraping the stone of the garden path. The noise was so slight that she ignored it at first, but as she heard it again and again, she finally turned to take a look.

Fiona choked back a gasp as she found someone standing by the side of the house.

Clasping a hand over her own mouth, she backed away into the clothesline, allowing the sheets to fall over and around her, hiding her from sight.

She tried not to move.

She tried not to breathe.

Trapped between the narrow textile walls of that cold dark prison cell, all she could do was listen to the creeping footsteps of the intruder as they moved slowly along the garden path.

Keeping her hands up and away from touching the sheets that hung in front of her, she sidestepped as quietly as she could until she felt the night air on her skin.

Holding her breath, she looked towards the house.

What she saw was not a man, but the absence of light in the shape of one. She watched him as he lurked in the window of the back door peering into her kitchen, long fingers caressing the glass as he searched for her.

She felt a sudden chill as she heard a *CLICK!*

The man was turning the door handle.

Panting heavily, she backed away into her hiding place and closed her eyes tightly, as she couldn't bring herself to watch him enter her home.

Swallowing tears, she covered her ears when she heard the low creak of the back door as he pulled it open, but then she surrendered to the need to listen to the dull squeal of metal as he released his grip on the handle.

And then nothing.

No more sound.

Why couldn't she hear anything?

Gathering herself, Fiona gave into her curiosity and chanced another look out from inside the clothesline.

The man was nowhere to be seen.

But the back door was hanging wide open.

She could see her phone, untouched, still sitting atop the kitchen table.

So close.

All she had to do was sneak a few yards up to the house and grab it.

Whispering a prayer to herself, Fiona bolted towards the open door. She made it inside. Her eyes darted around frantically as she made sure the room was empty, but she couldn't be certain. Heart pounding, she snatched the phone from the table and bounded back the way she came.

Shaking uncontrollably behind the cover of the clothesline, she typed out a text for her daughter.

EMERGENCY! DON'T COME HOME!!!

But before she could finish the message with *LOVE MOM X...*

"Hi, Mom! I'm home!" Her daughter's voice called out from inside the house.

"Jo, no..." Fiona gasped.

Tearing the sheets aside, she started to run for the back door when a long arm shot out of the clothesline and ripped her flailing body back into the hanging sheets by the soft flesh of her throat.

Seventeen-year-old Jo Mayfair's attention was fixed firmly on the small screen between her hands as she entered the kitchen and leaned against the doorframe.

"Mom?" She looked up.

Jo paused as she found the door to the backyard wide open.

She approached slowly, trying the patio light switch with no success.

"I know you're out there, so if you're trying to scare me, it's not gonna work." She tried the light again, but it was no use. "You forgot to hide the basket, Mom. Game over."

No response.

Rolling her eyes, Jo glanced down the length of the kitchen, her eyes searching for food, but a creak from the clothesline snapped her gaze back to the yard.

"Have it your way, old lady, but I know just how to find you," she said quietly to herself as she found her mother's number on her phone.

She pressed the call button and waited.

She heard the growing hum as a bright light illuminated the bedsheet before her like a shadow puppet show. The shape of her mother's figure stood there, unmoving.

"I can literally see where you are hiding now." Jo leaned her head through the back door. "Just quit it now, okay, Mom?"

Her mother gave no reply as she stood behind the sheet, perfectly still, arms dangling limp on either side.

"Mom?" Jo uttered again as she let the call go on. "Answer me, or I'm gonna lock you out."

"Don't do that, Joanna," a man's voice whispered.

The shadow of a third arm emerged from her mother's side as a hand reached for the edge of the sheet.

"I've been waiting for you all night," the voice told her as long fingers curled around into view.

"Mom…"

A bloodcurdling scream pierced the dark as something burst from the clothesline and raced towards the house.

Jo hauled the back door shut and locked it.

Huge pale palms slammed against the glass, startling her backward.

She bolted in the other direction, knocking aside everything in her path as she went. Fighting the porch lock open, she leapt out onto the front stoop.

She froze at the sound of a *CLICK!* as the security light snapped on.

The man standing beneath the blinding glare was tall enough to reach up and snuff it out, if he chose to. Instead, he leered at her with those empty eyes.

Jo spied the blood first still spreading down his shirt. Then she saw the smile.

He charged.

Lunging back the way she came, the front door slammed so hard that it bounced off the frame before Jo could lock it up tight.

As she backed away into the house, it dawned on her how ordinary the man on the other side of the door appeared to her. In his plain shirt and trouser pants, he could be a schoolteacher, or someone's father returning home late from work for the hundredth time. He could be anyone. He looked so normal, and with a face that you could easily lose in a crowd.

Except for that look in his eyes.

And the blood…

Her mother's?

She felt a chill that stalled her heart.

She cried out as the phone in her hand sent a surge up her arm.

The screen read MOM. She answered immediately.

"Mom!" She kept her eyes on the front door as she came to a stop. "Are you all right? Where are you?"

Something on the other end took a breath.

"Let me in, Joanna…" the voice from the clothesline said to her.

"What did you do with my mom?" she demanded through trembling words.

She saw the outline of the man pressed up against the front door. Her mother's phone cast a pale and eerie glow across the smile on his face.

Taking another breath, the man pushed a fingertip against the glass and slowly dragged it down the surface.

She winced at the squeal of his milky flesh on the window.

"What did you do to her?" she yelled out to him.

"Let me in…and I'll show you…"

Jo screamed as a needle the size of a barbecue skewer punched its way through the letterbox. Its razor tip stabbed the empty air as it twisted left and right, searching for innocent skin.

"Go away." The girl shivered.

"Oh, Joanna, Joanna, Joanna," the voice sighed. "I'm not going anywhere."

"Well, I'm not letting you in!"

"Silly girl," the man laughed. "I've already been inside your house once tonight. How do you think I know your name?"

The warmth drained from Jo's face.

"Can you guess if I found out where your mother keeps the keys?"

Suddenly, the needle retracted, slamming the letterbox shut. A thick drop of blood was left in its place as it slid down the door.

The lock below the handle made a few clicks before it started to turn.

Gasping, Jo headed for the stairs and raced up to the landing. Hearing the front door open below, she soundly followed the wall into the nearest bedroom. Her mother's room.

The left side was lined with pale closet doors, each one with its own lock and key. Jo crept over to the one at the very end, keeping an eye on the bedroom door as she unlocked it and climbed in. Pulling the closet door shut, she reached blindly for the back wall where she slid down to the floor. She held her breath while she listened.

Nothing.

Wherever the man had gone, he had not followed her upstairs.

Relieved, Jo took out her phone and called for help, watching the screen in her hand as she waited for a response.

The closet door flew open. For a moment she was frozen by the hypnotic way the light from her phone reflected in the pupils of the man's wild eyes as he stared down at her.

Jo screamed as he snatched both of her ankles and wrenched her out of the closet and onto the carpet at his feet.

Taking her by the throat, he rammed her upright against the door of the next closet, splitting it up the middle. She felt her windpipe start to cave in as the wood of the door splintered all around her, and then her feet left the ground as the madman hoisted her into the air.

Unable to beg for her life, Jo could only watch in silent horror as he drew out the large needle. He held it perfectly still as he raised it up to her eyeline. She let out a weak squeal of agony as he inserted it into the corner of her eye, and proceeded to push it deeper. Deeper. And deeper.

Her fingers twitched. Her nose bled. Her eyes stared off emptily in opposite directions.

Joanna Mayfair was gone.

3
The Message

No! Please, God! How could this be happening again? the mind of Ally Price screamed.

That face. That dead boy's face, decomposed and bloated, staring back at her from the body of a man as she opened the bathroom door. The sight of it startled her so badly that she slammed into the coat rack behind her.

"Hello, Ally…" it said to her in a horrid voice as it loomed over her.

Her heart sank into her stomach when it asked her where the baby was. When she refused to answer, it drew a weapon and struck her hard across the head.

Except this time, she didn't blackout. Instead it was as if she had become paralyzed with her eyes wide open.

She lay there on her side by the front door as she heard her attacker's footsteps moving through the house in search of her child. He would soon find her sound asleep in her crib, and there was nothing that she could do about it.

Carrying her out to his car, he slipped her into the passenger's side at the front, holding her body in place with the seatbelt. He finished the display by wrapping her up in a patterned quilt.

This man just abducted my baby and me, and everyone that sees me sitting in here will probably think that I've just fallen asleep next to this psychopath, Ally agonized as they drove through the streets of all the people she knew…but there was no way for her to ask them for help.

Before she knew it, they had arrived at the morgue. She could hear her child's cries, but she was unable to see her as their masked tormentor laid her down upon the embalming table.

"He still thinks you're the perfect wife, doesn't he?" the dead boy's face asked her. "The perfect mother. If only he knew…"

Then the scalpel came into view as he picked it up from the tray.

"What do you say we cut you open?" He stuck the blade into her stomach and started to carve away. "Bleed the truth out of you."

She didn't know if it was the shock of the instrument separating her flesh, but, somehow, she finally felt something, a strange sensation on her face. It was originating from her lips.

Ally Price found herself being kissed awake on a bright Saturday morning.

Her husband, Liam, hovered over her, smiling warmly as he brushed her frizzy blonde hair away from the hot skin on her forehead where he planted his next kiss. She hummed loudly as she stretched and smiled back at him.

"Someone's feeling much better," Ally said, yawning as she gently ran the tips of her fingers over the bandaging wrapped around his stomach.

There was a small but dry pink stain on the upper left side where the stitches were, hidden beneath the layers of soft gauze. The very spot where the man she'd had an affair with stabbed him moments before he was shot to death right in front of her. Her hand trembled as the memory became too much for her to bear.

"I'll be back in a moment," she told her husband as she got up and hurried into their bathroom.

Snapping the lock shut, she was hesitant before she turned and faced herself in the mirror.

If only it was just a nightmare. Tears rolling down her cheeks, Ally let out a long and heavy sigh as she slowly lifted the front of her nightgown.

There on her belly, in a series of crude but clean incisions, the Boatmore Butcher had marked her skin with a message. It was a message for Liam. And that message had only one word:

DADDY?

Somehow, the Butcher knew her terrible secret, and now her body was permanently scarred because of it. She wouldn't be able to keep it from Liam for much longer. He deserved to know the truth about his daughter. There was no denying that. Why fight the inevitable?

Ally dried her eyes as she collected herself. This time it didn't feel like the walls were closing in on her. On that Saturday morning, they couldn't have felt further apart, and that made her feel *alone*. Perhaps that's what she deserved at the end of it all.

* * *

A large wooden board leaned against the mantelpiece in the living room of Wendy Quinn's apartment.

It was covered, top to bottom, with newspaper clippings and photographs of different people, different locations, a roadmap with a route marked down on it that began inland and ended at the coastline, pieces of paper with notes scribbled on them; one read, *QUESTION GAS STATION ATTENDANT*, another said, *CCTV FOOTAGE*, while the largest note had the words *WHERE ARE YOU???* scrawled across it. And finally, in the center of it all, was the cutout of the banner headline:

LOCAL JOURNALIST BELIEVED
SLAIN BY ISLAND KILLER

Wendy sat on the sofa in her pink and baby-blue dolphin dressing gown staring at it all, an electronic ID card clasped between her hands. It was the one piece of evidence that linked her brother Jordan's disappearance to the Boatmore Butcher killings.

"If only I had gone with him," she said woefully. "I tried to."

"Your brother was a stubborn soul," her mother said comfortingly as she set a fresh mug of hot chocolate down on the glass coffee table. "And always so driven. There was no stopping him when he decided to do something. Don't blame yourself, my dear. If anyone's to blame, it's the police on that damn island for letting everyone believe that that monster was dead."

"Why can't they find his body?" Wendy tossed the ID card across the table. "Why does everyone else get their family back, and all we get is a piece of plastic with his name on it?"

Her mother put an arm around her shoulder as she sat down next to her.

"Wendy, don't you think-"

She was interrupted by a knock at the door of the apartment.

"Are you expecting anyone?"

Wendy didn't answer as she hurried to the peephole and peered through it.

"Ugh! It's Jordan's old boss from the paper," she scoffed before she opened the door to the balding man with the loose tie.

"I hope you don't mind…a neighbor let me in," he said sheepishly, hands jammed down his pants pockets.

"What are you doing here?" she demanded.

"You said to come see you if I ever found anything." The man held up a flash drive.

Wendy and her mother sat on either side of their visitor as he clicked away on her laptop.

"Where did you get this?" she asked.

"Friend of a friend," he simply replied as he opened a media file.

It was a video of Jordan Quinn sitting at the bar talking to another man, an older gentleman.

"Oh my god," Wendy's mother gasped soundly.

"Your brother was last seen leaving the bar of this ferry bound for Boatmore," Jordan's boss told her.

"Someone on that island knows who that man is," Wendy said as she pointed to the stranger sitting next to her brother. "I bet he can tell us something about what happened to Jordan."

"I certainly hope so, for your sake."

"Mom, we need to start packing." Wendy got up off the sofa and tightened the belt on her dressing gown. "We're going to Boatmore."

* * *

The center of Boatmore was situated on a gentle incline, which began with the new town hall at its very top and ended with the fishing pier as it curved out into the water like a giant stone hook.

The town hall itself, unlike most buildings, had a round structure, as it had previously served its purpose as a church for centuries. A church with round walls meant that there were no corners for the devil to hide in.

It was getting late on that busy Sunday afternoon, and the hall's interior was dressed for celebration. There were streamers, banners, and balloons, complete with catering and a hired DJ.

Liam watched contentedly as Ally's mother tried to play peekaboo with her baby granddaughter.

"Patty and her gang really went all out for Klaryssa's reception," he mentioned as he marveled at all the decorations. "We've got to do something to show our thanks for everything that she's done. It can't have been easy."

"I'm sure she appreciated the distraction," Ally remarked glumly. "After what happened to Harold and Tony."

"Are you okay, love?"

"I'm fine."

She wouldn't look at him.

"Are you sure?" He tried to touch her shoulder, comfort her. "You've been a little off since yesterday."

"It's nothing." She moved away, just out of reach. "I'm just not feeling well. I can't deal with being around all these strangers right now. It's making me crazy."

"Ally…" Liam looked at his wife in surprise. "You know these people. What's the matter with you? They are our friends. I love the way this community just comes together. It's like a family."

"Jesus Christ, Liam, you've got to stop romanticizing our reality!" Ally's chair squealed as she finally turned to face him. "What will it take for you to leave this island? We lost our son here. You killed a man. Your best friend tried to kill you. So please just tell me, exactly, what is keeping you here?"

"…I came here to build a life with you," he said sadly.

Ally nodded thoughtfully as she took in his answer. "Is that what it's going to take?"

On the other side of the hall, retiring news reporter Lezlie Graham Jones had come in from the mainland to film the final report of her career, the closing chapter of the Boatmore Butcher killings. In the middle of interviewing island residents, Carl had volunteered to become one of her last victims. With shiny golden curls and electric eyes, it was clear to all that her passion for her craft had endured through the years.

"Today, a new message of hope fills the air as people from all over gather in the town hall to celebrate the christening of Klaryssa Ben Price. The positive atmosphere is palpable, something that the good citizens of Boatmore certainly deserve after living through such terrifying times.

"I am joined now by the man appointed with the wonderful honor of being baby Klaryssa's godfather, close family friend Carl Oxspring, a long-time island resident who is also a well-loved and trusted member of the community.

"Carl, tell us, how are you-"

Lezlie and Carl turned to the sound of screams.

"You fucking bitch!" Liam erupted from his seat. "Do you realize what you've done to our family?"

"Liam, please, I'm sorry!"

Ally cried out as Liam slapped her hard across the cheek, sending a shockwave of gasps throughout the hall.

"Shut up!" His body shook madly as he screamed in her face. "Just shut up! How could you? I have been fighting with everything I have in me to be a better man for you, a better man for Christoph- Klaryssa! And what do you go and do? How fucking dare you? Who are you? I don't even know who you are right now. I don't recognize this person. The Ally I know wouldn't… She wouldn't… I can't do this."

Liam pushed his way through the nearest exit door, leaving the town hall in stunned silence.

* * *

"How can you be ironing right now?" Wendy asked her mother as she flicked through the channels on the small TV in the corner of their hotel room.

Sure enough, her mother sat on the end of her single bed using an old iron that she had found hanging in their room's sliding-door closet.

"Hmm, I probably shouldn't," she said as she concentrated on smoothing out a crease. "I remember this model from when I was a girl."

She looked up when Wendy finally put down the remote.

"What are you watching, dear?"

"The news," her daughter sighed. "Jordan always loved to watch the six o'clock news with dinner, and I'd always say that I hated it because I thought it was just too depressing. Funny thing is, since he's been gone, I don't think there's been one day that I've let go by without watching at least one news report."

"That's sweet, dear," her mother smiled. "It's so nice that you can remember him that way. Oh look, the news is in Boatmore."

"What?" Wendy sat up in her bed. "Are you sure?"

"Yes, I'm sure," her mother insisted. "That's the new town hall that used to be a church. Just listen to it."

"The positive atmosphere is palpable," said reporter Lezlie Graham Jones, "something that the good citizens of

Boatmore certainly deserve after living through such terrifying times."

"She's talking about the Butcher murders," Wendy uttered, suddenly transfixed.

And then she saw him.

"Oh my god…"

Standing next to the reporter was the man they were looking for.

"Mom, that's the man from the video!" she cried out as she ran up to the TV.

"Are you sure?"

"I'm dead certain."

"Well, did you catch his name, dear?" her mother asked.

Wendy nodded as she looked back at her from the television.

"Carl Oxspring."

4

The Sister

Wendy Quinn ordered a taxi from her room and met the driver outside the front of the Boatmore Hotel.

Climbing into the back seat, she slammed the door shut after herself and met his eyes in the rear-view mirror.

"Take me to Carl Oxspring."

A short drive later, Wendy found herself standing inside the entrance to the island morgue as the automatic doors closed behind her.

It was quiet, and even though some of the lights were still on at that late evening hour, the place felt abandoned.

The first door that she came to led her into the embalming room. Cold and empty, it held the heavy scent of industrial cleaning products in the air. Still, no amount of sterilization could protect her imagination from the purpose of that room, and she didn't want to be in there any longer than she needed to be.

Turning to leave, she stopped as she heard footsteps. Gently pushing the door closed, she left it open just enough for her to peer through. She caught sight of a small old woman in a violet raincoat as she rounded the corner at the end of the corridor.

When enough time had passed, she followed her there. Ahead was a set of double doors; above them, a sign read CREMATORIUM.

Taking a deep breath, she walked towards them and quietly slipped her way inside.

"I'm the reason Christopher died that day," Carl told Irene Birchwood as they stood by the cremator.

The machine hummed as its flames awaited the box of VHS videotapes that sat upon the gurney between them.

"What do you intend to do with the rest of the family?" Irene asked him. "The Boatmore Butcher is dead, and your revenge is only half complete."

"Well, Irene," Carl sighed. "Before this all began, the main cause of death on the island was either natural or accidental, so I guess I'll just have to bide my time, and wait for a few little accidents to happen."

Sliding the box into the cremator, they both stood by as they watched it burn.

* * *

Wendy's mother was still ironing when her daughter returned to their hotel room.

"Wendy, where did you go?" she asked as she set the old iron down by the window. "I was worried."

When she sat back up she found her still lingering by the door. She barely seemed to move as she stood there with a troubled look on her face.

"Carl Oxspring is the Boatmore Butcher," she said in her bewilderment before she walked straight into their bathroom and closed the door.

Ignoring her mother's knocking and the calling of her name, she sat next to the sink with her phone in her hands. Accessing her videos, she played the last file: a recording of Carl and his unknown female accomplice cremating evidence.

The drone of the cremator itself had aided in her entering the room unheard. Once she was inside the crematorium, she was able to hide behind another gurney, one that was trimmed with pleated black curtains around the sides.

Wendy gazed into the faint reflection of herself in the glass door of the shower.

I didn't come here for this. This is way beyond anything I could ever...

Shaking her head, she pocketed her phone as she got to her feet and started the shower water running while she changed into her dressing gown.

You came here for Jordan, she reminded herself as she looked into the bathroom mirror. *And he would want us to be safe. Show the video to the police in the morning. Let them deal with it. They will arrest him and question him, and then you'll finally get the answers you've been looking for.*

With that, she turned and knocked on the inside of the bathroom door.

"Mom?" she called out. "I'm just going to take a quick shower, and then we can talk."

"Okay, dear," her mother's voice replied. "I've ordered room service for our dinner tonight."

"Okay, cool." Wendy smiled as she slipped out of her dressing gown and climbed into the shower.

* * *

Last Point was a cliff face on the island of Boatmore famed for being home to the golden eagle. Islanders and tourists alike would walk for miles in all weathers just to catch a glimpse of the bird's majestic beauty.

It was also the one place that Ally Price knew she would find her husband on that late evening.

Liam laughed, infuriated, as he heard his wife's walking boots approaching.

Refusing to turn to her, he looked out over the darkening sea as he sat upon the grass a few feet away from the edge.

Ally stopped a few steps behind him and just watched.

They didn't look at each other.

They didn't speak.

They could only wait.

* * *

"I wouldn't have believed it if I hadn't seen it for myself," Wendy's mother remarked as she forked at the last of her plate of spaghetti.

"I know," her daughter sighed, captivated, as she watched the video for a second time. "He's still out there, and no one is doing anything about it."

"You will, dear," her mother reminded her. "You are."

A little blinking orange light on the floor caught Wendy's attention out of the corner of her eye. It was the old iron again, as it was still sitting under the window.

"Will you turn that frickin' thing off before you burn the carpet or something?"

"I just have one more round to do, then I'm done," her mother promised.

She collected Wendy's plate from her bed as she piled their trays together and carried them to the chair by the door.

"Mom…" Wendy's mouth went bone dry.

She hadn't watched the video this far until now. She wanted so badly to disbelieve it, but there it was, clutched between her two trembling hands.

Carl Oxspring was staring back at her from her own phone screen.

He knew I was there!

"Mom…" she said again as she rose slowly from her hotel bed.

"What is it, dear?" her mother asked, looking back over her shoulder at her daughter as she unlatched the door to put out their used plates.

There was a loud *CRACK!* as the door burst open, knocking Wendy's mother off her feet.

The woman spun as she fell fast and hard. The center of her forehead connected with the blunt corner of a bedpost, killing her instantly. She rolled onto her back, where she lay still. Her eyes were sad and lifeless as they stared up at the ceiling.

"Mom!" Wendy dropped to her knees by her mother's side, hysterical, as she tried to shake her awake. "Mom? Mom, please!"

She looked up from the body to the drowned child corpse face that was staring back at her. She screamed with a grief-stricken rage as she attacked the walking horror, pelting it with knives, forks, spoons, shattering plates, bowls, and glass tumblers.

As soon as it had backed out of the room, she drove her shoulder into the door, forcing it shut. Scrambling to her feet, she released the latch and locked it in place.

"Mom? Mom, no…" she wept as she tugged at her mother's hand. "I'm sorry, Mom…" She cried out as the door cracked behind her. Searching for a way out, she headed for the bedroom window, closing the curtains behind her. She gasped silently as she heard the door crash against the wall. That thing was already inside her hotel room. She listened for a moment and then turned to the window. Reaching up, she grabbed at the two handles to open it, but they wouldn't move. Confused, she felt along the edges of each pane with her fingertips until she realized everything was painted shut. She had to find another way out.

Turning away from the window, she held her breath as she parted the curtains carefully with a finger and quietly peered through the opening.

The Butcher was standing on the other side as he slammed the scalding hot plate of the old iron into her face. Wendy shrieked in agony as he rammed her back against the window. The curtain itself melted over her skin, into her eyes and mouth.

"No!" she wailed as window glass broke behind her head, cutting into the flesh of her neck and back.

The air from her cry blew a bubble of melted plastic that suddenly sucked down into her throat when she inhaled. In a terrified panic, she started to choke, letting out high-pitched guttural wheezes as she stumbled out from behind the curtain and ran blindly into the bathroom.

There was a scream, a chorus of fragmenting glass, and then nothing.

The Butcher found Wendy crumpled up by the tiled wall in a widening pool of her own blood. She had collided with the shower door in her haste to escape, the falling shards slicing her apart, amputating one of her legs like a glass guillotine.

She bled out in seconds.

* * *

Closed for the night, co-manager Rebecca Hayes sat alone in the empty hotel bar with her head in a bottle, the way she had done every night since the mutilated body of her twelve-year-old son, Paul, was discovered in the island morgue. He was murdered just days before his thirteenth birthday.

Tonight, her drink of choice was a bottle of Lighthouse Silver, a brand brewed in one of Boatmore's four world-renowned whiskey distilleries. Its sweet fire gently burned the back of her throat as it slid its way down like spicy hot liquid sugar.

Her red and sleepless eyes opened slightly as she heard someone enter the bar.

"Bar's closed!" she slurred.

"I'm sorry, ma'am, but something's happened," a nervous little waitress said. "Mr. Hayes needs you to come immediately."

The doorframe was splintered when Rebecca arrived at Room 119, but the way in was wedged shut as she tried to enter.

"Johnny?" she called as she knocked softly. The door jerked ajar as one of her husband's lanky limbs grabbed hold of her wrist and hauled her inside. She saw the old woman's body first, on the floor by the bed, a deep dent in the middle of her forehead which had turned a shade of blackish purple on her dead skin.

"Johnny, what happened in here?" The question wavered with her alarm.

Then she noticed the blood pooling on the tiled flooring by the open bathroom door.

"You don't want to look in there!" Johnny threw up his hands to stop her before she could even take a step. "Trust me."

"Well then why did you call me in here?" she fumed.

"Keep your voice *down*," he flapped at her.

Rebecca crossed her arms firmly over her chest as she glared back at him.

"Because I need you to tell me what to do," Johnny admitted as his body wilted against the wall.

"What?" His wife narrowed her eyes at him.

"We need to handle this the right way," he went on as he bowed his head solemnly. "The last time I made a decision like this…it was the mistake to end all mistakes…"

Rebecca sat down upon the bed, her head swimming from the whiskey. She almost lost her balance as she made sure her feet were nowhere near the old woman's corpse. Holding herself up, she closed her eyes and exhaled as a single warm tear ran down her face.

"We lost our son," she said. "We are not losing our business, too. We are not losing everything."

"What are we going to do?" Johnny asked her.

"*We* are going for a drive," she said as she got up from the bed and stepped over her former guest. "And *you* are going to bring our checkbook. We're going to the morgue."

5

The Promise

One Week Later

Liam Price found Ally already seated in the waiting area when he arrived at the doctor's office.

The room was tiny, with only one surviving plant which littered the laminated floor with its long dry leaves opposite a huge notice board overloaded with dozens of posters and pamphlets. A young mother was sitting in the corner by the window blinds pushing a stroller back and forth while her toddler played with a wooden abacus from the visitors' toybox.

He tried to smile at his wife as he went to sit down while at the same time she herself seemed afraid to smile back. The plastic chair next to her let out an obnoxiously loud creak as he lowered himself into it.

"Well, that couldn't have been more awkward," he joked.

Ally's tensed shoulders relaxed a little as she allowed herself a short laugh.

"I would have driven you here if you needed a ride," he told her, hoping that she would meet his gaze.

"I'd have turned you down," she said.

He noticed that her hands were shaking. Their eyes met for just a second as he reached out to calm them.

"Besides, I didn't think I'd be here this early," she confessed, her hands retracting slowly. "I've been sleeping in a lot lately."

"It's not been great for me either," her husband admitted. "Don't think I've slept more than two or three hours a night since…"

The door to the doctor's office clicked open, drawing the attention of everyone in the room, save for the toddler who was quite content with his abacus.

"Thank you very much, doctor," a frail voice uttered. "You have a lovely evening now. Goodbye."

Seventy-five-year-old Georgina Thompson hunched over her cane as she made her way towards the exit. Liam was quick to get the door for her.

"Oh, thank you, Liam!" she exclaimed gratefully. "God bless you."

"You're welcome, Ginny."

His response went unheard as she tended to her Scottish terrier, Donnie, who was tied up outside to a no parking sign. He watched the poor little soul give her a piece of his mind for leaving him out there for so long.

Liam turned to the sound of his name to find Ally standing behind him.

"It's our turn," she quietly told him.

"You know, all this wasn't necessary," Dr. Jacob Tree told them as the three of them sat down together. "I'm sure you realize you could have just-"

"I wanted it done this way," Ally said sternly, both hands clasped tightly together over her lap.

"Okay." The young doctor smiled as he unlocked the top drawer of the small filing cabinet underneath his desk and fished out a thin white envelope.

"If I could just stop you there for a minute, Jake," Liam said suddenly.

Getting down on his knees, he took hold of Ally's clenched hands and his touch divided them effortlessly. Her trembling fingers interlocked with his and he made them still with his caress.

"She is *my* daughter," he began. "She was mine before she was born. From the moment I knew she existed, I was her father. I will be her father now, and long into forever."

Ally's head and shoulders bobbed as she wept into her chest.

"Whenever you're ready," the doctor said kindly as he handed them a box of tissues.

Once Ally had collected herself and dried her tears, she gave him a nod.

"Ready."

He handed her the envelope.

She looked at her husband as she held it out to him.

Surprised at first, he accepted it. Carefully tearing it open, he pulled out the folded sheet of paper inside and set the empty envelope down on the doctor's desk. Along with his breath, Liam held back the beats of his heart as he unfolded the letter.

* * *

The automatic gate slid away as Liam and Ally arrived at Mayor Rori Fin's estate.

The driveway was smooth black tarmac, lined with deep red rose bushes on either side that soon opened out to unveil the mayor's Tudor-style villa. On the front yard, a picnic table sat by an old willow tree. The orange rays of a magnificent setting sun shone through its long falling branches on that cool spring evening.

Mayor Rori was already sitting at the table waiting for them with food and drink. As always, she wore one of her lavish lavender suits.

"I know we haven't seen each other since the funeral," the mayor sighed as she sat across from them, "but when you are a disgraced elected official because of your relation to an alleged serial killer, one feels less of a need to be social."

"You're looking well, ma'am," Liam said flatly.

"I'll get right to the point, as I'm sure you must be wondering why the hell I summoned you here," she began. "I heard about your altercation at the town hall. That there was an affair with my accused nephew, and that he sired young Klaryssa."

They opened their mouths to respond, but she cut off both of her guests before they could utter a word.

"What I would like to do is send the two of you on a lovely day trip to the Isle of An Dìomhair."

"The other island?" Ally gawked.

"Yes!" Rori laughed, "so the two of you can spend some quality time with one another and do some much needed healing; that way, I can make up for lost time and bond with my beautiful great-niece."

The nervous couple exchanged a sympathetic glance before Ally rested a hand upon Rori's arm.

"Actually, we got a test done," Liam told her. "And it turns out that I am actually Klaryssa's biological father."

"Ah...I see..." Rori slowly moved her arm away from Ally. "So my Martin really is all gone... Well, congratulations to the both of you. That's the way it should be..."

Ally got up and marched around the table and sat down by her mayor's side.

"Rori, before we found out, Liam told me he would always be our baby's father, no matter what the results were." She chanced an arm around the woman's shoulder. "Regardless of what anyone else on this damn island believes,

Marty was our family, so if you would still like to be Klaryssa's Auntie Rori, we would love that."

Rori's bottom lip quivered in her disbelief. She looked to Liam, who gave her his nod of approval.

"Yes, of course I would!" she cheered as she threw her hands up with joy. "I'd be honored!"

But her celebration was short lived. Her hands sank down from the air into the pockets of her lavender coat as she wandered away from the picnic table.

"I have to confess, though, my motives behind my gift to you both are a little bit selfish," she said as she leaned against the trunk of the great willow. "As you both know, there's the great whirlpool beyond the flooding bay of An Dìomhair. Martin wanted a portion of his ashes scattered there."

"We will take him with us," Liam said as he got up from the table.

"You will?"

"Of course, it's the least we can do," Liam promised her as he reached out and shook her hand.

"Thank you, Liam!" Rori gushed as she put her arms around him. "Thank you to the both of you. It is such a comfort to me just to know that Martin had such good people like the two of you in his life towards the end."

"We'll remember him the way he deserves," Ally said as she joined them. "As a hero."

6
The Other Island

The Isle of An Dìomhair was Boatmore's neighbor of the sea. At just over half its size, its inhabitants were a mere two hundred in total compared to its companion, which had a population of three thousand people.

Gul Bay seemed to spread out into eternity on either side with its miles and miles of slick wet sand. Better known to most as The Flooding Bay, it stretched the width of the island, and when the tide came in every evening, Gul Bay became completely submerged and the Isle of An Dìomhair became divided by the sea.

"Doesn't seem to end, does it?" Ally remarked as they walked across.

"If you could maybe not say things like that while I'm carrying this abnormally heavy picnic basket," Liam strained, "then that would be just peachy."

"Patty and her crew strike again," Ally giggled.

"I knew you'd find a way to flip that one on me." Liam shook his head with a smirk.

"No, you were right," she admitted. "They've done a lot for us, and they've been very kind towards me. Not that I deserve it."

With that, she reached over and took hold of one of the handles of the large basket so that they could share the weight for the remainder of their journey.

Liam poured each of them a glass of wine once they had set up camp on the rocky shores by the great whirlpool of An

Dìomhair, believed by some to be one of the five largest in the world.

Ally was mesmerized as she watched the foam of the sea spiral and vanish down into the dark mouth of the vortex.

"It's pretty far out there," she observed, holding her hair aside to stop it from whipping her face in the island winds.

"I'm sure the current will take him there eventually." Liam passed to his wife a small urn. "You do the honors."

"Why not you?" She looked at her husband in confusion as she tried to return it to him.

"This isn't about us," he reminded her with a pained expression.

Ally bit her bottom lip as she nodded and turned to the water. She opened the urn and closed her eyes.

"Goodbye, Marty," she whispered as she poured the remains of Martin Fin into the sea.

"Goodbye, Mr. Fin," Mr. Price said under his breath as tears choked him.

As he watched Martin's ashes glide over the surface of the water like a ghostly gray oil spill, somehow, he knew that they would find their way to exactly where they needed to go.

"Do you really believe the Butcher drove Marty crazy?" Ally asked him.

Liam gulped his wine down until the glass was empty before he answered.

"I don't believe it, I know it," he told her with certainty. "Somehow this bastard knows things about us. Memories that cut deep. When he got me alone, he showed me things, tried to mess with my head. This guy really wants to hurt us, and it's my fault, because of what I did."

"You know I've never blamed you for that," Ally said as she poured him another glass. "You did what you had to do.

What anyone would do to protect their own family. I just hope that one day I can make up for my mistake."

"I just wish you'd never told me about you and Marty," Liam remarked as he guzzled his second glass. "I wish I didn't know…any of it. I can't even give him a real goodbye…"

"Then why did you forgive me?" Ally cried out in her frustration.

"…I didn't," he replied as he caught his breath.

"*Will* you?" She squared up to him. "Will you *ever*?"

He couldn't even look her in the eye.

"Would I even be here with you if it weren't for your own guilt?" she asked with a trembling mouth.

"I dunno, Ally…" Liam said with a shrug before he glowered at her with a glare of distain. "I guess this is just me *romanticizing our reality*, right?"

* * *

All Liam could hear was the deafening thunder of rushing water and all he could see was the swirling void of the vortex as something lowered him headlong into a bottomless darkness.

"Liam!" … "Liam!"

He found his way back to consciousness upon the picnic blanket as Ally shook him awake. His head throbbed furiously and his eyes had to adjust as everything was now cold and dark. The sun had abandoned them. His feet were freezing, drenched by the sea that had crept up the rocks during his dreaming hours.

"How long have I been asleep?" he asked, sitting up with a groan.

"We both were," Ally replied as she looked around, disorientated. "I have no idea."

Despite the circumstances, Liam couldn't help but notice that their picnic was missing.

"Where's the basket?"

"Must've lost it to the tide," Ally shrugged, glancing over the rocky shore.

"Figures…"

"Jesus, Liam, we could've drowned." Ally got to her feet, resting her hands upon her hips as she looked back over the direction from which they came. "How are we even going to get back across?"

"Guess we'll just have to wade our way through it," Liam said as he joined her by her side. "Make sure we don't go too deep, and hope the current doesn't drag us both out to sea."

The two of them held hands as they helped each other walk through the deepening waters of Gul Bay. Shadows began to appear beneath the surface rising up as slippery dark masses.

"What are those?" Ally demanded as she cowered against her husband like a scared child.

"Oh, those?" Liam laughed. "Those are just a kind of tangled seaweed. Don't be scared of them. They might come in handy if we get separated and you need something to grab onto."

They had reached the halfway point, and all the while Liam had kept his eye on the small waves overlapping one another as they rolled in from the sea, filling up the bay little by little. It was then that he noticed that Ally had fallen behind, holding his arm back with her as she was lost in thought. They came to a halt as they locked eyes.

"I don't remember falling asleep," Ally said.

Suddenly, a blinding light flashed over the water as a vehicle approached, sending up torrents of foam from its wheels.

"Who is that?" Ally called out as she shielded her gaze from the beams.

The SUV stopped just a few feet away as a familiar old face leaned itself out of the window.

"It's Patty!" Liam cried out with relief.

"Come on, you two!" Patty waved them over with a huge grin.

"Thank God!" Ally huffed out a grateful sigh as she let go of Liam's hand and dashed towards the car as fast as the tide would allow her.

There was a shriek as a diver burst out of the slimy nest of seaweed in front of her. The eyes were blacked out, but the wetsuit was pale like fresh bone with that sickly stain of yellow marrow.

"Ally!" Liam screamed.

The diver jerked forward as they punched a harpoon through Ally's chest and into her heart. With a wet gulp, her eyes and mouth snapped agape from the shock.

Liam stopped dead in horror and disbelief. In those seemingly endless moments, there was no oxygen that could fill his lungs, and no pulse that could course his blood. This wasn't like Christopher. This was different. This was worse.

As the hooked blade was ripped back out, Ally's blood gushed out into the bay as she fell to her knees. Her body began to topple over onto its side, but Liam caught her before her head could vanish beneath the water.

"Liam!" Patty yelled from the window. "Get out of there! Get away, get away!"

The diver held the tip of the harpoon blade against his throat as he knelt there with his dying wife in his arms.

"Do it," he sneered through gritted teeth. "But if you go near my baby girl, I swear to God-"

It swung again, chopping the side of Liam's head with the blunt end of the blade. He slumped over, out cold, floating there on the surface of the bay as the pale diver dragged his wife's body off into the darkness.

7

The Widow

Liam Price remained unconscious in the back seat of Patty's SUV for the entire ferry ride back to the island of Boatmore, stirring only when he felt the swift sting of someone slapping him awake. At first, he saw the blurred mass suspended above him that was the roof of the vehicle. Slowly, he lifted himself upright and waited for his vision to improve. He scratched at his skin as it itched from the streaks of dried blood that ran down the side of his face.

Patty sat sideways in the driver's seat as she stared back at him, waiting for him to say something.

"Ally?" His voice was small, almost a whisper as he spoke with a bowed head.

"Gone," Patty told him.

"You followed us?"

"No." She shook her head. "I followed *him*."

"Who?"

"The man who attacked you."

Liam looked up as he met her eyes. "You know who it was?"

"I do." Patty nodded calmly. "And you know him, too. It was Carl Oxspring. Carl Oxspring is the Boatmore Butcher."

"Carl?" Liam scoffed at the man's name as his eyes narrowed in disbelief. "Carl? The man who is godfather to my baby girl? That Carl?"

"Listen to me, Liam," Patty said as she waved an angry finger at him. "You're not the only one on this island who has been affected by this animal. Now, for Klaryssa's sake, you'd better heed what I have to say."

Liam gave her his silence as he sat back, ready to listen.

"I had my early suspicions about him," she recalled. "Something not quite right. It never sat well with me that he had no idea Samuel was using the morgue to do all those horrible things to those boys. Then when the rumors started flying around the island that the Butcher was still on the loose, my Anthony mentioned to me one morning that some of them were planning on going after Gary Wright. Said they were going to take him somewhere secluded, rough him up a little, make him confess to his crimes. Next thing I knew, Harold and my son were dead. I should have tried harder to stop them from going. I later found out from one of Anthony's friends that everything was Carl's idea. From who to suspect to where they should take him. Everything. Furthermore, on that same night, both you and Ally were kidnapped by the real Butcher, and where were you found? The morgue. Once again, it all leads back to the morgue."

As Patty spoke, Liam became more and more aware of their surroundings, gazing out of each of the car windows at the dark street outside. Through the chilled glass it all began to look familiar to him.

"Where are we?" he asked Patty. "Why aren't we going to the hospital? Why aren't you calling the police?"

"He's here," she said. "Inside."

Liam's mouth fell open as he turned and rolled down the nearest window. There they were, parked outside the entrance to the island morgue. Without looking back, he climbed out of the car.

Throwing open the trunk of the SUV, he rifled through a heap of Harold's old belongings: a tire iron, a pair of hiking boots, some tools, a couple of fishing rods, and finally, a speargun. Ready as he would ever be, he closed the trunk and walked towards the automatic doors as they opened to greet him.

"I don't know why it took me so long to see it," Liam said as he found Carl waiting for him, standing on the other side of the far embalming table. "You sent me back into the church to die that day, didn't you? You knew Samuel would be there waiting for me."

Carl said nothing as the overhanging lamp cast an eerie light over his face as he stared emptily back at him.

"So, all this because I didn't want him to kill my child, huh?" Liam sobbed. "You killed my best friend. You killed my wife just because I protected my family?"

Carl's expression changed when he caught sight of the speargun in Liam's hand.

"Goddamn you, Carl," Liam exhaled as he took aim.

"Don't pull the-" The man started to wave his hands, but it was too late.

Liam pulled the trigger.

The worn rubber bands of the gun snapped in half, striking him hard as they whipped back into his face, knocking him off his feet.

Carl clutched the edge of the table, ready. He waited for Liam to get back up. He didn't. He listened for any groans of pain. There were none. The room was still until Patty walked in, shaking her head at the man's limp body.

"He can't quite get the hang of this killing thing," she remarked before she turned to Carl. "Can he?"

"Patty?"

"Patty Morris," the woman said, grinning as she nodded. "Formerly Patricia Walker. Alan Walker's widow. You remember him, don't you? You should. He died because of you."

"I didn't kill Alan." Carl growled, clenching his fists.

"Oh no?" Patty took a seat on the stool behind the opposite embalming table. "Because it's thanks to you that I made him confess to all the murders. How else could I get away with it? I couldn't just trust some strange child I'd never laid eyes on to keep my secrets."

"*You* get away with it?"

"Yes, I'm sorry to tell you." Patty pouted at him mockingly. "My Alan never killed anyone. He was just a sick little deviant who desired his young students more than he did his own wife. And he wonders why I had to kill them all. Then, one day, he lets one go. Not only that, he makes me promise to watch over him. I mean...it was the least I could do in return for his great sacrifice."

"You're lying..." Carl rasped, stepping out from behind the table.

"Well, none of that matters anymore." Patty kicked the stool over as she walked over to Liam's unconscious body and picked up the faulty speargun. "Thanks to you and your dead boyfriend's little whore. Now, I'm going to do what I should've done forty years ago."

The old crone screamed as she tore across the room towards him. Her teeth bared and her eyes wild, she was fast.

Carl batted the gun to the side as they collided, but she swung it back and drove the spear into the side of his belly. He roared with agony as he beat her over the head with his hammer, clawing a chunky flap of her scalp loose. Her body locked up as she let out a silent wail. A wide stream slathered down her brow like dark jelly. She tried in vain to blink the thick crimson goo out of her eyes as she slowly slid down to the floor. A meaty slice of her hair gleamed, fresh and wet upon the cold tiles, as she glared up at Carl with a trembling fury unlike any he had ever encountered in his lifetime.

"You have no idea what you've just brought upon yourself," she whispered to him as he knelt over her, her blood spreading out beneath her head.

Moments later, Patricia Walker Morris was gone.

8
The Wounded

"I need you," was all that Carl needed to say when Irene answered his call.

The hearse was waiting for her in the parking lot of Port Erin as she stepped off the ferry from the mainland. They didn't greet one another. They weren't among company. She simply boarded the vehicle and they drove away.

All the windows were thick with fog. She dabbed a clear hole in the misty glass with the tip of her finger, and then snuck a glance at the man beside her. He had to have been festering there by the water since he called her. She squirmed in her seat at the thought of his wet breath encapsulating them. It was everywhere, so she rolled down the window, breaking that liquid web of condensation. Horrified, yet relieved, it didn't occur to her that they hadn't spoken a word to each other the entire journey until the ground began to crunch under the tires as they drove up to the house.

She had never been to his home on the island before that day. The hallway was dark and narrow. A long raincoat hung on the wall to her left; a pair of tall muddied boots sat on the stone floor beneath it. There was a door to the right: the living room. The inside was exactly as she expected it would be. It had all the signs that someone lived there—water-colored picture paintings of lakes and mountains, clocks, candles, ornaments, and lamps—but nothing that could tell the casual observer anything about the owner. She knew what that place really was, just as she knew one other thing: it was devoid of the warmth of a real home.

Up ahead was a doorway of light at the end of the hall. The kitchen. This room was minimal, metallic, brazen heartlessness. Carl waited for her there as he set about preparing his guest something to drink. There was a pained hobble that he tried to mask as he moved from cupboard to cupboard.

"Carl?" She dared not remove her jacket, watching her host rattle as he resisted hunching over the counter.

"Take a seat," he managed with a heavy exhale. "I'll be with you in a moment."

The loud clang of stainless steel on marble rang in her ears as a teaspoon fell from his grip.

"Why don't I?" Irene was soft but insistent as she guided her ailing colleague to a chair at his own table.

A strained groan of agony no louder than a whisper escaped through gritted teeth as he carefully took his place.

She made them each a drink of hot tea. Sitting across from him, she quenched her dry throat with that first sip, keeping both hands pensively upon the cup as she set it down.

"Just let me say," Irene began before he could utter a word, "whatever it is you have to tell me, you should make it quick. I enjoy human suffering as much as the next sociopath, but this just won't do. You need to be seen by someone, and soon. Now, Carl…what on earth is going on here? What happened to you?"

Carl braced himself, inhaling deeply through his large nostrils, and spoke. "The wife is dead. I killed her in the water." Following his old friend's request, he wasted no time in regaling her with everything that had taken place up until the moment he called her. The confrontation with Liam, the truth about Alan Walker, the revelation of Patty's real identity.

And finally, the warning the dying widow left him with before she succumbed to her wounds from their brief but bloody battle.

"All this time." Carl's bottom lip trembled for a moment, something that Irene had never seen occur. "I've built my whole world, my entire existence around an idea of this man…and it was all a lie. I sacrificed everything. I risked everything. For nothing. I just don't know what to make of it all. What do I do now? It took me years of pained searching to find a purpose in my life. For all the things that I was feeling. I just… Where do I go from here?"

Irene stared at him for a few thoughtful seconds. Then she picked up her cup of tea and slurped it until it was empty. Placing the cup down hard upon the table, she sighed and said, "First, we are going to clean up this mess. We are going to get you the help that you need. You are going to focus on making a full recovery, and *then* you can think about what you're going to do next."

* * *

"Ally…"

Liam Price awoke to a cloudy darkness that throbbed to the distant beep of a heart monitor. A sound that grew ever more piercing the clearer it became.

"Ally…"

The flesh of his face was a pulsing mask of pain. He couldn't open his left eye, nor could he breathe through his nose as he lay there in that hospital bed. Searching the room with his good eye, he saw the nurse sitting to the side of him reading a magazine as she ate her lunch.

"What's going on?" His voice was a hoarse groan. "How did I get here?"

The nurse clapped her magazine shut and made her way to the door, taking her lunch with her. "Someone will be with you in a moment," she said without looking back.

"Wait!" Liam croaked at her. "What's wrong with my face?" But she had already disappeared.

Looking around, his gaze landed on the mirror above the sink by the wall. It was on the other side of the room, too far to get a clear view of himself, but he strained through his blurry vision.

"Jesus…"

His left eye looked like stomped fruit, as it was swollen shut. Gauze bloomed from his nostrils below the splint that was taped to a heavily bruised bridge. Shaken by what he saw of his own reflection, he drew in a sharp breath to the sudden squeal of a door handle turning.

"Hello, Mr. Price." Sergeant Cunningham smiled at him strangely as he entered the room, followed by another officer. "Nice to see that you're awake. How are you feeling?"

The sergeant settled into the wooden armchair where the nurse had been stationed while the other officer remained standing at the foot of the bed.

"How did I get here?" was the first thing that Liam said to them. "Can you tell me? What happened to me? To my face? Can somebody please tell me that?"

"You don't know?" the officer asked.

Cunningham raised a hand, telling his subordinate to say no more as he watched Liam shake his head in response. "What's the last thing you remember?"

"I-I'm not sure," Liam stuttered as he struggled to recall.

"All right, if you want to play it that way," the sergeant grumbled skeptically. "Yesterday evening, at approximately six p.m., you showed up at Carl Oxspring's place of work accusing the man of killing your wife. Lucky for the both of you, the weapon you attempted to shoot him with malfunctioned and knocked you unconscious. Mr. Oxspring called for assistance immediately, at which point you were brought here, which brings us up to now."

Liam was still as he gave no response.

"What I'm most concerned about is the claim you made about your wife," Cunningham said, leaning forward in his chair as his eyes bored into him. "What happened to her, Liam? What happened to Ally?"

The man sat there silently as tears began to fall.

"Liam?" Cunningham reached out for his shoulder.

"He killed her!" Liam erupted hysterically. "My wife… My wife… Ally… Oh, Ally…" His words were indecipherable. His entire body shook as he wept. Doubling over, he clasped his hands over his face, but they were not enough to stop his grief from raining down upon the sheets.

"Gentlemen!" Dr. Ahamed called from the doorway, her gleaming black locks flowing. "If you are quite finished with upsetting my patient, I am going to respectfully have to ask you to leave. I am sure you are aware that he is in no fit state to be talking to you right now. I can assure you that he is not going anywhere in his current condition, so you can leave him with me. Go on, you will have plenty of time to talk to him when he is feeling better."

"I'm sorry, Liam, if we caused you any distress," Cunningham said sheepishly, clearing his throat as he got to his feet. "Listen, when you're ready to be discharged, I will send my officer here over to bring you down to the station so we can ask you a few questions. Get your side of the story. If you have any legal representation, I suggest you give them a call at your earliest convenience."

"I shall see to it that he does that, sir." With a raised eyebrow, the doctor held the door open as she ushered the sergeant and the police officer out of the room, shutting it hard behind them.

Her hard stare softened as it turned to her patient. "Liam, I apologize that you had to be subjected to that."

"Where's Klaryssa? Where's my daughter?" Liam demanded breathlessly.

"She is fine, my friend, I assure you," the doctor informed him. "She is with your mother-in-law."

"Oh, thank God." He fell back against the pillows in his relief. "When can I see them?"

"During regular visiting hours," Dr. Ahamed replied. "Until then you should hydrate and rest yourself."

"Thank you, doctor."

* * *

"The doctor tells me the surgery went well."

Irene Birchwood found Carl sitting up in bed when she appeared in the doorway, carrying a jumble of get-well-soon items from the hospital gift shop.

"Yes…it seems there was very little damage to repair," Carl told her with a sigh. "I'm almost disappointed."

"Almost." Irene's smirk was as dry as her remark.

Carl huffed out a laugh as he watched his visitor set about placing an array of small cuddly toys along the windowsill. She then left flowers and a card on the side cabinet, and finished by tying a shiny helium balloon to his bedpost.

"You do put on a good show." He smiled at her at first until he realized that she had no intention of smiling back. "Irene? What is it?"

"You need to leave this island and never come back," she said gravely, her fingers tightly gripping the back of the visitor's chair as she stood behind it. "If you don't, someone is going to come here and kill you."

"What are you–" Carl began as he sat upright. He winced from a sharp shot of pain in his side. Clasping a hand gently over his healing injury, he gathered himself. "How do you know this?"

"Because that someone is my brother."

"Your brother?" Carl narrowed his gaze at her in his confusion. "You don't have a brother. You have a sister and a niece."

"No sister, no niece," Irene said as she shook her head. "Just a brother..."

"Irene, I–"

"Haven't you ever wondered what it was that drew you to me when we met at the university?" she asked him hopefully, her eyes wide, wet, and glistening. "Was there never even a flicker of recognition?"

"You're not making any sense at all now," Carl said as he looked away from her.

Irene's shoulders sank as she let out a weary sigh. "The first time you saw me was the day my father died."

Slowly, Carl turned to meet her sad eyes. "What?"

"And the first time we met was the night you caught me sneaking out of your room."

"No..."

"I'm sorry, but it's true," Irene sniffed. "I am the daughter of Alan Walker...and Patty was my mother."

Carl ripped the balloon from the bedpost as he lunged for the woman, wrapping the curling ribbon around her neck as he charged her into the bathroom.

"No, Carl, you're not being smart!" Irene cried out, her lower back ramming into the sink, cracking the mirror glass behind her, splitting it down the center.

"So, all this time, you were the monster from my childhood," Carl rasped furiously through clenched teeth as he tightened the balloon string around her throat. The crinkling of the material was so crisp and clear as it cut into her soft aging flesh.

"My brother is the real monster!" Irene managed, gasping and wheezing as she clawed at her own neck, struggling frantically for more air.

But he denied her, pulling the ribbon tighter.

"Please..." she begged through tears. "If you don't...listen...to what I have to say...you are...as good as dead..."

Carl pulled the string tighter still.

Irene's eyes bulged as she let out her final croak, and then...

The helium balloon exploded above her head as Carl punched it into the wall. The mirror glass shattered into the sink as he released the ribbon and dragged her out of the bathroom by her coat. He threw her into the chair where she coughed and spluttered as he loomed over her.

"This camaraderie of ours has reached its end," he said emptily. "Say what you have to say, and then leave."

Irene sobbed soundly as she carefully unraveled the bloodstained ribbon from around her throat. She had collected herself by the time she was done. Sighing deeply, she dropped it into the waste basket by the bed.

The monster was ready to tell her story.

"My brother was raised in hell. I don't know how old we were when she stole us, or even if she took us from the same family, but from the moment he entered that house, our new mother didn't love him. She wouldn't even give him a name. Whenever he broke one of her many rules, as punishment, she would bind him and put him under the floor along with the rest of her victims. Sometimes they were still alive...and sometimes they weren't. I knew he was down there and I never tried to save him. Not once. I was too afraid that the same might happen to me, too. I don't know how he survived all those years. I got away from her eventually, but I never stopped thinking about you...

"Anyways, in spite of everything she did to him, he still had a sick and twisted unbreakable love for her, and all that pain and suffering turned him into something unspeakable. *That* is the creature that is coming to this island to kill you, and if you're not afraid by now...then you're a fool, Carl Oxspring."

9

The Son & The Traitor

It had been quite a night at the Mayfair house.

When the sun came up, the neighborhood awoke to a horrifying discovery. The kind that they would remember for the rest of their days. A mother and her child found dead at their own home. A tragic and senseless double murder.

Of course, the newspapers would leave out that both Fiona and her seventeen-year-old daughter, Jo, were found outside in their yard, bound back to back against the clothesline, blood-soaked sheets scattered everywhere and draped over their faces. Those were facts, details, secrets that only a few souls were privy to. This made Walker smile as he walked through his apartment building, carrying one of those papers under his arm. He hated the place. It wasn't falling apart, per say. He didn't even mind the old and faded look. There was just something about it that seemed *unclean* to him.

His smile quickly disappeared when he saw the landlord squabbling with the tenants from next door again. This happened so frequently around here that it was just a weekend shy of becoming a daily occurrence. Today the mother was his sparring partner.

The landlord, Mr. Cary, was a morbidly obese atrocity who dressed to impress no one, and gestured far too much with his hands when he spoke.

"I can't keep having the same conversation with you," he fumed, chopping the air with his chubby fingers. "My inbox is always full of complaints because of you and your kids.

You've got to do something about it, or I will. Either you get the noise under control, or your family will have to leave."

Miss Boston, a young mother of three with a live-in boyfriend, was tiny, underfed, and perpetually coated in that fine sweat that can only come from over-exhaustion.

"Yes, Mr. Cary," she droned like a petulant schoolgirl. Despite a world of responsibility heaped upon her shoulders, sadly, for all involved, Miss Boston was no more mature than her offspring and showed no signs of improvement in all the time that she had been there.

Tired of hearing her sleepy false promises, the landlord threw those restless hands of his in the air and left.

"I suppose you complained to him, too, huh?" she accused her neighbor as he went to unlock the door to his apartment.

Removing the paper from under his arm, he held her gaze as he stood there without saying a word.

"Okay…" Rolling her eyes, the young mother shook her head as she retreated back into her nightmare of a life on the other side of the wall.

Walker marveled proudly at the front page of the newspaper as he sat in the living area of his apartment. A double homicide. Top story, too. There was only one person that would appreciate it just as much as he did. Picking up the cordless phone, he pressed REDIAL and waited.

"Hello, you've reached Patty Morris." The paper crunched in his grip as the recorded message began. "I'm sorry I can't come to the phone right now, but if you leave your name and number I will get back to you as soon as I can. *Please leave your message after the tone.*"

"Hello, Mother, it's me, again," Walker said sweetly. "Why haven't you been answering or returning any of my calls this week? Did I do something to make you mad at me? If that's true, I have some news I want to share with you that I know will make you very happy. Maybe you'll even forgive me for whatever it is I did. I love you, Mother. Please call me. I love you." He kissed the mouthpiece of the phone before he ended the call and burst into tears that were easily drowned out by the screams of children coming from next door.

"Hello, you've reached Patty Morris."

"Come on, come on, come on," Walker muttered impatiently as he marched back and forth through his apartment, twirling the long needle between his fingers like a razor-sharp baton. "Come on!"

"…if you leave your name and number I will get back to you as soon as I can. *Please leave your message after the tone.*"

"Yes!" He drew in an eager breath. "Mother, it-"

"*I'm sorry, but the voicemail inbox of the person you called is full. Please try again later. Goodbye.*"

His mouth had frozen open mid-word as he lowered the phone from his ear and stared at it in astonishment. It remained open until he realized that he had absentmindedly pierced the needle straight through his own thumb. His blood pitter-pattered down onto the newspaper on the coffee table where he had left it.

"No!" he cried out as he took the paper with him through to the kitchen sink along with his injured hand. There, he dabbed at the paper lightly with a soft sponge while his wound continued to bleed down his arm and into the small red puddle that was slowly forming on the floor, drip by drip.

"This is Officer O'Brian."

"Officer, thank you for speaking with me." Walker snapped forward on the sofa of his apartment, a tourniquet fashioned from a torn piece of dishtowel wrapped tightly around his thumb. "I'm sorry if it sounds like I'm raising my voice. I have some very noisy neighbors. Also, you may have to speak up a little so that I can hear you."

"That's not a problem. What can I do for you, Mr. Walker?"

"I'm worried about my mother, you see," he said into the phone, adopting a concerned manner. "I haven't heard from her in days. I'd like to make a request for someone to go out to her house and check on her for me. I just have this horrible feeling that something terrible might've happened to her."

* * *

Irene Birchwood walked along the pale sands of Windygo Bay as she listened to the waves that came rolling onto the shore, crashing, splashing, and hissing. She thought it was such a beautiful sound, one of the best sounds in the world. She came to a halt at one of the many mouths of the maze of sharp, black rock that lay at the very end of it all.

"You know, you may as well show yourself," she called out. "I haven't forgotten how much you enjoy the hunt."

Carl stepped out from one of the rocky openings to her left. This time he wore the pale hood and that grotesque mask of his.

"You didn't think to leave the island?" he asked her. "Save yourself?"

"Forty-two years ago, you became my entire life," she said sadly as she turned to face him. "That's all over now."

"You do realize that you are volunteering to suffer a most horrible end?" Carl began to walk towards her.

"I expected nothing less." She smiled as she too began to walk towards him. "Would you do a favor for an old friend?"

"We are no longer friends, but you can ask," he said as he came to a stop.

"Make sure it's something that people will talk about."

Carl couldn't help but laugh, and so he nodded.

Irene's smile widened as a tear rolled down her face. Then she turned and walked into the shadows of the cavernous corridor to whatever fate awaited her.

Unsheathing the metal pipe from the sleeve of his long raincoat, the man in the pale hood followed the woman into the labyrinth of black rock.

* * *

"Officer O'Brian!" Walker clutched the phone with a strained grin, baring all of his huge teeth. "Thank you for getting back to me so quickly."

"Mr. Walker, I'm afraid there was no response when we went to check on your mother," O'Brian informed him. "We spoke with her neighbors, but they told us that they hadn't seen or heard from her for the past two or three days, which they said was 'very unlike her.' Now, I understand your family suffered a great loss recently. Do you think your mother could be staying with friends?"

"No, she's not like that," he told him. His grin had shrunk to a sad smile. "My mother's always been very self-reliant."

"With your permission, we could gain entry to the property," O'Brian put to him.

"That won't be necessary, officer." He hung up before the man could respond.

Walker's smile was gone. He let the phone drop from his ear and watched the batteries as they spilled out onto the carpet and rolled under the sofa.

The entire wall behind him shook as something crashed into it from the other side, startling him from his thoughts.

Letting out a deep sigh through his nose, he tore out into the hall and beat on the tenants' door. Miss Boston's live-in boyfriend, Grell, was the one who answered. "Who is it?" He was the type that wore a baseball cap, a basketball jersey, and jeans that permanently hung halfway down his underwear. "Oh, hey, you're the neighbor, right?" Grell spotted the blood on the door first. Then the floor as it dripped from the tall man's trembling fist. "Hey, what are you-"

Walker drew the needle and moved in, stabbing the young man's trachea and jugular in quick succession. Eyes wide, he clutched his throat as he backed away, his legs tremoring for a moment before they failed him.

"Grell?" Miss Boston whimpered from the kitchen island, clasping an infant to her shoulder. Her son and daughter, no older than six or seven, raced over to their father, giggling wildly as they jumped up and down on top of him.

"Daddy, Daddy! Get up! Stop being so silly!" the girl cheered.

"Yeah, Daddy, you're so silly!" her brother chimed in.

The daughter started to cry, her hands shaking with fright as spouts of red sprayed across her face and hair.

Both children froze as Walker entered the apartment.

"Get out! Get out!" Miss Boston screamed as she cowered behind the island.

"Run, Jodie! Come on, run!" Her son led his sister past the intruder, escaping out into the hallway, the echoes of their little footsteps fading into the wails of the baby in their mother's arms.

Walker found the neighbors' phone on the counter. He dialed and waited as he stood over them.

"What are you doing?" Miss Boston sobbed.

The tall man raised a finger to his lips as he hushed her.

"Hello, police. Hi, I think I can hear a baby crying under the floor of my apartment. Please hurry and send someone to come and help the poor little angel out of there before she suffocates."

* * *

Irene had already screamed herself hoarse by the time Carl had finished tightening the bolts on the steel belt that pinned her neck to the front of the boat. The muscles in her face throbbed with agony as her jaw had become locked open. He had fitted her gaping wide mouth around the very tip of the bow. The belt around her neck was the only thing stopping her weight from tearing her cheeks apart. The rest of her body dangled down into the freezing water. She could no longer feel the parts of her that were submerged.

Despite the desperate shrieks and cries of his former friend, Carl's face remained expressionless as he walked calmly around the side. Crouching down on that small pier, he dropped the adjustable wrench into his toolbox before he carried it with him onto the motorboat.

Irene's face was thick with tears as he took one final look at her through the windshield. She tried to scream something at him, but her words were too muffled for him to understand. It didn't matter anymore. Whatever she had to say was no longer any of his concern.

He took the boat out, slowly at first, gliding smoothly across the deserted bay. His passenger let out an anguished groan as her eyes rolled over in pain. Her jaw had dislocated. He started to accelerate. Her cries became shrill and pig-like as she clawed at the hull. She tried in vain to hold herself up, but there was nothing she could do to stop the sides of her mouth from splitting open.

Carl turned the boat inland as they reached the towering black rocks at the end of the shore.

Then he floored it straight for them.

The icy waters splattered against his dead-boy mask as he sliced through the waves. Just before they hit, he killed the engine and watched through the windshield as the bow collided with solid rock. The impact pulverized Irene's skull in a glorious eruption of blood and foam.

He waited until he found a peaceful spot out at sea before he began removing what was left of Irene's head from the front of the boat, along with the rest of her body. As the steel belt came loose, he shoveled and peeled the slippery wet mess of brain, meat, and hair away from the bow, and then he dropped the remains of Irene Birchwood into the water.

He watched in fascination of how the redness bloomed and spread beneath the surface like a looming thundercloud of blood.

10

The Caretaker

It was an early morning start at the Price household. The sun was already shining bright through the kitchen window, which was still speckled with the drops of last night's rainfall.

Klaryssa lay back in her bouncy cradle chair, smiling away as her grandmother, Suzie, cooed, sang, and made funny faces to keep her amused.

"Yes, your Auntie Rori is coming to visit you this morning," she told her. "Yes, she is, and then your daddy is coming home today. You miss your daddy, don't you? Of course you do. Your daddy loves you very much, and so does your mommy."

Suzie cupped a trembling hand over her mouth as she turned away, hiding her worry from her grandchild. "I just hope she's all right..."

She cried out as something struck the back-door window. She checked on the baby first, who was still smiling as if nothing had happened. "No, I suppose after all you've been through, it'll take more than that to scare you, won't it."

Adjusting her dressing gown, Suzie got to her feet and retrieved a small set of keys from the top of the microwave. Unlocking the back door, she took a look outside. She found a red, white, and blue basketball on the stone patio rolling in the wind. Letting out a sigh of relief, she scooped it up and locked the back door again.

"I'm just going to see who this belongs to," she informed her granddaughter, carrying the ball underarm as she went. "Won't be a minute!"

The neighbors to the left didn't have any children, and the neighbors on the right weren't even home.

"So where did you come from?" Suzie puzzled as she returned to the kitchen. She unlocked the back door for the second time that morning, blowing raspberries at Klaryssa as she did so. "Well, you can stay out there," she decided as she tossed the ball back onto the patio.

Suzie carefully monitored Klaryssa's baby formula maker as the contraption whirred away. The black nozzle had just begun filling her bottle when, yet again, something hit the back-door window. This time Suzie did not cry out.

She ran out onto the patio, hoping to see something, someone, but no one was there. The ball itself was lodged under the lush evergreens that lined the fence.

There was a noise.

She looked up to the snapping of twigs. Raindrops glittered like shattered glass as they showered down from the restless evergreen branches before her. She heard someone breathing, raspy and heavy. She peered into the shadows behind the glistening rainwater. She saw mad eyes. She saw bared teeth. She saw the hot breath rising out from behind those teeth. She saw a foot move forward and a hand reaching. She threw the ball towards the evergreens and ran.

Bursting out onto the patio, the man in the pale hood caught up to Suzie before she could reach the back door.

* * *

"Ready to go?" Cunningham's officer asked from the doorway to Liam's hospital room.

"Yeah, thanks," he said as he put the last of his old clothes into his backpack. "Officer…?"

"Holden."

"Okay," Liam said with a smile. "Lead the way, Officer Holden."

Weaving through the foot traffic of the ground level, Liam spotted the mayor marching into the building as they approached the entrance.

"Rori?" His voice trailed off as he saw the worry in her eyes.

She was following a gurney. A gurney that was carrying Ally's mother, Suzie.

"Officer, wait!" he called to Holden as he pointed. "This is my mother-in-law."

"Liam…" Rori was on the brink of tears as they linked hands.

"What happened?"

"I found her lying unconscious on the kitchen floor," she told him. "It looked like someone broke in the back way and attacked her."

"Jesus Christ." He let out a heavy sigh as he watched Suzie disappear through a set of double doors.

"Liam," Rori shook his arm, a grave look on her paling face. "Klaryssa is missing."

"What?" he cried out in horrified disbelief as he backed away from her.

"I think they took her," she stuttered through her sobbing. "They took Klaryssa. I'm so sorry."

Before he could reach the support railing, Liam's legs gave out as he collapsed to the floor of that crowded hospital corridor.

* * *

The wet green grass was already soaking the bottoms of Sergeant Cunningham's trousers as the old sexton led him and another officer through the grounds of Boatmore Church.

"Found it this way this morning," the man said as he came to a stop beside a particular grave.

The sergeant muttered a curse to himself as he read the name. It belonged to Christopher Price. The plot itself was covered over with a pool table cloth, which was now sunken and soggy from the rain.

"Typically, we'll have artificial grass put down to make everything as pleasant and presentable as we can for our visitors," the church caretaker went on, "so I noticed something was wrong right away. Especially when you walk on it."

"Would you mind showing us what you mean by that, sir?" the other officer requested.

"Yes, of course."

Without hesitation, the man stepped onto the green cloth, the fabric squishing beneath his boots, and when he stepped off, they heard the distinct clatter of solid wood.

Immediately, the sergeant signaled his officer to assist the man. Together they carefully peeled away the cloth to reveal a panel of plywood. They all exchanged a wary glance before they lifted the panel as if they were opening a doorway into the earth.

Instead what they found was an open grave, and an empty coffin.

"Good heavens!" the old man gasped.

"This is all we need…" Cunningham grumbled under his breath.

"Did you or anyone see anything?" his officer asked the caretaker. "Maybe get a look at someone?"

"Not a soul," he replied. "I've been pushing to have security cameras installed ever since this Butcher business started up, but I've had no luck as of yet. Perhaps they'll listen to me now."

"Officer!" Cunningham exclaimed as Holden joined them in the churchyard. He pulled the young man aside. "Do we have an update on the mother-in-law?"

"She still hasn't regained consciousness," he reported. "They're doing some tests and x-rays, the works. We should know more soon. She's in good hands."

"Okay," the sergeant nodded thoughtfully before he met the officer's eyes. "Are you thinking what I'm thinking?"

"Yeah," Holden sighed heavily. "There's no way Liam Price did any of this."

"Agreed," Cunningham said as he took out his walkie-talkie. "I think we need to have another talk with Carl Oxspring. Where is Liam now?"

* * *

Liam anxiously tapped the end of his hospital bed with the toe of his shoe while the rest of him lay perfectly still. His eyes burned into the grim gray grid that was the ceiling.

Rori stood by him with Holden's replacement keeping watch over them outside the door.

"I know there's nothing that I could possibly say," the mayor said comfortingly, "but if there's anything I can do to help, you just let me know, and it's done. Whatever it is."

Liam remained completely silent, the IV fluids gently working their way into his arm.

"Just thought you should know that," Rori said as she reached for a visitor's chair.

"I can't believe he took my son..." Liam uttered, no louder than a whisper.

"What did you say?"

Liam shot upright in his bed. "I need to get out of here, and I need *you* to help me."

"What?" The mayor tried and failed to stifle her surprise. "Wait, where will you go?"

Just then, a loud buzz emanated from Liam's jeans pocket. Pulling out his phone, he unlocked the screen.

There was a new message waiting for him. And although its sender was unknown, he knew exactly who had written it.

Liam hit DELETE and then drew the IV drip out of his arm.

11

The Playground

It was nightfall on the island of Boatmore. The winds were stilled and the stars peeked through the clouds like eyes watching from the sky.

Liam saw the lights first; they were shining through the trees in the distance as he neared the metal gate entrance to the beachside children's playground of Yellow Bay. The engine of the ambulance he found parked there purred away as its headlights illuminated the climbing frames, the chutes, the bridges, and then there was the play tunnel in the center of it all.

"You bastard!" Liam screamed as he ran to the front of the vehicle, but there was no one inside, so he had no choice but to turn back to the sight that was before him. "God…"

The tunnel itself was plastered end to end with the bloody handprints of small children. Dozens and dozens of little palms. Hundreds and hundreds of tiny fingers. Dripping red and glistening from the beams as the decomposing body of Christopher Price lay against the heart of it. Both arms propped up, the young boy's corpse pointed in either direction.

Liam had always imagined that if he ever had to lay eyes on his son again that he would appear as if he were just sleeping. That wasn't the case here. Christopher's body was so far gone that he no longer looked like a real human being. Over time he had withered away into the husk of one. His skin, if it could still be called that, had turned a color that he had only ever seen in rotting fruit. Liam's head throbbed with a dull ache, as if he could feel his own mind locked in a violent struggle as it fought desperately to keep itself together inside his skull.

"Come on out!" he yelled with a broken voice. "You fucking monster…"

His breath caught in this throat as he could make out the cries of an infant echoing from inside the tunnel.

"Klaryssa!" he cried as he raced to one of the openings.

Crouching down, he shined the light of his phone into the tunnel. Sure enough, there she was, stashed away somewhere around the halfway point of that cold plastic passageway.

"I'm coming, angel," he reassured her as he crawled to his child on his hands and knees. "It's okay. It's okay, baby. Everything's going to be okay. Daddy's here."

She seemed unharmed as she was wrapped snugly in a fresh clean blanket, but as Liam continued to check her over, he soon realized that they weren't alone. There was something else in that tunnel with them. Liam lifted the light to find the bloated corpse mask of the man in the pale hood only inches away as it leered back at him.

"Are you frightened, Liam?" the dead boy's face asked him. "I'm sorry… I haven't been feeling like myself of late. I've found myself having to adjust to many harsh new realities. I believe you can relate. Heh…heh…heh."

"Fuck you!" Liam raged as he lashed out, knocking the mask to the floor of the play tunnel. He gasped as the face staring back at him was Patty's. Her teeth, tongue, and eyes had been removed, their bloody voids stuffed full of sharp surgical instruments. She had a ghostly glow to her from the phone hidden inside the mask. Its speaker crackled with Carl's cruel laughter.

"Tell me, how is dear sweet Klaryssa doing?" he mocked. "Come on, my little princess. Give your Aunt Patty a kiss!"

Liam snatched the phone from the mask and hurled it down the tunnel. He heard the rattle as it skidded and broke open upon the concrete outside.

Suddenly, he felt a deep roar rise up from the earth as someone revved the engine of the ambulance. "No!" he yelped in a panic, grabbing Klaryssa as tires screamed across the playground. "No, no, no!"

With nowhere to go and no time to think, Liam held his child to his chest as he closed his eyes and prayed that their deaths would be painless. There was a loud *CRUNCH!* as the entire tunnel caved in.

Liam slowly opened his eyes as he felt the night air on his skin. They were both safe on the concrete. Something had latched onto his ankles just before the ambulance hit. Scrambling to his feet, he spun around to meet their savior.

"Holden?"

"Are you both all right?" the officer asked as he dusted off his uniform.

"Yeah, we're fine," Liam replied breathlessly. "Thanks to you."

"There's no one in here," another officer said from the ambulance.

Moving alongside to the back of the vehicle, they found the rear doors hanging wide open.

"What? Where is he? Where did he go?" Liam held Klaryssa close, searching the shadows between the surrounding trees as more police began to descend upon the playground.

* * *

Carl Oxspring stumbled into his house, dragging his left foot along the stone floor as he limped his way towards the kitchen. He stopped cold by the doorway to the living room. There was someone sitting in the armchair by the empty fireplace.

"I used to live in a house like this," the man said as he glanced around the room with blank eyes.

"…I was once a guest in a house like this," Carl said in return as he studied the intruder's face. "What can I do for you, *Mr. Walker*?"

Clawing the arms of the chair, Walker climbed to his feet. "I'm here to make arrangements for Mother," he said, towering more and more over Carl the closer he got.

Humming to himself, Carl nodded and carried on into the kitchen. Walker followed.

Reaching the far counter, Carl picked up the cordless phone and turned to face his visitor.

"You callin' somebody?" A small smile grew on Walker's thin lips. "No one can help you now. I assure you."

"I don't need help from anyone," Carl said calmly as he heaved the phone across the room.

Walker stumbled back as it smashed against his forehead. Chuckling, he kicked the debris aside and drew out the needle.

Carl tore a drawer free, cutlery clattering everywhere as the tall man lunged for him.

There was a scream of metal as the tip of Walker's needle scraped down the base of the drawer.

Crushed against the counter, Carl sank an oyster knife into Walker's shoulder. With an enraged snarl, Walker spun Carl and rammed him towards the kitchen table. Tumbling over the top, Carl hit the floor hard.

Walker watched him escape into the hallway as he pulled the oyster blade from his flesh. With one sharp flick, he sent the needle spinning through the air. It lodged itself in the man's back before he could reach the front door.

Carl let out a shocked gulp as he felt it go in. Shaking, he plunged to his knees on the stone floor as his body failed him.

The water of the readymade bath was ice cold as Walker held him under. It wasn't until he pierced through the corner of Carl's eye that he started to struggle.

Bubbles roared from below as Carl screamed under the surface of the water. Wall tiles cracked as his thrashing legs kicked them. His fingernails clawed strips of acrylic away from the edges. Walker kept him firmly in place by the throat as he pushed the long needle deep down into the man's brain until it would go no further.

And then, everything was still.

Walker opened the front door and stepped outside with his arms raised high.

"I surrender myself freely," he declared as he sank to his knees on the gravel path.

Flashlights searched his body as the police moved in. One of those lights found a key in Walker's right hand.

That key led to a compartment that Patty kept under the floor of Harold's study. Inside it, the police would find just about everything they needed on Carl Oxspring: the *real* Boatmore Butcher.

12

The Farewell

Liam Price stood a safe distance away from the edge of Last Point as he paid the spot one final visit. Shielding his eyes from the blazing late morning sun, he could already feel his face going numb from the freezing winds.

"You're leaving the island then?" a familiar voice said.

Liam smiled as he glanced the shadow of Martin Fin out of the corner of his eye.

"Yup," he said with a sigh. "Boat leaves in one hour. No idea where I'm going or what I'm going to do. I just need to get away. Start somewhere new."

"I remember the night I found you up here."

"Jesus…" Liam chuckled as he shook his head. "If you hadn't shown up when you did, I dread to think what I might've done."

"You'd just lost Christopher," Martin said softly. "You thought your life was over. But you survived that, and you'll survive this."

"Thank you, Mar-"

As Liam turned, there was no one there. Martin was gone.

"He's right, you know," said another familiar voice. "You will make it. You'll survive."

"What makes you so sure?" he asked as he sensed Ally by his side.

"Because we both know that you'd do anything for the ones you love," she reminded him sweetly.

"I wish to God you were coming with us," Liam sobbed.

"Don't think I won't be watching over you."

"I love you, Ally," he said, feeling every word in his soul. He closed his eyes for a moment as he imagined her in his arms.

Then his dearly departed wife's smile faded into the morning sky as precious little Klaryssa began to stir in the baby carrier strapped to his chest.

"Come on now, my tiny angel," he hummed as he kissed her upon the forehead. "It's time we said goodbye to this place."

As the ferry sailed away, Liam took one last look at the island of Boatmore, the place where he thought he would live out the rest of his days in safety and happiness. Only now it was a graveyard for the ones he loved most.

Still, it did bring him some comfort when Ally's body was recovered and laid to rest next to their son, who was reburied alongside his mother the very same day. He could only hope the life that was still ahead for him and his daughter would not be haunted by their ghosts.

Death would be ever waiting, but at least they would have love. Whether it be for the ones they shared their lives with, or the ones they lost along the way. It would be love, all the same.

"Forever and ever," Liam whispered into his baby's ear before he carried her in from the cold winds of the sea.

Acknowledgements

To: J. Grell of The World According To J!, Rebecca Rowland, Lezlie of The Nerdy Narrative, Yvonne aka The Coycaterpillar Reads, the Bram Stoker nominated Ross Jeffery, Nichi of DarkBetweenPages, Heidi Hobbs Locke, Emily L. Terry, Gab Harvey, Josh of Working Man Reads, Melissa of Readingodysseysknbeyond, Brian Bowyer, Sharon Dwyer, Leah Lindeman of Pen to Paper, Dan Chadwick, and Dark Ink Books.

Thank you to all of you. To those who supported me, advised me, showed me kindness, and to those who gave me their friendship.

Last but not least, thank you to Donald, to my parents, and to my friends and family.

About the Author

L. Stephenson has been telling stories of killers and boogeymen to his friends and writing them on his computer since the summer before he began high school. A university degree in Film & TV Screenwriting, a handful of anthologies and a novella later, and not much has changed, it seems!

Stephenson's first short story was published as part of a Halloween-themed collection released by Dark Ink back in 2018. Nearly five years later, terror just came full circle as the author has returned home to Dark Ink to release his debut slasher novel, The Boatmore Butcher.

Printed in Great Britain
by Amazon

27295639R00216